UNDENIABLE PASSIONS

"It's the same sky in England," Christopher said, coming to stand behind her. "The same stars. It's a different world, true, but it has all the things you're longing for, Ariel. I can give them to you, and more. You only have to stop fighting me."

His hands slid across her shoulders, caressing her neck. Ariel closed her eyes, shutting out the darkness, letting the images he conjured come alive in her mind.

Christopher's hands slid down around her waist, and he bent to nussle her earlobe. His kisses sent delicious shivers racing through her. But Ariel needed to think. Turning in his arms, she tried to deflect his attentions as gently as possible.

"Christopher, please—"

"Anything you wish," he answered just before he covered her mouth with his. For a moment Ariel let the deliciousness of his kiss fill her, and the urge to push aside her thoughts and revel in the delights of his kisses was a powerful one. But she couldn't. She needed to think things out, and she needed to do it now.

Gently pressing her hands against his chest, she broke off their kiss. "Christopher," she tried again. He tipped her face up, and the tenderness she saw in his eyes sent a sensation of pure sweetness running through her. He only waited a heartbeat before dropping his gaze to her lips and dipping his head to catch them up in another kiss.

Ariel knew that if she gave in again, she would be lost forever.

CAPTURE THE GLOW OF
ZEBRA'S *HEARTFIRES!*

CAPTIVE TO HIS KISS (3788, $4.25/$5.50)
by Paige Brantley
Madeleine de Moncelet was determined to avoid an arranged marriage to the Duke of Burgundy. But the tall, stern-looking knight sent to guard her chamber door may thwart her escape plan!

CHEROKEE BRIDE (3761, $4.25/$5.50)
by Patricia Werner
Kit Newcomb found politics to be a dead bore, until she met the proud Indian delegate Red Hawk. Only a lifetime of loving could soothe her desperate desire!

MOONLIGHT REBEL (3707, $4.25/$5.50)
by Marie Ferrarella
Krystyna fled her native Poland only to live in the midst of a revolution in Virginia. Her host may be a spy, but when she looked into his blue eyes she wanted to share her most intimate treasures with him!

PASSION'S CHASE (3862, $4.25/$5.50)
by Ann Lynn
Rose would never heed her Aunt Stephanie's warning about the unscrupulous Mr. Trent Jordan. She knew what she wanted—a long, lingering kiss bound to arouse the passion of a bold and ardent lover!

RENEGADE'S ANGEL (3760, $4.25/$5.50)
by Phoebe Fitzjames
Jenny Templeton had sworn to bring Ace Denton to justice for her father's death, but she hadn't reckoned on the tempting heat of the outlaw's lean, hard frame or her surrendering wantonly to his fiery loving!

TEMPTATION'S FIRE (3786, $4.25/$5.50)
by Millie Criswell
Margaret Parker saw herself as a twenty-six year old spinster. There wasn't much chance for romance in her sleepy town. Nothing could prepare her for the jolt of desire she felt when the new marshal swept her onto the dance floor!

Available wherever paperbacks are sold, or order direct from the Publisher. Send cover price plus 50¢ per copy for mailing and handling to Zebra Books, Dept. 4207, 475 Park Avenue South, New York, N.Y. 10016. Residents of New York and Tennessee must include sales tax. DO NOT SEND CASH. For a free Zebra/Pinnacle catalog please write to the above address.

ELAINE KANE

DESERT FLAME

ZEBRA BOOKS
KENSINGTON PUBLISHING CORP.

ZEBRA BOOKS are published by

Kensington Publishing Corp.
475 Park Avenue South
New York, NY 10016

Copyright © 1993 by Elaine Kane

All rights reserved. No part of this book may be repro-
duced in any form or by any means without the prior written consent of the Publisher, excepting brief quotes used in
reviews.
If you purchased this book without a cover you should be
aware that this book is stolen property. It was reported as
"unsold and destroyed" to the Publisher and neither the
Author nor the Publisher has received any payment for this
"stripped book."

Zebra, the Z logo, Heartfire Romance, and the Heartfire
Romance logo are trademarks of Kensington Publishing
Corp.

First Printing: June, 1993
Printed in the United States of America

*For my daughters, Haley and Tess,
with love*

Chapter One

"I won't do it, Chedyla," insisted the young woman seated at the dressing table. Her skin was shaded softly golden by the equatorial sun and was well suited to the heavy tresses that flashed like dark Mediterranean honey as her duenna brushed them into a cascade of gold worthy of a sultan's vault.

"You can do nothing else, my child. For as long as the earth is old, this has been Allah's plan," the older woman replied without missing a stroke.

"Why should I marry him?" Determination sparked like dark spice in her nutmeg-colored eyes.

"A woman must take shelter under the roof of a man's protection with gratitude, and repay him by being fruitful and giving him children. Our beloved sultan knows this well."

"But not a man he's chosen from the thin air! That's not how it should be."

"It has been so for a thousand years. It is how I came to the sultan's harem. It is how his daughters have been married. It is an honorable thing he has done for you. By this union, the great treaty with King George will be sealed. It will mean much good fortune for our country."

"Why can't the treaty be signed without a marriage?"

Ariel asked, pressing long supple fingers against her brow.

"Because that is what Allah has destined."

"Do you believe Allah wants me to leave my home?" she asked. Ariel drummed her fingers against the tabletop in frustration. "I won't marry him."

"The sultan is Allah's chosen ruler. What he bids, Allah bids. You cannot fight Allah's will. No good can ever come of it."

Turning away from the table and her duenna's ministrations, Ariel settled her shoulders in an unconscious gesture of defiance. "Mohammed is only my guardian. He won't make me marry a man I don't want."

"Mohammed Ben Abdullah, great Sultan of all Morocco, will not change his mind," Chedyla stated with absolute conviction. "Not even for you."

"He permits me many other freedoms."

"And that is why he wishes you to marry the English duke. Already there is talk, and not only in the harem where they care only for talk. There is talk among the viziers."

Ariel bit her lip, the first seeds of doubt rooting in her mind. "What concern could I be to them?"

"They are reminded of your mother. They speak of the influence she held over him. They whisper among themselves that you will weaken him because you are Caroline's daughter. They have not forgotten how the sultan turned away from his advisors and listened to her."

"But I have no influence."

"You do not live in the harem. When you send a message to him, he grants you audience. This he does not do for his own daughters. It is said he speaks to you of government."

"Sometimes, if I come for a book in his study, he tells me of his dreams for Morocco. But it's only because I used to listen in the evenings when he spoke with my mother. It's not for any other reason. The viziers are wrong. This is my home, Chedyla, and all I want is to stay here."

"Daiwa is displeased. She says that such things are not for an outsider to know. The viziers listen to her. Like your mother she has much influence, but she is on their side."

Ariel made a dismissive wave with her hand. "Daiwa has hated me all my life. She's harmless."

"Do not underestimate the Hatum Kadin, child. Jealousy breeds much evil. Mohammed is sultan. He cannot ignore the rumblings of discontent. Many do not want this treaty with England. If you marry the English duke, they will be appeased. He must think of his people."

"My life is not a token to be used by Daiwa's hyenas. If the viziers don't want commerce with infidel countries, how long can this treaty last once they have what they want? They won't stop at having me out of the way. They'll want Mohammed to break the treaty. They'll find some way."

Chedyla shrugged. "It is out of our hands, my beloved. Allah moves the heavens, and with them, our lives. What is to be cannot be altered."

"Daiwa won't get her way in this. She has no right to command me."

"Watch what you say, child." Chedyla cast a nervous glance toward the open balcony doors. "Daiwa is the first wife. The mother of Mohammed's heir. As Hatum Kadin she has great power, and spies as well. The pact is being drawn. Only if the English sharif, this duke, chooses against it, will you avoid this marriage."

A slow, thoughtful smile touched Ariel's lips.

"Chedyla, it wouldn't be the sultan's fault if the duke refused the marriage, would it? The viziers couldn't blame him." Her mind racing, Ariel jumped up from the cushion and began pacing between her low, tapestry-strewn bed and the copper tabletop set on elephant tusks.

"The English sharif would not refuse such an honor," Chedyla warned. "To do so would show much arrogance, much disdain for Mohammed's great name. He is not even a prince, this man. He would not dare to refuse such a gift from the sultan."

"Oh, Chedyla," Ariel said, a motherly forbearance touching her classical features with reproach. "Not all men are honorable."

"You know nothing of this man."

"I know he's English."

"And so you condemn him. Not all Englishmen are like your father."

Ariel stopped mid-stride. "Of course not," she said with determined indifference. "But he's English, just as my father was." Ariel crossed back to the bed. "Perhaps he'll take a purse in exchange for releasing me from the contract."

"Ariel," Chedyla pleaded. "We are Allah's servants. We must not tamper with his wishes."

"If that doesn't work, I'll offer him something else. I'll deed him my land in England! It's of no use to me." She spun around, triumphant. "Somehow, I'm certain I can find a way to change his mind."

Ariel scooped her cashmere shawl off the bed.

"Where are you going?"

"To the ball."

"It is not allowed."

The sheer aqua silk of her harem pants swirled in a puff of air as she danced away from her duenna's restraining grasp.

"I'm only going to watch from the garden."

Chedyla pinned her with a horrified stare.

"I have to find out who he is. Then I'll come back, Chedyla. I promise." Ariel blew her a kiss and swept out of the room, her eunuch falling in stride behind her as she drew a sheer veil across her face and headed down the broad corridor.

"I have no intention of marrying anyone, regardless of how it might benefit England," Christopher Staunton repeated with controlled emphasis.

"This marriage is far more than a political maneuver. The sultan presented the idea personally." Robert Belmeth shifted in his chair beneath Christopher's scrutinizing stare. "An affirmative answer will seal our negotiations."

Christopher crossed the room in a handful of long strides and settled into a combative stance in front of the opposite chair. "You actually thought I'd agree to an arranged marriage, Robert? You should know better than to try coercing someone so familiar with your game into one of its roles. I've given you my answer, and I'll not change my mind, trade agreement, King George, and the sultan be damned."

"I can understand your reticence," the older man continued, meeting his nephew's scowl with an even look. "Under normal circumstances, I'd refuse to consider such an option. However . . ."

Christopher cocked a skeptical brow. "Yes?"

Robert ran a hand through his silver hair. "Lord knows, I wish politics could be played the way you handle your business. You can afford to be ruthlessly straightforward. But in this profession negotiations and concessions are simply part of the game, the necessary means to an end."

Christopher's aristocratic features remained stoically unmoved. "All this has nothing whatsoever to do with being offered the sultan's ward as a wife, or with being told that I should seriously consider the proposition. If it's not politics, why the sudden need for me to marry?"

"Christopher, you must provide an heir for the dukedom now that Stephan is dead. Isn't it about time you adjusted to your new mantle?"

Christopher pinned him with an unappreciative stare.

"You could have your pick of London's most beautiful women, more so in the two years since you've become duke. What are you waiting for?"

"I've been sailing ships most of my adult life!" he ground out with flaring impatience. "And now, thanks to you, I'm running diplomatic errands for the king. I've hardly been in London enough to form a liaison, much less find a wife."

"Liaisons aplenty, if even a portion of the rumors are accurate," Robert responded dryly. "I'm no prude, Christopher. They were all within reason—if a bit on the numerous side—while your brother held the title. But I assume that now you'll want to restore the family's good name on a personal level just as you have diplomatically and financially."

Christopher turned his attention to the crackling fire that had been set to dispel the chill of the desert night. "Haven't I done enough, Robert? Stephan left the estates in shambles and the creditors drooling for their chunk of the oldest properties in England. I had to restore everything whether I wanted to or not. And for what?" he asked, turning to his uncle. "So my father's reputation and bloodline wouldn't be destroyed. I'm sure he's turning in his grave at the thought of *me* saving the precious title he passed on to Stephan.

"I'm in no particular hurry to find a wife. Certainly not in a hurry to marry a woman I've never even laid eyes on."

"She's a beauty, Christopher. Well-educated. Refined. A stunning young woman who—"

Christopher slammed his crystal snifter on the marble tabletop and stood, heedless of the drops of aged brandy that stained the sultan's Persian carpet. In two strides he was across the room standing toe-to-toe with his uncle, using every inch of his height and build to intimidate.

"I agreed to join this political mission because of our relationship, Robert. I agreed to be an emissary and a conduit for England. But I will not be a pawn for her. If the sultan wants a titled Englishman as a husband for his ward, I can provide him with a long list of young fools eager to take her sight unseen, or dozens of money-hungry fops who'll trip all over themselves for any woman with a sizeable dowry. Let Mohammed choose one of them." He turned away and stalked to the double-set doors leading to the balcony.

"He wants you."

"Why? I've never laid eyes on the great sultan."

"It seems he's heard some tale about you saving the life of a desert sheik's son. Thinks you've got a Muslim's code of honor or some such thing."

"It was a caid's son," Christopher scowled. "Besides, that was years ago."

"No matter. It's to be you. You, specifically, for the girl."

"The answer is no, Robert. You'll have to find some other way to get the treaty approved."

A soft knock at the study door punctuated Christopher's words with finality. He brought his temper back into rein in time to greet Lady Belmeth as she entered the study.

"I'm sorry to interrupt you, gentlemen, but we're expected downstairs."

"That's quite all right, my dear," Robert replied,

13

pressing a kiss against her fingers. "I believe we're finished."

Christopher couldn't help noticing how neatly Robert relegated their conversation to the back of his mind. Unfortunately, the subject was not as simple for him to dismiss. He shrugged, easing the tension from between his shoulders while he watched Anne straighten Robert's lace-trimmed cravat. How could Robert seriously suggest that he marry the sultan's ward? But Christopher already knew the answer—politics.

"By the way," Robert said, pulling Christopher's thoughts back to the matters at hand. "I'm afraid that Prince Mohammed El Yazid is going to be a bit of a problem for us."

"More than a bit," Christopher replied dryly.

"You know him, then?"

"No. But if you don't know about Yazid, you haven't done your homework. The prince hates Christians. He's not particular about who they are or where they're from. He despises us all with equal fervor."

"Then, I'd best begin making headway with my campaign," Robert replied with a determined smile. He began to lead his wife out of the room, then stopped and turned back with a wry smile on his lips. "By the way, I did do my homework. I brought you along."

"If I'd known I was to be your sacrificial bargaining chip, I'd have refused the invitation."

"I knew nothing of the marriage proposition until we arrived last night. Anyway, you've already given your answer. Your value here is much greater than that, a fact the king knew when he requested your assistance in this matter."

"I'll help you in any way I'm able, Robert," Christopher said. "But I'm not a politician. Remember that."

14

His uncle gave an uncharacteristic snort. "Whoever told you that is a damned liar."

"You're coming, Christopher?" Anne interceded politley.

"In a moment."

Robert nodded. "We'll go on ahead."

Christopher propped one shoulder against the cedar door frame, sipping his brandy as he stared out at the mantel of darkness that had begun to drop over the vast gardens of El Bedi. Robert's words came closer to the heart of his feelings than he cared to admit. He was ready to go home for good. Much as he loved the sea, he was tired of constantly racing from Tangier and Rabat to London with cargos of leather, oranges and the other delicacies his fellow noblemen prized so highly. He'd hired an outstanding man to manage the shipping concern just before they'd left London. He was looking forward to taking some of the responsibilities for managing the estates off his mother's hands. But an arranged marriage?

He shook his head at the outrageousness of the idea. He had no doubt that he'd marry someday. But he would choose the woman. He lived by one rule that overrode all others. He alone was master of his destiny. He had learned at an early age, through his father's lack of interest in his second son, that there was no percentage in letting someone else's imperatives influence him. He did as he pleased, and although that included strong consideration for what was just, he consistently chose not to bend to influences other than his own.

As it was, he was quite content keeping Francene Girouard as his lover when he was in London. Francene had no ambitions of becoming the Duchess of Avon; her career was her true passion, and Christopher was content to keep it so. As for Robert, he would just have to find some way around the sultan's request.

15

As Meknes vanished into the dusk, Christopher abandoned the view and headed for the ballroom — the brandy and the marriage forgotten.

Chapter Two

One slipper in each hand, Ariel balanced unsteadily on the base of one of the fifty pillars that formed the colonnade between El Bedi's grand ballroom and the enclosed garden. It couldn't be too difficult to find the duke, she told herself. Diplomats from nearly every country in Europe, as well as many of the Mediterranean nations, were in attendance tonight, but only a handful were from England. The ballroom, like the rest of El Bedi, had been built by her guardian's grandfather. Moulay Ismail had reigned with an iron fist. He'd built the palace to prove Morocco was greater than France, and his own palace grander than the Sun King's Versailles. Now, awash in candlelight, the pearly hue of its alabaster walls inlaid with elaborate arabesques of lapis, malachite, and jasper lent a magical air to the festivities within and proved the fearsome Ismail had been right at least about El Bedi.

At one end of the ballroom, Muslim aristocrats milled around the entertainment. Jugglers, acrobats, dancing bears on closely held chains, sword-swallowers and myriad other amusements drew enthusiastic shouts of pleasure and encouragement. Nearer to Ariel, the Europeans, particularly the ladies, did their best to ignore such outlandish activities and danced to the excellent Parisian orchestra the sultan had recently acquired. The brilliantly hued dresses of the ladies as they floated gracefully across the ballroom floor were like so many jewels scattered across the room, as if the sultan had carelessly spilt the riches of his treasury here. For a moment Ariel's heart caught in her throat, recalling watching her mother dance on just such nights as this.

Demure and delicate, Caroline had exuded a quiet peace that strange looks or whispers had never been able to disturb. Ariel's mother had been a perfect diamond, her clarity and brilliance speaking for itself. She had been Mohammed's most beloved possession. And yet, beautiful as she was, Ariel's memories of Caroline were also filled with the warmth and love her mother had given to her freely and constantly. They had been as close as a mother and child could be. Ariel could not remember a day when her mother hadn't been close by, watching her play as she embroidered in the shade, or reading her the stories of the Arabian Nights Ariel had come to love so well. For so long after her mother's death, Ariel had been alone and lost. No one, not even Chedyla, had been able to comfort her. Ariel had sat day after day in their little garden, waiting for Caroline to come. Even though she'd been all of eight years old when Caroline died, Ariel could not accept that her mother was gone. Even now, after so many years, the ache was still in her heart, and Ariel felt it acutely tonight. And as she watched the festivities in the ballroom, she knew, as Mohammed knew, that the most dazzling jewel of all was missing.

Letting out a sigh, Ariel returned her thoughts to her purpose. She did not have much time to linger here in the shadows. Intent as she was on surveying the dance floor for the duke, Ariel kept a constant watch on the two enormous black African guards who stood at attention ten meters farther down the colonnade, their sickle-shaped scimitars gleaming from scarlet waistbands. She couldn't stay long with the two Bukhariyin, Black Guards, nearby. From her vantage point behind the pillar, she could see most of the dancers. One by one she evaluated the gentlemen, discarding each in turn. No one seemed likely to be the person she sought. Ariel knew nothing about the duke, but she knew a great deal about the husbands the sultan had selected for the princesses. At last she turned her attention to those men talking and drinking along the colonnade, and her attention settled on a gentleman standing a bare two meters away.

Elegantly dressed in olive breeches and a striped frock coat, she judged him to be in his early fifties. A diamond stick pin winked from his jabot, and he carried himself with a grace that bespoke position and breeding. He seemed the most likely candidate of anyone she'd seen so far, and Ariel scrutinized him, looking for telltale flaws in his actions that would indicate his true character.

He was deep in conversation with a much younger man. Leaning forward, he communicated something in an intense whisper, and the younger man threw his head back and laughed. It was a deep, full, masculine laugh filled with appealing confidence. Ariel's attention turned to him, the germ of interest blossoming into intrigue and then alarm when he looked directly at her, pinning her with an intense, blue-eyed stare that reflected none of the laughter in his voice.

She ducked behind the pillar, but as she did one of the slippers she held caught on the marble fluting.

Dropping the slipper, she grabbed for a hold on the column in an attempt to regain her balance; but her toes lost their hold on the narrow ledge, and she began to slip off the base. Her hands slid across slick, smooth marble finding no place to take hold. Losing her balance completely, Ariel grabbed at the air, searching for anything that might break her fall as she tumbled backward. At last her fingers touched something pliable and soft, and she curled them around the cloth, pulling it with her as she went down. She heard the heart-stopping tinkle of crystal breaking and squeezed her eyes shut, uttering a desperate prayer. Don't let the Bukhariyin see me, she pleaded silently. Anything but that humiliation. Still, she steeled herself for the worst, prepared to scramble away the moment she hit the floor.

Then suddenly, instead of landing on the mosaic tiles, she was being jerked upright and set roughly back on her feet, pinned between the pillar and a snow-white linen shirt.

"What in the name of God do you think you're doing?" Christopher stared down at the woman in his arms with cold suspicion. Her slender figure trembled beneath his fingers, yet she faced him with haughty disdain. Her eyes shone with proud challenge, daring him to question her. They were extraordinary eyes, the color of spiced nutmeg, an amber hue flecked with bits of gold as if the hand of God had swept down and liberally dusted them with that precious ore and then trimmed them with thick, golden lashes. A lock of gilded, coppery hair was caught between his fingers where they bit into her bare arm, pinning back her head to reveal a long, slender column of neck below her gossamer veil.

Even with the veil, there was no doubt that she was

a rare beauty, and he squelched the urge to unhook its flimsy clasp and feast on the full glory of her face. Instead, he captured another inch of her hair, pulling her head even farther back.

Tears of pain glazing her eyes, she glared up at him. "The Bukhariyin," she said with quiet intensity.

He eyed her skeptically, then glanced over his shoulder at the two guards. They had taken a sudden interest in the activity around the pillar, and hovered not three meters away. He turned back to her. His eyes bore into hers, assessing her. "Don't move," he commanded, pulling her against his chest.

Barely turning to look over his shoulder, he called a sharp order in fluent Arabic to the guards. "It's all right. Don't concern yourselves."

The Africans eyed him suspiciously, and stepped forward.

"I said, it's all right. My friend has had too much to drink. I'll take care of it. There's no need for you to assist us."

The two Bukhariyin snorted insolently, as though they expected no more of an infidel. But they did as he said and turned away, walking to the end of the colonnade where they could observe him more discreetly.

"Thank you," Ariel said, barely daring to breathe beneath the penetrating scrutiny of his blue eyes.

The icy stare softened ever so slightly, and he cursed beneath his breath. "It doesn't mean I won't call them back."

"That would cost me everything."

"Then, tell me why you were eavesdropping on my conversation."

He held her so close she could feel the heat rising from his body, scorching hers. He was tall and dark.

And menacing. Mahogany hair lay tossed in careless tufts across his brow, and his eyes were a startling blue in the rugged, bronzed face. Her nostrils filled with the mingled scents of warm skin, musky cologne and spilled champagne. Her skin prickled where his rough palms gripped her bare arms, and the crisp linen of his shirt brushed against her breasts.

"I wasn't eavesdropping."

His eyes narrowed with a combination of suspicion and disbelief, though he couldn't quite bring himself to believe she was guilty of treachery. He glanced at the Bukhariyin meaningfully.

"Please don't call them over."

"What were you doing?"

She gave him a mutinous look. "I can't tell you."

"No?" He half-turned toward the Bukhariyin.

"Don't!" Ariel grabbed his arm as he began to signal to them. "Please. Don't call them."

"Tell me what you were doing hanging on the sultan's pillar like a juggler's monkey." His words bore an icy polish that brooked no refusal.

"Let me loose first," she said. He loosened his grip ever so slightly, letting her hair slip from between his fingers. Blood rushed back into her cheeks as she eased the cramped muscles of her neck.

"Now," he demanded. "Tell me."

"Not here." Ariel stood on tiptoe, trying to locate the guards over his shoulder.

"I believe," he said, dropping his gaze to her feet, "that is precisely what got you into trouble in the first place."

Indignant, Ariel returned her heels to the floor.

"Not that I intended to let you ogle me for much longer anyway," he added. His gaze travelled appreciatively over her sheer silk tunic and loose trousers.

"I was *not* watching you, sir," Ariel gasped, her cheeks burning in humiliation.

"No?"

"No!" Casting a worried glance down the colonnade, she returned her voice to a whisper. "What interest would I have in you?"

"My question precisely."

"Please," she begged anxiously as the Africans began sauntering back in their direction. "I can't stay here."

"Where would you suggest?"

"The garden." She nodded toward the darkness. In her determination to escape, Ariel didn't give his surprised look a thought.

"As you wish. But unless you're planning for us to waltz out into the night, I think you should let go of me first."

Ariel's gaze dropped to where her fingers still clutched the cobalt blue sleeves of his jacket. She was clinging to him like a frightened child, although he had released her arms. Mortified, she dropped her hands to her sides and stepped back, wishing she could melt into the mosaic design of the floor.

Their separation didn't last long. She didn't even have time to look up when he hauled her back against him, dragging her into the shadowy darkness of the garden. He didn't let go of her until they had crossed to the far side, where an ancient wisteria, heavy with spring blossoms, twined along a pillar providing a secluded niche in the garden. The minute he let go of her, Ariel backed into the spiky leaves, consumed with anger and humiliation. He had towed her out into the night like a beggar being expelled from the palace grounds simply because he wanted an answer to his questions. She had half a mind to call the

Bukhariyin out here herself. What right had he to order her about?

"You very nearly stepped right into their arms." An amused half-smile tipped his mouth to one side.

"What?"

"The guards were right behind you."

Ariel's eyes widened with understanding, and her anger dissipated in the cold night air. "You could have warned me," she said, her words tinged with injured pride.

"And given you away? We've both gone to too much trouble for that, don't you think?" A dazzling, boyish grin swept across his face. It had a devastating effect on Ariel, seeping like thick, hot coffee through her veins.

Unaware of the seductive nature of her action, she closed her eyes against the sensation, tipping her head back as she let the breeze fan away her confused embarrassment.

A sharp cough brought Ariel's eyes open again.

"You were about to tell me why you were peeking around that pillar like some ten-year-old spying on her parents' fete."

For a moment, Ariel considered fabricating a story, but as if reading her thoughts, he narrowed his eyes into two blue sparks of warning. "I was looking for someone," she admitted finally.

He eyed her skeptically, and waited for her to continue.

"Actually, I *was* hiding. And looking for someone," she said, surrendering her pride with a surreptitious smile.

"And were you able to find him in that crush?"

"Yes." Then looking at him with renewed trepidation, she asked, "How did you know I was looking for a man?"

"It seems a safe guess with beautiful women."

Staring self-consciously at the toe of her slipper, her heart made a ridiculous leap at his compliment. Then realizing his implication, her head snapped up. Ariel couldn't help noticing how the slightly menacing quality of his chiselled features softened as he smiled at her in amusement.

"I wasn't seeking him out! I was avoiding him."

"This sounds like some convoluted affair of the *ton*," he said with dry humor. "What is it that this gentleman did to warrant you trying to spy on him and avoid him all at the same time?"

"He wants to marry me."

"And you object to his suit?"

"It's a marriage purely for political gain."

"Ah, he sounds like a perfect monster. But isn't that how marriages are usually handled here?"

"Sometimes. But I'm not a princess. There's no reason that I should be forced to leave my home."

"We all have to leave home someday."

"Not to leave the country and never return."

"Is he a diplomat for the sultan? Is that why you'd leave Morocco?"

"He's a diplomat for your king."

"You're betrothed to an Englishman?"

Ariel was taken aback by the sudden intensity of his tone. "Yes. It's to be part of the treaty."

"And the name of the gentleman you were searching for this evening . . ."

"The Duke of Avon," Ariel replied.

For a moment his face took on the cast of an emotionless mask, shuttered and unreadable. Ariel had forgotten that he knew the man. She looked away, un-

25

comfortably warm beneath his sharp appraisal. "You were speaking to him just before I fell. I'm sorry if he's a friend of yours. I didn't mean to offend."

"You don't want this marriage?"

"Would you want to marry a stranger?" she asked. "I'm only a bargaining chip. Someone wants me sent away, and in exchange Mohammed gets his treaty."

"Why?"

She laughed bitterly at the irony of her situation. "The viziers think I'm a threat. They believe I'll encourage relations between Muslims and infidels."

"The English are infidels, yet the viziers are willing to condone the trade agreement just to be rid of you?"

"So it seems." Her reply was a mere whisper, choked by angry tears.

Christopher lifted her chin between his thumb and forefinger, and slowly unhooked the veil that masked the lower half of her face. She stood very still, looking up at him with determined pride despite the moist glaze of frustration that shone in her eyes.

So this was his intended bride. A momentary pang of regret filled him. Under different circumstances he would have liked to taste the promise of the finely set mouth. Full, yet not overly so, he thought. Infinitely kissable. Her nose was straight and slim, and her chin small, with just the hint of a point to it. Her cheekbones were high, and colored pink with what he knew was embarrassment at his perusal.

He brushed his thumb along the line of her jaw; her skin was like satin beneath it. "You don't seem capable of treachery to me."

"A few minutes ago you were ready to turn me over to the Bukhariyin yourself," she accused softly.

"A few minutes ago I didn't know you."

"And you know me now?"

"I know that the viziers are a greedy lot, overwhelmed by their own insecurities. I know they have nothing to fear from you."

"They will banish me unless I can convince the duke not to accept their terms."

"Perhaps I can do that for you," he told her gently.

"You? Why would you do such a thing for me?"

"I'm here to help with the treaty. And I believe you."

"You would speak to the duke? You know him that well?"

"I know him better than anyone."

"What is your price?" she asked, her nutmeg eyes suddenly wary.

Christopher cocked one brow in surprise. So she believed his offer was mercenary. So be it, he thought. If he was going to help her escape their marriage—a marriage neither of them wanted—his price would be a taste of what he was giving up.

"A kiss."

"What?"

"A kiss. It's a small price, wouldn't you say, to talk the duke out of signing the agreement." He watched her carefully, judging when to continue. "That's what you want, isn't it?"

"Yes." Ariel didn't hesitate in her reply. It seemed simple enough. All he wanted was a kiss, and tomorrow she would be free to stay in her adopted homeland.

He stroked her cheek, a soft caress that sent a shiver of apprehension running down her spine. It was only a kiss, she reminded herself, but the chill stayed with her as though in warning that once made, there would be no turning back from her decision.

Ariel looked at him. In the moonlight he seemed more sculptured stone than man. The half-moon frosted the untamed tufts of his hair, and the shadows carved his face into a pattern of planes that accentuated the deep set of his eyes and the strength of his jaw. For a moment she pictured him atop a sand dune deep in the Moroccan desert, the west wind curling through his dark hair like a lover's fingers. Startled by the sensuous image, she blinked the vision from her thoughts.

When she looked up again, there was no mistaking the smoldering intent of his gaze. Despite her apprehensions, some small part of her softened, becoming pliable and open to the promise there. She turned her face up, ready to pay his price and gain what she desired. She had no doubt that he could sway the duke. He did not seem a man to make idle promises. His mouth was next to hers, his breath a warm caress against her cheek. Ariel closed her eyes, waiting for the touch of his lips on hers. His arms closed around her like a warm blanket, and he drew her against him. She pressed her shoulders back, arching into him as his lips descended upon hers. He nuzzled at the crease of her lips, sending a trickle of warmth running down her spine. Then his mouth covered hers fully, and a volcano of hot, vibrant colors exploded within her. His kiss deepened, urging her to respond. She pressed her body to his, molding to him as molten lava spread through her limbs. Her fingers loosened their stiff splay across his chest, and she curled them into the soft linen of his shirt, sliding them upward across the fine nub of his cobalt jacket until her arms twined around his neck.

He pulled her closer against him, and she felt the demanding press of his manhood against her leg. Her breath caught in her throat, and a soft, erotic moan escaped as the muscular curve of his chest teased her own softly yielding body. This was what they spoke of in the harem. The experience one and all lived for, to be held like this. To please and be pleased. The scent of jasmine filled the night. Leaves rustled in the cold desert air. Ariel sensed it all anew, suddenly more attuned to the world than she had imagined possible. She felt drugged, and yet alive as never before as all of it blended with this man and the heat of their shared intimacy.

Suddenly there was the crush of grass under foot not a meter from where they stood. Ariel froze. Her breath caught in her throat as icy fear gripped her heart. His lips were gone, replaced by a calloused finger, still warmed from where it had pressed against her own flesh. And as she stood motionless, reason, cold and vicious, swept the cobwebs of desire from her mind. A kiss. It was to be only a kiss. But a kiss for which she could lose her head if discovered. It had never occurred to her that they might be found or that a simple kiss could last so long, or evolve into something with the same name but a new meaning altogether.

Surely the man standing on the other side of the wisteria was a Bukhariyin. But what did it matter if he wasn't, she thought hysterically? If they were found, she'd have no further worries about the English duke. She'd be stoned by the harem, or banished to the desert. Then what good would her freedom from a marriage contract do her? she thought in shame.

Christopher relaxed as the Moroccan moved away from the copse. The heavy, sweet odor of an opium pipe left little doubt that the man was none the wiser to their existence. Still, Christopher was furious with himself. She was the sultan's ward—the woman he had refused to marry, and had just now promised to extricate from any marriage pact. He'd been a fool to kiss her here in the sultan's palace. The last thing he needed was to be murdered for violating the sultan's ward. He reached for her hand, meaning to escort her to whichever escape route she had from the garden. She shoved his hand away, refusing to look at him, but he forced her eyes to met his.

"I shall have an answer from the duke tomorrow," he told her. "Meet me at the stables at noon."

Without replying, she turned away from him. She would have fled, but he caught her arm, drawing her against him again. "You'll be there?"

"And if I'm not?"

"Then, the duke will sign the pact."

"I don't even know your name."

"My name is Christopher Staunton."

"I'll be there, Mr. Staunton," she replied.

"And your name?" he insisted, angered by her dismissal.

"Ariel."

"The air sprite," Christopher commented to the night, for she was gone, darting like a hummingbird into the darkened doorway of the adjacent room.

Chapter Three

Soft morning sunlight streamed through the latticed balcony doors of Ariel's room. A fire already crackled in the hearth, and a breakfast of orange slices sprinkled with cinnamon and a sweet almond bun lay on a silver tray before it. But as Ariel sat up in her bed, drawing her legs beneath her chin, she could not enjoy the beautiful morning. Images of last night flooded her memory, and a flush of heat ran from her chin to her brow. Ariel scowled and kicked her blanket away. She'd been a fool to trust him. No Englishman could be trusted.

He hadn't kissed her. A kiss, from what she'd heard in the harem, was something sweet and deliciously promising. His kiss had been an assault, a searing demand, a hungry passion that had roared through her senses like a sandstorm, shattering her reserve, bending her to its will as it dragged unbidden emotions from her. Her fear turned to anger as she recalled Christopher Staunton's order that she meet him in the stables at noon. His lips had still been warm from their kiss when he'd snapped out his demand as if he were a nobleman himself, and she his property!

Arrogant infidel! From the moment she'd met him he'd made nothing but demands. Demanding to know who she was, accusing her of spying on him, threatening to give her to the Bukhariyin! What Yazid said was true. Infidels were nothing but pompous jackals who dined on the leavings of honorable men. But she needed this jackal. The kiss had been part of a bargain, and she'd paid. She owed him nothing, but he owed her much. He owed her his part of their agreement, his promise that he would convince the Duke of Avon to refuse to marry her. He'd said he knew the duke better than anyone. Certainly he'd not made an idle boast when he told her he could talk his friend out of the marriage. He was arrogant, she thought, but he didn't seem a man to make a pact he couldn't keep.

Ariel stared hard at the flames as they licked away the morning cold, and resolve bandaged her injured pride. No matter what had happened last night, she wouldn't let him intimidate her. She had willingly entered into their bargain. She would meet him at the stable. She would collect her due, and then she need never set eyes on Christopher Staunton again.

"Good morning, *ya hagga*." Rhima peeked in the door and went to inspect Ariel's breakfast. Seeing it was untouched, she left the tray and crossed the room, pushing the latticed screens open. Sunlight streamed through the open doorway, and with it came the lilting notes of instruments being tuned in the garden below. Climbing from her bed, Ariel helped herself to an almond bun and a glass of papaya juice, and walked out onto the balcony. The garden was enclosed by the palace on two sides, and a tall, pierced screen sealed it from the outside. She rested her arms on the balustrade and watched as a group of concubines and their children filed into the garden under the watchful eyes of eunuch guards.

Soon the odalisque musicians began a sprightly tune. The music set a happy mood, and the children settled in small groups to play while the women began a light-hearted game of tag. Ariel smiled down on the scene.

"They are very happy today," Rhima called from the bedroom as she tidied up. "The sultan has announced a *fantasia*."

"Really! When will it be?"

"After evening prayers on the morrow."

"It's been too long since the last *fantasia*. No wonder they're so full of play," Ariel laughed. Most of the concubines were her age or a bit younger. They darted in and out of the lemon trees, chasing one another in circles around the small pond. Their squeals of laughter, mingled with the music and the high-pitched babble of their children, made a delightful euphony.

"Your bath is ready," Rhima said, stepping out into the sunshine.

"Good," Ariel replied, the specter of her impending meeting with Christopher returning to her mind. "I feel in need of a bath this morning."

By the time Ariel looked down from the balcony again, nearly two hours had passed. The concubines now rested on divans that had been set amid the flower beds, while the children curled into drowsy balls on the grass. A quiet, almost haunting melody filled the air. As Ariel watched, her smile turned melancholy. She would like to have children someday. But she didn't know how she would ever have children without paying the price the concubines paid. This was their whole life. Silly games in the garden, and hours of gossip while they made themselves desirable and prayed that Allah would turn the sultan's eyes on them when he called for a lover each night. One young concubine stroked another's arm.

Ariel shook her head sadly. "The sultan doesn't love those girls. He beds them when his thirsts require quenching. That's all."

"He is generous and kind to them," Rhima replied quietly from the doorway. Ariel hadn't intended for anyone to hear her, but she didn't mind that Rhima held a different opinion than her own. To Rhima, a concubine's life must seem the pinnacle of satisfaction.

"They'll never know love."

Rhima shrugged. "What is love, my lady? If I had a warm fire at night, food to feed my family, and a tent to shield me from the sun, I would surely love the man who gave me such things."

"You would be grateful to him."

"No," the slave girl replied, her voice filled with practicality. "I would give him my allegiance and my fidelity. I would follow him where he went and make a welcome home for him. I would love him."

Ariel watched as the concubine's hand slipped lower on her companion's arm until their fingers intertwined. Her mother had described love as a man and woman bonded not solely by sensual gratifications, but also by like minds. Two souls made one by common goals and dreams. Something complex and touched with magic. Ariel looked down over the women in the garden. They had been bought for pleasure. That was what the sultan proposed to do with her: sell her to a stranger so that she could give him pleasure. Trade her happiness for English guns and trinkets. Last night she had traded for her freedom. Perhaps she was no different from the concubines. She had only one thing to bargain with, and like them, she had used it to her own gain.

The women stirred. One by one they collected their children, and soon the garden was deserted except for the odalisque musicians, who played in a sparse patch of late morning shadow. Ariel's hips began to sway in rhythm with the music.

"Can you stay a few minutes more?" she called down.

The lute player nodded, and Ariel's face lit with happiness. A minute later she was in the garden. She stopped just long enough to kick off her slippers and slip the leather straps of her finger cymbals in place; then she crossed the cool grass to the musicians. Finding a sunlit spot a few feet away, she closed her eyes and waited.

When the music began again, Ariel tilted her head back and closed her eyes, letting her thoughts dissolve amid the veil of colors the sunlight created against her lids. Slowly her hips began to sway. Her arms rose like the graceful necks of two swans above her head, and her fingers clicked the tiny cymbals together in rhythm with the song. Its sweet strains wound around her like a tantalizing odor, drawing her into its spell, demanding that she translate its notes into movement. She swayed and dipped, turning again and again in slow circles.

The music beckoned to her, awakening some primitive need deep within that inflamed and soothed her soul at one and the same time. Oblivious to everything other than the tale the music conveyed, her heart beat in tandem with the hand drum; her chest rose and fell with the notes of the lute as they drifted across the breezeless heat of the garden. She lost herself in the music, letting it sweep all thought from her mind. Then, just as the song reached its crescendo,

35

the music stopped abruptly. Ariel opened her eyes, looking in bewilderment at the odalisques as they raised their veils to cover their faces. Following their stares, she turned toward the doorway where her gaze locked with a pair of crystalline blue eyes.

One shoulder propped casually against a wall, Christopher watched Ariel with frank approval. Her arms were bare except for wide bands of gold that encircled her wrists, accentuating their delicacy. A butter yellow silk tunic fell in loose folds from her shoulders, and a thin belt of twinkling gems caught the sheer fabric close at her waist. Beneath its seductive transparency, he could see the outline of slim hips. The thick plait of her burnished bronze hair just touched her waist, where it still swung to and fro in rhythm with the now silent musicians. She was a golden siren, seductive beyond belief, and the memory of her kiss was becoming all too much of a habit.

He smiled lazily at her, hiding the intense reaction her dancing had drawn from him. "Good morning." Crossing the lawn that separated them in long, sure strides, he looked down at the rising color in her cheeks. They were like fresh peaches, a harvest of pink and gold that begged to be touched.

"I'm afraid your guard is a bit remiss in his duties," he said, nodding to where her eunuch sat snoring in the shady doorway.

"You can't be here," she replied, ignoring his greeting.

The calmness of her own voice surprised Ariel. Disregarding the wild thump of her heart, she continued. "These gardens are for the harem. If you'd passed by a few minutes earlier, you'd have come upon half of the concubines. Spying on the harem is an offense punishable by death."

"I knew they had left. I wanted to assure myself that you intend to keep our appointment."

"I said I would be there, Mr. Staunton. My word is good. However, since you're here, you can tell me the results of your meeting with the duke now." As she spoke Ariel waged a furious battle within. He was as calm and cool as an iced drink, sauntering into the garden as though he had every right in the world to do so and then questioning her word. She ached to show him that this was her home. She should order him out, call the very guards he had threatened to set on her the night before. But she didn't dare. She needed his answer first.

In the light of day, he was taller than she recalled. His stature and the straight, unyielding carriage of his broad, square shoulders all combined to his advantage, making him the most intimidating man she'd ever seen. There was a rugged strength about him that permeated the air, and Ariel's nostrils flared at the scent of the same musky cologne he'd worn the night before. She choked back her ire. It would do no good to vent her aggravation until she knew the duke had refused the contract.

"You've spoken to him?" she asked.

"Not yet, he's touring the stables with the sultan soon. I'm headed there now."

Ariel looked up at the overhead sun. "It will be midday very soon."

Christopher's gaze followed her own. "So it will." He pinned her with an unswerving look and smiled. "Come prepared to ride. I'll have what you want."

"I can't ride! Women aren't allowed outside the palace. I can't imagine how your king allowed you to come here on a political mission without knowing a thing about our customs."

"Oh, I know all about the customs," he said, unconcerned. "And I know that anyone who sneaks around ballrooms can figure out a way to ride."

Before she was aware of his intention, Christopher swept her hand to his mouth and pressed a kiss on the back of it. "Until then." He smiled at her, a smile full of mischievous challenge. Then he strode out of the garden without a backward glance, stepping over the peacefully sleeping eunuch as he went.

Christopher strode along the walk that led to the stables. The sea green tiled roof of the imposing white building shimmered like the Mediterranean in the waves of heat that rose before it. Two long wings extended to either side of the main structure, marked by an even line of stall doors and a walkway of pink marble chips shaded by an overhanging portico. As he made his way down the rows of stalls, he could see Robert and the sultan engrossed in conversation.

"Lord Staunton," the sultan called out as Christopher approached the small group of men. "Surely, in your travels throughout Morocco, you have ridden our fine Arabian horses. Do you not find them superior to your English Thoroughbreds in speed and agility?"

"Each has its place, Moulay Mohammed," Christopher explained, stopping between the sultan and his eldest son. "The Thoroughbred is well suited to the long stretches of roads and rolling hills we ride. The finest English Thoroughbred, however, couldn't last a week in the Moroccan desert. Your Arabians were created for the dunes."

"Quite a diplomatic answer. Substantially different from the hot-tempered legend I've heard about," the sultan said with an approving smile. "Your demeanor suits you well."

Christopher inclined his head. "I believe experience has tempered the irascible nature I was sometimes accused of possessing in my younger days, Moulay. My uncle can attest to the pliable and level-headed temperament I've sported the past several years."

"My sources are not as completely unreliable as you'd have me think," the sultan returned good-naturedly.

"What's your opinion of our Thoroughbreds, Moulay Mohammed El Yazid?" Christopher asked, turning pointedly to the sultan's heir. Yazid was, from all that Christopher had been able to discern through his contacts, the perfect heir to the throne. Intelligent, shrewd, and wildly popular. No one denied his hatred for Christians, but every sultan in the last four hundred years had hated Christians. Mohammed Ben Abdullah was the lone exception, and though he had brought a long-awaited prosperity and unity to the nation, many of the Moroccans were more comfortable with Yazid's blatantly aggressive personality.

"Your horses are inbred and weak in my estimation, Lord Staunton," Yazid stated without bothering to hide his contempt. "I find them nervous and easily winded. Certainly I would not place my trust in one. I would ever be wary of receiving a vicious bite."

The barely concealed slur turned Christopher's eyes flinty as he parried Yazid's thrust, the battle of wills engaged.

"Perhaps, Moulay, it's your inexperience in handling steeds of a Thoroughbred's stature which makes you fearful of them," Christopher commented deftly. El Yazid's face lit with fury at his suggestion.

The knowledge that Robert, and therefore England, knew so little about Mohammed El Yazid bothered him. The heir's renown as an equestrian and swordsman was legendary, as was his popularity. But Christopher lent more weight to the stories about El Yazid's enormous ego, and his abiding hatred of foreigners. Rumors abounded that El Yazid more often rallied support with the Arab and Berber leaders of the Makhzan for the banishment of foreign diplomacy than for the peaceful treaties put forward by his father. But he worked in the shadows, never opposing the sultan outright. Christopher wondered if Mohammed even knew it was his son behind the rumblings against his policies. If he did, he didn't acknowledge it. Yazid's disdain for the English could easily bode ill for the treaty, depending on the extent of El Yazid's influence with the sultan. Just how much the sultan would be swayed by El Yazid's opinion was something Christopher didn't know. Yet.

"There isn't a stallion in all of the British Empire I could not conquer," El Yazid declared, the deep olive of his complexion tinged with scarlet indignation.

Christopher lifted a skeptical eyebrow, watching the muscle in El Yazid's cheek twitch in outrage as he continued.

"Some men see the Arabians' small size and are fooled into believing they are weak. But the Arabian horses are swift and sure-footed. They'll carry a man until they fall dead beneath him. They know how to survive, and Allah's *baraka*, his protection and grace, is upon them." El Yazid stared at Christopher, his pale green eyes filled with challenge. "Have you heard of the *fantasia?*"

"Ah, yes," Robert cut in. "Isn't the *fantasia* some kind of military training maneuver?"

40

"It is much more than that," the sultan replied proudly. "It is not unlike your ancient English tournaments. The finest horsemen and soldiers of our armies charge in a mock response to the call to battle. In one great line they thunder on their horses directly toward the audience. When they reach a designated point, they stop and fire their guns into the air."

"It must be quite exhilarating to see," Robert said.

"It is a true showing of the might and skills of my countrymen, Lord Belmeth," the sultan replied. "And yes, it is something one must see to fully appreciate. We are holding a *fantasia* tomorrow night. You shall see then why our pride is so great in our horses—and our warriors. Mohammed El Yazid shall lead the *fantasia*."

El Yazid's eyes were hooded as he executed a smooth bow, but in the few seconds before his face was hidden from view, Christopher's watchful gaze caught the hard glint of disdain flicker across his face.

"Tell me your opinion of this animal," the sultan said, turning his attention to a beautiful gray stallion being led out of his stall for their inspection by a spindly-legged stable boy. The brown slave boy trotted the young stallion up and down the marble-chip path in front of them, his face beaming with pride as the horse arched his neck and flagged his tail behind him.

When he brought the stallion to a halt before the group of men, Christopher ran an experienced hand down one foreleg, checking it for strength and straightness. "He's spectacular, Moulay Mohammed," he said, stepping back to admire the stallion again.

"Sirocco will be a king of the Arabians," El Yazid stated. "One day he will lead much greater things than just the *fantasia*. He has the blood of a war horse in his veins. He will be the pride of all Morocco."

As the boy led Sirocco back to his stall, Christopher caught a glimpse of a white djellaba trimmed with blood-red disappear around the corner. A moment later a turbaned head appeared there and a pair of eyes that had haunted him ever since he'd first looked into them.

"There are a few other horses you must see, Lord Staunton," the sultan said.

"I would be honored to see them, Moulay. However, I was hoping to ride today. If I might beg your indulgence, I'd like to see them another time."

"Of course," the sultan replied with genuine understanding. "One would always prefer to ride. I give you freedom to choose whichever of my horses you like. I will see you this evening, Lord Staunton," he continued, becoming more somber. "There are certain points of the trade agreement between our two countries to be considered."

"There are indeed, Moulay," Christopher said, watching for the scarlet-trimmed djellaba beyond the sultan's bejeweled turban.

Chapter Four

Christopher waited until the other men disappeared into the cool darkness of the stable, then turned as Ariel joined him outside Sirocco's stall. She was dressed in the loose cotton pantaloons and scarlet robe of a royal guard. The abundant white material of her pants was tucked into soft suede boots, and the black sash that held her tunic accentuated her slim figure beneath it. A snowy turban crowned her head, completing her disguise. She was as beautiful swathed in yards of cotton as she'd been in the sheer yellow silk he'd found her dancing in, Christopher noted.

"I said you should come prepared to go riding, not dressed for a trip into the desert," he chided good-naturedly.

"Do you think I should have come with my eunuch, Siad, and announced to the sultan that I've decided to take in the scenery?" she asked, irate. "That would have been akin to asking that I be locked in my room until I was safely married off. Now, if you have something to tell me, please do so before someone comes by."

"That's why I suggested we go riding."

Ariel shot him a furious glare. "I have no horse, Mr. Staunton."

"Do you know how to ride?"

"I do. Although it's been many years since my mother took me riding with her," she said uncertainly. "I may have forgotten most of what I knew."

"It will come back to you quickly," Christopher assured her with irritating confidence. The stable boy appeared as if from thin air and, without giving Ariel so much as a second glance, hurried to follow Christopher's instructions to saddle a quiet mare.

"You were talking with Prince Yazid just now." Ariel commented, unable to keep her interest to herself. "How did you find him?"

"I found him abrasive and immature," Christopher stated flatly.

Ariel cocked her head defensively. "Yazid will be sultan some day, and he believes a sultan is entitled to behave in such a manner. Isn't it the same with your King George?"

"Not to that degree," Christopher said pointedly.

"Yazid can't help being the way he is." Ariel gave a dismissive wave. "His mother has filled him with grandiose ideas since he was born. She fawns over him, and lets no one forget that he will be sultan. You know the mother of a sultan has great power, and Daiwa is very hungry for that."

As she turned to mount her horse Christopher scooped her up and set her on top of the dappled white mare.

She looked down at him with a startled expression.

"I think you are too familiar with someone who is supposed to be a guard of Morocco."

"A rather puny guard."

Ariel threw him a frustrated look. "I am not enjoying this, Mr. Staunton. We have a bargain, and I wish to know if you have kept your portion of it.

44

That's all. Now, if you don't mind, can we please find somewhere where we may talk in private."

"As you wish, Lady Ariel." Christopher swung atop the Arabian stallion the stable boy had brought and fell in beside Ariel, who was leading the way toward the main road.

"Did my disguise trick you?" she asked after a short silence.

"Not at all."

Ariel made a childish face at him. "Well, I attempted to grow a beard to complete my disguise, but I was unable to manage the feat. I imagine that if I'd had a bit more time, I might have been able to concoct some vile liquid that would create one."

"It would have been a crime. Nothing should hide a face like yours. Not a veil and certainly not a beard. Besides," he added quietly, "your eyes would always give you away."

Ariel turned away, busying herself with straightening the long scarlet tassels that decorated the mare's reins.

"Are you close to Mohammed El Yazid?" Christopher asked suddenly. The muscles in his back tensed unaccountably as he waited for her reply, and he scowled to himself. What difference did it make to him how Ariel Lennox felt about the prince? After tonight he would have nothing at all to say to the little chit. The only tie that bound them now was a mutual desire to extricate themselves from a ridiculous contract that would create a highly unsuitable marriage. He should have told her this morning that "the duke" had agreed to refuse the sultan's offer and been done with it.

But he couldn't really do that. As of yet, Christopher hadn't spoken to Mohammed Ben Abdullah on that particular point. That was to be discussed to-night, and one thing the sultan did not like was having his schedule changed. When Mohammed was discussing horses, you discussed horses. You didn't suddenly bring marriage into the conversation. Christopher wasn't even sure why he'd insisted that Ariel take this ride with him. He didn't have an answer for her. He looked at Ariel from the corner of one eye. Despite her inexperience, she sat astride her horse as proud and secure as any Berber warrior. A reluctant smile touched his mouth. She was all the more beautiful for her self-assurance. He was attracted to her. There was no denying that. Why shouldn't he enjoy her while he could?

"I grew up with Yazid in a way. But I'm a woman and he's the heir. He hasn't time to be concerned with me," Ariel said. "He, and Suleiman are the only children of the sultan older than I, and when my mother wanted me to be educated, I studied under their tutors — though separated, of course. I haven't really seen them much since my mother died. And now they are men, and it would be wrong to see them often. Although," Ariel added after a moment, "I did see Yazid in the sultan's library not more than a month ago. I don't think he knew who I was at first, and then he just stared at me. It was very unsettling.

"I don't know why I'm confiding all of this in you," she said self-consciously. "I shouldn't even be here. And I wouldn't be," she added, glaring at Christopher before turning pointedly away, "if it wasn't absolutely necessary."

With her hair tucked beneath her turban, Ariel's high cheekbones were accentuated, and her beauty ignited a flame of desire in Christopher's belly. His gaze settled on the long, slim column of her neck, and it

occurred to him that he had never seen a more eminently appropriate place to plant a warm kiss. She
turned to look at him just then, her gold-flecked eyes
wary.

"You did speak to the duke, didn't you?"

"I know what his answer will be. But we'll wait
until we're somewhere less obvious to discuss that."
Christopher was beginning to dislike all these half-
truths. He ought to tell her who he was and be done
with it.

"We can turn off the road at the grove just ahead,"
Ariel told him, pointing to the lines of trees that began just ahead of them. "Beyond it is a place where
we can stop. I remember it from riding with my
mother."

Christopher didn't respond. He was battling with
his conscience.

"Do you like oranges?" Ariel asked with a note of
pride in her voice as they entered the grove. It ran as
far as the eye could see on either side.

"The English would pay a king's ransom to possess
a grove like this," Christopher said, forcing aside the
debate running in his mind. "My cargos are specially
packed, crated, and cushioned. Still, the oranges arrive in London bruised and sometimes spoiled. Few
Londoners have ever seen a perfect orange."

"You're a merchant?" Ariel asked, with sudden interest.

"In part," Christopher said. "Although I no longer
captain my ships."

"Oh, I see."

Christopher had the distinct impression that she
was disappointed to find he wasn't a swashbuckling
sea captain.

"I own a fleet of ships," he continued, suppressing a

grin. "If I took the time to captain one of my own ships, the others would suffer from lack of attention."

"You oversee all the ships, then?" she asked as if trying to anchor an image of his work in her mind.

"My overseer and managers do that."

"Then, what is it *you* do?" she asked doubtfully.

"I make certain that everyone does their job, and I negotiate for the goods my ships will carry."

"But now you're at El Bedi to help with the trade treaty?"

"Yes," Christopher responded carefully.

"Then, you'll be going back to England as soon as the duke refuses marriage to me."

"Perhaps the treaty will be ratified without the marriage," he suggested.

"If the viziers can't rid themselves of me with the treaty, they'll never agree to it. Mohammed won't invoke a disagreement. Peace among the tribes is tenuous, and much too important to risk."

Christopher contemplated that bit of information in silence. They had passed through the orange grove to a series of parklike gardens. A long wall of yew ran along one side, and Ariel turned into a small opening in the growth.

As they emerged on the other side of the hedge, a crystalline pool forty meters across spread before them. All around it trees blossomed in their spring finery, their colors a soft pastel wash in the calm water. At one end a man-made waterfall cascaded into the pool. At the other end stood an intimate pavilion.

"It's just as beautiful as I remember it," Ariel breathed, taking in the scene before them.

Christopher looked at her and nodded. She couldn't possibly know the purpose this secluded pavilion with its waterfall and pool had been intended for, he told himself. He slipped off his stallion and lifted her easily to the ground, leaving the horses to graze on the carpet of emerald grass. Ariel walked before him, leading the way directly to the pavilion. She stepped under its arching dome and crossed to the side nearest the pool, where three marble steps led into the water.

Christopher watched as she settled on the uppermost step and proceeded to pull off first one suede boot and then the other. She pushed the loose cotton of her pantaloons up to her knees, exposing a pair of shapely legs and smooth, lightly tanned feet.

Christopher was just contemplating the impression that the sun-burnished color of her skin appeared to continue well beyond the portion of her leg revealed to his gaze when she tossed her turban beside the discarded boots. Her hair tumbled from its prison like a rope of bronze. She lifted her hands to her nape, and ran her fingers through the thick, straight tresses, slowly dropping her head back to shake them loose. He stood frozen above her. The memory of her in his arms swam before him, and the palm of his hand suddenly ached for the buttery softness of her skin. Every movement she made was seductively enticing, yet he knew she did so innocently, not intending to add tinder to the bonfire of desire that roared through him.

Everything in his nature cried out for him to pull her into his arms and crush her against him, to let her see the power her beauty and her seductive charms held over him. Never in his life had any woman so inspired his desire or so tested his willpower. But he was about to tell her that she was free from the threat of marrying him. How could he do that and satisfy his hunger for her at the same time?

49

He let out a ragged breath and retreated to a safer distance, settling against the arched entrance to the pavilion.

Ariel dangled her feet in the crystal clear water, enjoying its refreshing coolness while she breathed in the blossom-perfumed air. She smiled at Christopher, who had become unaccountably quiet. "This was built by Moulay Ismail as a trysting place," she said, reciting the stories her mother had told her. When Christopher only shot her a humorless stare, she continued with determined brightness. This was her first time away from the palace in eight years, and she was enjoying herself immensely.

"They say he had over five hundred concubines and only a handful fewer children. Whenever he purchased a particularly beautiful new concubine, he would arrange for her to be brought here on the first couching night.

"I can't think of anything more wonderful than to be here at sunset, blossoms dropping into the pond, the sound of the water rushing from above to join with the stillness of the pool, being held by strong arms . . ." Ariel faltered and blushed furiously as she realized how childish she must sound. She looked up at Christopher. His eyes had warmed to a midnight blue, and he watched her with frightening intensity.

"Do you dream of a tryst, Ariel?" he asked huskily.

"No." She turned away to stare into the pool, refusing to look into those hypnotic eyes. She did not want to repeat last night's mistake. "Tell me about the duke," she asked, changing the subject. "He's agreed to my request?"

"He has."

She ventured a peek at Christopher's deeply tanned face and found to her relief that the strange intensity was fading, although his eyes were dark and brooding. "I have your promise on this?"

Christopher nodded. "He believes we can convince the sultan and his advisors to sign the treaty without the marriage, and like you, Ariel, the duke has no interest in marrying for political gain."

"He doesn't need my estates, or the prestige my name would lend him?"

Christopher laughed, and Ariel made an irritated face at him.

"The sultan has told me I have estates and houses of great value in England, and that the cachet of marrying a countess who is also the ward of a great sultan would make me a good match for any Englishman."

"Pull in your claws, little tigress," he chuckled. "I didn't mean to offend you. But the house of Avon is an old one. The duke has more estates than he cares to even consider. And as for your money," he continued, a dark shadow falling over his face, "marrying for money would have been the easy way out. He could have done that a long time ago if he was that kind of man."

"You like him, don't you," she said quietly.

Christopher laughed again. This time, though, the sound was tinged with cynicism. "Sometimes I'm not really sure who he is." He paused for a moment. "Why wouldn't the Makhzan approve the treaty without a marriage?"

Ariel shrugged. "It will be much like the treaties with France and America; a trade agreement, goods which you produce in exchange for our fruits, leather and copper."

Christopher nodded, and Ariel continued.

"The sultan believes these treaties are very good for

51

Morocco. He says we must work with other countries if the Maghreb is to prosper."

"And the viziers?"

"Their opinion depends upon which tribe they come from. There are many different opinions."

"What about Yazid?"

"I don't know what Yazid thinks of the treaty," she said, cocking her head to one side thoughtfully. "But he doesn't agree with the sultan about prospering through commerce. I've heard them argue about it. Yazid thinks Morocco should shun the other countries. He says they weaken us."

"And what do you think, my little politician?" Christopher asked with a lopsided grin.

"I don't know enough to say," Ariel responded, blushing.

"You haven't formed an opinion about your guardian's policies?"

"I only think that he is right in his thinking and Yazid is, well . . . inexperienced," Ariel said after a long pause. She didn't want to criticize Yazid. Although she'd shared hardly a dozen words with him in years, she still thought of him as the closest thing she had to a brother. It wouldn't do to have anyone, especially someone from the opposing delegation, think she might not respect his opinions. "I'm certain that in a few more years he'll come to agree more thoroughly with the sultan."

"I'm not sure the prince is deserving of such loyalty, Ariel, although I commend you for it. It's not often that a person is able to see the flaw in someone's character and forgive them for it."

Warmed by the gentle timbre of his voice, Ariel looked up into Christopher's devastatingly handsome face, and then away, staring at the goldfish that nibbled boldly at her toes. Something warned her that she should get up and go now. Christopher had lived up to his promise and convinced the duke to give her back her freedom. There was nothing else to be said, and no reason to linger by the water.

But the afternoon was still young, and it might be another eight years before she came back to the trysting pool. Christopher reminded her just now of the sultan. The way he asked her about her thoughts, and took an interest in what she was doing. She'd have liked to look forward to another afternoon ride with Christopher Staunton. But he was an Englishman and an infidel. It was just as well that after today their paths never cross again.

Ariel's heart leapt into her throat as Christopher's knuckles brushed her cheek. She hadn't even noticed that he'd left the archway, yet now he knelt beside her, his eyes once more dark and intense.

"I think you'd do better to lavish your loyalties on someone who might hold you in as much regard. Someone who would show you the true magic of a place like this."

Ariel knew he meant to kiss her again. She also knew that there was something more than just the sensation of his lips against hers that pulled her to him and made her welcome his kiss despite her earlier resolve. He was handsome and witty, and this afternoon he'd made her feel valuable as no person had made her feel since her mother's death. He would be gone soon—if not tomorrow, then the day after. Ariel wanted the memory of this afternoon to savor. She wanted one kiss that was not part of a bargain. One kiss that was real. And looking into the midnight depths of his eyes, she knew that this one was.

She laid her hand on his sleeve as he drew her into

his arms and turned her face up to his, eager to taste his kiss again. As her gaze met his she thought hazily that his eyes bore the haunted depths of a man on the verge of some infinitely sweet torture. He was a mass of contradictions. Hard sinew and muscle. Soft, velvet blue eyes. Intense, bold, and demanding. Gentle, warm, and enticing. Then his lips descended upon hers, and all thoughts fled, vanquished by the tender warmth of his mouth moving on hers.

Ariel's hands slipped around his neck. Her fingertips touched his hair and dug deep into its dark silk as she fit her body against his. A flame of desire licked to life at his touch, and she melted into its heat, flowing like molten wax into a new form. It was like last night had been. She was intoxicated by him. One kiss became a thousand. He showered her face with their warmth. Her eyelids. Her brow. The sensitive skin where her jaw met the lobe of her ear. An indefinable urge rose within her. It was exciting. Tantalizing. Overpowering. Her lashes fluttered against her cheeks as he pressed kiss after kiss along her neck. Then his lips took hers again, this time more insistently. His tongue flickered across her teeth, running along the inner edge of her lip, then dipping into the well where lower lip met upper. His mouth pressed hers open, and she yielded. Immediately his tongue dove deep within, caressing the inner walls, drawing her own tongue into titillating play, and a bloom of new sensation sent rushes of heat curling through her. He drew her tongue into his mouth, introducing her to new intimacies there. And she followed eagerly. The flame spread, nourished by emotions she had discovered with him and kindled to increasing heights by the urgency of his mouth, his own shortened breath, and the soft groan he uttered as she boldly slid her tongue into his mouth once more. She wanted the heat of his body mingled with hers, to breathe in the smell of him until it obliterated the sweet scent of cherry blossoms and the water's icy chill on her feet.

His fingers caressed her hair while his other hand moved to the soft roundness of her buttocks, molding her to his own length, sending tingling fingers of warmth spiralling through her as a breathless whimper escaped from her. His fingers were at her sash, and Ariel felt her nipples tighten in anticipation of his touch. He drew his mouth away from hers as he spread the djellaba, revealing her full, firm breast to the sun.

"Temptress." The word was a ragged whisper against her mouth. His kisses wandered lower, trailing along her neck. His tongue painted a line along the crest of her shoulder as his hand cupped her breast. A moment later his mouth closed on the jutting peak of her nipple. She moaned at the indescribable pleasure and pulled his head down upon her with fierce need. He nibbled gently, then suckled, sending fevered chills, one upon another, bolting through her.

"Please," she whispered through the strangling charge of emotion that warred within her. "Please, don't."

Christopher looked at her, his eyes haunted and bleak. Slowly he drew away from her.

A chill swept through Ariel as a dark rain cloud obliterated the sun. She was still on fire, and the sudden breeze covered her skin with a rash of goose bumps as she pulled her clothes into place and knotted the sash. How could she feel so wonderful one moment and so desolate the next? she wondered, drawing a jagged breath. And why was the man who'd set this fire raging within her sitting there, his fingers tangled in his hair as hers had been moments ago, with a look as grim as death upon his face?

"We'd better start back," Christopher commented, nodding at the black clouds rushing toward them.

Ariel nodded silently and began to pull on her boots. As she piled her hair atop her head and artfully wound the long white cloth about it recreating the discarded turban, Christopher remained ominously silent. Finishing, she tucked the tail of cloth into place and walked back to her mare. She felt Christopher come up behind her, but swung into the high-pommeled saddle before he could offer any assistance. Frustrated and angry, she turned the mare and slipped through the cypress, not waiting for her companion.

Christopher pursed his lips into a thin line and mounted his horse. He caught up with Ariel easily, riding in silence beside her. He'd acted like a fool of the worst sort, he told himself angrily. Stealing a kiss last night had been a mere act of curiosity, and that had gone badly enough. But succumbing to his attraction to Ariel today, when he was about to renounce her guardian's offer, was nothing short of stupidity.

If only she weren't so innocently seductive, he railed, staring at the branches of the orange trees as the wind began to toss them wrathfully. How could she not know the temptation she presented sitting there, her legs bared and that cascade of gold streaming down her back? He had intended only to convey the message that "the duke" would not marry her. Instead, he'd abandoned all reason for one more taste of her. A taste of sweet desire that she had returned in full measure.

There had been no peck with sealed lips to tease him. Ariel had met his ardor with her own unsequestered passion. He could still feel the press of her hips against his own, the soft curve of her buttocks in his hand, and the way her tongue had driven him insane with its darting explorations. He'd wanted her so badly then, he'd have stopped at nothing.

And she would have gone with him.

Something told him that. It was only his own hesitation that had frightened her. Otherwise he would, at this moment, be pouring his seed into her.

Christopher groaned and pushed the torturous image away. He set his jaw with steely anger as the first heavy drops of rain splattered against his face. It was impossible! He didn't want to marry her. He'd told her — given her his word — that the Duke of Avon would reject the sultan's offer. His behavior was pure adolescence. He was allowing his desires to override his common sense, a liberty Christopher never permitted himself. Such indulgences only led to disaster, a fact he'd seen confirmed time and time again.

The heavens opened up like a bursting goat skin. Ahead of him Ariel urged her mare into a headlong gallop for the stables. Christopher watched her go, holding the nervous stallion at bay as a bolt of lightning split the blackened sky, followed by a menacing growl of thunder. The deluge beat down, battering horse and rider in its ferocity. Christopher held himself there, setting his resolve as he steeled himself against the storm. He desired Ariel Lennox, he wouldn't deny that, and she desired him.

But he did not want her. Not at the price the sultan demanded.

And Ariel certainly did not want him.

It wouldn't happen again, he vowed as another fork of lightning lit the black sky. Tonight he'd tell the sultan there would be no marriage, and his golden temptress would be out of his life forever. Hauling on the reins, Christopher wheeled the Arabian stallion around, and horse and rider bolted forward as one, ready at last to come in out of the rain.

Chapter Five

Christopher returned to his rooms dripping rain water, but the hot bath and brandy he'd barked out orders for had done much over the past hour to alleviate his vile mood. Tucking the tails of his shirt into his breeches as he dressed for his meeting with Mohammed Ben Abdullah, Christopher reminded himself that there were hundreds of women in the world, and that he was not about to be spurred into making an irrational change of plans by one particularly challenging sprite no matter how stunning a beauty or how responsive a lover. He stopped mid-stride on his way to pick up the evergreen vest he planned to wear as a knock sounded at the door. Before he could utter a response, the door burst open, and Fatim stood in the doorway, hands on his hips, and legs akimbo in a flowing djellaba and turban.

"I could not believe it when Moulay Mohammed Ben Abdullah, great leader of all Morocco, spoke your name! I had to see for myself, and now I have the proof of his words! Aiyee!" he cried, throwing his hands heavenward with enthusiastic relish as he strode across the room. "Welcome, son of my father's tent. Allah smiles on me today!"

The mountain Berber grasped Christopher's wrist, pulling him into a brusque embrace. Christopher returned the gesture, genuinely pleased at this unexpected visit.

"Fatim, what are you doing here?" Christopher asked the bearded young man as he stepped back.

"Ah! I came to speak to our great sultan at the request of my father. I am afraid I was not the bearer of good news for him. But, do not concern yourself with that. Let me look at you!" He grinned ear to ear before clamping Christopher in another infectious embrace.

"My mother and sisters will be displeased when I tell them you are in Morocco and have not come to see them," Fatim said with a sober shake of his dark head. "You must give me some fodder with which to appease their injured vanity."

"I planned to come when I could take a few days. I'm working for the king, so my time isn't my own this trip."

"At least it is a bone for them to chew upon." He shrugged. "But you must make good on your vow to come, else my life will not be worth living, Brother." He rolled his eyes heavenward. "I warn you, my sisters fight constantly over which will marry you and become a great English sultana. I tell them you will not marry until you are a gray-bearded old man, by which time they will be many years married with a brood of chicks to look after and a thick waist to prove it."

Christopher chuckled, pulling on his last boot as Fatim dropped into the opposite chair, his legs sprawled in a carefree flop.

"Each year as they come of age and my father, in his wisdom, marries them off, I think my life will become easier," Fatim continued with a woebegone face. "But the older ones live close by and visit often. And the younger ones! Aiyee! I vow they are more head-strong than the others. There is no peace for me. As Allah is my maker, life with ten sisters is a trial. I cannot see how The Great One could have overlooked providing me with at least one brother for my own defenses!"

Christopher relaxed in his chair, casually propping a booted ankle across his knee as he watched Fatim's happily overwrought face. "I'd help you if I could, Fatim, but I'm afraid you can't count on me to relieve you of one of your sisters. Besides, I doubt there is a more doted-upon male in Mohammed's kingdom. It seems to me you thrive on your sisters' affec-tions."

Fatim grinned broadly. "It is almost like possessing a harem, is it not? And without any of the expense. I suppose we must all trust Allah's wisdom and bear our trials as best we are able. Now," he said, jumping up from the chair, "what is this business you are here to conduct for your king?"

Christopher shrugged. "My uncle is negotiating a trade agreement between Morocco and England. He asked me to come along, knowing my familiarity with the land."

"Then, your father's brother believes there may be some trouble with this new treaty?"

"My mother's sister's husband," Christopher cor-rected with a smile, "and perhaps he simply wants to put the Makhzan more at ease by using some of the language and knowledge I can give him."

"A wise man this uncle," Fatim stated unequivo-cally. "He is blessed to have you here."

"Because of your information for the sultan?"

Christopher asked, then added, "If your father has sworn you to secrecy, I will understand, Fatim."

"I have trusted you with my life! Is there anything of greater value I would not be free to tell you?" he asked, indignant. "No! Of course not!" Fatim paced the room in a fit of energy. "We are brothers by vow. Among the Berbers that is an even greater bond than blood." He looked across at Christopher, and grinned. "But, of course, you are too honest a man to pry and possibly dishonor me. So I am not insulted by your remark."

"I'm pleased to hear it," Christopher remarked, eyeing the overly enthusiastic younger man. "Perhaps you will tell me what your father's message was before I have to change for supper."

"Of course! Ten days ago my father was called to a Berber Council of the Bilad al Siba."

"They meet several times each year," Christopher interjected.

"Yes. That is true, Brother. But while he was there, my father overheard some talk of affairs within the Bilad al Makhzan. You know the cities are governed by the sultan's Arab government. The Makhzan is made up of the leaders of the cities. This is different from the Bilad al Siba, which is all the leaders of the Berber mountain tribes. We are freer to do as we please with our people so long as we do not disobey the sultan's laws."

Christopher nodded. He was familiar with everything Fatim told him, but it was what he implied that caught his attention. Fatim's father, Khalif al Rashid, was among the most respected and powerful of the Berber caids, the leader of a tribe numbering nearly one thousand. The fact that he had *overheard* some rumor of the Bilad al Makhzan made the possibility of the rumor more dangerous by far than something he may have been told outright.

"The men my father overheard spoke of revolt. This is not unusual. There are always rumblings of revolt in Morocco. If we cannot dream of a new and better freedom, then we are as despondent and listless as the captured butterfly. But the words of these men my father overheard were precise and well thought-out. They were not the dreams of jaded old men. They spoke of the sultan's own guards. The Bukhariyin."

"The Black Guards?" Christopher scrutinized Fatim's dark, almond eyes.

"I know," Fatim replied to Christopher's sharp look. "Even my father could not believe his own ears. It is a testament to Allah's favor on our great moulay that he led my father to the shadows near these two men. He would not otherwise have heard this. No one would dare to speak of such things against Mohammed Ben Abdullah in my father's presence."

"Then, Khalif al Rashid has been able to confirm the conspiracy?"

Fatim nodded.

Christopher pressed his fingers together beneath his chin and stared at the patterned rug. "What did Moulay Mohammed say when you gave him your father's message?"

Fatim pursed his lips into a thin line. "He said very little. What could he confide in me? He listened and then sent his wishes for good life and Allah's blessing to my father."

"With the Bukhariyin within the palace walls, a revolt could defeat the sultan before a war even started," Christopher said quietly.

"Such were the words of my father. It would be a

time of great mourning in our land, for it is certain that along with Mohammed Ben Abdullah, his wives and children would be massacred. Whoever leads the Bukhariyin would not even allow a pregnant concubine to live. There could not be any heirs."

Or wards, Christopher thought, if the viziers were at all involved in the plot. The image of Ariel defying the sultan's usurpers flooded his mind. He had no doubt that she would fight, and a fiery spirit was not something Islamic warriors appreciated in a woman. They would beat the pride out of her if she was caught. And she would be caught if the Bukhariyin were able to pull off a coup within the walls of El Bedi.

"It's good that you came, Fatim. You may have saved the sultan and his government."

"It is a good thing your mother's sister's husband brought you with him," the Berber prince responded. "He will need to work quickly to secure a treaty for your king, and perhaps he will wish to be away from here soon and take roads unknown to most travelers. Paths which you are familiar with, no?"

"Robert is not a man to run from danger if he can offer his allies help of any kind."

"Then, he has a warrior's soul like yours, my brother, even though he is not a blood uncle."

Christopher nodded distractedly. "You can judge for yourself."

"Ah! I shall meet this relation of yours, then?"

"Unless you have other plans. And even if you do, you'll have to change them. We need to inform Robert of your message to the sultan."

"I shall be at your side, as ever, my brother," the young Berber announced, chasing after Christopher, who hadn't bothered waiting for his long-winded reply. Half an hour later Robert had been informed by Fatim of everything he had told the sultan. But Robert responded much too casually to the implications of Fatim's information for Christopher's tastes. He paced the drawing room in brooding silence, stopping occasionally to stare out into the night as though he might catch one of the Bukhariyin sneaking over the balcony at any moment.

"The best thing for us to do," Robert was saying, "is get the treaty signed as soon as possible. Then we'll have a legitimate reason for assisting Mohammed. England can supply weapons for his defenses."

"It's not that simple anymore," Christopher countered. "The revolt changes things."

"It may be weeks, even months, before anything comes of it," Robert returned. "Besides, that's not our business here. Mohammed has been duly warned. Certainly he'll see that the ring leaders are rounded up and taken care of."

"My father was able to confirm that a revolt is being planned," Fatim interjected. "But we have no knowledge of who leads these ignorant heathens."

"He has only to convince a few of the Bukhariyin that it is in their best interests to name their leader. I believe such persuasions are one of your government's strengths, aren't they?"

"When the terrible Moulay Ismail reigned as sultan that was true. But Mohammed Ben Abdullah is a man of learning. He has no stomach for traditions he calls 'barbarian.' Ismail killed for his enjoyment; this is not the way of our current great sultan. Surely you have seen this for yourself."

Robert crossed the swirling inlaid woods below his feet in agitation. "In the last two hours I've uncovered deep dissension among the viziers regarding this treaty. It appears that the only thing that might save our mission here is the prospect of the sultan's ward marrying. And that is not going to happen," he finished, stopping beside Christopher. "I know you've spent a great deal of time in Morocco, Christopher, but becoming embroiled in their internal affairs would be suicide right now. You must remember that you're representing the king here. One does what is necessary for *England's* good. This is the sultan's concern."

Christopher turned to Robert as a facade of deadly calm settled over his features. "There's something I have to do," he said, striding to the door. "Excuse me." Turning to Fatim, he added, "Can you meet me back at my rooms later tonight?" The Berber nodded. "Good."

Robert started after him. "Christopher, for God's sake, this once take my advice. You're only one man; what can you do?"

"I'll explain later, Robert," Christopher said without looking back. "There are a few pieces to this puzzle you haven't seen yet."

The sultan's gilded anteroom was hot and cloying. Trails of smoke from incense sticks curled toward the ceiling, undisturbed by any breeze since the shutters had been closed against an impending second cloudburst. While he waited for the sultan, Christopher reconsidered the course he was about to embark on. This afternoon he thought he'd washed Ariel Lennox out of his life in the fury of the downpour. Now the specter of their proposed union rose again, reborn more complex by far. Christopher held no illusions about Ariel's fate if she stayed at El Bedi. He didn't know the names or faces of her enemies, but they were there. Between the viziers who wanted her out of the way and the Bukhariyin who would create a bloodbath in the palace, she had no chance of surviving the spring. He had told her this afternoon that she wouldn't have to marry "the duke," but if he kept his promise, her golden beauty would be snuffed out far too soon.

Damn it, he swore to himself. He wasn't going to let her meet that fate. The image of enormous, nutmeg eyes reflecting the golden afternoon sun rose in his mind. It was more than just saving a life, he admitted. He wanted her. And the intensity of his desire was new to him—something he hadn't felt toward any other woman. The only problem was that she didn't want him, and his male pride was loath to enter into a marriage with a woman who abhorred the very idea of marrying a duke.

The opportunity to marry into one of England's finest families with half a dozen estates and over a million acres of property under its protection could hardly be considered a dire fate. Countless mothers preened their daughters at the start of the London Season harboring just that glimmer of hope. And if all their carefully laid plans met with success, it would be their own sweetly simpering daughter, plumed and beribboned, who would lead him to that highly desirable altar.

It was time ill-spent from Christopher's perspective. He watched the Season's ambitious mothers urging their daughters on him with acid amusement. The debutantes reminded him of a flock of twittering finches with their nervous chirping and over-valued virginity. Inevitably, at the first ball of the year they would make their way, one by one, demurely across the floor, pretending not to notice him until they stood directly in his path and he was no longer able to ignore them without creating a stir at his lack of manners. Christopher would listen politely to their attempts to converse as they plied him with comments on the weather, their newest dress, or various manner of flattery as he waited for an opportunity to hand them over to someone more eager to listen to such drivel.

"My, how muscular you are, Your Grace," one particular brunette had panted only a few months ago. Beating her fan coyly about her face, she had looked up at him with vacuous blue eyes.

"Why, thank you, Miss Westbrook," Christopher replied with a mocking bow.

"You must exercise quite vigorously. Are you a boxer?"

"Don't you know of his reputation?" Christopher's companion chimed in.

"Why, no," the young lady breathed, her eyes wide with excitement.

"The duke is a renowned lecher, Miss Westbrook," Lord Smithston continued in his most conversational tone. "It's all the exercise he takes in the company of innocent young ladies that accounts for his build."

Melinda Westbrook gasped in paralyzed horror, staring at Christopher's broad shoulders as though a writhing serpent had suddenly appeared there. "I . . . I cannot imagine . . . ," she stammered.

"Perhaps you would care to take a stroll with me through the garden, Miss Westbrook?" Christopher inquired with a sardonic cock of one brow. The overwrought Miss Westbrook squealed in terror and fled to the protective arms of her mother as Christopher threw back his head and roared with amusement.

"You really shouldn't have, Michael, but thank you anyway."

"Don't think of it, Christopher. You had her quaking in her pretty pink slippers as it was. One more of those brutally scornful looks from you and she would have turned on her heels and run anyway. I simply added a bit of fun to the inevitable."

"The gossips will be working overtime tonight with the fodder you've given them," Christopher commented dryly as he noted the furtive glances already aimed his way.

"If you cared about gossip, you'd have changed your disposition years ago," Michael Smithston had chuckled as the two men had excused themselves and headed for the gaming room.

How indescribably different Ariel was from those dull, preening chicks, Christopher realized. Just as different as she was from the women his name had been linked to romantically over the years. He enjoyed having a ravishing beauty on his arm, and in his bed. That was true enough. But the beautiful women he'd taken to his bed were experienced lovers who enjoyed his virility, and knew better than to let their aspirations show. When the flirtation was over, they went their own way. Christopher was always careful to see that his dalliances were discreet and that any lady whose favors he'd enjoyed was not left without an escort once he had tired of the relationship. There was always Michael Smithston or Berkley West. Both were more than eager to pick up wherever Christopher left off with a lady.

Not one of those women had ever given Christopher even a moment's pause regarding marriage. And now he was about to marry a woman he'd known for less than a day, a woman who considered marriage to the Duke of Avon an unbearable disaster. A disaster he'd sworn to prevent. But that had been when she believed Robert was the duke. Certainly knowing the truth would change her feelings. Christopher recalled the mutinous determination on her face when she'd told him about her plan to somehow nullify the agreement, and he frowned. Certainly she was smart enough to realize that her dream of staying at El Bedi could never come true now, he told himself. And then with an irritated twist of his mouth, he added a final unbidden caveat.

The trouble was, she was just stubborn enough to refuse to acknowledge it.

Christopher didn't have time to continue that particular line of thought as the double cedar doors were thrown open by two slaves preceding the sultan. Mohammed Ben Abdullah entered, taking a seat at the circular table set in the center of the room without acknowledging Christopher's presence. At his signal, a black slave set two scrolled documents before him on a silver and horn tray.

"Lord Staunton?" The sultan nodded toward the waiting documents. Christopher took the quill, dipping it into the ink well while his eyes swept over the document, catching her name written in sweeping script; Lady Ariel Lennox, Marchioness of Hurstbeck. He signed his name in bold, sure strokes, then repeated the signature on the other copy. The sultan did the same. A slave moved quickly to the papers, sprinkling sand over the damp signatures and dripping blood red wax upon the lower corner. Handing the seal to the sultan, he stepped back as the sultan pressed his royal mark into the warm wax.

" 'Tis done." Mohammed smiled with satisfaction. "Let us celebrate." Sweet, hot Moroccan tea was poured into the tall glasses and presented to each of them.

Christopher raised his glass in a returning toast. " 'Tis done," he repeated.

Chapter Six

"You have your treaty," Christopher remarked, entering the parlor of his uncle's suite. Ignoring the look of shock that crossed Robert's face before his politician's mask dropped into place, he helped himself to a liberal dose of brandy.

"You're not telling me you've agreed to the marriage, are you?" Robert asked incredulously.

"Your surprise is showing, Robert. I thought that was strictly forbidden in your field."

"All politicians have their moments. But aside from that, I believe congratulations are in order for both of us," Robert replied. Pouring himself a brandy, he raised his glass. "To the treaty. King George will be pleased. And I look forward to meeting the marchioness." He sipped his drink and added, "I met her mother on a few occasions years ago in London."

Christopher shot his uncle a dark scowl at this piece of information that Robert had somehow managed to overlook during their discussions. "Is that so?"

"How else do you suppose I knew the sultan's ward would be suitable for you? Lady Caroline was a stunning beauty. Her eyes were the most unusual color—almost golden as I recall—and she quite captured the heart of every eligible young man that Season."

"And her father?"

Robert winced, remembering. "Evan Lennox was a dreamer. Oh, he was a handsome devil, which must have been why she ran off with him. But I always thought there wasn't much substance to the man."

"What do you mean she ran off with him?"

"Her parents wouldn't approve the match. They had quite grand plans for Caroline, and Lennox wasn't much of a catch except for his looks."

"So they eloped?"

"I believe the story I heard was that they were married in Dover and sailed immediately afterward for the Continent. They were probably planning to honeymoon a bit while her parents reconciled themselves to the marriage. They never had the chance, however. Lennox convinced Caroline to travel across the strait, and neither one of them ever returned."

"She stayed here," Christopher remarked, filling in the part of the story he knew from Ariel. "But what happened to him?"

Robert shook his head. "That I don't know. There was a great deal of speculation about them. Rumor got around that Caroline was here, and that she'd had a child. But her parents wouldn't confirm or deny a thing. Whenever they were asked outright about her, they said their daughter was dead."

Christopher made a sound of disgust. His own father would have done something just as callous. The English aristocracy were nothing more than a pack of selfish tyrants at times. The real nobility among them, he could count on one hand. Robert and Anne numbered among them, as did his mother. Unfortunately for Ariel, it appeared that her grandparents did not. "Well, you'll have your chance to meet her tomorrow. I was hoping you and Anne would entertain her at dinner."

Robert smiled. "We'd be delighted."

It was well past midnight when Christopher finally returned to his own rooms, having satisfied Robert's curiosity with a much abbreviated version of his change of heart. He opened his door to find Fatim asleep in a chair in front of the fire. Running his fingers through his hair, Christopher walked over and shook the Berber awake.

"You would try the patience of Allah, Brother." Fatim scowled groggily. "I ride a day and a night to reach the sultan; then you drag me around the palace and leave me to wait for you until the dawn returns again. My mother will be displeased with you if she hears of this."

"Tell her I'll seek Allah's forgiveness for abusing her son, Fatim. But personally I doubt a few sleepless nights will do you any permanent damage."

"We shall see, my brother. Now, I hope this reason you had for depriving me of my rest is worthy of the price I have paid. Tell me what the sultan said. If I can be of aid to you in any way, you must tell me. Remember," he said as the grin returned to his face, "I am in a debt of life to you, and you must offer me every opportunity to repay you. Such is the law of Islam."

"I'm afraid you'll have to remain in my debt for a while longer, Fatim. My business was not of a life-threatening nature. I'm getting married."

"Aiyee!" Fatim came wide awake as he smacked the palm of his hand against his forehead. "My sisters shall surely have my head on a platter alongside the mutton when I return home! My heart is filled with joy for you, Brother—although I cannot believe these words of yours. Who is the woman who has captured the heart of my English brother? And what has this to do with our great sultan Mohammed Ben Abdullah?"

"You've heard of Lady Ariel Lennox, the sultan's ward?" Christopher asked, surprised at his own pride in his announcement.

"The English sultana?" Delight lit Fatim's olive face.

74

"Of course! Who has not sat at the tent fires on star-filled nights and traded stories of the mysterious English sultana. Her beauty is said to rival the sun itself. She is gold and bronze, and as untouchable as a palmful of hot Saharan sand." He crossed the room to embrace Christopher. "She will make a fine first wife for you. As a second wife, no. Your first wife would make life unbearable for you with her jealousy."

"She will be my only wife, Fatim. And she doesn't know about our marriage yet."

"Ah, it is part of this treaty you work on! A good bargain, my friend. We get cloth and munitions, your king gets leather and fruits, and you get a beautiful wife. Trust me, I shall not divulge your confidence to anyone. But you must promise to bring her with you when you come to visit my mother," he added gleefully. "It will be my finest hour of justice seeing my sisters' faces when you announce that you have taken the English sultana as your wife."

Christopher nodded. "You have my promise, Fatim. But for now, let's both get some sleep. We can finish this discussion in the morning before you return home."

"Until then, my brother," Fatim said with a final embrace. "Allah Akbar! There is but one God, and he is Allah!" he proclaimed as he swept out of the room in a swirl of white djellaba.

"And he'd better lend me a little inspiration tomorrow," Christopher said to the empty room. Despite his explanations to Robert and Fatim, he had yet to think of a satisfactory method of telling Ariel that he was the Duke of Avon, and that he had changed his mind about marrying her.

Ariel lay the leather-bound volume facedown on her knees. She had given up any attempt to sleep over an hour ago. Christopher Staunton's face and overpowering masculinity haunted her thoughts, making sleep, and now even her reading, impossible. Determinedly she burrowed farther into her chair and returned to the same page of *One Thousand and One Arabian Nights* she had started on half an hour ago. But the story did little to cool her thoughts.

Sheherazäde's sultan repeatedly took on the visage of the handsome Englishman until she thought she would scream for want of some control over her own mind. Ariel snapped the volume shut impatiently and walked to the balcony door.

Concentrating on the night's cold touch, she leaned against the open door. Puddles from the afternoon's storm reflected the moonlight, and she looked up into the cloudless, black sky mentally tracing from star to star the familiar forms of the constellations. Her gaze crossed to Orion, her favorite of all the constellations. She loved the tale of the powerful warrior with his brilliant star-studded belt slung low across his hips. And tonight it occurred to her that his eyes might have been as blue as the desert sky when he was flung into the heavens a thousand years ago.

Ariel wound one honeyed tendril thoughtfully around her finger, then tossed it over her shoulder in disgust. She was acting just like one of the young princesses, pining over every handsome man who passed beneath her window. Spinning back into her room, she marched past the beckoning fire to the bookcase. Her fingertips brushed over the intricate openwork that decorated the corners, sliding with pleasure over the inlaid mother-of-pearl swirls along the top. They shifted restlessly across the titles as she searched for the one she wanted.

At last, unable to locate the book of verse, Ariel straightened, the toe of her slipper beating a soundless tap upon the thick carpet. She had been reading it in the sultan's study when Yazid had haughtily ordered her out yesterday, Ariel remembered at last. Silently she contemplated retrieving her book. Siad had retired long ago, and Chedyla was sound asleep in the cell adjoining Ariel's room. She had no desire to wake either of them. Certainly she could walk to the library and back again unnoticed, Ariel thought. She wasn't tired in the least. And the night loomed endlessly ahead of her. Her mind made up, she slipped out the door and, with a surreptitious look in either direction, headed for the library.

The candles in the wall sconces had burned low, and the palace was eerily quiet at this hour. She hurried, trying to reason away the nameless anxiety that settled into a heavy lump in her stomach. As she approached the far end of the hallway, Suleiman's voice rose from the staircase. Yazid's joined in, and Ariel scurried even faster, not wishing to face their inevitable reprimands if caught. She reached the corner, but before she could round it Suleiman's greeting stopped her. Reluctantly, she turned toward them.

"Are you well, Ariel?" Suleiman queried as the two approached.

"I'm fine, Suleiman, thank you. I just couldn't sleep, and thought I'd fetch something to read from the Moulay's library." Ariel stared down at the toe of her kid slipper.

"Where is Siad?" he continued. "You are not properly covered, Ariel."

"I'm sorry Suleiman," Ariel replied, wishing she could escape this interrogation.

"Let her be," Yazid cut in. "She will not be subjected to our laws much longer. Let her learn to expose herself as an infidel's woman would. She already rides like one."

Ariel stared at Yazid in astonishment.

"That was many years ago," Suleiman chided. "She is no longer a disobedient child, my brother. She is a woman, and knows her duties."

"As always, Brother, you are too soft. Ariel deems it her right to go out on horseback unescorted whenever she pleases," Yazid mocked.

"I was not unescorted, Yazid." Ariel bridled with indignation at his tone.

"Of course. You were in the company of your future husband which, I suppose, is why you thought nothing of going out without a chaperon. But didn't anyone tell you, Ariel, that even *Christian's* do not condone a man and a woman being alone together until the marriage vows are exchanged?"

"What are you talking about, Yazid?" Ariel watched him warily.

Suleiman's eyes moved from his brother to her, questioning. "Yazid, I'm sure you are mistaken," he insisted. "The duke would not . . ."

"Your betrothed, Ariel," Yazid continued, ignoring Suleiman. "The Duke of Avon. The man you were riding with."

Ariel stared at him blankly.

"Pretense is of no use. I know the comings and goings of everyone. The duke has shown no interest in young boys, and your silly disguise did not trick those who saw you."

"I was not with the Duke of Avon, Yazid." Despite the strength of her voice, Ariel was reeling. What Yazid implied was just not possible, she told herself. Trying to quell her increasing uneasiness, her mind raced from one thought to another without purpose. How had he known about their ride? Did he have spies everywhere in the palace as he claimed? And what possible interest could she be to him that he would spy on her? Her thoughts stirred like a boiling caldron, but she could make no sense of it.

"I was with Mr. Christopher Staunton. An English merchant and a diplomat here to finalize the treaty. I didn't ask Siad to accompany me because I knew I would be perfectly safe with Mr. Staunton," she admitted finally. She held her head high, but as she watched the caustic smile spread across Yazid's mouth, a horror began to seep through her. Sickening betrayal began to shake her ordered world.

"You really don't know, do you, sweet Ariel?" he said with sham sympathy. "Christopher Staunton *is* the Duke of Avon. Whatever tales he spun about being a merchant may not be outright lies, but he has deceived you with his omissions."

"You'll be pleased, Ariel," Suleiman said gently. "He is a fine man. The sultan has chosen well for you."

She looked at Suleiman in confused disbelief. How could he know her so well and yet not know her at all? She couldn't marry this man or any man who would take her from El Bedi. This was her home. And worse, she had been duped by the very man she had confided in. The man she'd turned to for help. Slowly phrases from the past two days began to congeal in her mind, and she recognized the vicious web of lies he'd woven around her.

Christopher Staunton had known from the moment he met her that she was looking for the Duke of Avon. She'd even asked if he knew him. "Better than anyone," he'd said. He'd lied to her. Deceived her. Tricked her. He had demanded a kiss for his assurance that he would speak to the duke, telling her that the duke had indeed agreed to release her from the marriage. The duke! He was the duke! Ariel's face burned with humiliation. Worst of all, when he had kissed her, she'd let him. She'd wanted his kisses. Moaned and sighed in his arms and tried to pull him back to her when he'd drawn away. Ariel felt nausea rise, bilious and bitter in her throat, and she was afraid she was going to be sick.

Rooted against the marble wall, she was shaken be-

79

yond her wildest imaginings. Her eyes flew to Suleiman, searching his face for a denial. But it was clear by the consoling expression on his face that the only error had been made by her.

"You'll change your mind, Ariel," he said, reading her expression. "A good husband will give you great happiness."

But Yazid knew her better. The calculating gleam in his pale green eyes read her deepest thoughts and put words to them. "He's deceived you, Ariel. You trusted him enough to slip away and meet him in private, and all the while he was lying to you." Commiseration softened his olive-toned features. "It brings me great sorrow to know that you must marry such a man, Ariel. I would have chosen a man of strength for you. A warrior and a sharif of the Moroccan people. A man who is not afraid to face a mere woman with the truth. But it was not given to me to decide," he ended with a meaningful shrug.

Her voice was a whisper. "You're certain they are one and the same?"

"You doubt my word?" Yazid demanded. Then he shrugged. "The Duke of Avon and Christopher Staunton are one and the same. Suleiman, is it not so?"

"My brother speaks the truth, Ariel," Suleiman replied. "We met the duke just this morning. He was much taken with the royal stables."

Ariel's heart clutched in a tremor of anger. What a fool she was! Didn't she know better than to put her faith in any infidel? Hadn't she learned from her father how deceitful the English were. How full of lies. She had given her trust to Christopher Staunton. And he had used it against her.

"Suleiman," Yazid ordered angrily, waving him away. "Go to our father's rooms. See if he is still awake."

Suleiman nodded respectfully to his older brother and

disappeared the way they had come.

Yazid slid a comforting arm around Ariel's shoulders and drew her against him, pressing her head gently against his chest. "Perhaps something can yet be done to purge this viper's poisonous bite."

Ariel turned into El Yazid's embrace, happy to have the comfort of his strength to hide her shame and fury in. "What can be done, Yazid?" she asked as thick, syrupy tears of remorse flooded her eyes.

"I will do whatever is in my power, Ariel. I promise you." Triumph glimmered in the depths of Mohammed El Yazid's eyes. His fingers lightly caressed her back. He would have his way yet, he thought, smiling into the dark. There were many roads to victory, and a wise man took whichever presented the simplest route. He lifted a lock of her hair between his thumb and finger and rubbed it between them, measuring the worth of its gold. What a delightful bonus she would make. The stupid English infidels believed they'd secured their vile treaty tonight, and his father thought he possessed the loyalty of his governors. How sweet would be his victory over them all.

He would celebrate it with the sweet nectar of the one woman forbidden to him, he thought with a cold smile. He would enjoy her immensely. Even more, he would enjoy eradicating her infidel pride while he taught her submission.

Ariel looked up at Yazid. He was the god of her youth, and all her life she had longed for this brotherly affection from him. Strange, she thought as her lips curved into a brave, tentative smile, that now when she needed an ally the most he should come to her rescue.

"You must trust me, Ariel. Finally you have learned that the infidels are unworthy."

Ariel nodded. His words were like a soothing balm to her injured pride. She brushed away all memories of the

Christopher she had thought existed, sweeping them aside like dusty old cobwebs that had no place in the new view she forged now of the Duke of Avon. Slowly her mind began to clear, the pain in her breast turning cold and heavy, stiffened by the scarring tissues of her wound.

"I won't marry Christopher Staunton," she vowed, the cold pain within her obliterating all other thoughts of him as it grew.

"You will not have to," Yazid replied with a narrow smile. His nostrils flared, and the black pupils widened in his light eyes as she looked into his face.

"Our father is not there," Suleiman announced, returning from his mission.

Yazid broke his hold on Ariel, setting her apart from him.

Suleiman looked at him strangely, then turned to Ariel. "Are you all right, Ariel?"

"Yes. Yazid has promised—" She broke off her words as Yazid pressed his finger to his lips, behind Suleiman's back.

"Yazid has promised what?" Suleiman queried.

"Nothing," she amended hastily. "He has just promised to speak to the sultan on my behalf."

"This will do no good. The contracts are signed. The marriage is law now."

"Christopher Staunton is a deceitful, conniving liar. The sultan doesn't know that. Yazid will speak to him, and I will present my plea also. Between the two of us, I'm certain he will see that he must rip that vile contract to shreds. After all, he is the sultan," she finished in a cold voice.

"Yes, he is," Suleiman replied quietly. "And he is a man of his word as well."

"You are not the heir to the throne. You may be powerless to sway the sultan, but Yazid is the heir."

Immediately Ariel regretted her words. Suleiman had always looked on her with the indulgent smile of an older brother. But she couldn't understand why he would side with Christopher Staunton when she so clearly despised the idea of this marriage.

"Enough," Yazid ordered. "There is nothing to be done tonight anyhow. Return to your rooms, Ariel. We will speak again in the morning."

Obediently Ariel headed back to her rooms. But when her hand clasped the brass knob of her door, she pressed her forehead against the cool cedar and sighed. Despite her exhaustion she could not let the night pass without mending the rift she'd torn between herself and Suleiman. Quietly she turned away from the welcome comfort of her bedroom and headed back down the corridor.

When the door opened, Ariel was not certain how she had reached Suleiman's room. Her knees shook so beneath her she could not account for how she was standing. She had never taken such a liberty with either him or Yazid. But Suleiman didn't question her appearance at his door. He took her hand, ushering her to a pile of cushions beside the fire. Sinking onto a pillow beside her, he watched and waited, his face an artwork of concern.

"What is it?" he urged. "You are as pale as the snows on the High Atlas."

Ariel stared down at her hands, mesmerized by her fingers as they unraveled the pillow's scarlet tassel seemingly of their own volition.

"I came to apologize, Suleiman."

"There is no need, Ariel."

Suleiman's gentle forgiveness was her undoing. Ariel squeezed her eyes shut as tears sprung from between her lashes, streaming down her cheeks and dropping onto her tightly clenched hands. "I didn't mean those things

. . . ," she stuttered between sobs. "I was trying to hurt you. Trying to s-s-stop you from saying anything good about . . . ," Ariel faltered, unable to make her lips form Christopher's name.

"Your betrothed," Suleiman finished for her.

She looked at him through the watery curtain of her tears. "Do you have to call him that?"

"That is what he is."

Ariel gave him a baleful look. She no longer had the strength to argue. The night seemed endless already. All she wanted was to stop the whirling thoughts in her mind. All she wanted was blissful, dreamless sleep.

"My father loves you, Ariel," Suleiman continued, his voice condoling. "Many nights he has spoken to me of you. It was your mother's wish that you return to England. As well, this marriage will bring great prosperity through the treaty. I do not know the duke well, yet I sense a fair and good man in him."

His words were sincere. But Ariel didn't want to hear them. She stared down at her lap, vainly trying to smooth the maligned tassel back to its former state. Her fingers froze as Suleiman's hand came to rest on hers. He drew them out of her lap, until their hands were clasped midway between them in a gentle embrace of respect.

"Do not let your father's shadow keep you from happiness, Ariel. I would not see you hurt any further by him. Free yourself of his evil *baraka*. Open your heart to Allah's will. Give Lord Staunton an opportunity to prove himself to you."

Ariel looked into Suleiman's benevolent face. She smiled regretfully.

"I can't, Suleiman. I can't forgive either of them for their lies."

Chapter Seven

Ariel had slept little during the night. Wringing her hands in frustration, she'd paced a well-worn path between the chair and her bed. At an outrageous hour she'd called for a bath, and lay immobile in the enormous sunken tub, willing her frustrations from her exhausted body until she could only think of sleep. It was near dawn before she finally climbed out of the tepid bath. Her skin still damp, she had dropped the turkish towel in a heap on the rug and fallen into bed.

Now, despite the bright sunlight that told her it was midday, she was still exhausted. A lethargic malaise lay over her like a thick, woolen blanket. Her skin was so swollen and sensitive from the long, enervating bath that even the hand-worked frills of her sheets felt vicious. Ariel forced her sleep-laden lids open and groaned as she rolled over and buried her face in the goose-down pillow. No nightmare could be worse than the reality of last night.

How could she have let Christopher Staunton deceive her so easily? The night of the ball he had given her no choice except to confide in him. It was that or face the Bukhariyin. But in retrospect, she'd have taken her chances with the fearsome Black Guards rather than put her trust in the deceitful hands of that English asp! She was betrothed to a man whose heart was surely as cold as stone. A man who would take her away from the place she loved, knowing that her greatest desire was to remain here. She was betrothed to a liar, a man who felt no compunction about dealing in deceit, who, in fact, appeared to enjoy it.

To her utter horror, his image filled her vision, and it was not the portrait of a slithering, shifty-eyed snake she conjured up. It was a composite of muscular stature and the charge of power that emanated from him like the confluence of opposing forces. Forces that created a tempest in Ariel that was both frightening and exciting at one and the same time. With shameful clarity she recalled the thrill of his arms encircling her, and her own ecstasy as he drew her into his embrace. She could almost hear her own slanderous moans of delight.

Ruthlessly Ariel cast aside her traitorous thoughts. The man who had bought her for the price of oranges and leather was none of those things. The ride to the trysting pond, their encounter in the garden, even her rescue from the Bukhariyin at the ball had all been pieces of her degradation. He had created a false image. A person who didn't exist. He was not the merchant with the easygoing humor she had found so irresistible. Beneath his devastatingly handsome skin he was a conniving animal of the lowest order. While he consoled her with understanding and took liberties with her, he had laughed at her trusting nature.

She hated Christopher Staunton.

The cold, hard lesion that had begun to form in Ariel's heart the night before expanded, blotting out the warmth she had once felt for him. She swallowed convulsively, and sent a silent prayer of thanks to Yazid for warning her. Lord Staunton, she railed silently, was no different than her father — a titled English nobleman. What had he been but a liar and deceiver who abandoned his pregnant wife in an unfamiliar land? Ariel's mother had assured her that her father did care about them. She often repeated the certainty that he died attempting to return for them. But the furtive whispers in hallways and behind doors told Ariel otherwise. No ships had floundered, no foreigners were attacked and held for ransom, not even an unforgiving Mediterranean storm had occurred in the months after Ariel's birth to toss an Egyptian ship bound for the ports of Tangier or Salé off course. He had gone off to see the pyramids, saying he would return in time for her birth, but like Christopher Staunton, he had lied.

She closed her eyes, wishing desperately that she could be anywhere else, that somehow this unimaginable fate could be willed away. As she lay amid the scattered bedding of her sleepless night, Yazid's promise came back to her, and her spirits buoyed somewhat. Swinging her legs over the edge of the bed with a bit more purpose than she'd possessed a moment ago, she steeled herself for the day. *First I will see the Sultan,* she decided with stubborn determination. *Between my plea and Yazid's influence, surely he can be swayed.* But if she was to do so, she would have to hurry. Moulay Mohammed had been busier than usual the past few weeks. She might have to wait hours for a chance to catch his attention.

Sweeping up the wrapper that lay across the foot of her bed, Ariel crossed the room and flung the shutters open. The sun poured in, warming her chilled mood. Ariel moved to the wardrobe and was just lifting a shell pink tunic with matching harem pants from the rod when Chedyla slipped in followed closely by Rhima bearing a tray.

"Put down your gown and break the fast," Chedyla said. "You must eat."

Still holding her clothes, Ariel eyed the bowl of fresh figs without enthusiasm. A pot of mint tea stood by a small pitcher of creamy goat's milk and a plate of crusty herb bread on the tray, but none of it held any appeal. She smiled regretfully at Chedyla. "I can't eat. I must see the sultan immediately."

"I do not think that is possible," Chedyla warned, setting a small vase of flowers beside Ariel's breakfast. "The palace is in an uproar. I doubt the sultan, in his great wisdom, will see you this morning. So you have more than enough time."

"Something may have gone amiss with the English treaty," Ariel ventured hopefully, glancing sideways at Chedyla.

She shrugged in reply. "Such things are not my concern. Our moulay will take care of whatever problems have arisen. My concern is to care for you, and that, with the help of Allah, is what I shall do."

Ariel rubbed her temples in exasperation.

"And you, my child, need time to accept Allah's will before you face other people."

"If you're referring to that awful marriage contract, I won't listen to a word of it," Ariel insisted, her head beginning to ache from lack of sleep.

Chedyla took the tunic from Ariel's limp hand and passed it deftly to Rhima. "I shall miss you, child of my heart. But I am full of gladness knowing you will finally find your place in life."

Ariel glared at her, but the devotion that looked back at her from Chedyla's kohl-rimmed eyes held a lifetime of love. Suddenly, the tears she had been unable to shed during the night spilled down her cheeks as she melted into Chedyla's comforting embrace.

"What shall I do? I have been tricked, and used and . . ."

"What are you talking about, child? There is nothing to be so distraught about." Chedyla's hand moved in rhythmic circles across her back.

"There is everything to be distraught about," Ariel sobbed into her shoulder.

Chedyla's voice was a seductive chant as she coaxed Ariel to her bed. "Lie down, my child. You need rest. You need time."

Ariel wanted to say that Yazid would be looking for her, that she needed to speak to the sultan and that each moment she delayed sealed her fate more irrevocably. But her body rebelled against her wishes. She yearned for the comfort of her bed, the cool, inviting sheets, and the comforting touch of Chedyla's hand as she gently massaged away the tension that gripped Ariel's body.

"Rest . . . ," Chedyla murmured soothingly.

The scent of warmed oils drifted through her mind as Ariel gave in to her exhaustion. She needed rest. Then she would be able to think more clearly.

But as Ariel drifted at the nether edge of sleep, one thought haunted her. Chedyla was wrong. Allah would not plan this for her. He would never wish to separate her from El Bedi. This was not his plan; this was Christopher Staunton's plan. Her shoulders clenched in anger, and Chedyla's hands moved adeptly across them, chasing the reaction away with gently kneading fingertips.

Christopher's lies, she thought, slipping nearer the sweet oblivion of sleep. Sparkling blue eyes and a breathtakingly handsome face smiled down at her from the netherland of her dreams. He spoke, but the words were caught on a breeze and spirited away. The image faded out of focus and the face changed. The eyes that looked into hers were green, not blue. And the face, though still handsome, was darker. Shaded with olive, not bronze. Yazid, she thought, drifting at the edge of sleep. It was Yazid holding her, comforting her. And now she could hear what he was saying.

"Trust me, Ariel."

She smiled.

Then the face was Christopher's again. "Trust me."

The breeze strengthened, growing without warning into a sirocco, a sandstorm of awful proportions. The images in her dream swirled and mixed until they were a blur. And then there was nothing. Nothing but the storm raging all around her in a world where nothing was familiar. The sirocco seemed to last a lifetime before she drifted into the black slumber of exhaustion.

Chapter Eight

Ariel popped another wedge of fig into her mouth with a relish that bore little resemblance to her earlier lackluster mood. If she could just avoid Christopher Staunton, she thought determinedly — be absent whenever he expressed an interest in seeing her — she would be able to delay any commitment on her part until Yazid had resolved things with her guardian. The helplessness which had beset her that morning had vanished, replaced by resolve. Ariel knew Christopher wouldn't deal lightly with anyone who crossed his will, but daunting as those steel blue eyes could be, she was determined to be the victor in this battle. The Duke of Avon would simply have to learn that there was no room in her world for his kind, she decided, her mouth set at a stubborn slant. Siad appeared at the door, and Ariel leapt up from her meal, drawing the eunuch to one side so that Chedyla would not hear the nature of the errand she had sent him on.

"Will my guardian see me?" she asked eagerly.

"My apologies, beloved mistress," he whispered humbly. "But I was not able to deliver your message. I was told that our holy moulay is in meetings of great consequence and not to be disturbed for any reason."

Ariel noticed the eunuch's keen discomfort, and her

brows drew together in concern. "What is it Siad? What's the matter?"

"I do not know. But there is great tension in the palace. I fear for the Maghreb this day."

Ariel's heart soared. Yazid had spoken to his father! The marriage banns were broken, and with them the treaty! The sultan was probably at this very moment dealing with Christopher and his contingent. Ariel nearly burst with delight as she savored her victory. She was free! She'd won without even engaging the battle.

She had to see the sultan. She would throw herself upon his feet in thanks. And Yazid. She must thank him also. "You've brought me better news than I could wish for!" she exclaimed, wrapping the eunuch in an impulsive hug.

"I do not understand," he declared, knitting bushy black brows beneath his glistening, bald pate. "But my heart sings with delight at your joy."

"We must go to the throne room. Let me get my veil."

"Ariel!" Chedyla chided from across the room. "You must not! No woman is permitted in the throne room without the moulay's express permission. The viziers are there. You may be seen. And you must think of your betrothed. He would be shamed."

Ariel grasped her duenna's hands between her own. Nothing could dampen her spirits at this moment, not even Chedyla's growing concern for Christopher Staunton. "Please, Chedyla," she pleaded. "I'll go into the sultanas' adjoining room. I shall take care. I won't let myself be seen. I have always practiced caution, haven't I?"

"Only as you know it," Chedyla replied softly. But Ariel was already gone.

Ariel let Siad approach the two guards who towered like twin minaret's on either side of the sultan's throne room door while she slipped behind the screen that shielded the entrance to the sultanas' room. They were not the usual Bukhariyin that guarded the sultan, she noted, watching through the pierced fretwork. What was more, she was not comfortable with the way their eyes kept glancing beyond Siad, as though they were watching for something or someone. But these new guards were the only sign that anything was different today. Ariel reprimanded herself for being so jittery. She *wanted* things to be different. The extra guards only confirmed that something was amiss, and she was certain that could only be the treaty and her impending marriage.

Siad crossed back to the screen and bowed before Ariel. "I am displeased to say that these Bukhariyin have no respect for the sultan's beloved ward. They say he is no longer here, and they refuse to divulge his whereabouts. Such precious information should not be denied to the sultan's beloved ward. I tell you, most wonderful mistress, I do not like these guards. They possess stomachs filled with rot," he concluded with a disgusted gesture.

"Never mind, Siad. Did they at least tell you if the sultan will return?"

"Yes. After much arguing they have revealed that the great moulay is expected to come back. But they do not say when. Perhaps it will be many hours before Moulay Mohammed returns. I think it is best if we return to your chambers and you allow me to await the sultan."

Ariel shook her head. "I'll wait. By the time you came to get me, he might be gone again."

"As you wish. I shall remain in the company of these two apes who call themselves men, and see that they care for our purpose."

Ariel let herself into the small waiting room. As she'd expected, it was empty. A low, brass table stood in the center of the room atop a colorful Persian rug that covered much of the polished tile floor. All around it pillows and cushions had been arranged for the comfort of those awaiting the sultan's pleasure. The single narrow window was heavily shielded from the outside world by a decorative iron grill. Still she could feel a very slight breeze, and the sun had not yet come to this side of the palace.

Ariel made herself comfortable, relaxing on the two tasseled pillows nearest the window. So much of life seemed to consist of waiting, she thought. She envied men their right to take action, to be decisive, while she must sit in this small, stuffy cubicle and wait for the right even to speak her gratitude.

She must have drifted into sleep, because when she heard muffled voices in the next room the cubicle had become a steam bath and a light film of perspiration coated her face. Taking a ragged breath, Ariel scrambled up from the pillows and smoothed the spider-web pattern of wrinkles from her silk tunic. She pressed her palms against her cheeks, willing herself to be calm. She would not go before her guardian dishevelled and frantic.

Why hadn't Siad come to tell her the sultan was back? she wondered. It wasn't like him to be remiss when someone put him on edge as the Bukhariyin had. Ariel listened at the door connecting the harem room with the sultan's throne room. She had already begun to turn the knob when she realized that two voices were coming from the other side of the door. If the sultan wasn't alone, she couldn't go in. She would have to get Siad and have him announce her so that the room could be cleared—if the Black Guards let him. Ariel pressed her cheek against the door, trying to decide on a course of action. The conversation in the throne room had stopped, and she wondered, hopefully, if the audience might not be over. She'd wait here a little longer, she decided. If she could steal the few minutes she needed with the sultan without having her eunuch announce her, then no one would even know she'd been here. And if the viziers were very displeased about the dissolution of the proposed marriage, it would be less obvious that she had been the one to thwart them.

Suddenly the door was wrenched open from the opposite side, and Ariel was standing face-to-face with the one person in all of El Bedi whom she had hoped never to see again.

"Do you make a habit of constantly spying on people?" Christopher demanded in a tone that immediately set her hackles on end.

"I could ask the same of you, but my manners are considerably better than that," she shot as she shifted to look beyond the wide shoulders that blocked the larger portion of her view.

"I'm looking at some maps the sultan left for me," he responded obligingly. "And you?"

"I am waiting for my guardian." Ariel struggled to compose herself and managed a tenuous hold on her emotions. Mere inches separated them, and Christopher's height as well as the confidence of his manner all worked against her own self-assurance. Her pulse pounded at her temples. And despite herself she knew that she was afraid of his reaction now that she'd won her victory. At the moment she didn't feel very much the winner. Instead she felt like an errant child caught in some gross misdeed; as though she was the betrayer rather than the betrayed.

That thought sent a rush of resentment surging through her. He was the one who didn't belong here! Not the other way around. What arrogance he possessed demanding to know what she was doing here! Ariel squared her shoulders and tipped her chin resolutely just as her gaze settled on the man standing by the table. Her rage multiplied tenfold as she looked at the false Duke of Avon, the man Christopher had knowingly let her believe was her opponent while the true duke commiserated with her.

Christopher met her accusing stare with a grim smile. As he assessed the rebellious tilt of her head and the glittering anger that sparkled like hard, golden nuggets in her eyes, a cold fury settled over him. Obviously his concern about how to explain his real title and the change in his intentions to her had been time wasted. She already knew.

He turned to one side, allowing her a full view. "May I introduce Lord Robert Belmeth, Marquis of Simsbury. Robert, Lady Ariel Lennox, Marchioness of Hurstbeck."

"Marchioness," Robert replied with a low bow.

"Your Grace," she said, laying heavy sarcasm on the words.

"Please," Robert replied congenially. "I'm afraid I don't merit quite that degree of courtesy. I hope you're not disappointed that I'm not a duke."

"Not in the least, Lord Belmeth," Ariel cooed softly. "However, it seems I was misled into believing you were indeed a duke."

Christopher watched her silently as his own anger swelled. He had told Mohammed Ben Abdullah in no uncertain terms that he would be the one to tell Ariel his true identity. Whoever had relieved him of that right was playing a vicious game with Ariel's feelings at his expense. This was precisely the scene Christopher had been determined to prevent, and he intended to find out exactly who had interfered so effectively with his plans.

"I didn't tell you Robert was the duke, Ariel," he said with a steely calm. "You came to that conclusion on your own."

"How dare you!" she hissed low enough to prevent Lord Belmeth from hearing. "How dare you stand there like some innocent bystander pretending you did nothing. You deceived me. You cultivated my trust when all along you knew who I was looking for. You led me on while you fabricated stories to entrap me. As though, as though . . ." she sputtered, unable for a moment to link his behavior with anything human or animal that would adequately convey her contempt. "You gave me your word that you would prevent this marriage at the same time you were orchestrating it! You are the most vile, lowest of snakes. The most—"

"That's enough, Ariel." Christopher's voice was flat and cold.

But Ariel was like a spitting lioness bent on revenge. Her slender frame seethed with a rage that made her shake. "Enough? I've barely begun, Your Grace. That is the correct address for you, isn't it?"

Christopher gripped her wrist and bent his head to her ear. "Would you have me make a fool of us both in front of my uncle, or will you hold your tongue long enough to hear me out?"

Looking into the midnight intensity of his eyes, Ariel knew he would do precisely as he threatened. Her chest heaved as she held her unabated fury in check, but muted hatred emanated from the core of her being like red-hot embers.

Christopher relaxed his grip on her wrist, and she ripped her hand away. He gave her a warning look, but she only glared back at him, lifting her chin an imperious notch despite its trembling.

"I'm perfectly capable of standing still without any assistance."

Christopher cocked a doubting brow, but made no further attempt to restrain her. "I agree that there are things I have to account to you for. I'll explain as I escort you to your room, Ariel," he said, taking her elbow. Ignoring her attempts to wrench free, he steered her out the door. "I'll see you in an hour, Robert."

"It was a pleasure meeting you, Lady Ariel," Robert called after them. "I look forward—"

The rest of his sentence was cut off by the cedar door as Christopher propelled Ariel across the waiting room and past the guards. He didn't even glance at Siad as the eunuch fell in step behind them.

It wasn't until they were well beyond the Bukhariyin's view that Christopher slowed his pace.

"Take your hands off of me," Ariel hissed furiously.

"Not until you are safely deposited where you belong."

"I haven't seen the sultan, and I have every intention of doing so. So if you'll just say whatever it is you have to say, I can go back to wait for him."

"The sultan has his hands full today, Ariel. You might as well wait in your rooms."

"That's for me to decide, and at any rate I'm perfectly capable of returning to my rooms on my own."

"I'm sure you are. But there are a few things I have to discuss with you, and I think that is best done in private."

"Nothing you have to say would interest me."

"I think our marriage is one subject we might cover."

"The marriage has been revoked," she burst out angrily before calling back to her eunuch. "Siad, Lord Staunton seems to be unable to keep his infidel hands off of me. Perhaps you could assist him."

Siad made no move to obey her. In fact, he seemed to have disappeared into thin air, for there was no sign of her trusted guard at all. Was no one on her side? she ranted silently. Siad had been guarding her for years, and now, just because he believed she was betrothed to this barbarian, he was willing to let him treat her any way he chose.

Christopher stopped dead in the hallway and pulled Ariel around. "Who told you the marriage was revoked?"

Ariel tossed her head. "The prince."

"Then, the prince is misinformed. The documents are signed, and the sultan is very pleased." He took a deep breath before continuing in a more tempered tone. "I intended to tell you who I was, and why I decided to go through with the marriage later today. And I'll see to it that whoever took that right away from me pays for his loose tongue."

"I don't think so," she retorted. "Mohammed El Yazid told me everything last night, including exactly who Lord Christopher Staunton was. If it hadn't been for him, I would doubtlessly still be charmed by your deceiving ways, Your Grace. You would likely have had no qualms about leading me on right up to the moment that the Imam performed the ceremony. I'm sure it would have suited your perverse sense of humor to see my surprise when it was you and not Lord Belmeth I found standing at the altar."

Christopher silently cursed Yazid. He'd suspected something like this. The prince had succeeded in creating a knot that would require all of Christopher's concentration to untie at a time when he needed to focus on other problems. "Yazid did you no favor."

Ariel's anger erupted into molten fury. "On the contrary, my lord. I shall be indebted to him for as long as I live."

"Don't be a fool, Ariel. There's more to all of this than there appears."

They'd arrived outside her bedroom door, and Ariel turned to glare at him as threateningly as possible. "If you have even a shred of honor in that black soul of yours, you'll give me what I want and end this mockery immediately."

Christopher leaned over her, his eyes nearly black with anger. His dark hair brushed her brow, and his lips moved against her ear as he drove home his point. "Let me make one fact very clear, Ariel. I do not enter into agreements lightly, and I do not, ever, renege on an agreement once it's made."

"Then, you have erred greatly." Pulling away from him, she gripped the doorknob with white knuckles. "Because I will fight you with every ounce of my being. If what you say is true and the banns have not yet been revoked, they will be." Ariel jerked the door open, intent on slamming it in his face, but she was jerked back into the hall. Christopher pulled her against him, molding her body to his in a crushing embrace. He looked down at her, the steel hue of his eyes brooking no challenge.

"Believe me, Ariel, when I told you I had no interest in marrying you the other day, I meant it. But things here aren't all that they seem. There's danger I can't tell you about just now. I agreed to this marriage for one reason alone. Because you're too stubborn and naive to protect yourself from the holocaust that is about to envelop this place. And in a fit of obvious lunacy I thought you would be glad of my protection.

"The damned prince you hold so dear, is the one you should be wary of, not me. If he cared so much about you, would he have told you something that only your guardian or I had the right to? Perhaps you should look more closely at Yazid's motives, Ariel."

"Don't you dare slander Yazid. He has . . ."

"He has what?" Christopher demanded, tightening his hold on her arms.

Ariel took a deep, steadying breath. She wouldn't arm Christopher with knowledge of Yazid's promise. The less prepared he was for her eventual victory, the better. "He's concerned about me."

"Don't put your trust in him, Ariel," he replied darkly. "He's not what he appears."

"Spoken by someone truly familiar with a deceitful nature," she shot back angrily.

"I never deceived you, Ariel. Everything I told you about myself was true. Since I had already decided to refuse the contract, I saw no need to frighten you by revealing my title. For that, I apologize."

"We had an agreement."

"Things have changed. Aren't you willing to listen to

100

anything other than what you wish to hear?"

"I'm not in danger, and if I were, I can take care of myself. I've survived very well on my own so far, and I promise you, I shall continue to do so without your brand of so-called protection!"

"Over confidence is a dangerous thing, Ariel," Christopher warned softly. "Don't fall prey to it." His features softened ever so slightly as he stared down at her, and a hunger that she was becoming all too familiar with deepened the color of his eyes. "For now, little one, I have more important concerns to attend to than easing your vanquished pride."

Without further warning he kissed her, his lips taking possession of her mouth as though a familiar owner. The crushing warmth of his mouth on hers brought back all the memories of their embrace at the trysting pond, but this time there was a palatable demand in his touch. He urged her lips apart hungrily, no longer an explorer, but a man well familiarized with the territory he moved upon. His tongue plunged boldly into the recesses of her mouth, demanding succor for her lashing out at him. And as he asked, so she gave.

While her mind cursed him, her soul warmed to the passion of his embrace. The memories that she had thought banished flooded back in warm waves that crashed over her as they washed away her fury, and with it, her resistance. She melted against him, her hands slipping to his shoulders, escape forgotten. Her tongue met his and gave thrill for thrill back to him. She was lost, sinking under the spell his embrace cast upon her. His arms crushed her to him, and he cupped the swell of her buttocks in his palms, sending cascades of titillating ecstasy pouring through her. The kiss deepened, and their bodies molded to one another. Somewhere in the recesses of her mind, Ariel tried to remember that this was the man she had sworn to defeat, the man who had lied to her and would spirit her away from her home. But the assault on her senses diluted her resolve until all thoughts of what should be were swept away in the swift current of her desire.

When Christopher at last drew away, his thumb gently brushed along the rise of her cheek, tracing a line to her jaw. Tipping her face to his, he demanded that she acknowledge him. His eyes shone dark with the intensity of his desire, but a gentle understanding played at their corners.

"Tonight I'll make amends. I will tell you whatever I can about what has happened."

Recalling her vow to resist him at every turn, Ariel was mortified by how easily he had dissuaded her from her purpose. Pulling away, she spun on her toes and was halfway through the door before Christopher blocked it.

"Don't think for even a second about coming into my rooms, Lord Staunton. I'll scream at the top of my lungs, and Siad will cleave you in two before he bothers to ask why. Don't be fooled by his seeming sloth or compliance. He would give his life for my defense in an instant."

"I've no doubt of that, Ariel," Christopher replied flatly. "I simply wanted to invite you to supper this evening. I'll come for you at eight."

"I will not sup with you," she told him haughtily. Her hands shook as she clenched them in the folds of her pants, but she'd never let him see how he had unnerved her.

"I will be here at eight. Is that clear?"

"Oh, absolutely clear, my lord and master," Ariel retorted. "Perhaps you had best bring along a few Bukhariyin, though. 'Tis the only way you'll force me to accommodate even the smallest of your wishes. A moment's kiss won't alter my mind. I don't want to marry you, and nothing will change that. Now, if you'll kindly take your hand off my door, I would like some privacy."

"Just one thing more, Ariel," he said as he stepped aside.

"Yes?" she demanded in exasperation.

Christopher smiled down at her with sardonic intent. "Despite what you say, you do want me. A kiss like that doesn't lie."

Ariel slammed the door with all her might, whirling as she stamped across the room. Damn him! And damn herself for letting him kiss her. It would never happen again, she vowed. She would defy him at every turn until he was so tired of having to deal with her that he would beg Mohammed to nullify the contract. And nothing, nothing would make her give in to him. Christopher Staunton would learn that he couldn't scare her into marrying him any more than he could trick her into it. He would rue the day he'd traded his lies for her kiss.

Chapter Nine

Half-hidden by billowing clouds of steam, Ariel lay naked on a black-veined marble bench in the harem baths, listening to Carmela's excited chatter.

"The women are talking of nothing else!" the dark-haired Spanish concubine continued. "It's been too long since the last *fantasia;* everyone is looking forward to the excitement."

Ariel concentrated on the conversation and tried to forget, for the moment, that she had been unable to speak with her guardian and that she might still be legally betrothed. She ran a finger along the side of her face, freeing the long tendrils of hair that clung to her damp cheeks, prisoners of the wet heat.

"It's been so long since the last one," Ariel commented, sitting up to face Carmela.

"My Gypsy blood is boiling for the excitement! The men, the horses, the guns! It reminds me of the caravan — the food, the celebration . . ." Carmela sighed. "If only there were a little wine to wash it all down with. And a man, a dark, gallant caballero who would carry me away on his stallion."

"Isn't that how you ended up in the harem? I think you're well away from gallants who sweep you off your feet."

"I swear by the sainted mother Mary I'll never forgive Paulo for selling me to that filthy slaver just to fatten his purse for a few *pesetas*. He said he loved me!"

"And you still dream of being with him?" Ariel shook her head.

"Ummm, Paulo had a treacherous heart, but his face still warms my dreams. The scent of his sweat in the hot Seville sun makes me long for his arms around me. I admit it"—Carmela made a hopeless gesture at Ariel's askance look—"I am a woman, and when I think of a strong, virile man taking me in his arms— ah, *mi amor*—my blood rushes through me like a herd of wild horses, and I want him, heartless flesh-trader that he is. You'll soon know what I mean." Carmela shot Ariel a knowing glance. "I haven't seen your English duke, but others have. They say he's as handsome as a Gypsy king. That he walks with the confidence and power of a lion."

"And he has the heart of a liar just like your Paulo," Ariel added quickly.

"What! You've met him? Tell me. What happened?"

Taking a deep breath, Ariel related everything to Carmela from meeting Christopher at the ball to his parting demand that she join him for supper this evening. The only thing she left out of her story were the kisses they had shared, first in the garden, then by the pool, and finally the searing kiss that ended their confrontation earlier.

"You have Gypsy blood in your veins, Ariel," Carmela claimed adamantly. "I don't care what high-and-mighty bloodlines your *madre* and *padre* carried. You met your duke without Siad or your duenna and took him to the trysting pool?" She hooted with glee. "That is why we are *compadres,* my friend! It was your Gypsy blood that saved my head from being severed when I was first brought here, and now it is heating to a boil at the sight of your handsome, soon-to-be husband."

"You'd better talk more quietly, Carmela," Ariel warned, noting the glares they were receiving from the other concubines, and wishing desperately to turn the topic of conversation elsewhere, "or Raisuli will take advantage of your behavior and slit your Gypsy throat."

"He'd like nothing better," Carmela agreed, returning her voice to a whisper. "He keeps his scimitar sharp enough to split a hair just for me. But he will never have his revenge. I'm much too sly for Raisuli. Besides, it's you he despises for shaming him. And he cannot touch you."

"He still scares me," Ariel admitted, thinking of the glaring hatred that filled the small beady eyes of the harem's head eunuch whenever he saw her. It was one of the reasons she rarely came into the harem. Ariel had stopped him from killing Carmela. During her first days at El Bedi the Gypsy had fought like a wildcat. No one could get near her, and the odalisques were unable to perform the necessary toilets to prepare her for the sultan. Raisuli had lost his temper, deciding that this woman was not worth the trouble despite the price he'd paid for her foreign looks. But Ariel had been there that morning and taken pity on the fiery young woman. She'd understood how strange the ways of the harem must be to foreigners, and been certain the Gypsy was only scared and not evil, as Raisuli claimed.

The eunuch's oiled chest muscles had heaved with fury when Ariel used her position to stay the powerful eunuch's scimitar. She'd known she was courting danger as well as far over-stepping her rights as the sultan's ward, but Ariel's conscience had refused to let him murder the woman because she fought for what remained of her dignity with a spirit that Ariel felt a kinship to.

Raisuli had finally backed down, but Ariel had won his enduring hatred. The fear he incited in the harem was well earned. The mere sight of his feral black eyes and hard, black-skinned muscles could cause a palatable tension to settle over the harem. Although it was never spoken aloud, the women knew he was Daiwa's henchman. The Hatum Kadin's insane jealousy of anyone who became a special favorite of the sultan had proven a perfect foil for his ambition. And like Raisuli, Daiwa reserved a special hatred for Ariel, who was a daily reminder that her husband had put her aside for years while he favored an English marchioness with his exclusive attentions.

Carmela might believe that by living outside the harem Ariel was safe from Daiwa's vendetta or Raisuli's hate, but Ariel was far less certain. Although she made light of it, particularly in front of Chedyla, Ariel knew that if Daiwa had her way, she would be shipped off to England on the next boat to leave Salé's harbor. She had been the first wife for a very long time, and she was Yazid's mother which made her all the more powerful. There were stories — some told to her by Chedyla — about favorites, or the newborn son of a favorite, disappearing forever from the palace. If Daiwa didn't have Yazid as living proof that someday she would be the most exalted woman in the land, a right reserved exclusively for the mother of the sultan, the steps she might take to secure her powers did not bear imagining.

Ariel shuddered inwardly despite the warmth of the baths, "I'm sorry, Carmela, did you say something?"

"I only said that I think you are making a bonfire out of a candle's flame."

"The *fantasia?*"

"No, you goose, your betrothed. Did you really think he'd tell you he was the duke when you had just finished telling him you wanted no part of him? Ariel," Carmela said, tossing her heavy black hair over one wet shoulder, "only a man who wants to see you squirm like a worm on the fishing hook would reveal himself to you after that."

"It wasn't that he didn't tell me at the ball or in the garden afterward. There wasn't any time," Ariel replied. "But at the trysting pool, Carmela, it was as if . . ." Ariel hesitated, uncertain she wanted to put her thoughts into words. She'd been so attracted to him. It went beyond the pact they'd made, Ariel admitted, although her honesty was painful. She had *wanted* him to kiss her. She'd been on the verge of committing the same error in judgment as Carmela. The Spanish Gypsy's impetuous, romantic notions had gotten her nothing but the life of a captive. Christopher was nothing more than another Paulo. Ariel would not make the same mistake as Carmela, ending up locked behind a beautiful facade with only brightly splashed memories to keep her company. She would never again succumb to him, nor let his touch divert her purpose.

"I give up!"

"What?" Ariel asked, bewildered by Carmela's sharp words.

"There is no use talking to you today. Your head is up among the palm fronds. Besides, I've had enough of the baths. I cannot lie here all day in an opium haze waiting for the sultan's call like these other women. I have to *do* something, even if it's just changing my tunic seven times a day."

Ariel smiled at her friend's boisterous energy. "I'll see you at the *fantasia,* then."

"Before sunset tomorrow. At the harem tents," Carmela called back as her naked, overripe body disappeared into the steam. "And enjoy your lion tonight."

Ariel frowned. Tonight was approaching far too quickly, and she hadn't been able to get even a message to her guardian. As long as the marriage contract was still valid, Ariel was legally bound to Christopher and to his wishes. Spurred by that thought, she quickly rose from the bench, making her way past glassy-eyed concubines as they languished half-submerged in the pools. Carmela was right, she thought sadly. The baths were too mesmerizing and comfortable by half. One could lose all interest in the outside world here, leaving life to lead you around by the hand.

She wouldn't be led, Ariel thought as she silently accepted her caftan from the odalisque at the door. There were still a few hours before the evening meal. If the sultan was locked behind the doors of his meetings, she would at least speak to Yazid. He'd promised to help her; perhaps he had an answer by now.

Time was running out. The sun cast a satin sheet of pink across the sky as the Imam called the faithful to evening prayer. Ariel lay across a pillow in her room, elbows sinking deep in goose-down stuffing as she drummed her fingers impatiently against her cheek. Why was he so long! Two hours had passed since Siad had returned with Yazid's message saying he would speak with her shortly. It could only be that there were problems with the treaty. And if that were so, then

Yazid must be succeeding in extricating her from any promise of marriage. She wouldn't allow herself to believe anything else. It had to be. But Christopher's adamant denial poked insistently into her thoughts, and Ariel didn't feel nearly as confident as she'd been that morning.

Rolling onto her back, Ariel looked out at Allah's artistry. Her heart clutched with a sickened longing at its beauty. How could she ever leave Morocco with its stunning palette of orange, lemon, and azure blue? All its beauty, all the people she held dear, hung on a thread that was spinning thinner and thinner with the passing minutes. What would become of Siad if she was not here. And Chedyla? She would be cast back among the concubines where she was ridiculed for tying herself to Ariel. The three of them were a family. Small and unorthodox, no doubt, but they needed her just as she needed them.

"Allah," she prayed, squeezing back the tears that sprang suddenly into her eyes. "Please let Yazid come with the answer I pray for before Christopher finds me. I can face him as long as I know there's hope for my cause, but if I have to face him as his betrothed . . ." She let out an uneven breath. A sharp knock on the door abruptly ended her prayer. Jumping to her feet, Ariel nodded for Siad to open the door. A second later Ariel uttered another prayer, this one a prayer of thanks as Yazid stalked angrily into the room, his face set in the jagged contours of fury.

"Yazid," she said, too anxious to be wary of his venomous attitude. For a moment the prince glared at Ariel with eyes the cold, green color of thick mountain ice. Then the look was gone, replaced by something calculating and very nearly as chilling to Ariel. Driven by desperation, she paid no heed to the inner voice that warned caution, and hurried toward him.

"Yazid," she repeated, unconsciously clutching his long robe. "I've been so worried all day. I've sent message after message. Thank you for finally coming." She felt his chest muscles jump beneath his djellaba as his eyes narrowed suspiciously. "Have you spoken to your father?" she went on in a burst of anxiety. "Will he revoke the marriage contract?"

Yazid relaxed noticeably beneath her hand, and his arm snaked around her waist, drawing her closer. She was suddenly, startlingly aware of his taut thigh between her legs. "I have not spoken to my father about your problem yet, sweet, sweet Ariel," he said, taking her chin between his forefinger and thumb as he tipped it up.

She had no choice but to look directly into his almond-shaped eyes. Her heart pounded with uncertainty, but she dared not move, afraid to invoke his anger and lose his help. "But do not doubt me. I will see that you never marry the infidel swine. He is not good enough for you."

Yazid's face hardened with anger again. "He is an interloper, interfering where he has no rights. And my father, the sultan"—he almost sneered at the title, his fingers tightening cruelly on Ariel's chin—"my father asks the advice of an infidel. He invites him to ride in our most honored war ritual. He goes too far!"

Ariel winced in pain as Yazid's fingers bit into the soft flesh of her face and the crushing power of his arm cut off her breath.

"Am I hurting you?" Yazid asked, a strange smile curling his upper lip.

He loosened his hold slightly. Ariel gulped air into her lungs, wanting desperately to free herself from Yazid's arms, yet unwilling to surrender her last hope

111

to a nameless fear.

"You forgive me, don't you, Ariel?" Yazid relaxed his hold further without allowing her to move even a centimeter from his hard body. "This has been a difficult day for all of us, but I have not forgotten about you, Ariel. Lovely, Ariel."

Ariel felt his fingers caress the sheer fabric at her waist as he spoke, and she squirmed uncomfortably.

"The infidel Englishman will never have you. One way or another, I will see to it."

She should have been pleased by his promise; instead Ariel's heart contracted in fear. Her instincts warned her away from Yazid, but he was the only person who promised her what she most desired. Ariel swallowed back her discomfort, reminding herself that he was her ally and her prince.

"What a touching scene," a deep voice drawled from the open doorway.

Before she even saw him, one arm casually propped against the portal, Ariel recognized Christopher's voice. Dread surged through her veins. The two of them standing here, alone except for Siad's motionless figure in the shadow of a potted palm, Yazid's arm wrapped around her as he pressed her against his thigh; there was no denying what conclusions Christopher had jumped to. His face was as hard as Yazid's had been a moment ago, but unlike the prince, Ariel couldn't read his emotions. His was a cold, deliberate facade, as shuttered and expressionless as a death mask.

He spoke to Yazid, looking through Ariel as if she didn't exist. "I take it Mohammed Ben Abdullah has finalized his plans." His familiar use of the sultan's name was like a well-thrown dagger, and Yazid responded, his shoulders stiffening. Ariel could feel the

112

fury emanating from Yazid in a nearly palatable wall of heat as he set her aside, momentarily discarded. Relief gave wings to her feet as she sped across the room, propelled by instinct to put a wide margin between herself and the heir.

"You concern yourself too much with the affairs of my country," Yazid replied.

Christopher shrugged nonchalantly. "I have a stake in the outcome of your affairs. After all, I have responsibilities to my king, and I take the expedient accomplishment of his wishes very seriously."

"The treaty is secure. You have seen to that quite handily." Confused by the look Yazid directed her way, Ariel looked at Christopher. She may as well have been a vaporish spirit for all the acknowledgement he gave her.

"I hope that's so," Christopher stated in a voice that reeked of sarcasm. "Until it's signed and in my hand, however, I'm sure you won't mind my looking after things myself — even though you have things so well in hand," he added, twisting the blade of his disdain deeper.

The heir's hand flew to the jeweled dagger thrust into the sash of his robe in white-knuckled fury. "You mock my honor, infidel," he hissed through clenched teeth. "And that of my father."

"No, Moulay Yazid. I am merely concerned with the welfare of King George's treaty. I have the deepest respect for your father." Christopher flashed a casual smile. "But what I think doesn't matter anyway, does it? Unless I've forgotten, the Koran teaches that only Allah can be your judge."

Yazid's hand loosened on the hilt the slightest degree, but his anger hung in the air like the foreshadowing of a storm.

Ariel watched the exchange in growing trepidation. Christopher reminded her of a skillful snake charmer enticing the hissing, furious cobra from its dark basket. Yazid was his snake, and Christopher was toying with him, goading and then retreating, testing his limits, studying his flaws and his strengths.

"Then, you have no business here, Lord Staunton," Yazid challenged.

"Unfortunately, I do have business here. You see, I came to collect something of mine. And much to my surprise I find her in your keeping."

"Ariel does not wish your protection. She finds my presence more comfortable."

"Nevertheless, I have the papers to prove she's mine," Christopher commented icily. "I'm sure you know better than to doubt their authenticity."

Ariel stared at Christopher in white-faced disbelief. How dare he talk about her as though she were a misplaced belonging! If she had despised Christopher Staunton for his deceit, that could only be described as distaste beside the black hatred that bellowed in her ears at this moment. She opened her mouth intent on delivering a scalding tirade, only to wordlessly drop her jaw in disbelief at Yazid's reply.

"Take her," he said coldly. "I have better things to do than waste precious time over a *woman*." His final word carried such disdain Ariel reacted as though she'd been slapped across the face. Numb, she watched Christopher give Yazid a barely recognizable nod. A moment later he was at her side, his hand clamped around her elbow in a vise-like grip.

"Let's go," he ordered through tightly clenched teeth.

Ariel made no attempt to move, obstinately refusing to acquiesce to even the smallest command he made.

"You've already pushed my patience beyond imagination, Ariel," he warned her. "I wouldn't count on your good fortune holding out much longer."

"I have no intention of going anywhere with you."

"You made that crystal clear this morning."

Yazid crossed one arm over the other, watching them with smug satisfaction. "Is one young woman more than you can manage, Lord Staunton? I see now why Christians have so few wives."

Without a backward glance Christopher jerked Ariel off her feet and carried her from the room.

Gasping in indignation, Ariel struggled to free herself, hurling every viperous imputation she knew at Christopher's chest. "Pompous, egotistical son of a bazaar woman!" she hissed from between clenched teeth, barely stopping for a breath. The litany continued unabated. The more blatantly he ignored her, the more scathing her appraisal became. The breadth of her vocabulary would have impressed her tutors had they been privy to the scene as Christopher strode down the hall in frigid silence. At last her flailing feet found a mark on his shin.

He dropped her unceremoniously to the floor, leaving her to fend for her lost balance.

"I am not one of your misplaced possessions!" she snapped, snatching up the slipper she'd dislodged when Christopher released her. "Nor am I a recalcitrant child to be carried off for punishment!"

"Then, stop acting like one," Christopher shot back. He started down the hallway again while Ariel stared after him in disbelief. He hadn't gone four meters when he turned back to her.

"Ariel." He ground out her name like a vile medicine he had no choice but to take. "I am giving you a

115

chance to prove yourself capable of being a lady. Look on it as an opportunity. One way or another you are coming to dinner. If you prefer that it be over my shoulder, I will be more than happy to accommodate you."

Tears of impotent rage threatened at the corners of her eyes as she swept past him. She'd done nothing to warrant his malicious treatment, she railed silently as she marched in the direction of his suite. If he wanted to believe there was some taint of impropriety in her relationship with Yazid, so be it. If he had asked her, if he had even acknowledged her existence rather than treating her like a pest, she would have explained. Of course, leaving out their plan to break her betrothal, she amended as a tinge of guilt colored her thoughts. Instead, he had called her his possession. His possession!

"We're eating in here," Christopher announced icily. He had stopped several doors short of where Ariel stood.

"Of course," she retorted, spinning on her heels as she retraced her steps. She had supposed Christopher would have been put in rooms farther along the passage, but she was very rarely in this part of the palace. Perhaps some of the rooms had been altered. Given the events of the past few days, she thought grimly, nothing should seem unusual to her anymore.

Ariel stepped into the lavish gold and cream rooms generally reserved for high-ranking official visitors, and froze.

"Good evening, Lady Ariel. It's a pleasure to see you again. May I be among the first to offer you congratulations on your betrothal to my nephew."

Robert Belmeth stood beside an intimate table for four that sparkled with crystal and silver. At his side, an elegantly dressed woman whose silver hair was swept into a refined twist offered a smile of encouragement.

This was no quiet dinner for two where they might discuss the impossibility of this marriage as Ariel had expected. This was to be a celebration! A celebration when he knew she wanted no part of marriage to him and, judging by the frigid mask on his face, a marriage that Christopher no longer looked upon with any great relish either.

Chapter Ten

"Lord Belmeth," Ariel replied with a curtsy, doing her best to cover her flustered state.

"May I introduce my wife, Anne, to you."

Ariel smiled hesitantly at Anne Belmeth. "I'm pleased to meet you, Lady Anne."

"The pleasure is all mine, I assure you, my dear." Anne Belmeth swept across the room, ignoring both her husband and Christopher and took Ariel's hands, giving them a warm squeeze. Her smile was filled with understanding.

"I know this is all somewhat of a shock to you. My nephew has explained the confusion that occurred at your first meeting, but we are so pleased to have you as a member of our family. I know his mother will be just as delighted. Welcome."

Ariel's numb fingers received another squeeze as Lady Anne kissed her gently on the cheek before stepping back beside her husband. Assaulted by a barrage of conflicting emotions, Ariel stood mutely in the center of them, desperate for something light or witty to say. But the only thoughts that sprang to mind were quite the opposite. The Belmeths seemed to be genuinely nice people, and she had no desire to insult them by telling them that she considered their nephew a liar and an opportunist, and despised the mere suggestion of this proposed marriage. Instead she stood there struggling in silence for some kind response to Lady Anne's welcome. She needn't have worried, for Christopher stepped into the breech, his demeanor as social and pleasant now as it had been hard and unwavering a few moments ago.

"You'll have to excuse Ariel, Anne. She's just come from a disturbing meeting with Prince Mohammed El Yazid. I'm sure that when she's had a few minutes to collect her thoughts, she'll be more talkative."

Ariel didn't miss the emphasis Christopher placed on Yazid's name, nor the edge to his voice. But she refused to let him humiliate her in front of his relatives. Instead she turned on him with a smile intended to melt the snow from the highest peaks of the Atlas.

"Thank you, Christopher. But you entered into the conversation rather late, and I don't want you to worry unnecessarily in my behalf. Actually," she continued sweetly, "Yazid gave me news of a very encouraging nature. You'll understand, Lady Anne, if I ask that you allow me to keep the content of Yazid's message private."

"Of course, my dear," Anne replied. "Shall we have supper now?"

When she was seated, Ariel found Christopher in the chair opposite. He gave her a coolly appraising look while he cocked a dark eyebrow in challenge. "How fortunate that the prince had good news for you. You'll have to share it with me when we have an opportunity to be alone."

Ariel glared at him with frigid distaste while Lord Belmeth seated his wife. "I doubt there will be a chance for us to be alone," she replied, her voice dripping sweetness. "It's forbidden for a woman to see a man alone, particularly her betrothed. It would be a bad omen," she warned ominously. "I shall be in seclusion until the ceremony." And with an imperious dismissal, Ariel turned to Lord Belmeth, whom she intended to engage in any subject that would keep her from having to look at Christopher's black scowl.

An hour later Ariel was still regaling Robert and Anne with charming conversation. Christopher had to admire her determination. She was managing to exclude him quite completely. Rolling the fine French burgundy wine on his tongue, he listened to Ariel's soft laughter as she responded to one of Robert's quips. Except for treating him as though he didn't exist, her demeanor throughout the meal had been stunning. She'd risen to the occasion with more aplomb than the most highborn of women. In fact, he was certain that she was charming both Anne and Robert quite thoroughly.

Anne had been furious with Christopher that afternoon when he'd explained Ariel's misconceptions about the Duke of Avon. She'd empathized with Ariel's point of view, and Christopher had realized just how much right Ariel had to some feelings of betrayal. He'd steeled himself for that reaction from her, and had told himself that no matter what she did this evening to aggravate or defy him, he would be understanding. However, none of those things had included walking in on that touching little scene in her bedroom.

As Christopher listened to her describe her adopted country to Anne, he wondered if Ariel's reasons for wanting to stay in Morocco might be considerably different from the ones she'd given him. Maybe she aspired to become one of the prince's wives. His stomach tightened in anger at the possibility. He knew all too well how it felt to be someone's second choice. He wasn't about to find himself in that position again. Not ever again.

Christopher's gaze settled on the vision across the table from him. In the candlelight her untouched wine goblets sparkled before Ariel like a ruby and topaz necklace, but the string of jewel colors didn't compare to her beauty. Her complexion shimmered in the soft light, and as she spoke her lips moved in a rhythmic cadence that evoked disturbingly sensual memories of her kisses. A streak of warmth shot through his loins, and Christopher shook himself abruptly. If Ariel was on intimate terms with El Yazid, he wanted to know. He had no intention of being cuckolded.

At last Robert suggested they move to the fire. Christopher pushed back his chair and bore down on Ariel, determined to put an end to the icy shield she was erecting.

By the look on his face, Ariel was not certain whether Christopher intended to escort her to a chair or throttle her and hang her from her feet to age. But whichever it was to be, she refused to cower before him. She took the arm he thrust before her and glanced up at him. Despite her resolve not to be intimidated, Ariel was still bruised by the caustic treatment she'd received in front of Yazid. She wasn't at all certain that she could win against him. She was accustomed to standing in rooms with sultans and kings, but Christopher was different. He emanated a presence of such magnitude that it had taken every fiber of her being to stand against him. The tight control of his jaw and the unyielding authority that radiated

121

from him now were evidence of the very invincibility that put her in awe of him.

As they neared the warmth of the fireplace, Christopher steered Ariel toward the settee. Seeing she had no choice but to accept or make a scene, Ariel perched herself on the outermost corner of the little sofa. Christopher settled into the seat beside her, casually draping one arm behind her as he stretched his long legs at an angle that gave him a far larger portion of the settee than was left to her. When she turned to say as much, there was a distinct threat in his blue eyes that dared her to make a comment, and Ariel snapped her mouth shut rather than be humiliated by some caustic comment she didn't doubt he'd let fly in front of the Belmeths.

"I assure you, Lady Ariel, you'll enjoy the flowers in England," Lady Belmeth said, picking up the botanical conversation they had begun at dinner.

"I've heard your gardens are wonderful there," Ariel agreed. Anne Belmeth shared her love of flowers, and her lively discussion of the lush private gardens in England as well as London's public parks had been a highlight of the dinner. "They sound so different from ours here."

"It's a shame you've never seen your parents' homeland," Lady Anne replied sincerely. "But they both died while you were very young, didn't they? You know, Robert and I both knew your parents, although only casually. Your mother was a delightful woman, and your father . . ." Anne Belmeth smiled. "It was no wonder she chose him. He was quite handsome, and very romantic."

Ariel stiffened at the mention of her father. Clearly Lady Anne knew nothing of how he had deserted her

122

mother. But Ariel's memories of the years after her mother's death were vivid and poignant. She had been so torn between hope that he would come back for her and an equally strong dread that he would take her away from what had become her home that at times she felt as though she were being torn in two.

"I never knew my father," she replied in a voice that revealed more emotion than she intended. "But Moulay Mohammed has been a wonderful guardian."

"I'm sure he has," Lord Belmeth said, reaching out to pat her arm as he tactfully changed the subject. "You must tell my wife what to buy while we are here. She's announced that she intends to visit the souk tomorrow."

"You've never been to the marketplace here before?" Ariel's eyes lit with pleasure. "It's a wonderful place. Everything seems to happen at once in the souk. Delicious smells fill the air, merchants call out as you pass by, entertainers wander through the streets vying for your attention. I'm sure you'll find it unlike any place you've ever been before. The outdoor bazaar has everything you can imagine, and it's all for sale, although I warn you much of it you'd be wise to avoid."

"Which are the best buys?"

"That depends on what you like," Ariel teased merrily.

"What would you buy there, Ariel?"

It was Christopher asking the question, and the interest in his voice caught her off guard. She turned to look at him, surprised to find the tight anger he'd worn throughout the evening greatly lessened. For a moment it was as though they were back at the trysting pool. Confused, Ariel faltered and dropped her gaze to where her intertwined fingers lay in her lap.

"I haven't been to the souk in years," she admitted quietly. "But were I to go . . ." Her eyes filled with imagined possibilities. "I would visit the silversmith and the leather merchants. Perhaps I could find a necklace for Chedyla or something for Siad."

"Why did you stop going?" Lady Belmeth asked.

"Now I would be required to cover myself. I've never gotten used to being swathed in material from head to foot. I'd rather stay here where I can wear a tunic and pants."

"When we traveled from Salé," Anne remarked thoughtfully, "I wore a veiled hat. Christopher assured me it was modest enough for me to go about in public. Will the same attire suit for the bazaar?"

Ariel nodded. "My mother used to visit the souk dressed the same way. A high-necked gown, gloves and a veiled hat will protect you from any disparaging looks. I'd be happy to send my eunuch with you. He knows the bazaar well, and his English is excellent."

"You must come, too, Ariel," Anne insisted with sudden enthusiasm. "I have an extra traveling outfit. The dress may need a little altering, but the hat and gloves will be perfect. It's more confining than what you're used to wearing, but perhaps it would be fun. You could show me the bazaar yourself."

Ariel began to say no, but talking about the souk had brought back so many memories. She hadn't realized how much she missed it. Suddenly she smiled and nodded. Why not? She would bring along a second eunuch just to be sure. There was no reason not to go, and Chedyla's name day was coming up. Ariel could purchase a gift for her.

Ariel's decision put a spark of excitement into the air of the parlor. Lady Belmeth's blue eyes fairly crackled with delight, and her husband made light-hearted jest of the losses he was certain to incur as a result of their foray the next day. Even Christopher seemed genuinely pleased by her decision. The watchfulness seemed to ebb out of his demeanor, and he even joined Robert in his ripostes about the day at the souk.

Although Ariel dared not give him more than a sideways glance as he relaxed beside her, the warmth of Christopher's enthusiasm and his good-natured humor affected her. Without realizing it, her ramrod posture slackened as she joined their light banter. Glancing outside at the stillness, Ariel sensed that it was quite late. Still, she didn't think of going until Christopher's hand gently brushed across the crown of her head as he reached for his brandy. Suddenly aware that she was sitting far too close, Ariel adjusted her weight away from him. Keeping her gaze lowered, she made her excuses and thanked the Belmeths for a lovely dinner.

"I'll send the gown and hat over first thing in the morning," Lady Belmeth assured her.

"It's very kind of you," Ariel responded. "I'm looking forward to the trip. Shall I come by for you at ten?"

"Is that the best time?" Anne inquired.

"The merchants rest in the afternoon. Besides, we'll want to be back in time to change for the *fantasia* tomorrow evening. You won't want to miss it, Lady Belmeth," Ariel assured her, smiling in response to Anne's questioning look. "If we go in the morning, we'll have plenty of time."

"Then, ten it shall be."

"Thank you again," Ariel said.

Christopher stepped out into the hall with her. Ariel looked nervously at the tall, powerful figure beside her. "It's not necessary for you to walk me to my rooms. Siad has been waiting to escort me."

"I don't mind," Christopher replied casually. "I'm still full from dinner. The walk will do me good." Siad slipped into place half a dozen strides behind them, and not knowing what else to do, Ariel started down the hall in silence while Christopher took possession of her arm. The wall sconces threw flickering shadows across their path as they walked. She was at a loss for something to say. The friendly warmth that had permeated the parlor seemed merely illusion now, and their light, easy banter tinny and false.

She glanced up at him through long, golden lashes. Why was he always so calm while she was so ill at ease? His fingers on her elbow seemed to burn her flesh even through the sheer silk sleeve, and she jumped at the slightest change in the pressure of his hand. Somehow he seemed always to have the advantage in this game they were playing. Either he was so charming that he cajoled her from her determined hatred or he was so calmly detached that her anger didn't touch him at all, and she felt as though she were the miscreant rather than he.

But it wasn't she who had lied, she reminded herself resolutely. Nor had she made demands of him that he was unwilling to accept.

They arrived at the door to her room, but this time instead of trying to flee inside as she had this morning, Ariel turned to face him. He was a harlequin, she thought, hiding her perusal of him in the shadows of the dark hallway. There was no gray about him. He was all black or white; either charming and seductive

126

or scheming for his own purposes. Ariel was not at all certain that she knew which was real, and the two images clashed and struggled between themselves in her mind.

"Did you enjoy yourself tonight, Ariel?"

She opened her mouth, intending to bite out a scathing denial, but choked on the falseness of such a reply. She had enjoyed herself, more than she'd thought possible. But she wouldn't let that confuse her determination, or excuse Christopher's deception. "I enjoyed Lord and Lady Belmeth very much."

"Then, the evening was a success." He brushed a kiss against her forehead and held the door to her room open for her. "Good night, Ariel. Sleep well."

Ariel gave him a quizzical look as she slipped under his arm. "Good night." The door closed behind her, and she leaned against it, listening to the fading sound of Christopher's footsteps.

"You have returned, my child." Chedyla appeared from her cubicle, eager to help Ariel undress. "You spent much time with your betrothed. Perhaps you have come to know him this night. Perhaps you have seen that the sultan indeed chooses wisely. You are very fortunate. Rare is the woman who is allowed to meet her husband before the marriage and overcome her fear of what is unknown."

Ariel didn't respond, and Chedyla continued her one-way conversation while she helped Ariel into a sheer nightdress. When, at length, Ariel was ready for bed, Chedyla stepped back, looking at her charge. The golden copper of her hair hung like a sheath of satin to her waist, but her eyes were clouded tonight. Chedyla could not read how the meal had gone, and this troubled her. Ariel was destined to return to England, to complete the circle of life her mother and father had begun. This finishing of the circle of life she must not attempt to change.

Chedyla considered it her final duty to her charge to see that she accepted this destiny. But Ariel was so full of fire and temper that sometimes it was like trying to guide the course of a spring stream overflowing with mountain snow. From her post in the corner she could hear Ariel's rhythmic breathing, signalling that she was at last asleep. Chedyla turned and passed through the doorway to her bedroom. She walked straight to the small cupboard that housed her prayer rug. *I must continue to seek Allah's guidance,* she thought. *His capable hands will guide the child of my heart to her destiny.*

Chapter Eleven

Ariel stared at the image reflected in the full-length mirror, but it was her mother who looked back at her. When she'd awakened, Lady Belmeth's gown, hat, and gloves lay already pressed and altered across the chair in her room. Now as Rhima hooked the long row of buttons up the back of the celadon gown, Ariel could not reconcile the image in the mirror with herself. The slightly taller than average frame, carefully shaped by the tucked waist of the dress, the long neck, exposed to view by the upswept hairstyle Chedyla had labored over, the high cheekbones and straight nose seemed not to be hers anymore. Although her memories of her mother were dim, if there was one picture that Ariel carried in her mind of her mother, it was this.

Picking up the broad-brimmed straw hat from the table, she lowered it onto the elegant coiffure Chedyla had insisted was needed for an English gown and hat. The hatband came to rest directly over the place where Christopher had kissed her brow the night before, bringing back all the conflicting feelings she'd felt at this gentle side of him. Ariel snatched the hat from her head, pulling loose several long, dark-gold strands of hair and dropped it in her lap, crushing the broad brim between nervous fingers. "I'm not going."

"Of course you are going," Chedyla chided as she swept the straw hat out of her hands. "But I cannot follow along behind you repairing your appearance. Don't you remember the things your mother taught you?"

Chedyla carefully tucked the stray strands back into place, and placed Lady Belmeth's hat on Ariel's head. She pierced one side of the crown with a long hatpin, securing it in place before Ariel could protest and send it sailing across the room. The yellow diamond at the end of the hatpin winked at Ariel from the wide green ribbon that decorated the crown, reminding her of a spring crocus. She no longer knew what to think of Christopher Staunton. If he had remained withdrawn and angry, it would have been much easier to hate him. But last night he had been charming. As they sat around the fireplace she'd found herself enjoying his company. Then he had planted that gentle, chaste kiss on her forehead, and Ariel hadn't known how to react.

She'd been prepared for another wanton, demanding kiss. In fact, she'd been waiting for it, planning exactly how she'd reject him, making it clear that she didn't want any part of his plans to make her his wife. Instead, he'd given her a tender kiss on the forehead that was more brotherly affection than the fiery demand of Christopher's other kisses. Ariel knotted her fingers together in frustration. The sooner Yazid implemented a plan to break the marriage contract, the better. She didn't want to marry Christopher. But, she admitted reluctantly, neither did she wish to see him humiliated by an outright rejection of his offer. She had no desire to rekindle his wrath after what she'd

130

seen yesterday with Yazid. Sucking in her cheeks to form a thoughtful pout, Ariel dropped the opaque silk veil over her face and stared resolutely back at the mirror. *I am not Caroline Lennox,* she repeated to herself. *And I am not going to England.*

At exactly ten o'clock Ariel rapped on Lord and Lady Belmeth's door. Behind her Siad stood at attention, his left hand on the hilt of the ever-ready scimitar. A second eunuch stood farther back, holding a heavily laden picnic basket in his arms.

"Lady Ariel," Lord Belmeth greeted her with a crisp bow. "Come in. My wife will be here momentarily. I've come to the conclusion that the London shops bore her to distraction, judging by her excitement over this sojourn into Meknes."

Ariel's rejoinder was cut short by a wry comment from behind her.

"Didn't your mother teach you always to check the doorway before closing it, Robert? You might slam it in someone's face."

Ariel whirled around to find Christopher lounging against the door frame, his face filled with warm amusement.

"Didn't yours teach you not to sneak up on people unannounced?" Robert retorted in good humor.

"Of course she did," Lady Belmeth added airily as she swept into the room, wearing a sherried pink dress of identical cut to Ariel's. "Elizabeth has flawless manners, and she passed everything she knows on to both her sons. I have it on good authority, however, that Christopher was not wont to pay attention to his lessons as a boy."

In an instant Christopher's mood changed from one of joviality to brusque tension. He cocked an impas-

131

sive brow at his aunt. "I don't think this is the time to regale Ariel with stories of my childhood." A long, silent void in conversation followed, and as the minutes drew out, Ariel felt compelled to fill the widening gap.

"I've taken the liberty of having a picnic lunch packed for us, Lady Belmeth. I hope you don't mind."

"I'd like nothing better. And please call me Anne. You'll soon be my niece, and I can't imagine such a distant relationship." Ariel looked quickly at Christopher and back to Lady Belmeth.

"Of course," she replied lightly, but beneath her easy demeanor Ariel was fuming. Christopher still hadn't told the Belmeths the true circumstances of their betrothal, and she had no intention of going along with his deception. Well, she thought resolutely, if Christopher wouldn't tell them, she would. It would only make it harder in the end if she didn't. Better that they understand the situation than be taken by surprise later when they might misunderstand and think she was at fault. She'd have a perfect opportunity to explain everything on the way to the souk.

"Shall we go?" Lady Belmeth asked brightly.

"Yes, of course. I thought you might be uncomfortable with only Siad accompanying us, so I've brought along another eunuch."

"I let him go."

Ariel turned to stare incredulously at Christopher.

"I'll be there, and Siad agreed that three men weren't necessary for protection."

"Siad agreed . . . ?" The words died on her lips as she absorbed this sudden change in plans. "Are you coming also, Lord Belmeth?" she asked, swinging around.

"No. I'm afraid shopping is not my particular forte. I'm planning a quiet day at my desk. I have several letters to send off to the king."

Ariel shot Christopher an accusing look, but he only grinned back at her.

"You need two body guards, and I'm available. Why tie up another guard?"

"Why indeed," added Lady Belmeth. "I feel perfectly safe with Christopher. After all, he's conversant in the language, and given his experience in dealing with Moroccan goods, I'm certain we'll win the best prices from the vendors."

Ariel started to say that she had quite a bit of experience bargaining with the merchants and that Christopher's expertise wasn't required. But she kept her thoughts to herself. If Sahlib had already been dismissed, it would take precious time away from their trip to find a replacement, and Ariel didn't want to deny Lady Belmeth her full day at the souk. Instead, she nodded her agreement and brushed past Christopher without so much as a backward glance.

Any hopes Ariel harbored that Christopher would do the gentlemanly thing and stay home were quickly dashed. The sound of his easy, long-legged stride behind her made it clear he was unconcerned if his presence ruined her day. From the bantering conversation he carried on with his aunt, he couldn't care less that he was an unwelcome guest. A fact that only added tinder to Ariel's flaring temper.

Reaching the carriage, Ariel dashed up the steps without so much as a glance at the footman's proffered hand and dropped into the farthest corner. By the time Lady Belmeth and Christopher reached the carriage, she'd fumed enough to dissipate the hottest portion of her anger. Having regained a modicum of her composure, Ariel flashed Lady Belmeth what she hoped was a cheerful smile as she settled onto the opposite seat.

A moment later Ariel's good mood evaporated.

Christopher's broad shoulders filled the carriage doorway, and before she had time to absorb her shock, he climbed into the compartment and took the seat beside her. Ariel turned to him in frantic agitation. "Your horse is waiting for you outside."

Christopher made himself comfortable against the squabs, stretching his legs at an angle across the compartment that encroached substantially on what Ariel considered her section of the interior.

"I thought it best to have a horse along in case you ladies are overambitious in your shopping. But why should I ride in the sun when I can enjoy both your company and the coolness of the carriage?"

Ariel glowered at him before she turned to stare out the window, studying the palace grounds as if she'd never laid eyes on them before. Why couldn't he put up with a little heat? Here she was, crammed in this stuffy box, swathed in pound upon pound of heavy fabric, and *he* couldn't bear a little sun and wind. Arrogant, pampered jackanapes! What happened to the swashbuckling sea captain he'd described himself as, she thought derisively. Bluster, all of it. Every word he had spoken to her, everything about him, had been feint and flourish. Now she was seeing his true nature. Dandified aristocrat. Duplicitous schemer. Attributes that appeared to come quite naturally to him, Ariel noted as the carriage lurched into motion.

As they rolled down the main artery of traffic within the palace walls a trickle of perspiration ran

down the valley between her breasts and met the bod-
ice of her dress where she could already feel a damp
spot forming. Another threatened at the small gap at
her waist. And having Christopher so close wasn't
helping her deal with the suffocated feeling that
threatened to envelop her. The hard muscle of his
thigh pressed against hers and the uneven roll of the
carriage created a patch of hot friction there despite
her layers of dress, petticoat and stockings. Ariel
squeezed farther into the corner of their conveyance
and plucked at the folds of her skirt, trying to maneuver away from Christopher without giving him the
satisfaction of knowing he was the cause of her discomfort.

Anne Belmeth reached over, giving her nervous
hand a reassuring pat. "I know it's difficult adjusting
to my voluminous skirts when you're accustomed to
something much lighter," she prompted with a smile.
"But I've always found that the less I move about, particularly in the heat, the more comfortable I am."

Ariel froze mid-fidget, wordlessly clasping her
hands together in her lap. But she refused to relax her
ramrod posture, despite the jostling of the carriage. A
conspiracy, she thought to herself, returning to her
absorption in the passing scenery. How could she have
entertained the idea of talking to Lady Belmeth? she
wondered hysterically. Every comment Lady Belmeth
made was in subtle support of her nephew's position.
How could she ever have hoped that the Belmeths
would understand her position? Their allegiance
would naturally be with Christopher.

Ariel's sense of well-being was deteriorating with
every passing minute and thought. Why was everyone
lining up with the opposition? Lady Belmeth, her

guardian, Chedyla, and Suleiman all stood behind Christopher. Only Yazid was on her side. Without him, she realized bleakly as they passed through the main gate of the palace and headed into the heart of Meknes, she stood no chance at all of escaping Christopher's grasp.

But Yazid was the sultan's heir. If Moulay Mohammed would listen to anyone, it would be Yazid. And Yazid had promised he would do whatever was necessary to convince his father. If she was to have only one ally, she decided, Yazid was the best. Surely by tonight, he'd have spoken to her guardian. All she had to do was pass the day with Christopher and his aunt. In fact, she realized as the carriage slowed and began its crawling pace along the outer fringes of the souk, the longer she kept Christopher out of the palace, the more time Yazid would have with the sultan. A slow smile curved her mouth. It was a small sacrifice, keeping Lord Staunton busy in town while Yazid lay Christopher's lies and deceptions before her guardian.

"Oh, my . . . ," Lady Belmeth whispered in astonishment as the carriage rocked to a halt. "This is quite a reception." The souk had become silent. There was no more bustling activity, none of the happy chatter amid the call of merchants to prospective customers that had filled the air a moment before. Ariel touched her hat, reassuring herself that it was straight and that her face was appropriately shrouded by its veil. Then, turning a cold shoulder to Christopher, she gave Lady Belmeth a brave smile, "We've arrived."

They emerged from the carriage into a sea of prone bodies. All around them faces pressed worshipfully into the dirt-packed street; merchants, shoppers and tradesmen all huddled in prostrate obeisance around the carriage that bore the sultan's coat of arms.

"When will they get up?" Anne Belmeth whispered in dismay, glancing to all sides for some sign of movement.

"When we leave."

The look of astonishment on Lady Belmeth's face only added to the grim discomfort that had blossomed in the pit of Ariel's stomach. "It's true," she continued, pursing her lips into a thin line of resignation.

"But we're not royals. We're just visitors. Surely they don't recognize you; you're covered from head to foot."

"I had forgotten about this. When I was small, no one paid the least attention to me, but I remember that whenever the sultanas came to the market it was like this. And we came in the sultan's carriage. For all they know we might be sultanas who are having a little fun playing dress up."

"Surely not," Lady Belmeth argued, but her words died on her lips as Ariel gave a chagrined nod of her head.

"Just a few months ago a merchant continued to haggle over some goods with his customer when one of Moulay Mohammed's wives stopped at the neighboring booth. She took exception to the fact that they didn't recognize her in her European dress and hat."

"And . . . ?" Lady Belmeth asked in trepidation.

"And she had them both beheaded."

"How horrid!"

"Then she had the heads displayed for four days in the center of the marketplace as a lesson to others," Ariel finished. She didn't dare look at Lady Belmeth. She was too afraid of what she would see on her face if she did. She was ashamed by the admission she'd just made. Ashamed for her country, and ashamed for the sultan. Ashamed that any woman would have committed such a heinous act for the sake of her vanity.

Christopher lounged against one wheel of the carriage, his posture belying the intensity of his thoughts as he watched Ariel. Her voice had lowered until it was nothing more than a dark whisper, and despite the gauzy drape from the brim of her hat he could see the stony color of her face as she stared over the backs of the crowd. Undoubtedly the sultana who'd ordered such senseless murders hadn't given it a second thought, yet Ariel was suffering her disgrace for her. He knew instinctively that Yazid's mother had been the one who'd ordered the executions. If she was capable of that, she was capable of ridding herself of Ariel in just as mean a fashion. Any remaining doubts that Ariel needed protection from the Hatum Kadin and her pack of mongrel viziers were swept forever from his thoughts.

"No wonder you stopped coming." Lady Belmeth laid an understanding hand on Ariel's arm. "Perhaps we can skip the souk. The truth is, I'm famished. Is it possible to picnic now rather than later?"

"Perhaps you're right," Ariel agreed quietly. "It'll be easier to find a shady spot now." She turned back to the carriage, too wrapped in her own thoughts to notice the thoughtful look on Christopher's face.

Christopher handed his aunt into the carriage behind Ariel and called up an order to the driver before joining the two ladies. The ride into the foothills offered none of the amusements he'd enjoyed on his way to the souk. Before, although Ariel had been furious,

138

he'd thoroughly enjoyed her feisty defiance. Even beneath her drape her spirit shone through, drawing him like a welcoming flame in the window. Now, however, the thought of such senseless cruelty had snuffed out that light. He wanted nothing so much at that moment as to gather her into his arms and brush away the cloak of shame that burdened her spirit.

Christopher scowled. She wouldn't even stand for him touching her, much less offering her comfort. Ridiculous little hoyden. When was she going to see that it was Morocco and its people who were hurting her, not him!

The driver called the team of matched gray Arabians to a halt beside the ochre walls of the old fortress. Christopher descended from the coach first, perusing his choice with a critical eye before Ariel stepped out behind him. Situated on the highest of the foothills overlooking the city, it provided a panoramic view in all directions. Below them, Meknes was a maze of whitewashed walls and tiled roofs as intricate as any Moslem artwork. In the shade of the wall, a grove of scruffy eucalyptus trees protected a scraggly patch of grass from the heat and wind. It would provide a comfortable spot for their picnic.

As Ariel climbed down the carriage steps, a light breeze cooled her skin, tickling the few loose strands of hair at her neck. She walked to the far side of the hill and looked down over the city. The souk was once more a bustle of activity, easing her conscience somewhat. Pulling the pin from her hair, she removed the straw hat and veil. She closed her eyes and let the breeze sweep away the nauseous humiliation that filled her each time she saw how closely she was associated with Daiwa's hateful vindication. Lady Belmeth had been right to suggest they leave, and Ariel recognized the gesture for what it was, a true offering of friendship.

Christopher's deep voice behind her pulled her from her reverie.

"Everything has been set out. Anne is overwhelmed by the view; she'll enjoy having you to point out the various sights to her."

Ariel turned to Christopher, toying with the rim of the bonnet before she looked shyly up at him. "She's very nice, Christopher."

"She'd be happy to hear you say so."

Ariel looked at the town below them. It was strange, speaking so civilly to each other again. As if the events of the past day had never occurred and they were back to the easy comradery of their ride. But the contract did exist, as did Christopher's betrayal. Not knowing what to say, she walked to the picnic blanket, leaving Christopher alone on the bluff.

"You'll have to tell me what all of this is." Lady Belmeth nodded at the array of silver bowls forming a circle in the center of the colorful blanket that had been laid out for them. Ariel settled herself on a plump cushion, holding her hands over the proffered basin as a turbaned slave poured rose-scented water over them. Another waited beside her with an embroidered towel. Indicating that Lady Belmeth should follow suit, Ariel accepted a plate laden with their picnic feast.

"This is an olive and mint salad, and this salad is made with oranges and carrots. Use your bread to scoop a bit of the salad up, like this," she explained, demonstrating with her slice of the knobby pita.

140

"There's also *kibbi,* and stuffed chicken. And for dessert, a special treat—*kab ghazal.*"

"And I thought last night was a feast!" Anne exclaimed. "What is the dessert? *Kab*—"

"*Kab ghazal.* Gazelle hooves."

Anne blanched at Christopher's comment as he came over to the blanket.

Ariel shot him an unappreciative glare. "The name stems from their delicate shape, like a little gazelle's foot. The filling is almond paste, nothing more."

Anne smiled quickly. "Then, I can't wait to try one."

Ariel happily entertained Lady Belmeth for the next hour with stories of the Casbah in its glory. Her vivid images of Ismail the Great's troops guarding the city from attacks and the twenty thousand slaves and artisans who worked on the construction of El Bedi kept Anne spellbound, and the afternoon flew by.

As they ate, Ariel watched Christopher out of the corner of one eye. Early in her narrative he'd excused himself, taking his plate to a lone olive tree where the horses stood. Now he was engrossed in conversation with Siad. It was evident in the deference Siad displayed that her eunuch's admiration for him was growing by the moment. Siad was always obedient and kind to her, but this was a rare display of respect for someone he barely knew. He had not always been a eunuch as most of the women's guards. Instead he had been shorn of his manhood as an adult, an operation that often killed the men it was performed on. Rather than making him compliant, he had become difficult, and his back bore the scars of innumerable whippings. The first time Ariel had seen him he was sick and weakened from a beating, yet she saw a gleam of pride in his eyes that tore at her heart. She'd

141

gone directly to the sultan to ask for him, and since that day he was always at her side. Distracted by her memories, Ariel was caught by Christopher's inquisitive look when he turned to glance at the picnickers. She turned quickly away, embarrassed for having been caught staring.

"I think I'll take a little walk," Anne announced as Christopher headed toward them. She stood to dust off her skirt and then, with a nod to her nephew, blithely deserted Ariel.

Not wishing to answer Christopher's inevitable questions, Ariel feigned a sudden attack of hunger. She nimbly plucked a *Kab ghazel* from the platter and took an enormous bite of the thickly frosted delicacy that a moment ago she'd been too full to even contemplate. Glistening almond paste oozed from the pastry, and before she could prevent it one large dollop landed with a plop on her skirt.

"Allow me." Christopher dropped to one knee beside her, and with an expert touch wiped away the sweet confection, leaving behind only a small stain. "There, I'm sure that can be cleaned later."

Ariel, her mouth still stuffed with the pastry, gave him a deprecating look and continued to crunch the *Kab ghazel*. As the seconds strung out like an endless strand of pearls, her face began to burn in mortification. Yet Christopher made no attempt to allay her embarrassing predicament by filling the void with idle small talk; instead he merely watched her, one arm propped on his knee while she did her utmost to finish her mouthful without resorting to unladylike chomping.

"I'll have to see to it that the moulay feeds you better," Christopher speculated with amused gravity. "We

142

can't have you stuffing yourself with sweets; you'll become ill. Or thick-girthed."

"I have no intentions of overeating," Ariel announced, her pride stung to the quick.

"I'm pleased to hear it. It would be a crime to lose such a shapely figure to an over affection for sweets." His gaze roved meaningfully along her curves with an audacity that set a billow of angry smoke rising in her as Ariel swallowed the last of her pastry.

"What gives you the right to comment on my person?" The words were out of her mouth before she could call them back.

"We're betrothed; you haven't forgotten, have you?" Christopher asked in the lightest of mocking tones.

"No, I haven't forgotten! And might I remind you that the matter is not settled. In fact, I think Lord and Lady Belmeth deserve to know that our marriage is not at all a fait accompli."

He paused, giving her a measured look. "I think we need to talk, Ariel. You should know why I agreed to this marriage."

Ariel's eyes darkened to a piqued, angry café noir. "What I need is to stay in Morocco, not to be part and parcel of some politician's maneuvering."

Christopher tucked his knuckle under her chin and tilted her face up. Ariel jerked away reflexively.

"Hold still," he commanded. Dabbing an errant drop of almond paste from the corner of her mouth, he gave her a nonchalant smile. "Things are not always what they seem, Ariel. Not Morocco. And not me. Remember that." He lifted the dot of filling to his lips, his eyes never leaving hers as he licked the sweet from his finger.

Ariel's face went hot, and she looked away, making

much of brushing flaky crumbs from her dress. Christopher caught her chin between his finger and thumb, and applied a subtle pressure until she had no choice but to look at him. His index finger was still damp where he'd licked it a moment ago, and the wet intimacy of it, combined with his words, made Ariel's stomach melt into a hot, molten pool despite the rebellion that raged in her mind. She forced herself to remain rigidly still.

"You trusted me at the sultan's ball, and you trusted me at the trysting pool. But now you won't trust me enough to look me in the eye."

Ariel glared directly into his face, refusing to give any quarter. "You betrayed that trust. It suited your needs to string me along with your promises. I'm sure it was quite entertaining for you to play your little charade at my expense. I image you and Lord Belmeth had quite an evening recounting my stupidity and lack of worldliness at being duped by you both."

Christopher's face hardened, his brows coming together in a dark, angry slash over his eyes. "No one did anything of the sort. And I'd like to know just who fed you that lie."

"I doubt it's a lie, my lord. I'd wager it's more a case of your being discomforted by the image in the mirror now that I've stripped your mask away," Ariel retorted, squaring her shoulders defiantly.

"Just be careful who it is you choose to trust," Christopher growled.

Ariel flushed. "You're quite sure of yourself, Lord Staunton. How is it that you know who I trust?"

Christopher leaned over her, his head bent too close to hers for Ariel's comfort. She was painfully aware of his broad chest, the crisp linen of his shirt beneath his exquisite moss green jacket. He was waiting for her to look at him, and with an ageless, nameless certainty Ariel knew that if she did so, all her attempts to remain unaffected by him would be for naught.

"I make a point of knowing what I want, Ariel. And I let nothing prevent me from having it," he said gravely.

"You want the treaty; you don't want me," she said, rising from the blanket.

"Is that what you really think, or does that somehow save you from a guilty conscience?" he asked, joining her. "Do you know what you want, Ariel? Would you honestly be happy in Morocco forever? Would you be satisfied by an Islamic husband with other wives? Would you be happy locked behind the door of his house, unable to step outside without wearing a haik?"

Christopher's scrutiny was unrelenting. Ariel's breath shortened, and her heart began to beat uncontrollably in her breast. She felt like a wounded bird trying vainly to fly. Ever since Christopher Staunton had stepped into her life, things had become so complicated. Questions that a week ago wouldn't have required a second thought suddenly seemed mired by doubts. He couldn't know about Yazid, she thought, frightened by the very idea. And she prayed he didn't know how wildly her heart was beating just now.

"I don't know," Ariel whispered. She wanted to go, to be anywhere but under the insistent gaze of those all-seeing blue eyes, but Christopher's hand restrained her. His grip was gentle in its insistence, and she turned back, looking up at him in confused despair.

Seeing the self-doubt that marred her proud fea-

145

tures, Christopher realized he had been thinking too much of himself. "I'm sorry," he said quietly. His single-minded pursuit of an answer to the puzzle of Yazid had gained him nothing and robbed Ariel of much. For now Christopher put the vision of Ariel in the prince's arms firmly out of his mind. He leaned across the picnic blanket, intending to wipe away the tear that threatened to roll down her cheek, but Ariel turned away, dashing the tear impatiently with the back of her hand.

"I've laid my cards on the table. I have no more secrets, Ariel. I had no intentions of marrying the sultan's ward to facilitate a treaty between our countries. I have as little taste for being used as you do. But after meeting you, I wanted to protect you. Things are changing here. Whether or not you believe it, you aren't safe here anymore."

Ariel kept her head turned, looking out over the barren, crusted ground to where Anne idly enjoyed the view. "Tell me what this great danger is."

A picture of Yazid and Ariel in her room filtered back into Christopher's mind. No matter how much he wanted to tell her, to once and for all make her understand that he had not intended to betray her, he couldn't risk the safety of all those involved by divulging his information to her when she might take it directly to Yazid. For although he had no proof at all, he didn't trust the prince. When Yazid had proven himself trustworthy, or when Christopher knew that Ariel was not involved with him, then he could tell her, but not now.

"I can't," he said.

Chapter Twelve

Ariel swallowed her tears and turned to glare at Christopher, frustration replacing the wounded uncertainty of moments ago. "You mean you *won't* tell me," she corrected icily. "You expect me to simply accept whatever fancies you concoct without the smallest shred of evidence. You expect far too much, my lord!"

"To the contrary, Ariel. I've come to expect nothing of you but bared teeth and drawn claws." With that, Christopher leapt up and strode toward the horses.

Ariel sat in the last wisp of shade, her jaw clenched against the tight knot in her throat. His words had hurt her deeply. Was she mean-spirited as he implied? Her own instincts wouldn't accept his appraisal. If she didn't defend herself, who would? Christopher had given her no choice in the matter. She watched him mount the stallion that had been tied to the back of the carriage and signal brusquely to the servants to gather up the picnic. Ariel stood and headed toward Lady Anne. She held her head high despite her still-trembling chin, and by the time she was at Anne Belmeth's side, she felt able to speak without her voice catching in her throat.

"It's a beautiful country, Ariel," Anne said, delicately

skirting any mention of Christopher. "I'm sure it will be difficult for you to leave."

Ariel's gaze followed Anne's across the panorama. "It will be very, very difficult."

The ride back to El Bedi was accomplished in near silence. Christopher rode just ahead of the carriage, and Lady Anne soon abandoned her attempts to draw Ariel into conversation. For Ariel, although she didn't mean to be withdrawn, was lost deep in her own thoughts.

When the driver finally pulled the team to a halt before the entrance to the palace, Ariel heaved a sigh of relief. Her head ached and she was miserable, hot, and dusty. She wanted nothing so much as a bath to wash away all thoughts of this disastrous day and let the evening start fresh with the celebration of the *fantasia*.

But it was not to be.

Ariel didn't have the energy or the will to fight when Christopher helped her down from the carriage. She let him hand her down, then turned to say goodbye to Lady Anne.

"Thank you so much for a very enjoyable day," Anne told her the minute she was on solid ground.

"I'm afraid nothing went quite as planned."

"Nonsense, my dear. It was a perfectly wonderful sojourn. I'll keep my friends agog for hours on end when I return to London with the stories you told me. And, after all, what more can one wish for?" she said with a twinkle in her eye.

"You're kind to say so," Ariel replied. "At least you have the *fantasia* to look forward to."

"Will I see you there?"

Ariel hesitated. She hadn't considered sitting with the Belmeths. Carmela expected her to watch with her, and the thought of having Christopher sitting beside

148

her while she cheered on Yazid and Suleiman did not appeal to her in the least. "I'm afraid I was planning to sit in the section draped off for the harem. But you'll have Christopher and Lord Belmeth with you."

"Christopher has other plans this evening, but Robert and I will be quite well taken care of, I'm sure. The sultan has seen to our every whim, and I've no doubt he will in this case also. Please don't worry about me, my dear," Anne continued with an understanding smile. "You should be with your friends this evening."

"I'll come by during the tournament," Ariel promised. "Then I can explain the history of the *fantasia* to you."

"Perfect," Anne agreed.

Ariel turned to Christopher. "Thank you for escorting us, Your Grace," she said, doing her utmost to show him that she was capable of being pleasant. "I hope whatever business keeps you from the *fantasia* is profitable for you."

"Thank you," he replied, the slightest hint of a smile touching his mouth. "Perhaps you will see me tonight. I'm not certain yet where my business will lead. May I walk you to your room?"

"No, thank you. Siad is here."

"Of course," Christopher replied dryly.

Ariel was just turning to leave when a fourth voice joined the group.

"Ah, such a tranquil scene. Charming. Isn't that how you English would say it?" Astride Sirocco, who pawed impatiently at the crushed-marble drive, Yazid threw back his head and laughed—a cold, caustic sound that sent a chill up Ariel's spine. Lady Anne dropped into a curtsy as Yazid swung his leg over Sirocco's head and slid to the ground, using the back of a slave who had dropped to all fours as a stepping stool. Dressed in a tailored gold jacket that fell to his knees and a pair of billowy black pants that matched his jewel-studded turban, he handed his whip to a second slave and sauntered toward them. Behind Anne, Ariel could see Christopher acknowledge the prince with a barely discernible nod, his face devoid of emotion. The air crackled with the charge of animosity between the two men.

"For a moment," Yazid said, strolling in a leisurely circle around Ariel, "I thought I was seeing an apparition step out of my father's carriage. It was as if our dear Caroline had come back from the dead."

Ariel felt him stop behind her, his breath warm against her neck.

"But it was you, of course, sweet Ariel. The very image of your mother. The resemblance is quite astonishing."

Ariel stood very still. "Thank you, Yazid."

"Caroline had a hypnotic beauty. The power to render a man senseless with desire. Do you have such powers, sweet Ariel?" It was no more than a whisper in her ear, but his words startled her and set an icy dread spreading deep in the pit of her stomach.

"I don't know what you mean, Yazid," Ariel replied, keeping her tone lighthearted. "But right now I doubt I could render anyone senseless except by virtue of my extraordinarily dirty state. I was just saying goodbye so Lady Anne can retire to rest before the *fantasia*."

"Then, I shall walk you to your room."

He turned and strode into the palace without acknowledging either Anne or Christopher. Ariel cut off her intended reply, left with no choice but to scurry after him. She still hadn't caught up with him by the time he passed the great hall.

"Yazid," she called out. "Please slow down. I can't walk very quickly in these heavy skirts."

Alone in the hall of the sultan's private wing, Yazid turned on her so abruptly that Ariel plowed right into him. Before she knew what was happening his hand shot out, and he pulled her into the inky darkness of an alcove with a brutality that snapped her head back like a whip. He yanked the straw hat off her head, tearing her hair from its roots. His fingers dug painfully into her arm as he hauled her against him, shaking the crushed hat in her face.

"Never! Never let me see you wearing such a costume! You insult the very soil you walk upon. I thought you did not want this marriage with the infidel swine. Perhaps, I was wrong. Perhaps, sweet Ariel, you grow fond of the Christian snake."

"No! I swear it, Yazid." Ariel's voice sounded sharp and hysterical in her own ears, and drawing a ragged breath, she forced it to a calmer note. "I promised to take Lady Anne to the souk, that's all. I didn't know Christoph — Lord Staunton, was going to join us. But once I saw he was determined to come, I thought I could be useful to you by keeping him away from the palace for the day. I thought you would have more time to speak with your father and bring this vile charade to an end."

Yazid glared at her, his pale green eyes narrowed with suspicion. "So you sought to help me. How wise of you, Ariel. How thoughtful. But I don't need your assistance, or have you forgotten that it was you who came to *me* looking for help?"

"Of course not." Ariel knit her brows in piqued frustration. "You're my only hope, Yazid. Everyone else thinks it will be a wonderful match. My future lies in your hands. I know you won't fail me."

The prince's eyes filled with a satisfied gleam. "That is so. Your future, indeed, lies in my hands."

Ariel had to resist an urge to pull away from him as he ran his thumb across her cheek, stroking it as he would a cat's. "Yazid," she said in a weary voice. "I'm very, very grateful for your help. But I'm tired. You're right, these clothes do not suit me. I want to change and be ready for the *fantasia.* Please."

He stiffened visibly, his expression regaining its cynical veneer. "A woman does as a man wishes, not as she wishes."

"Do you ride tonight?" Ariel asked quickly, knowing that the only way to allay their differences was to sidestep them.

"I shall lead the charge."

"Then, you will wish me to be there as witness to your glory."

Yazid glared at her before he thrust her from him as he would a leper. "Go!"

As she headed toward her rooms, Ariel felt no satisfaction at her escape from Yazid. His moods were so changeable. One moment he was sharp and haughty; the next he seemed to want to coddle and stroke her like a favored pet. Ariel shook her head. She was growing more and more wary of Yazid. If there was anyone else who would help her, she would gladly have released the prince from his vow of assistance. But he was the only person beside herself who was opposed to a union between Christopher and herself. And she needed his help. Reaching her room, Ariel gratefully turned herself over to Chedyla.

One look at her charge's drawn face and Lady Anne's ruined hat and the old duenna sent servants scurrying in every direction. Soon Ariel was chin deep in scented water. Leaning her head on a linen towel she gazed up at the thousands of tiny mirrors imbedded in the domed ceiling of the bathing room. The flickering candles set about the floor filled the dome with tiny lights like the starry heavens that carpeted the Moroccan nights.

She hoped it would be such a night tonight — a perfect night for the pageantry and excitement of the *fantasia*. She regretted that Christopher wouldn't be there. His taunt about the many wives Moroccan's took had struck home. Marrying a man with a bevy of wives and concubines was not her concept of the life she wanted. She still clung to her mother's description of love, hoping that someday she would find a man who wanted only her. One who loved her to the exclusion of other women and who would share his life and love with her. Surely there was such a man waiting somewhere on the vast plains of her adopted homeland.

If Christopher could only see the *fantasia*, it would explain so much to him, she thought as she towelled herself dry. He would see why her heart was so irrevocably bound to this land. He could witness the pride and honor of Berber and Arab alike, their love of the land. How could England, or any land, equal the breathtaking majesty of the Maghreb when the sky was painted amethyst and claret by the dying sun and the red earth thundered with a thousand hooves? That was the *fantasia*, the life's breath of the Moroccan soul. Slipping into a sheer caftan, Ariel passed into her bedroom and turned herself over to Chedyla and Rhima's care. It would be a wondrous night tonight. A truly Arabian night.

Ariel made her way toward the far end of the harem tent. It was a task not as easily accomplished as she had anticipated. Everywhere she looked women attired in brightly hued harem dresses and richly embroidered

153

vests much like her own chatted excitedly in the generously sized tent. Individuals crisscrossed the layered Persian rugs that covered the bare ground as they passed from one set of friends to another, and everywhere, eyes watched. Jealous eyes, wary eyes, calculating eyes—eyes that played the game of guessing who the sultan would call for next, who might become a favorite and jeopardize the chances of all.

Carmela, whose dark-brown eyes were encircled with the same black kohl that decorated Ariel's, squeezed between two blackamoor slave girls and waved, trying to draw her attention, but Ariel didn't see her and headed in the other direction. With a curse, Carmela shoved through the center of one circle and reached for her friend's hand.

Her long, cool fingers made Ariel jump involuntarily as they wrapped around her wrist. The Andalusian shook her head. "You are as restless as a wounded impala who smells the lion."

"Anyone would jump if they were grabbed in this crowd. Where is Raisuli?"

Carmela tossed her head in the direction Ariel was headed. "You would have walked right into him."

Ariel sighed. "I can do without that tonight."

Carmela let out one of her deep, throaty laughs and clasped Ariel's shoulders. "Intrigue is the pepper of life. Without it our existence would be so bland! The Gypsies have hatreds and vendettas such as you've never imagined. Bloodthirsty quests for vengeance that go on for generations. Sometimes a clan can't even remember what they're fighting over. Honor!" She shrugged and waved her hand. "But who cares! So long as the desire to fight, to be a victor, boils in the Gypsy's blood, that is all that matters. If that ever died—then my race would die. Forget Raisuli. He can do nothing to you here.

Let's find a seat for the *fantasia*. I want to be able to see every man who rides tonight. I see a man so rarely these days," she added with a mutter.

"Carmela," Ariel retorted impatiently. "Life is more than handsome men with thick arms and well-muscled chests. I think the sultan—" Ariel looked at Carmela. "What?"

Carmela said nothing. She only nodded, never taking her eyes from their target just beyond Ariel's left shoulder.

Ariel swung around. "Raisuli!"

"Lady Ariel," he said with a bow. His face was obedient, yet hard. His long, drooping mustache barely moved as he spoke, the oiled expanse of his chest seemed like a wall of iron before Ariel, and his thick, oversized hand, resting on the hilt of his scimitar, was like an ominous warning that for a moment obliterated all sensible thought from her mind.

"There is a messenger waiting for you outside the tent. He says he must speak with you."

It was a minute before Ariel was able to reply. "Is it Siad?"

"No," he replied, curling his thick lips in disgust. "This man carries a seal."

Confused, but impelled by Raisuli's last comment to see the man, Ariel glanced at Carmela, whose barely perceptible nod told her she understood. Ariel followed Raisuli to the tent's entrance. A messenger carrying a seal could only be from the sultan or one of the princes. Lifting her veil in place, she stepped outside the tent. The flap dropped behind her, and for a moment she thought she was alone in the empty space that separated the harem's tent from the sultan's. Then a movement in the shadows caught her attention.

A man dressed in a black djellaba and turban

155

stepped from between two tents. *"Ya hagga."* He bowed, calling her by the Arab word for lady. "Come." With a flourish of his hand he indicated that she precede him down the narrow passageway between the tents. Ariel didn't move, and he again indicated the passageway. "Come," he repeated, this time with a note of impatience.

"Whose seal do you carry?"

The man pulled a long black cord from inside his djellaba. At its end was the small cloth bag of amulets that all Moroccan's wore; even Ariel never removed her own precious amulets from around her neck. Threaded through the cord next to the amulets was Yazid's seal, the sign that this was one of Yazid's servants, although Ariel was certain she'd never seen him before. His face was almost flat from forehead to chin, and his skin bore a yellowish cast, devoid of either the warm olive of the Arab clans or the fair tones of the Berbers. His eyes were small, mere slits with no discernible lid, and his patchy beard hadn't been clipped in far too long.

"Now, come," he repeated as he hid the amulets and seal inside his clothing. Reluctantly Ariel started down the narrow corridor. The messenger followed behind her, but when she reached a cross-path at the end of the tents, his hand shot out to stop her.

"Wha—"

He held a finger to his lips and stepped in front of her. When he had checked the cross-path in both directions, he stepped aside and signalled for her to proceed. At the end of the second set of tents, Ariel stepped into another cross-path. Yazid was waiting there, impatiently snapping his whip against his boots.

"You are nothing better than a snail!" he snapped at the black-garbed messenger.

"Your forgiveness, great son of our sultan and descendant of the Holy One. The woman would not come unless she saw your great seal."

"Go to stand guard. Let no one approach." The messenger bowed and backed away with his hands pressed against his nose in supplication.

Yazid turned to Ariel. His gaze swept the length of her white silk pants and richly embroidered knee-length tunic. A smile curled the corner of his mouth. "Ah, Ariel. You are a sweet morsel of delight. My mouth waters at the very sight of you. It pleases me that you have taken such care tonight. It shows you honor me. I shall lead the first charge with your name upon my lips."

"Thank you, Yazid. I am honored."

His smile widened. "That is good."

"Why did you wish to see me?"

Yazid closed the gap between them, taking her hand in his as he pulled her against him. "Tonight I put an end to your marriage, sweet Ariel. It is not done yet, but it shall be. Before the morning dove sings, you shall be freed from your betrothal. I wanted you to have this knowledge, so that you might savor it and your enjoyment of the *fantasia* be heightened just as the opium pipe heightens one's enjoyment of Allah's world."

Ariel tensed against Yazid's chest. His hand roved up and down her spine, caressing her waist in a most inappropriate manner, but recalling his anger only hours before, she dared not protest.

"What will you do, Yazid?"

"That is of no concern to you. All that you must know is that as I have sworn to you, you shall be released from the infidel marriage."

"Moulay." His eyes down-cast behind Yazid, the messenger's whisper was filled with urgency. "I beg your forgiveness, but the sun sets. You must come."

"Go!" Yazid ordered, his fingers digging into Ariel's flesh in anger "The *fantasia* will wait for me." He turned back to Ariel, his eyes intense as he looked down at her and pulled her veil aside. "I must go. But I would leave to lead the charge I dedicate to you with the bond of your kiss between us."

Ariel pursed her lips and leaned up on tiptoe, intending to plant a sisterly kiss on his cheek. Instead Yazid turned his face and pressed his mouth against hers. His kiss was hard and demanding He forced her lips apart and plunged his thick tongue into her mouth as his hands fell to her buttocks. Lifting her off the ground, he pulled her hips against his with a guttural groan.

Ariel pushed with all her might against his chest, gagging on his tongue as it drove into her mouth, trying desperately to separate herself from the appalling intimacy of his body as it pressed through his clothing. His arms held her like iron manacles, and then, as abruptly as he had forced this intimacy on her, he released her. She dropped onto her feet and nearly fell, for her knees would not hold her up.

Yazid's face was flushed, and his eyes lit with a maniacal gleam. "This night you shall see the power of Mohammed El Yazid. This night, sweet Ariel, I shall free you."

Without another word, he left, his scarlet cloak billowing in his wake. A moment later, Ariel heard Sirocco's trumpeting whinny and the thunder of the young stallion's hooves as Yazid galloped to the front line of the *fantasia*. From minarets throughout Meknes, Imams called the faithful to prayer until the air rung with the sound of voices. Ariel's entire body shook as she stood alone in the dust. Yazid's words filled her with dread when they should have brought her joy. Turning to the west, she knelt in the dust, bowing her forehead to the dirt. "Allah," she prayed, "help me. Yazid is my ally, yet he frightens me. Christopher is my enemy, but I am drawn to him. Help me, please."

Ariel sat back on her heels, hot tears threatening at the corners of her eyes. Determinedly she pushed her fears away. It was the *fantasia* that had made Yazid treat her so horribly. Yazid was a warrior at heart, and the excitement of the *fantasia* was coursing through his blood tonight. He'd been caught up in the anticipation. That was what had prompted the intimacy of his kiss. She would put it out of her mind, forget that it had passed between them. Instead of being afraid, she should be grateful. After tonight, she would no longer have to worry about how to free herself from her betrothal. This was what she had prayed for. But if that was true, Ariel asked herself as she knelt alone in the dusty corridor, why was she chilled to the very depths of her soul?

Chapter Thirteen

By the time Ariel stepped back into the harem tent, the front had been drawn away in preparation for the *fantasia*. Carmela caught her attention, signalling that she had saved a spot for her, and Ariel gratefully threaded her way through the women to her friend's side.

"Where did you go?" Carmela whispered as they watched the parade of warriors pass the tent.

"Yazid wished to speak to me."

"Yazid? What would he speak to you about?"

Ariel was listening to Carmela with only half an ear as she anxiously perused the face of each warrior for Yazid. She had to know what he planned. Walking back from their clandestine meeting, she'd asked herself how Yazid would speak to the sultan tonight. The *fantasia*, and the following celebration, would last into the early morning hours, and she just couldn't imagine Yazid making his case amid the milling festivities that would surround his father. The more she thought about his pronouncement, the stranger it seemed to her. She was thankful that Christopher wasn't planning to attend. He and Yazid were at loggerheads already, and she had no doubt that actually contesting the issue of her marriage with the sultan in front of him would result in an outright battle.

Ariel chewed at her lip, ignoring the pomp and pageantry in favor of trying to decipher Yazid's intentions, but the more she contemplated an answer, the more she doubted that it was possible. Still, Yazid was the prince and heir. If any one could do it tonight, he could. At last Ariel pushed her concerns aside and focused her attention on the sights and sounds of the *fantasia.* Flags of the two hundred tribes gathered for the *fantasia* snapped in the evening breeze — turquoise and sapphire for a coastal tribe, emerald with silver stars for one from the lower Atlas, saffron cut by a black slash for a third. The freshly lit torches had yet to cast a shadow, for the sun still cast its hot light across the plains even as it dipped below the horizon. When the parade ended, each warrior went to his tribe's camp to check his weapons and water his horse. Over one hundred meters away lay the starting line.

Already, mounted riders were gathering along it for as far as the eye could see. They were the finest fighters in the land, and they had brought their tribes' most outstanding examples of horseflesh with them. Ornamented in their finest, the Arabian horses pranced and snorted as they collided with one another, everyone vying for a place in the formation. From every breastplate hung long, colored tassels that matched those adorning the bridles' brow bands. Bells jingled from ornate, high-pommeled saddles, and braided ribbons had been wound through their luxurious manes and tails, glorifying the steeds that were treated by Arab and Berber alike as beloved family members.

161

Full darkness would not fall until the second or third charge, and while the light was still fair, the women buzzed with delight at being able to look upon so many unknown men. The single glimpse they stole of some handsome caid would feed their hunger for the outside world on many a long, lonely night. As Ariel listened to their excited whispers, her thoughts drifted back to the picnic that afternoon, and from there to Christopher. He had been friendly and entertaining until she'd provoked him beyond the duration of any man. Grudgingly she admitted that he had made every attempt to be cordial and mend the rent in their relationship. He'd attempted to apologize for his lies, and almost apologized for offering to marry her.

Ariel smiled, but it was a wan attempt, tinged with an inexplicable sadness. Who would believe she wanted him to apologize for such a thing? Knowing that by dawn their betrothal would be broken, she suddenly wished she could see him once more.

"Mierda!"

Carmela's expletive jolted Ariel out of her melancholy reverie. "What is it?"

"You're back?" Carmela gave her a mocking look.

Ariel began to protest before Carmela stopped her. "From *tierra del sueño,* that dreamland you went to. You haven't heard a word I've said for ten minutes."

"I wasn't dreaming. I was watching the riders."

Carmela snorted derisively. "Then, you will know what I'm talking about."

Ariel grit her teeth in frustration at being caught in her half-lie. "Well, I don't know what you're talking about. There are over a thousand men out there; you could be looking at any one of them."

"Perhaps I was not looking at a man at all," Carmela suggested.

Ariel rolled her eyes. "You wouldn't try to tell me it's a *horse* you're having palpitations over?"

"All right. It is a man. What a man! Every woman in the harem is breathing heavier since he appeared."

"Where?"

"There." Carmela pointed to a knot of horses that was at least two tent lengths from them. In the growing dusk and the churning sand that was thickening the air by the minute, it was difficult to see anything.

"Carmela, I don't see—"

"There," her short-tempered companion cut in, pointing harder. "He rides a black horse that is hands taller than any other, and he is dressed in black. How can you not see him?" she demanded shrilly. "He is like a black panther, with eyes as blue as the Mediterranean."

Ariel's entire body tensed. She squinted, peering through the dust, knowing before she saw him who he was. The rider broke from the knot of men. He spun the sleek stallion around, and the animal reared onto its hind legs. The horse was as black as night, a color as rare to its breed as was its size. Its hooves flashed in the torch light, and the stallion let out a shrill whinny, its white teeth and flaring red nostrils in sharp contrast to the otherwise unbroken blackness of its noble Arabian face.

A gasp went up in unison from the harem as the warrior rode straight toward their tent. His djellaba was tucked into soft black boots, and the black cotton binding of his turban was broken only by a single twisted rope of silver. Silver tassels decorated his saddle, but the stallion sported no bells or charms. The

163

warrior was stunning. His outfit was stark in contrast to the frills of the others, yet the pair was anything but plain. They emanated power and restraint. And magnetism. In a moment he was at the harem tent. The women were partially protected from view by a low screen, but because they needed to see over the upper edge to view the riders, a bold warrior could look in if he rode close enough. As he faced them, concubines and odalisques alike ducked behind shawls and veils. It was one thing to watch the warriors from the protection of the screened tent, but quite another to have a warrior poised directly before them, as if he was looking in!

"He's a bold one!" Carmela laughed, tossing her black hair seductively over her shoulder. She sat straight up on her pillow, thrusting her full breasts forward. "He looks here."

Ariel also sat upright on her cushion. She had frozen there the moment he'd broken from the group, her heart caught in her throat. He was magnificent. No man among the thousand could compare to him. And she had known from the moment she'd fastened her eyes on him through the dust and the quickly fading light who he was. She hadn't needed to see his face. She knew by the way he sat in his saddle, by the square, broad expanse of his shoulders beneath the flowing black cape, that it was Christopher.

As he wheeled the stallion before the tent, their eyes locked. It was only an instant, but Ariel felt his eyes on her as though he had touched her. He masked all expression on his face, but his eyes seemed to be assessing her somehow. It was as though he asked for assurance of some kind from her, but before Ariel could begin to fathom what it was, he wheeled the huge stallion and galloped for the starting line. The second he was gone, the tent erupted in an explosion of talk. His boldness sent shivers of excitement through the women. But stronger than their excitement was the speculation that began to blaze like a brush fire through the harem. Who had he come to see?

None doubted that one of them had taken this man as a lover. But the boldness of his appearance, the incalculable danger he had put himself and the concubine who was his lover into by his blatant interest in the sultan's harem, was like a drug on all of them. Each turned to scrutinize her companion, driven by jealousy, and anger, and a twisted loyalty to their common prison. They would stop at nothing to uncover the transgressor. There wasn't one among them who didn't wish she were the black warrior's lover, but they would find the woman who had betrayed her sultan, and see her punished. Like a pack of jackals, they scavenged the harem tent, intent on devouring one of their own without a moment's remorse.

"He looked here!" Carmela repeated, her eyes ablaze with lust.

"I know," Ariel replied. Her voice was low and quiet.

"I have never seen such a man! Paulo would be a mouse, an *ant,* beside him. Look, quickly. We must find out which tribe's flag he rides under."

The warriors had formed a line that reached as far as the eye could see in either direction. The diplomats and politicians in the tents and the tribes people who sat in the open air hushed expectantly. Ariel could hear the rustle of canvas in the evening breeze. The horses snorted, pawing the ground, impatient for the charge. Even the harem had quieted, all eyes on the line of men. Then the crack of a gun splintered the silence. The charge was on!

The line of horses shot forward, each rider leaning close against his steed's neck, pressing his horse faster as they raced directly at the crowd. All was silent except for the thunder of four thousand hooves pounding the barren Moroccan soil. The flags snapped; the air quivered with the sound of cloaks flapping in the wake of pumping muscle and the power that rushed toward the tents. Each man carried his gun or scimitar horizontally before his chest. Closer they rode. And closer. All around Ariel women clutched one another, sharing the thrill and fear of the stampeding charge that was nearly upon them. Then at the final second, when nearly half the harem had begun to scream in fear as the horses seemed ready to trample the protective screen and charge over them, the warriors came to a halt that set every horse on its hind legs, hooves striking at the air.

With a mighty cry they shouted in unison, and the night exploded with gunfire. "Allah Akbar! Allah Akbar!" The air reverberated with the bellows of the warriors. Scimitars gleamed golden in the firelight, their long, curving blades arcing through the night as men slashed at the air. The horses were so close Ariel could hear their labored breathing, smell the sweat on their heaving sides, feel the heat radiating from their muscles in the chill night air.

In the furious charge Ariel had lost sight of Christopher, and as she scanned the line of warriors she spotted Yazid. He was directly before the sultan's tent. Sirocco reared again and again as Yazid whooped and hollered, his gun held high over his

166

head. Standing high in his stirrups, every muscle was tensed, and his eyes shone with the same maniacal gleam Ariel had seen just before he'd ridden away from their rendezvous. Beside him, Suleiman also hooted and swung his scimitar over his head. Astride his handsome gray stallion, however, Suleiman bore none of Yazid's intensity. It was clear by the easy way he relaxed in his saddle that this was nothing more than a game to him. But for Yazid, she knew that it was much, much more. Yazid gave the signal to regroup, and the leaders of each tribe shouted orders, assembling their men for the second charge.

"The black warrior should have been at the front of the charge," Carmela said, her voice hoarse from her own screaming. "I did not see him, did you?"

Ariel shook her head. She was wondering the same thing as Carmela. What had happened to Christopher?

The tent had once again filled with the buzz of nervous laughter, but the tension had grown even more palatable. Ariel glanced across the sea of women, her nerves on edge as much as anyone's. The high-pitched chatter was giving her a headache. She looked over at the doorway, wondering if she shouldn't take Siad and go to sit with the Belmeths. Besides getting her away from the harem, she was certain they would know what Christopher was doing riding in the *fantasia*. She had just decided to make some excuse to Carmela when she saw Daiwa making her way in their direction. Dread spread through her like an icy mountain wind. She was certain Daiwa was coming over to them.

"There he is!" Carmela moaned like a she-dog in heat. "Look at him. He rides two men from the prince. Even the future sultan cannot challenge the black warrior's stature."

"They are equal in height," Ariel said, suddenly irritated by Carmela's infatuation with Christopher.

"But the black warrior is like the panther while Mohammed El Yazid is the lion. The lion is powerful and awesome, a true king of the desert. But the panther . . . mmmmmm." She licked her lips, and Ariel turned away, disgusted. "The panther is mysterious and full of secrets, cunning, and graceful, and clever."

"You speak as though you know him, Carmela."

The two young women turned in unison, and stared up at the Hatum Kadin.

"No, Sultana," Carmela replied, her face suddenly wary, and closed. "I have never seen him before, but like every other woman here, I am intrigued."

"Yes, we are all intrigued. I would like to know who he is, and which tribe he comes from. I would bestow many gifts on the person who could tell me these things."

"I know nothing of the man, but should I learn anything I will come to you immediately, Daiwa."

"Many of the women saw him look here."

"A whim, I fear. Nothing more."

"Of course." Daiwa smiled thinly, and her eyes glinted with suspicion beneath narrowed lids. She abandoned her questioning of Carmela and turned her attention to Ariel. "He is quite magnificent, don't you agree, Ariel?"

"I do, Daiwa. Handsome, and talented with a sword. Very mysterious. It's an irresistible combination, isn't it?"

Daiwa smiled rancorously. "Indeed. It's so unfortunate that your marriage is already arranged. If my husband had but known of this man, perhaps he would have aligned you with him. Instead you are betrothed to a pale Englishman. Such a shame. But then, you must prefer marrying one of your own kind."

"I am well pleased with the sultan's choice of a mate for me, Daiwa," Ariel lied blithely. Never, even in her most desperate moments, would she admit anything else to the woman who had treated her mother as an enemy. Moreover, it gave Ariel a distinct sense of pleasure knowing that Daiwa so completely miscalculated Christopher. "You must meet him someday soon. Perhaps he will surprise you."

"Very little surprises me, Ariel. For there is very little I do not know." Daiwa turned to go. Over her shoulder, she called back. "I will be waiting to learn more of the black warrior, Carmela. I trust you will come to me soon."

When she was out of earshot, Ariel turned to Carmela in warning. "She believes you know him."

"I told her the truth when I said I do not," Carmela said with a nonchalant shrug. "But I would give much to change that."

"Carmela, you are being a fool. She means to coerce you into finding out about him. Surely you can see that when you bring her your information, she'll accuse you. She'll say that you have betrayed the sultan by lying with him."

"The black warrior would be a man worth dying for."

"How can you say such a thing!"

"I can say this," Carmela retorted. "One night in arms such as those would be worth a thousand nights in the harem. What have I to live for? What, I ask

169

you! The sultan does not care for my attributes. It is clear that he will never call me to his bed again. So I have endless days of nothing stretching out before me, nothing except to stay one step ahead of Daiwa and Raisuli. What life is that? Why shouldn't I sacrifice such a tawdry existence for one more chance at delight?"

Ariel stared at her, unable to speak. It was as if she was seeing her friend's life for the first time. Ariel had assumed from Carmela's spontaneous nature and her carefree attitude that she was at least content. Of course, she had been sold into slavery, and Ariel harbored no illusions about the horror of that event. But she had believed Carmela had adjusted to life as a concubine, that she took what she could get from life and let the rest be. Now, seeing the pain and anger in her black Gypsy eyes, Ariel's heart broke for her. Carmela knew nothing at all about Christopher, and she was so desperately lonely that she was willing to die for one night in his arms.

Ariel pursed her lips into a thin, thoughtful line. She couldn't tell Carmela that Christopher was the black warrior. She would never understand how Ariel could reject a life with the man she would die for. There was no way to explain it to her. She would simply think Ariel a fool. Carmela's vision was so black and white. She couldn't understand the shades of gray Ariel was forced to deal with. It wasn't as simple as desiring a man, because Ariel knew all too well that she *did* desire Christopher. Her body betrayed that fact every time she was with him. But that didn't alter her determination. This was her home. Mohammed Ben Abdullah, Chedyla, Yazid, and Suleiman were her family. They had kept her when she had nowhere else to go. If they did not love her as her mother had, then at least they had earned her loyalty. A loyalty her father had lost forever by deserting them.

Carmela leaned over, taking the lapels of Ariel's embroidered vest in her hands. "I tell you, Ariel," she whispered desperately. "I would gladly die for just one more chance to feel alive. You must thank God that you are going to be free from this land. It is a prison here. A chamber of torture. Take your duke and run, Ariel. Run and never, ever look back."

Ariel tore away from Carmela's grasp, her eyes wide with shock and confusion. "You're wrong!" she whispered. "You're unhappy, Carmela, and for that I grieve. You were brought here against your will, taken from your homeland. But this is my country. I cannot leave it."

"Why?" Carmela demanded. "The sultan barely has time to notice you. Daiwa despises you, and she feeds her hatred to her son—the future sultan. Things will not always remain as they are. You are being offered escape, Ariel. Take it!"

"I don't want to escape," Ariel cried, choking on tears of frustration. "Why can't anyone see that?" She couldn't bear to stay with Carmela even one second more. The harem tent was stifling, and Ariel thought she would suffocate if she didn't get away. She jumped to her feet just as the second charge began.

Fleeing from the tent, she ran into the empty passageway between the tents and then behind the sultan's tent. She didn't think about where she was going until she was at the entrance to the tent set up for the foreign visitors. Lord and Lady Belmeth would be in there, but the last thing Ariel wanted just then was to be near anyone that reminded her of Christopher.

171

Slowing to a walk, she passed the next two tents and found herself at the edge of the open field set off for the townspeople and tribal families who had come to see the spectacle. The image of the souk that morning materialized in her head, and she suddenly yearned to walk among the crowd as one of them. Ariel lifted her veil into place and stepped out from the shelter of the tent.

The air exploded with gunfire as the second charge drove to a halt, and a roar of approval went up from the crowd. Ariel was far to the rear of the area, and as she threaded her way toward the front, her eyes darted from rider to rider, looking for Christopher. She couldn't find him in the melee, nor did she see Yazid or Suleiman, but with so many riders, she thought nothing of it. It was unlikely that the princes would perform so far from the sultan's tent. They had made the first charge directly in front of him, and would certainly continue that way.

All around her people cheered the riders. Children tumbled in the dust, mock warriors performing their own *fantasia*, while women covered from head to foot in simple black haiks comforted squalling babies. As she looked around, Ariel began to feel uncomfortable. The clamor had died down as the riders returned to the starting line for a third charge, and although the air was still charged with excitement, she knew she was drawing attention. Her silk tunic, though long and opaque, was far finer than anything worn by the people gathered here. Her veil was too flimsy and revealing, and she could feel hundreds of eyes on her as more and more people took notice of her. A small circle of space was forming around her, and Ariel suddenly realized as she turned to look over her shoulder that Siad wasn't with her.

Her eyes flashed from face to face. The men leered, their gestures and guttural sounds saying all too clearly that they thought she was a prostitute. The women gathered their babes to their breasts and turned away, shunning her. Behind her, Ariel heard the third charge begin. The ground beneath her feet trembled with the power of the assault. Lifting her chin, she squared her slender shoulders despite the tears that stung at the back of her eyes. She was not what they thought, but neither was she one of them — free to walk among them as an equal. Without looking to either side, Ariel took a step back toward the tents. It was as though she was walking back to an opulent cage. Never before had she felt her confinement so keenly, or understood how narrow was the path upon which she might safely and freely tread.

She concentrated only on getting beyond their line of vision, finding a place to shed her tears in private. Her enlightenment had been too quick, too shocking. She felt the on-coming brigade behind her, heard the trumpeting horses as they slammed to a halt, listened to the blast of the guns, the scimitars singing through the air; but she didn't look back. Only a few more steps, she concentrated on that one thought. It was only when the call was sounded for the second time that it penetrated Ariel's mind. She froze, listening again, not willing to believe that she had heard the words correctly. A second later the shout came again.

"Death to all infidels! Death to the English!" And its echo was repeated by hundreds of voices. "Death to Mohammed Ben Abdullah! Traitor! The Maghreb needs no ally but Allah!"

All around her the world burst into frenzied panic.

173

No one knew where the first shout had come from except that it was the voice of a warrior. A shot rang out that was not part of the *fantasia*. From the opposite end of the line, a war cry pierced the confusion. A scimitar sliced into unsuspecting flesh, and madness broke out amid the festivities. In the passing of a second, fighting broke out everywhere. The crowd around Ariel became a writhing monster, and she was caught in its tidal wave of panic. Women screamed and ran in every direction, calling frantically for their children. Men and boys raced for any weapon they could find. Beside her a Berber tribesman pulled a burning timber from a fire and hurled himself toward the horsemen screaming, "Allah Akbar! Sultan Mohammed Akbar! Our sultan is good."

Ariel didn't know which way to turn first. The invisible line that had separated the *fantasia* warriors from the crowd disappeared as man fought against man, pushing the haunches of their steeds into the hysterical crowd. She knew she had to get away from the open field if she was to save herself from being trampled or split in two by a scimitar. But as she pushed through the tangle of people, her eyes never left the riders. Where was Yazid? Where was Suleiman? Where was Christopher?

From behind her someone plowed into her side. Her knees buckled beneath her, and she slammed face first into the dirt. She threw her arms over her head as a man's foot landed so close to her face that her veil was ripped away. Ariel tried to pull herself up, but the weight lying across her legs prevented her from moving at all. Choking on the dust, she turned on her elbows to find a child clinging to her ankles. His face was buried in the dirt as he choked and sobbed. A woman tripped over the child and cursed hysterically before struggling up and running off. Quickly Ariel pulled the child loose and dragged him into her arms. A horse snorted from somewhere far too close. There was a scream of pain, and Ariel again threw her arms over the two of them, shielding the boy's head with her own body as she waited for the sting of a blade in her back. Instead a tremendous weight fell against her, knocking the air from her lungs as it landed.

Ariel opened her eyes to find a dead man staring into her face. His head hung back at an unnatural angle, and one limp arm was slung over her shoulder. Ariel felt a trickle of warmth run down her arm and realized that the man's blood was coursing from his throat. Using every ounce of strength she possessed, she shoved the corpse away. His head snapped back into place atop the severed neck.

Ariel clenched her jaw against the nausea at the back of her throat. Jumping up, she pulled the child against her and ran. She ran as she had never run in her life, dodging campfires, and people, and animals. Her foot landed on a soft mound, and she looked down to find herself standing on the broken body of a young woman. She clutched the boy tighter and ran again. At last she found the passageway between the tents and slipped into it. At the entrance to the first tent, one of those assigned for the use of the foreign visitors, Ariel ducked inside. There would be servants of the sultan and the Bukhariyin here. They would be safe. But what she found inside the tent made her knees turn to liquid.

Carnage.

Nothing moved within the vast expanse of the tent. Bodies covered the ground everywhere, strewn like

175

discarded rag dolls across bolsters and tables. The carefully laid rugs were dyed scarlet by a hundred rivers of blood. Ariel bolted from the tent, her mind screaming denials. At the next tent she hesitated only for a moment before stepping in. The scene was a repeat of the last tent. But this time Ariel didn't turn and run. Kneeling beside the entrance, she tried to pry the child's arms from around her neck.

"I won't leave you," she crooned softly. "You'll be safe here in the corner. I'll be here." The child's arms only tightened until Ariel could barely breathe. His face was buried against her neck, and except for the warmth of his breath against her skin, she wouldn't have known for certain that he was still alive.

She had to look for the Belmeths. She could have no peace until she knew if they were among the bodies here, but she didn't want the boy to witness the scene. If he would only sit in this corner, most of the slaughter would be beyond his vision. But trying once more to separate herself from him, she saw that there was no use in that plan. With a ragged sigh, Ariel pushed a strand of hair off her face and, cradling the boy with one arm, began to look from corpse to corpse for Lord and Lady Belmeth. The smell of blood was overpowering; the job she performed, debilitating beyond endurance. But Ariel forced herself to look at the face of each body, determined that she would not leave until she knew whether the Belmeths were among the dead. At the front of the tent, one side of the wall that had been opened to view the *fantasia* had fallen completely, and the other hung in shreds that left only a small opening to the field.

Ariel moved among the dead, her hands shaking as she looked into the lifeless faces of body after body.

176

These were the faces of people she had never met, but whom she knew. Only a handful of days ago she had watched them laugh and dance in the ballroom, and now they were just more mutilated bodies among hundreds. She was nearly to the front of the structure when the fighting closed in around the tent. Ariel jumped at the sound of a pistol firing just on the other side of the thin canvas wall. Not two meters from her, horsemen galloped past, followed closely by a second group, clearly in pursuit. A lone rider returned, and a moment later was joined by another. Ariel threw herself and the child on the ground, praying that the child would remain silent. Her only hope was that anyone who might peer into the tent would think they were just two bodies among the others.

"Have you searched all the tents?" a sotto voce demanded.

"I have. Certainly she was taken with the other women to the safety of the harem. I shall go. I left her side. I shall find her."

Relief flooded through Ariel's veins as she scrambled awkwardly to her feet, the weight of the child making her clumsy. She stumbled over bodies without noticing, so eager was she for the sight of the two men beyond the ruined tent wall. Unmindful of the sight she presented, Ariel plunged through the small opening and came to an unsteady halt beneath the nose of the enormous black stallion.

177

Chapter Fourteen

Christopher was off his horse and beside her in a moment. If not for the honeyed gold of her hair, he might not have recognized the woman who careened out of the tent with a small child in her arms. Her pants were ripped to ribbons and her tunic covered with dirt. What he had hitherto thought of as the cascading waterfall of her hair was a tangled mass, clotted with the same blood that covered her left side from shoulder to knee. Scrapes ran across both cheeks, her nose had been bloodied, and he had no idea whose child it was that she clung to as though her very life depended upon the warmth of his body against her own.

"Where are you hurt?" he demanded, running his hands over the caked blood, determined to stem its source. Ariel stared at him dumbly, as though she had no idea what he was talking about. "Where are you hurt?" he repeated urgently.

"I'm not hurt."

"The child?"

"The child is only afraid, not injured." Her eyes filled with the horror of some sudden thought, and she turned, as if she intended to return to the tent. In her flustered determination to finish the task she had set for herself, she nearly tripped over Siad, who had fallen to his knees at the sight of his mistress.

Christopher pulled her back. "Where do you think you're going?" he demanded.

"Lady Anne and your uncle," she stuttered. "I haven't looked at the rest of the bodies."

Christopher gathered her into his arms like a small, confused child. Between them the little boy squirmed ever so slightly. "Anne and Robert are safe, Ariel. You needn't search for them anymore."

"But the call to arms," she insisted as though Christopher was not in possession of his complete faculties. "It was against all English, and inside the tents —" her voice broke.

Seeing her struggle to regain control of her emotions, Christopher raged with anger against the Bukhariyin who had created this butchery.

She looked up at him, the pain in her eyes obliterating their golden lights. "The tents are filled with the dead."

"I know," he said, stroking her head gently. "I've seen them. Anne and Robert didn't come tonight. I suspected danger, and Robert agreed to be prudent."

"They're safe?" Ariel looked up at him with such relief that it tore at his heart as he nodded. Ariel crumpled in his arms then, her legs no longer willing to hold her upright. He swept her off the ground, setting her on the black stallion. Swinging up behind her, he pulled her against him, sheltering both her and the child with his arms.

"Siad. Ride with us to the palace."

Without a word, the eunuch leapt onto the horse he had taken from a dead man and drew his scimitar. He followed in Christopher's wake, guarding his back as

179

they rode at breakneck speed away from the fighting.

Ariel must have fallen asleep, because for a moment she remembered nothing of the *fantasia* or the bloodbath that followed it. Christopher was holding her in his arms, speaking to her in a soft, low voice, and she felt safe and secure. It was dark, but torchlight cast a warm glow across his face. She pulled the warm bundle in her arms against her, cuddling it. And then she remembered. Horror flooded back with the power of waters held behind a dam. The blood, the stench, the mindless fear of the peasants as they trampled over their own people. It was far too real, as real as the young boy who lay asleep in her arms.

"I have to return to the battle, Ariel," Christopher was saying. "Siad will take you to your duenna and guard your door."

Ariel clutched his black cotton djellaba and looked into his face. He was more Berber warrior than any man she'd ever seen, and she could almost believe that he returned to the fighting in the defense of the sultan and under the protection of Allah. But she couldn't possibly run to hide in her room when everyone she loved was in danger. She had to know what had happened and why. Christopher had been part of the *fantasia,* and he said he had suspected trouble. Their differences were of no account now. She couldn't let him go without at least a few answers. "What happened?" she asked. "Who did this?"

"I'll tell you everything I know when I come back. For now, we need to get you safely behind a locked door."

"No! You can't dismiss me like some child who must be taken away for her own good. I must know if the

180

sultan is safe. If you won't tell me, I'll find someone who will."

"Mohammed Ben Abdullah is safe. Those still loyal to him saw to that."

"The Bukhariyin?"

"No," Christopher told her in a low voice. "Not the Bukhariyin."

Ariel knit her brow. Much was going unsaid, and she wanted answers badly. But Christopher was clearly anxious to return to the field, and she could leave her questions about the Black Guards until later.

"Go with Siad, Ariel."

"One more question," she said, holding his arm. "Suleiman and Yazid rode in the *fantasia*. Have you seen them? Do you know if they're safe?" Christopher glared at her as though he'd like nothing more than to skewer her through with a scimitar himself, and Ariel balked at his disposition. "They are my family. Surely you're not so cruel as to keep news of their welfare from me!"

"I don't know their whereabouts, Ariel," he said in a voice that was hard and bitter. "I saw Suleiman at the start of the last charge just before the fighting broke out, but I haven't seen Prince Yazid since before the second charge."

Fear shot through Ariel, and she put aside her pride to beg for Christopher's help. "Please, I beseech you. Look for the princes. Bring me back word of their safety."

"I'll find out what I can." Christopher glared at her.

At any other time Ariel would have bristled at him, but she was too exhausted and too glad just to be alive. She had simply asked after the welfare of men who were like brothers to her. She had no idea why he should treat her request with such disdain, but she was beyond

181

caring. She wanted to know that the princes were safe, and despite their differences, she knew of no one better suited to find them and, if need be, protect them than Christopher.

"Thank you," she replied humbly.

"You're welcome, Ariel. Now, for once do as you're told and go to your room."

Ariel jerked her head up, stung by his tone and his unwillingness to make peace between them. "As you wish, *Your Grace.*" She swept around and marched up the palace steps with the child in her arms, refusing to look back. But her pique didn't carry her far. Even as she climbed the steps she felt exhaustion begin to buckle her knees. It took every ounce of strength she possessed to go on, but she set her sights on the iron gates that had been locked against the aggressors and forced herself to reach them. The moment she was shielded from Christopher's view, she fell against the wall, her entire body shaking. Siad was there, lifting her into his arms.

"I can walk, Siad. I just need to rest for a moment."

"No. I will carry you or I will crawl and you shall ride upon my strong back. But I shall not abandon my duty to you again. You are too weak to walk, and you have the child to carry."

"But everyone will think I'm hurt, and there are so many others . . ." Her words dissolved into nothingness, for simply to speak was beyond her.

"We shall speak of this no more. It is now as it shall be."

Ariel didn't try to fight Siad's wish. If he acquiesced now, she knew she wouldn't be able to carry out her intentions anyway. Her energy was ebbing like water being sucked down a whirlpool. Her arms ached from holding the child. She was beaten and tired, and the safety of her own room was a sweet and welcome thought in her exhausted mind.

In minutes they were there. Siad knocked once without setting Ariel down, and Chedyla threw open the door. She fell on Ariel, weeping and moaning and praying her thanks to Allah all at the same time. She had stoked the fire to a roaring blaze in anticipation of Ariel's return, and Siad set Ariel in the chair next to it. Rhima was also there, and when she saw what Ariel held in her arms, she gasped, her eyes wide with shock.

"A child!"

"He fell against me when the fighting broke out. He would have been trampled," Ariel explained in an exhausted daze. "There were people falling everywhere and others running—running in all directions."

"It is over now, and you are both safe," Chedyla whispered as she gently accomplished what Ariel had been unable to and loosened the boy's hold enough to separate the two. She nodded to Rhima, who came forward to take the child. "Rhima will see to the boy. Now we must see to you. Drink this." She held a tall glass to Ariel's lips.

"The blood is not mine," Ariel explained. "A dead man fell on me. The Belmeths are safe." She knew her mind was skipping from thought to thought, losing track of sequence as the herbal drink Chedyla had just given her began to take effect. But before she could give herself over fully to its influence, Ariel had one last thing to do.

"Siad," she called the eunuch to her side softly. He knelt before her, and although she saw by the look of guilt on his face that her question would hurt him, she had to ask. "Why did you leave me? Why weren't you waiting outside the harem tent?" It never occurred to Ariel that her faithful servant of so many years had de-

183

serted his post. She expected him to tell her he had been lured away, threatened, chased, or in some other way forced to abandon his post. So she was not prepared for his reply.

"I believed you safe. You were in the harem where there were many guards. I never thought you would leave there."

Ariel's surprise was so complete she could do nothing but look at him, befuddled.

Siad hung his head in shame. "I saw treachery, beloved mistress. I heard men plotting the death of my mistress's betrothed. I felt it my duty to protect this man who will be your husband, and so I left you to stand at his side and protect his back from the blade of a villain. In doing so, I endangered your own life. I cannot ask you to forgive me for this terrible sin." Siad took her hand in his and pressed it to his lips, and then, his forehead. "I do not deserve to live."

Ariel looked at the eunuch, her friend for more than half a score years, and her heart burst with love. There were many, many questions, but they would wait. She gently pulled her fingers from his desperate grasp and, bending over him, took his face between her palms and kissed his bald head. He had given her every day of his life, this gentle giant. He had been brutally robbed of his manhood, robbed of a man's voice and body, and ordered to do her bidding. Yet his loyalty had directed him to protect the man who he believed would be her husband.

If what he said was true, Ariel thought guiltily, Christopher might still be in danger. She had sent him out to see to the princes' safety without ever considering his own.

"Go back to him, Siad. Keep him safe."

The eunuch slave looked up at her, his face filled with

184

pride. "He is a great man, this English caid whom the sultan chooses for you. He is a far greater man than many who call themselves sons of Allah. I will bring him back to you. I will not fail you again."

"I know, Siad," Ariel said softly. "Now go. I'm well cared for here."

Without a moment's hesitation, he was gone. Ariel had the distinct impression that he was relieved to be sent back to Christopher. Perhaps battle gave him the chance to feel whole again. Or, she wondered, frowning, did Siad believe that Christopher was still in danger and needed him more than she did? All at once a terrible thought came to Ariel; then just as quickly, she dismissed it. Surely Yazid wasn't the one Siad had heard plotting to kill Christopher. Yazid had said he would free Ariel from the threat of their marriage, but he would never stoop to murder. She certainly had never wanted such a thing. She couldn't bear to go through life with Christopher's blood on her hands.

Ariel sat up straighter in the chair, ignoring Chedyla's efforts to wipe her face. She tried to recall Yazid's exact words. Had he said anything at all about killing Christopher? Ariel racked her brain, forcing herself to recall every aspect of their conversation despite the increasing power of Chedyla's medicine. No, she decided at last, sinking back into the cushions. Yazid had said nothing about murder. He had only said that by dawn she would be free.

It had been so important to her then, breaking their marriage contract. But in view of everything that had occurred since, whether or not she married Christopher seemed a very small thing. It wouldn't be so terrible to marry a man that every woman sighed over — a man who was as strong and handsome and brave as any man she'd ever seen.

185

Rhima slipped quietly into the room and, seeing that Ariel was still awake, crossed to the chair and bowed. "The child sleeps. He has been bathed and fed." She smiled. "He devoured four almond buns, a bowl of tabbouleh, and a pitcher of goat's milk."

Ariel smiled groggily. "Has he told you his name?"

"He does not speak to us yet, mistress."

Ariel nodded. "He's been through a terrible experience."

"As have you," Chedyla clucked gently as she washed the blood and dirt from Ariel's arm.

The child was well. The sultan was safe. Siad was with Christopher, and Christopher would see to the princes' safety. Ariel closed her eyes as exhaustion overtook her at last.

As she drifted into sleep the dream came back.

Christopher was with her as they stood by a tent laughing and talking. Then suddenly from behind him, a hand emerged from the tent holding a dagger. Ariel tried to scream, but no sound came out of her mouth. The dagger came down, and down, its glittering point bearing directly at Christopher's back. And then, suddenly he changed, and it was Yazid standing with her. He was laughing, too. But the sound was hard and cold. And as she looked away from him, she saw that he held a dagger in his hand, and all around them for as far as she could see, they stood in a river of blood.

Christopher galloped Hannibal up the main street of Meknes, toward the front gate of El Bedi. Although he relaxed in the saddle, he watched each alleyway he passed for shadows. There was little chance of attack now, but wariness was too imbedded in him to do otherwise. The rebels had been driven beyond the walls of the city, and Siad rode on his flank, the sultan's banner snapping from the staff he held high in one hand. It would be dawn soon. Already palest pink streaked the sky. He was tired to the very marrow of his bones, dirty, and thirsty.

All night long, he and Siad had ridden through the city helping any group of warriors they could. He'd found Suleiman early in the fighting. A large contingency of the sultan's soldiers was with him, and they were fighting in the souk. They'd beaten the insurrectionists back after over two hours of hard combat, and Christopher had been impressed by the younger prince's ability. He had seemed so quiet — almost gentle — in their previous meetings that Christopher had wondered if Moulay Suleiman was capable keeping himself alive in a battle. But the prince had more than proven his courage and skill, and Christopher had a new respect for the young man. That was about the only good thing to come out of the past twelve hours. The fighting had been hard, he was exhausted, and he hadn't been able to find Yazid.

It was more than his pledge to Ariel that bothered him. Yazid was nowhere to be found in the city, and that stunk of something very foul. He had no proof against Mohammed El Yazid, just his instinct. He should have been leading a charge like his half-brother. With his known skills as a horseman and warrior, Yazid should have been the one to rally the sultan's forces when the first cries of revolt had been sounded. But he hadn't, and the loyalists had lost precious minutes trying to organize without a leader. Hundreds of men were cut down needlessly because the heir to the throne didn't take immediate command of his men.

Christopher had seen him at the first charge. But at the second, he hadn't been able to find Yazid, and by

187

the third, every muscle within Christopher was tensed and alert. His instincts warned him that what his informers had hinted at was imminent. And he hadn't been wrong. Now, the more time that went by without any sign of Mohammed El Yazid, the more convinced Christopher became that Yazid stood on the very cusp of the insurrection.

They passed through the gates of the palace. Christopher pulled the black turban off of his head and dropped it in his lap, letting the wind run through his hair as he rubbed his hand across the back of his neck. At least Ariel was safely within the walls of El Bedi. He slowed Hannibal to an easy trot, and momentarily closed his eyes. He couldn't get the image of her as she'd burst from the tent out of his mind. Her strength amazed him. She was so slight, soft and feminine and breathtakingly beautiful, yet within her was fire and steel and passion. She had been glorious, all the more so because she'd stood before him, her head held high despite the dirt, and blood, and scrapes that she bore. Exhausted, and frightened as a doe, she'd been determined to find Anne and Robert, people who had been strangers to her less than two days ago. And she'd carried that boy through God only knew what horrors, yet she didn't even know his name. For all she knew he could be the child of a man who sided with the revolutionaries. But that thought clearly hadn't occurred to Ariel. For all that she could be as stubborn and single-minded as a camel, Ariel wore her heart upon her sleeve.

For everyone except him.

He thought about how she'd paled when he'd told her he hadn't seen Yazid. She crossed him at every turn, refused to give him the least quarter in their private battle of wills, yet she'd given nary a thought to begging

188

him to protect Yazid. If Yazid *was* involved in the coup, was Ariel also part of the treachery? No, Christopher thought, shaking his head. Her fear, and her demands to know who was behind the insurrection, had been too real. But that still didn't clear Yazid. He would have kept Ariel in the dark. He wouldn't tell a woman anything that mattered. They were all one and the same to the prince. He was blind to the differences between Ariel and other women. He understood nothing about the rarity of her. The beauty that went far deeper than the glory of her face. It infuriated Christopher to think that she wanted a man with so little regard for her, to know that she would willingly subjugate herself to his enormous ego.

And yet she had sent Siad back to his side. . . .

To help him protect her precious prince. The image of Ariel standing in Yazid's embrace made Christopher grit the sand between his teeth. She had run after him, following meekly in his wake when he'd announced he would walk her back to her room upon their return from the souk. Was Yazid already her lover, or did she only hunger for him to be so? Was that what Ariel wanted? To be treated no better than a slave? Christopher had wooed her, served as her escort, and cajoled her with food and good company, only to gain her spite. He knit his brows in frustration. When she'd fallen asleep in his arms as they rode back to El Bedi, she'd stirred a deeply protective side of his nature. She'd lain trustingly against him, warm and vulnerable. It was an image he couldn't forget any more than he could banish the taste of her kisses from his mouth, or the memory of the fiery sparks that lit her eyes when she faced him down so fearlessly.

He was more than half in love with her, he admitted silently. And that was beginning to look more and more

189

like a mistake. His reasons for accepting her hand in marriage ran deeper than a simple fear that her life would be in danger if she stayed in Morocco. He wanted her. He wanted her more completely than just having her in his bed, although he wanted that greatly. He wanted to see her passion and strength turned with him, not against him. He wanted to unite their abilities, to work together side by side, because he knew with an abiding certainty that together they would be far better than either one of them could ever be alone.

But if it was a mistake to fall in love with her, it was because she was too stubborn to see the reality of the world she lived in. He would just have to make her see. Her wit was too sharp and her face too full of natural wisdom for her to turn blindly to Mohammed El Yazid. He pulled Hannibal up before the front entrance to the palace and jumped off the black stallion's back as a bony stable boy scurried to catch his reins.

"Be certain he's well rubbed down," Christopher warned. "Only small amounts of water, and no grain until he's cool."

The wide-eyed boy nodded and led Hannibal away while another took Siad's mount. "I go now to guard my mistress," the eunuch told Christopher.

"I'll go with you. I promised to tell her the news."

Siad nodded and bowed, letting Christopher lead the way through the palace. When they arrived at the double-doored entrance, Christopher knocked twice, and Chedyla appeared at the door.

"Is Lady Ariel asleep?"

"No, my lord. She is not here."

"What!" Christopher could not believe his ears. She refused to do even this one small thing he had asked of her, and he'd only asked it for her own safety. "Where is she?"

"She went to see the child," Chedyla responded calmly. "He woke and could not be calmed by the other women."

Christopher knew he should have relaxed at that, but he didn't. He couldn't forget that she had once again disobeyed his instructions. "The child could have been brought to her here," he barked at Chedyla.

"The child was inconsolable. My lady feared that he would only be more distraught if he was forcibly brought to her."

"Where are they now?"

"The boy is being kept in the princes' old room. Siad knows the way."

Christopher turned, and barked furiously at the eunuch. "Let's go!"

Siad bowed and led the way back from where they'd come, but when he stopped and indicated a door, the eunuch who guarded it held up his hand, denying them entrance.

"We come to see the child and the Lady Ariel, ward of the sultan," Siad told the other eunuch, making it clear that no delay would be broached.

"The Lady Ariel, ward of the great sultan, is not here," the eunuch announced, settling his arms defiantly across his chest.

"We will see this for ourselves," countered Siad.

"She is not here. And no one may pass by me without the express permission of the lady."

"Get out of the way," Christopher demanded between clenched teeth as he stepped in front of Siad. "I am the lady's affianced husband, and I want to see her *now*." Furious at being delayed, he strode to within an inch of the eunuch's beardless face and wordlessly dared him to defy his wish.

Seeing the muscle that leapt in the tall, battle-toughened man's rigid face, the guard backed away. Bowing and gesturing suppliantly, he slid away from the door, hoping that the black-garbed caid would soon forget his face and this unfortunate encounter.

Christopher burst into the room, sending the door crashing against the wall. The two women who sat near the child's bed—neither one of which was Ariel—screamed. They leapt from their chairs, dragging the frightened boy with them, and were soon cowering against the wall.

"Where is Lady Ariel?" Christopher demanded, his much strained patience at an end.

One of the young women stepped gingerly forward, the circles of white around her eyes giving Christopher a clear indication of her fear. She spoke to him from behind one hand, which she kept over the lower part of her face. "My mistress was here; but the boy fell asleep, and she said she would return to her room to rest more."

"How long ago?"

"Perhaps an hour."

"Well, she's not there!" *Damn her,* Christopher swore. This was all he needed. With traitorous viziers and the sultan's wife still roaming freely about the palace, anything could have happened.

"On the grave of all holy men," the girl stammered. "I swear to you that is what she told me."

"What is your name?" Christopher asked curtly.

"Rhima, my lord."

"And you serve Lady Ariel?"

The girl nodded.

"Then, go back to Lady Ariel's rooms. Tell the duenna . . ." for a moment Christopher searched his mind for her name. "Chedyla. Tell her what you know. Tell her that if your mistress should return, she must send you to Lord Belmeth at once with a message that she's safe. He'll get the message to me. Do you understand?" he asked, giving the slave girl an ominous look.

"Yes, my lord. I understand."

"Then, get going. And *don't*," he called after her with a growl, "let anything waylay you from going directly to the duenna."

The girl nodded and fled from the room. Christopher spun on his heels and stalked out of the room without a backward glance at the remaining servant and the child left hunkering in fright in the corner.

Chapter Fifteen

His longest stride couldn't carry Christopher down the hall fast enough. At his aunt and uncle's room he stopped and, with his fist raised to knock, forced his features into a smooth mask. Christopher was surprised at Anne's quick response when his hand finally lowered against the door. She put her hand to her heart in relief at the sight of him.

"Thank God!" she sighed, leaning up to kiss his cheek as she pulled him into a motherly embrace. "Robert has been pacing the floor all night."

"And you did none of the pacing, my dear?" Christopher's uncle commented, coming up behind his wife. He clamped a hand on Christopher's shoulder. "Come in, will you? The sultan's counsel meets within the hour, and I want to know everything that's happened — not to mention that I'm damned glad to see you safe, my boy."

Christopher gave them a thin smile. "I can't stay. Ariel is—"

"Right here," Anne finished for him.

"What!" It was more of an explosion than a comment. Christopher strode past both of them to the middle of the room and turned, looking around.

Silently Anne nodded to where Ariel was curled into a ball on the chaise in a darkened corner of the sitting room. "And if you don't lower your voice, you'll wake her."

"I damned well will wake her. And I've got half a mind to do it with a willow switch."

"Christopher!" his aunt reprimanded sharply. "How can you say such a thing? She's been through a terrible ordeal."

"Do you have any idea the ordeal she's just put me through?" Christopher barked. "I came here to tell you I was about to launch a full-scale search for her, and here she is fast asleep on *your* chaise longue."

"She came here to see for herself that we were safe," Anne told him softly. "How can you be angry at her for that?"

Christopher ran his hand through his hair and stared at the floor. "She was supposed to stay in her room."

"How could she when she was so worried about the other people she felt responsible for? That child, for instance."

"Everyone else in the palace has," Christopher retorted, but even as he spoke, he knew it was a lame attempt to hold on to his quickly ebbing anger.

"She's not everyone else, though," Robert said, coming to stand beside the chair. "Anne and I saw that very clearly tonight."

Christopher looked down at Ariel, who continued to sleep despite their noise. Dark shadows lay beneath the crescent of her lowered lashes, and her normally golden complexion was paled by exhaustion. She looked like a small kitten curled beneath the cashmere throw that covered her, soft and innocent, sleeping a deep, dreamless sleep. His anger melted away. How could he be angry with her when she was safe? He was pleased that she'd felt comfortable enough with Anne and Robert to come here. Slowly he walked back to the doorway, signalling Siad.

"She's safe, Siad. Go tell Chedyla and the serving girl. Then get some sleep yourself. She's going to need you with her at all times once she wakes up. Until then, she's safe here."

The eunuch bowed as Christopher closed the door behind him. "How long has she been here, Robert?" He was calmer now, his anger replaced by a muscle-deep tiredness. There was no time to sleep, however. If the Bilad al Makhzan was gathering to meet within the hour, he needed to brief Robert about everything he'd seen during the night. Foremost among the things he wanted to discuss with Robert were his concerns about Mohammed El Yazid.

"She arrived not long before you. Thirty minutes or so, wouldn't you say, Anne?"

Anne nodded. "Poor dear. She could barely keep her eyes open. It was as though just seeing us allayed her fears. The minute she knew we were safe, exhaustion simply overtook her."

"We asked her in, of course, since we were both awake and glad for the company," Robert said, picking up the narrative.

"At first I didn't think she would stay," added Anne. "Then barely a moment after she sat down, she was sleeping as soundly as a lamb."

Christopher said nothing for a minute. Their story just didn't jibe with the other information he had gathered. If Ariel had come straight here after leaving the little boy's room, she'd have been here longer than half an hour. He had covered the distance between the two rooms in bare minutes. Where had Ariel gone between the boy and here? he asked silently. Had she seen

196

Yazid? And where the hell was the heir to the throne, anyway?

"Why don't you let me order you a bath, Christopher," Anne was saying. "After what you've been through, I'd think one of the sultan's luxurious baths would be just the thing."

Christopher shook his head. "Thank you, Anne, but I have to bring Robert up to date before he sees the sultan. You do have an audience with him, don't you, Robert?"

"Of course. It was put on his schedule before the *fantasia*, just as we agreed."

Christopher nodded, satisfied.

"Now, tell me what you believe is going on. Who is leading the revolt? The Bukhariyin as we suspected?"

Christopher opened his mouth to reply affirmatively, and then closed it again, his gaze falling on Ariel sleeping peacefully in the semi-darkness of the corner. "Maybe I will take that bath. Anne, would you mind asking one to be prepared? And, Robert, why don't you come along. I'll tell you everything while I get cleaned up."

Robert followed Christopher's line of vision and gave him an incredulous look, but withholding any comment he followed Christopher down the hall to his room.

"You don't think Ariel has anything to do with this, do you?" he asked the moment the door was shut.

Christopher crossed to the window, listening to the quiet of the morning for a moment before he replied. "No," he said at last, turning back into the room as he stripped off his cape and djellaba.

"Then, why wouldn't you discuss the revolt in front of her?"

Christopher sat down in the chair across from Robert and pulled off his boots, tossing them aside angrily. What *did* he think? Did he really think Ariel, who professed to love her country too much to leave it, was part of the insurrection? Did he really believe that she would abandon all her values for the prince? Put that way, he couldn't reconcile such actions with the woman he knew and was planning to marry. Ariel was too proud, and too guileless. Whatever she was thinking was always there for everyone to see. No, he couldn't — wouldn't — believe that she was involved.

"I think Mohammed El Yazid has some part in this," Christopher said at last, watching his uncle's expression closely. "Ariel is inordinately loyal to the two princes. I couldn't tell you about my suspicions and take a chance that she might overhear us before I could tell her myself."

"And will you tell her yourself?"

Christopher looked at Robert and met his uncle's straight look with one of his own. "Not immediately. She's too close to Yazid. If I told her about my suspicions, she might feel it was her duty to go to the prince himself with her information," Christopher said, thinking that was *exactly* the kind of thing she would do. "I can't take that chance."

"She's going to be your wife, Christopher," Robert counselled him. "Maybe you should trust her."

"Not with this, Robert. Not yet."

"Ariel . . . Ariel . . ."

Someone was calling to her from far across the desert. Ariel opened her eyes. Christopher sat beside her holding her hand between both of his.

"Good morning," he said, smiling down at her.

"Good morning," she replied, and then waking more fully, "What are you doing in my room?"

"I'm not in your room. You fell asleep in my aunt and uncle's apartment. Don't you remember?"

Ariel knit her brow, trying to recall. At last she nodded slowly. "I wanted see that they were all right."

Christopher smiled again, and Ariel couldn't help noticing how attractively the dimple in his left cheek deepened. He was tired and battle-worn, but even so, he was the most handsome man she'd ever seen.

"But I didn't mean to fall asleep. They must think I'm a barbarian."

"Quite the contrary, they think you were the picture of thoughtfulness to be so concerned about them. And they knew you were exhausted."

"What time is it?" Ariel asked, still groggy from her rest.

"Nearly nine in the morning."

"Nine!" Ariel shot bolt upright on the chaise. "Where are Yazid and Suleiman?"

Christopher held her shoulders and looked at her. "What are you so concerned about? Was something supposed to happen by this time?"

"Happen?" Ariel looked at him in blank confusion that quickly turned to irritation. "How should I know what has happened or what is supposed to happen. *You* were the one out there fighting, and," she said, pinning him with an accusing stare, "you promised you'd come and tell me everything as soon as you got back to the palace. Do you know I was up the entire night *waiting?* I don't know anything thanks to you!"

"I returned less than two hours ago, Ariel."

"Oh," she said weakly. Ariel felt Christopher's hold on her shoulders loosen, and she sensed that for some reason he was vastly relieved by something she had just said. But she couldn't imagine what it had been, and at the moment her priority was to be sure the princes had also returned safely.

"Well, I should return to my room and see if anyone there has any information. At least the harem is bound to be buzzing with news."

As she began to rise from the sofa, Christopher pulled her back. *"Don't* go to the harem."

She looked up at him, almost frightened by the ferocity on his face.

"Do you understand me?" he demanded. *"Don't* go to the harem until I tell you it's safe."

Ariel nodded, her eyes wide with trepidation. Despite her feelings that the harem was a perfectly safe place for her to go, she sensed he had reached his limit of understanding with her and decided it would be best not to cross him in this one thing. "I won't," she said quietly.

"Promise me."

"I promise, Christopher. I won't go to the harem."

Beneath the silky fabric of her tunic, Ariel's nipples brushed against Christopher's chest. Their touch sent an irresistible wave of desire crashing through him. Her skin, where his fingers held her shoulders, was like velvet, and he brushed a thumb across it, savoring the enticing texture. A long, silken expanse of throat was in clear view as she tilted her face back to look up at him. Her lips were parted and her eyes closed—expectant and daring as she waited for him to kiss her. She was innocence, and challenge, and seduction all wrapped into one, and he willingly succumbed to her powers.

Bending his head to the hollow at the base of her throat, he trailed kisses across her shoulder, gently thumbing aside the silk tunic. Her scent was intoxicating—jasmine and spice mingled with the warmth of her skin. He tore his lips away, taking an unsteady breath. Dragging his mouth roughly across her cheek, he seized her mouth with his as he pressed her back into the bolsters. His tongue traced the rim of her lips, and Ariel willingly parted them. A moment later her tongue moved across his in imitation. Christopher groaned, and when her tongue began to explore the inner walls of his mouth, he thought he would lose all control.

His own tongue plunged into her mouth, darting in and out in rapid thrusts. Her hands played across his back, ranging over every inch, touching, stroking, running light as a feather up his spine to the base of his neck where her fingers wound themselves among the ends of his hair. He felt alive as he had never felt before. Her every action was as seductive as a well-trained courtesan, as though she knew instinctively where to touch him and how to arouse his desire to unbearable levels. Christopher pulled his mouth away from hers and rained kisses over her face, wanting to claim every part as his own. He encircled her ear with his tongue, nibbling gently at its lobe before trailing kisses down her neck, forging a path that led to her tunic.

Christopher dragged the gauzy silk lower, and for one moment stopped to admire the expectant, hardened peak of her nipple. His heart slammed against his ribs, and he cupped her full, young breast in his hand, drawing the rosy tip into his mouth, suckling at its sweetness. Moaning, Ariel arched backward, pressing his head down, asking him for more. He knew that if he did not stop now, there would be no stopping. Anne had gone with Robert to await the results of the sultan's meeting with the Bilad al Makhzan. They might return at any time, or they might not be back for hours. But

Christopher knew he wouldn't chance compromising Ariel. Not here, or now.

He reached back and pulled one hand from his neck. Slowly he drew her index finger into his mouth. He felt a shiver snake up her spine, and releasing her finger, he lavished the same attention on another, and another, until each glistened damply. Then he kissed the palm of her hand, trailing his tongue up her arm to the sensitive place in the very crook of her elbow.

"Christopher," she moaned, and he covered her mouth with his once more, thinking his name had never sounded as perfect as it did coming from her lips.

"On our wedding night, I'll show you many more of the delights of lovemaking," he whispered against her mouth. "But for now, you'll have to wait, little one."

The passion that had swept away all other thoughts was suddenly beaten back by Christopher's words. Ariel had wanted him to kiss her; she'd willingly followed his lead, going where he directed her. And now he was chiding her for her wanton behavior, warning her that *he* would not go so far. She felt cheapened as she had never felt before. Why was it that they could never be alone without Christopher dragging her into his arms? And why couldn't she ever seem to resist him? "Let me go, please," she whispered. "I'm sure you're in a hurry to be off to other matters."

"Ariel, I'm thinking of you. Surely you must know—"

"Indeed," she cut in, turning her head away so that he couldn't see the tears threatening to overflow the gates of her lashes. "I know that you wanted nothing to do with this marriage, just as I want nothing to do with it. And that you only agreed to my guardian's terms out of some misguided theory that I'm in danger. I suppose I owe you thanks for your chivalry, but I can't thank you

202

for the unwilling bondage your thoughtfulness will mean for me. This interlude was a mistake. I fully intend to pursue release from our engagement to the very last possible moment. Now, if you'll excuse me." Ariel was at the door before Christopher made any reply.

"Do you want to hear how the princes have fared?"

Ariel stopped where she was. She desperately needed to prove to Christopher that she could resist him, that she wasn't interested in him, or anything he might have to say. But her concern for Suleiman and Yazid was too deeply imbedded in her. How could she walk away without knowing that they were safe? Chedyla may have heard news, but Christopher had been there. Still facing the door, Ariel nodded. "Yes, I would very much like to hear that they're safe."

"They are safe."

"Where?" Ariel asked, letting out a long breath that she hadn't realized she was holding.

"They've set up headquarters at the Casbah."

"Then, the revolt has been repelled?"

"They were beaten back beyond the wall of the city. The fighting has stopped for now; I think the Bukhariyin will need to regroup and rest. But they'll be back. They did a great deal of damage. Many men were lost."

"The Bukhariyin?" Ariel turned to face Christopher in disbelief. "They're the sultan's most trusted regiment. You must be wrong."

He shook his head. "No, Ariel. I'm not wrong. It's the Black Guards who have lead the revolt. There are others, too. Some of the Arab tribes, even members of the government have joined them. Only half of the viziers appeared today when the Bilad al Makhzan was convened by Mohammed Ben Abdullah."

Ariel shook her head at him, refusing to accept what he was telling her. "But why?"

203

"I don't know that yet," Christopher said. "The treaty is part of it. Many Moroccans don't want to change the old ways. They see Mohammed's ideas about commerce and the exchange of ideas between Morocco and other countries as blasphemous. But there's something more. Some other reason." He shrugged in a way that said everything and nothing at all.

She knew there was more, but she had grovelled enough to learn that Yazid and Suleiman were well. She refused to stoop to cajoling more information from him. She would simply find out for herself. "Thank you," she said quickly, and before he could detain her in any other way, she left.

Ariel was deeply relieved to find Siad waiting just outside the Belmeths' door. He fell in behind her, but Ariel slowed, dropping back to walk beside him. There were guards everywhere in the palace, men she didn't recognize, and none of whom wore the scarlet sash of the Bukhariyin. "What happened, Siad?" she whispered as they walked down the hall.

"It is best if we say nothing until you are safely behind the doors of your own room."

Ariel shot a surprised glance at him. "Is it so dangerous even within the palace?"

"There is no knowing who to trust, beloved mistress," the eunuch explained out of one side of his mouth as he stared straight ahead. "Yesterday the very men who would kill our great sultan, descendant of Allah, were standing guard outside his door. Who knows that these men who replace them are not their brothers, that tonight they will not raise their weapons against every man, woman, and child who sleeps within these walls."

Ariel shuddered, thinking that she had escaped yesterday's massacre at the *fantasia* only to become a prisoner here. Arriving at her quarters, Ariel asked Siad to come in. She dismissed Chedyla, suggesting that she check on the child as an excuse to get her out of the room. She didn't want Chedyla to hear whatever terrible stories Siad might have to tell her.

"Did you see the princes?" Ariel asked as soon as they were alone in the room.

Siad nodded. "Your future husband fought at Moulay Suleiman's side during the night. Together they broke the spine of the Bukhariyin revolutionaries. It was that battle which turned the tide of the night, and began their retreat from the city. The English caid fought with the strength of ten men. He towered above the others and was an easy target once word spread that the black warrior was a Christian who brought the treaty. Many of the traitors came after him, thinking to topple one of the infidels. But he never lost. He left a trail of blood wherever he went, and the men that fought with him — Moulay Suleiman's troops — began to call him 'Sohda Agadir,' the black fortress. They say he has Allah's great *baraka* upon him. That he cannot be defeated."

"And Yazid," Ariel prodded. "What of the heir?"

Siad looked at her, perplexed for a moment before answering. "We did not see Moulay Mohammed El Yazid, although the English caid looked throughout the city for him. I have heard in the palace that he fought at the gates of the city. He was the first to chase the cowards of treachery from Meknes. He pursued them, I am told, far onto the plains, but he turned back to reinforce the city. The princes have taken the old Casbah as theirs."

Ariel nodded. "I've heard."

"It is a good place. From there they may see all who come for many miles. The sultan shall not be defeated. This is as Allah wills."

205

"Thank you, Siad."

The eunuch pressed the palms of his hands together and touched them to his forehead as he bowed. "As you wish. I await your pleasure, beloved heart of the great English caid."

Ariel frowned at Siad's back as he took his post outside her door. She was vastly relieved that the battles had gone well, but the entire slant of his conversation made her uneasy. What had he meant by calling her Christopher's "beloved heart"? He had spent the entire night with Christopher, and clearly he had developed a deep respect for him. But he assumed much if he assumed Christopher *wanted* to marry her.

Traitorously, her thoughts returned to the Belmeths' sitting room, and her heart began to race. Groaning, she turned and threw herself upon her bed. This growing fascination with Christopher Staunton was nothing more than a woman desiring a man, she scolded herself. She didn't want him. She didn't even like him most of the time, although at the moment she couldn't think of any of the things she truly *dis*liked about him. What she felt toward Christopher was only the most base of attractions between man and woman, and she would not let it cloud her concentration on her true desire. Morocco was her home, and she meant to stay here, despite Christopher, and Daiwa, and everyone else who thought she'd be better off gone.

Rolling over, Ariel stared up at the swirling arabesque pattern of the ceiling. She could picture Christopher fighting beside Suleiman, meeting the enemy's onslaught thrust for thrust. She'd meant to tell him how relieved she was that he had returned safely. But he'd so unnerved her by implying she couldn't wait until they were in their marriage bed that she'd forgotten. Jumping up, Ariel crossed to the door and signalled to Siad.

"Please go to Lord Staunton's room, and tell him I've asked for him, Siad."

The eunuch bowed. "I am sorry, but I cannot. He is gone."

"Gone?"

"Back to the battlefields. The rebels, spawn of all evil that they are, have again breached the city walls."

"I see," she said quietly. "You'll tell me as soon as he returns, Siad?"

"*Inch* Allah, beloved mistress."

"Yes," Ariel replied, leaning her forehead against the door as she closed it. "If Allah wills."

Chapter Sixteen

At the knock on her door, Ariel looked up from where she and the little boy sat casting stones into a circle she'd formed with a length of woolen yarn. Chedyla answered it, first peeking through a small crack, then opening it completely to let Christopher in. He was once again in English attire, undeniably handsome in an evergreen dinner jacket, fawn breeches that hugged his muscular thighs, and polished black boots. But despite his clothes, the shadow of the desert warrior still clung to him. The hawkish perception in his eyes and the air of confidence Ariel had come to recognize as uniquely his were honed to a fine edge tonight. They defined him. Watching him cross the room, she realized that despite the many faces he sometimes sported, his core never changed. He was the same man whether he called himself merchant, duke, or warrior.

She started to rise, but Christopher waved his hand. "Stay where you are." Crouching beside her, he smiled at the little boy and, in Arabic, asked him how he was feeling. The child stared at him, frozen with his handful of stones.

"I think he's afraid of you," Ariel said, speaking softly in English so that the child couldn't understand her. "Rhima tells me you terrified both of them. She thought you were a madman, a djinn coming out of her dreams. I doubt the child thought any less."

Christopher gave her a chagrined scowl. "That reminds me, when this is all over there is a particularly obstinate eunuch I intend to have a few words with."

Ariel laughed lightheartedly. "Zaiani comes from the Rif; they are all very stubborn there."

"I've yet to meet anyone in this country who isn't."

"And everyone in England is as meek as a lamb?"

Christopher's eyebrows shot up as he rubbed his chin in mock contemplation. "I can't recall a single acquaintance at home with a stubborn streak."

"Really? I had no idea there weren't any looking glasses in England."

"Looking glasses?" Christopher asked.

"How else could you have avoided seeing the wide stubborn streak running through your own face."

Christopher threw back his head with an easy laugh. "Maybe so, but you know what they say . . ."

Ariel tilted her head quizzically, waiting for Christopher to finish.

"They say that it takes one of a similar bent to recognize it in others."

Ariel made a face of mock insult and then laughed, joining him in the joke. It felt good to be so at ease with him. Sitting on the floor with the child nearby, there was a comfortable warmth between them, and she silently acknowledged the moment for the treasure that it was. Christopher seemed so willing to accept her for herself. Yes, she was stubborn. But his glib jibe had been said with a note of respect. How different that was from the Muslim attitude. Even the women chided her for her tenacity, and it felt wonderful to have someone admire the quality for once.

"How is the boy?" Christopher asked.

Ariel sighed, and gently combed the child's unruly black curls with her fingers. "He won't speak. Or else he can't. I've had the physician and the Imam both see him. The Imam says that sometimes when a child has been through a terror such as yesterday, he may not speak for days. Sometimes," she said, looking up at Christopher, "they never speak again. He says this is Allah's way of protecting them from the atrocities they've witnessed."

"I'm sorry," he said earnestly. "I hope I didn't make things worse by bursting into the room this morning."

She shook her head. "The field where he collided with me was far worse than any scare you could have given him. I hope with some kindness and a few nights' rest, he'll begin to talk. I can't find his family until I know his name. They must think he's dead. I want to put their minds at ease."

"What will you do if his family was killed?"

Ariel looked down at the little boy. "He's a precious child," she said as he laid his head in her lap. She began to stroke his back in the same rhythmic circles Chedyla used to soothe her. "He must have some relatives who survived, grandparents, aunts."

"Sometimes a child can be better off without his parents."

She looked up at him in surprise. "How can you say such a thing?"

"Not all children are loved, or wanted, by their parents, Ariel. Sometimes it's less painful to never see them again than to live day in and day out knowing you aren't wanted. Let me find out about the boy's parents. Maybe he'd be better off with you."

Ariel watched Christopher intently as he picked up the pile of stones abandoned by the little boy and began to toss them one by one into the circle. She knew intuitively that he was talking about himself, and she wondered what had happened in his childhood that would cause him to believe he wasn't loved by his parents. Lord and Lady Belmeth spoke of his mother with great affection, and Christopher had seemed to feel the same. He had never mentioned his father, though, and Ariel had made an assumption that he was dead. She thought of her own father, a man she'd never even seen. She'd always thought that anything would be better than not even knowing your parent, but after Christopher's words she could easily imagine how much more painful it would have been if he had been here and treated her without love. Her heart ached at the thought that Christopher may have lived with such a father. She reached out and touched the unruly tips of his rich, brown hair, much as she had touched the child's.

Christopher looked at her, his face questioning.

"Would you like to stay for supper?" she asked softly. "You must be very hungry, and I'd like to hear about today's battle. I've heard little, you know," she added, giving him a sideways glance. "I've been in my rooms since I left you."

Christopher smiled at her, and Ariel's heart somersaulted. "I'd like nothing better."

Suddenly Ariel felt as though they were locked in a bubble where nothing else existed. He was so close his breath fanned her cheeks. She could see the tiny lines of exhaustion that radiated from the corners of his eyes, and a small scar that ran from the outer corner of his eyebrow to his hairline. Without thinking, she reached out to soothe away the things that had hurt and tired him. His fingers intercepted hers. He drew them to his lips and, without taking his gaze from hers, kissed the tips of them one by one.

Fussing over the dressing table, Chedyla surreptitiously watched the two young lovers in the mirror and smiled. They *were* lovers; at least they were in their hearts, where it mattered. A few more days, a few stolen hours alone, and Ariel's heart would teach her what her head was refusing to see. The English duke was as wise as he was handsome, she acknowledged with growing respect. There was no greater persuasion than laying siege to a heart with patience and persistence, and this man with eyes the color of Allah's heavens knew this well. But there was a time for loving, and this, with her in the room, was certainly not it. She finished straightening, picked up Ariel's horn hairbrush and dropped it with a clatter on the marble floor.

Ariel pulled her hand away from Christopher with a gasp. Then, grabbing a pillow to put beneath the boy's head, she jumped up off the floor and began a flurry of inane straightening activities that she hoped would prevent Christopher from noticing that her cheeks were burning and she was finding it hard to breath. How could she have let that happen in front of Chedyla? And he hadn't been simply kissing her hand. It had been much, much more. He had been seducing her as surely as she'd been letting him. Thank God Chedyla was in the room. Ariel felt a shudder run down her spine at the thought of what might have happened if they'd been alone.

She desperately needed to put some space between Christopher and herself. How could she think with him here? He could make her forget everything that mattered to her. She had to keep her mind clear. Her feelings for Christopher, whatever they might be — and she had no intention of examining them too closely — couldn't change her purpose. She belonged here,

212

among these people. That was the most important thing.

Christopher straightened, stretching his cramped legs. "So what's for dinner?"

Ariel swung from the dressing table she'd been rearranging. Her jaw dropped open as she stared at him.

"You haven't forgotten?" he asked.

She bit her lip in anguish. She *had* forgotten. And more than anything she needed to be away from Christopher. But there was nothing to do for it now; she'd invited him and she couldn't very well take back her words. She'd just have to keep some distance between them. Then she'd be fine. "Chedyla, Lord Staunton will be dining with me. Could you please see that sufficient food for two is sent up."

"You'd better make that three," Christopher said, stretching first one leg, and then the other. "I missed the noon meal, and all this riding and fighting has left me starving."

"Shall I take the child?" Chedyla asked.

Ariel looked over to where he slept beside their game. The sight tugged at her heart. She'd never cared for a child before, and she was enjoying her time with the little boy very much. "Yes," she said with an unconscious sigh. "Sami will probably sleep straight through to morning. But call me," she said, following Chedyla to the door, "if he should wake and be frightened."

"Of course," Chedyla agreed as she carried the boy from the room.

"Sami? When did you start calling him that?" Coming up behind her, Christopher brushed her hair away from her neck as his lips caressed her skin. Ariel jumped, but held her place despite her heart's wildly beating warning that his kisses could destroy her self-possession.

"Just now, I suppose. I can't keep calling him nothing."

"Someday we'll have children of our own, Ariel. Many of them, I hope," he whispered against her ear.

Ariel flushed crimson and knotted the tail of her tunic around her fingers as she stared at the floor. What was she going to do? They were alone again, and he could unsettle her with a single touch. Every look from those midnight eyes struck straight to her core. Why, she hadn't managed one moment of self-possession since she'd set eyes on him. Somehow she had to break the cord between them. Somehow she had to make him give up this quest, this insane impossibility that they would be together. They could never, never be together. Her world was here, and his was England; and between them lay the chasm she would never cross.

"I can't marry you, Christopher."

"Why not?" he asked, peppering soft kisses across her shoulders.

She sighed. Turning in his arms to face him, she squared her shoulders. "I belong in Morocco. How often must I tell you?' "

"Until you say otherwise."

Ariel looked away. "I shall never say otherwise."

"Why? Who holds such a rein on your heart here?"

"No one," she insisted. His face was inches from hers, and she could feel his eyes on her, searching. But she couldn't look him in the eye for fear she would lose whatever remained of her control and agree to anything he wanted. Frustrated and heartsick, she tore away from him. "There is no one, Christopher. Just me. Just my own wish to stay here. Why do you ask me over and over if there is someone else?"

"Because I can't believe you'd throw away everything, your life included, for a *place*."

"For my *home*," she said emphatically. She crossed the room and stepped out onto the balcony overlooking the garden. Christopher followed her. He was trying to understand, she knew that. And she wanted him to understand, because she could no longer deny that she cared about him. Even now her skin tingled as the sleeve of his jacket brushed against her arm. He was handsome and kind, and she felt things she'd never dreamed of when he was with her. But the Maghreb, the land of the West, was her country, and she would remain loyal to it. She would not leave.

"My father left before I was born," she whispered, staring across the garden, and over the walls. "My mother died when I was eight. Whatever family they had never bothered to come after me. I think they'd heard the rumors that I was Mohammed's child. They must have been repelled by the thought that I might be some brown-skinned half-Moroccan. Chedyla, Siad, Mohammed—they're the only ones I have. They're my family, and I won't leave them."

"Ariel, it's not the same now."

"How do you know?" she said bitterly. She turned to face him. "I won't be what my father was. I won't be like his family, and turn my back on mine. I know what it means to be loyal, to be there when they need you."

"You're like a salmon swimming upstream, can't you see that? There's a difference between cold-heartedly abandoning someone, and leaving home because you've grown up. If your father and his family were guilty of the first, I'm sorry. But you can't remain a child forever, Ariel."

"I'm not a child!"

Christopher snorted. "Sometimes I think you're less equipped to face the world than that scared desert half-pint you found. He, at least, has his eyes open. You, on

215

the other hand, insist on hurtling around blind as a beggar while you dream up a landscape that's more to your liking. But it won't last, Ariel," he warned. "You're going to have to see the real world you live in one of these days. I just hope for your sake it's sooner rather than later." Angrily he strode to the far side of the balcony, and took up watch with one side shouldered against the wall.

Before them the sunset was fading from brilliant oranges and reds to a deep purple. The air was perfumed with the first opening sprays of night jasmine, and a nightingale sang sweetly. Ariel's eyes smarted with tears she refused to shed. Her heart ached as she silently watched the first stars appear overhead. She yearned for Christopher to wrap his arms around her, to kiss away the doubts she was beset by more every day, to love her as she had only dreamed of being loved before meeting him. But she knew he wouldn't. Not after what had just passed between them.

She turned to go inside, hesitating a moment to see if Christopher would look at her. Instead he let her pass, his gaze anchored on the darkness. Her heart sunk lower still. There was a soft knock at the door, and Chedyla entered, followed by half a dozen servants bearing their supper on silver trays. As they began to prepare the room, Ariel watched Christopher leaning tensely against the balcony. She tried to memorize everything about him at that moment. His strength, his warmth, the powerful contours of his back, the softly curling ends of his hair. Her fingers tingled with the memory of its thickness. For the first time in her life, she wished she was somewhere else. Somewhere where it would be possible to have all that she wanted—to be able to at least consider marrying Christopher, and still have her "family."

"Why couldn't you really have been a Berber warrior? Why did you have to be English?" she whispered to herself.

"The meal is served, Lord Staunton," Chedyla announced from the doorway.

Christopher looked over his shoulder at the diminutive duenna. She knew Ariel better than anyone, but revealed almost nothing about her charge. She and Siad were shadows, yet he sensed they were both on his side and wanted this match as much as he had come to want it. "Thank you, Chedyla."

"If there is nothing more you wish for, I shall see to other matters. I entrust my charge's welfare to you until I am able to return."

So she was leaving them alone. "I'm honored," he said, acknowledging the unspoken pact they entered into with a bow. Chedyla bowed in return and backed away. Sighing, he ran a hand through his hair. He was beginning to doubt his own sanity. He'd never pursued a woman with even a tenth of the determination he'd already invested in Ariel, and God only knew why. She was infuriatingly childish at times. So single-minded in her loyalties, so rooted and unyielding, that it was hard to believe she was the same woman who responded so sensitively to his touch. When he kissed her there was no pretense, not a drop of stubbornness. She was eager for every new sensation, and gave back twice what she took. She was an infuriating virago one minute, and a shy, eager woman-child the next. He was completely certain of only one thing: with Ariel there was only one hundred percent. Whatever she did, she did with her entire self. Whatever she believed in, she believed in completely, and that, combined with the promise her body held, was enough to drive a man insane. And insanity, if that was to be his fate,

217

would be worth it if he had Ariel in his arms.

Christopher straightened and stepped toward the room where Ariel waited. He stopped dead in the open doorway. The room had been transformed from a playroom for the little boy to a den of seduction. Candles had been set on every available surface. They warmed the room, yet left a canopy of darkness hanging from the domed ceiling overhead creating a cloak of intimacy. Before the fire a small table had been set with plates of gold and crystal goblets. Jasmine branches, set in tall vases, had been placed around the room, and he smiled as the first strains of a lute drifted up from the garden.

Ariel stood by the fire, unaware of his approach. Golden light framed her, outlining her slender form beneath her lilac tunic. She had drawn the sides of her hair back with a set of ivory combs, leaving the rest to cascade down her back in a sheet of honeyed gold that fell to her waist.

"You're more beautiful every time I see you," Christopher breathed. But Ariel was too lost in her own thoughts to hear him.

Coming to her side, he stretched his hand toward hers. "May I?" She jumped at the sound of his voice so close by, then smiled shyly at her reaction.

Despite her smile, he saw sadness in her eyes when she looked up and nodded. He wanted to pull her into his embrace and soothe away the cause of her unhappiness, but he stayed himself, determined to woo her gently, to prove his friendship first, and his desire after. Tucking her fingers into the crook of his arm, he led her the short distance to the table and held her seat. She murmured a quiet thank you as he took the opposite chair, and then silence settled over them.

Christopher watched as Ariel fidgeted with her tableware and finally settled for staring down at her hands in her lap while the meal was served. Was she so uncomfortable because of the tongue-lashing he'd given her? If anything, he thought she could use one or two more, but as the minutes stretched out and her quiet mood continued, Christopher began to feel tinges of guilt. He would tread a little more lightly with her in the future.

"The Bukhariyin were pushed back beyond the city again today," he commented, aware that any information on the revolt would draw her out of even this melancholy temperament.

Ariel looked up, her sadness fading as her interest was piqued, and Christopher couldn't help wondering again why her interest was so strong.

"The sultan's forces were able to follow them for quite a while; they're in the desert now. I think in a few days they'll be routed completely."

"What's left to be done?"

"The leaders still have not been identified. Until they can be captured or forced to surrender, the men who fight under them may continue to regroup and come back."

"How will we do that?"

"There are several possibilities," Christopher explained. "But I don't know what Mohammed Ben Abdullah is planning. I wasn't able to speak with either Suleiman or Yazid. Although it's understandable that Mohammed has been too busy to see him, Robert is hoping for an audience with the sultan tonight."

"Did you see the princes?"

"Not today, but they are both uninjured and at the Casbah."

"And the city is secure?"

Christopher nodded. "Much of the countryside surrounding Meknes as well."

"Then, there would be no danger in my going to the Casbah tomorrow."

Christopher frowned. "Why would you want to go there?"

"To see Suleiman and Yazid for myself."

"Ariel, they are fighting a battle for control of the country. They're not sitting around smoking a hookah all day. Even if I took you to the Casbah, there's very little chance either of them would be there."

"But if I sent a message?" she persisted.

"They can't schedule when there will be a battle and when there won't, Ariel."

"I know that," she said impatiently. "But neither side can fight in the dark out on the plains. There's no moon, and it's bound to be as black as pitch tonight. Surely, if we go late in the day, I can see them."

"It would mean staying overnight. It wouldn't be safe to come back in the dark, moon or no moon."

"Then, we'll stay!" Ariel cried in glee.

Christopher pinned her with an exasperated look. The little witch could connive her way into anything, he thought irritably. The last thing on earth he wanted was to take her to the Casbah. The trip might be achieved safely enough if they took a full guard with them, but the headquarters of a fighting army was no place for a woman. Mohammed Ben Abdullah would never approve of such a scheme, which meant he'd have to take her there without telling the sultan, and he didn't like that either. He had half a mind to say no and be done with it, but the thought of having her by his side for so long was tempting. And it would serve another purpose.

Taking Ariel out to see the princes would be the perfect opportunity to see Yazid. Despite all reports that Yazid was at the forefront of the fighting, Christopher

220

still had a keen sense that the heir was not all he appeared. Besides rumor and clandestine reports from informers, there was no other way to evaluate Yazid's actual threat.

"Christopher, please," she begged.

It grated on him that once again she was willing to beg for Yazid's sake when nothing else would have convinced her to be so compliant.

"I stayed in my room all day, just as you asked. I've heard nothing about their welfare except what you've just told me. Take me to see them. If you're there, what harm can come to me? I'll stay with you the entire time, I promise, and the next morning we'll come back. I just want to see them. Please."

He knew there was every likelihood that she'd go on her own if he refused her, and that he couldn't countenance. He leaned back in his chair, letting the steaming bowl of couscous before him cool. "All right," he said quietly. "Tomorrow, if it's safe, we'll go."

"Thank you, oh, thank you!" she cried, nearly leaping out of her chair.

"I haven't finished," he asserted, interrupting her euphoria. "Beginning with the moment we set foot outside the walls of El Bedi and ending not one minute sooner than our return, you will stay with me. You will ride with me, eat with me, and do whatever I tell you, *without question*. Aside from our sleeping arrangements, you're to be at my side at all times. Is that clear, Ariel?"

Ariel's eye shone mutinously, but she gave him a curt nod. "I understand."

"And you agree."

She rolled her eyes in exasperation. "I agree. Now, can we please finish supper. I thought you were starving."

Christopher leaned over the couscous, ignoring it.

"Don't misunderstand, Ariel. Both our lives may depend on it."

"Sometimes you're very melodramatic."

"Sometimes you're very naive."

"We'll be with Suleiman and Yazid. I can't imagine a safer place," Ariel told him.

"Don't take anyone for granted, Ariel. Not even 'family.' "

"Don't you trust anyone, Christopher? It must be difficult going through life like that—always looking over your shoulder. Always being alone."

He stared at her. She couldn't possibly know what she was talking about, but he felt like she'd pulled the dust cover off wounds he'd thought were long forgotten. "Trust isn't part of a man's natural tendencies," he said, his jaw tightening so that he had to consciously unclench his teeth.

"Nor is it something withheld without reason," she responded blithely, resuming her meal. "I'll be right by your side tomorrow. You needn't wring promises from me."

Christopher attacked his meal, tearing the meat off a roast leg of pigeon with his teeth in cold silence. Damn her, he thought, tossing the bird down on his plate. His appetite was gone. Chedyla's efforts with the music, flowers and candles were wasted. The past had seeped into the room, and he could no more think about seducing her here than if his father had been standing beside him.

He sat back in the chair and took a long sip of wine. Why was she always getting under his skin, uncovering thoughts he'd rather forget, asking him to rethink decisions he'd made years before? Did she deserve his trust simply because she'd never done anything outright to earn his *dis*trust? Every one of Christopher's instincts

222

had been honed on his belief that you trusted no one at first blush. But this wasn't the first time he and Ariel had been together. She'd honored her promises to him: She'd been there at the stable. She'd come to the dinner, and even if he had found her with Yazid, he'd had no proof that she'd been eluding him that night. She hadn't wanted his company the other day on the trip to the souk, but she'd been honest in that at least.

He watched Ariel across the table, where she was keeping a wary eye on him while she ate. Maybe Robert was right. She was going to be his wife. Maybe now was the time to put the past behind him, and start trusting. It wouldn't be much of a marriage without it. He wanted her to have the life she dreamed of, a life she could never have here. But he couldn't give that to her without trust. Maybe this was a chance to put his father's cruelty, and Stephan's stupidity, behind him. Maybe Ariel was the key that could free him.

Chapter Seventeen

Ariel clipped another snow-white calla lily and laid it in the straw basket hanging from her arm. Shielding her eyes with one hand, she peered impatiently at the sun.

"Planning a rendezvous this afternoon?"

Ariel slanted Carmela a piqued look. "I just 'wondered' what time it was," she said, avoiding either an affirmation or denial of the comment.

"Then, this makes the tenth time you've wondered since we came out. The only time I ever cared so much about the time was when I was meeting Paulo in the woods behind our Gypsy wagon."

"Carmela, I am not sneaking off to meet anyone."

"Not even the black warrior from the *fantasia?* Everyone has heard that he was your duke in masquerade. *Mierda,* you should have seen Daiwa! She was furious. I had such a day watching her fume. Ariel—" Carmela turned somber and laid a warning hand on Ariel's arm—"beware of her. She hates you more than ever."

Ariel pursed her lips and nodded. It was true, but there was nothing she could do about Daiwa, except stay out of her way. The two women moved down the long rows of flowers in the walled garden, each lost in her own thoughts as they plucked the freshest blossoms for their bouquets.

"Hmmm, smell this," Carmela said, holding a blood-red rose out to Ariel. "This is a rose to swoon over! A rose to dance with, to toss to your lover as a secret signal for him to meet you when the campfires are low and the old women sleep." Dropping her basket on the grass, Carmela clutched the stem between her teeth and began swaying and twirling in a circle around Ariel. Over her head she clapped her hands together and tossed her black hair about her shoulders as she whirled. Dancing in front of Ariel, she pulled the rose from between her teeth and dropped it at her feet, then ran to hide behind the narrow trunk of an almond tree.

Ariel laughed. "I'm coming, my love," she called, snatching up the flower as she joined the game. Carmela ducked beneath the low branches and scooted to another hiding place behind the fountain while Ariel gave chase. Five sprints later Ariel gave up, tossing the rose at Carmela as she dropped onto the grass. "You're too evasive!" She laughed. "This man hasn't the stamina to catch you."

Carmela collapsed beside her, lying on her back to look up at the morning sun. "You don't understand desire. Paulo would never have given up. But then, he would have caught me at the almond tree." She sighed.

"There's no use pining over him, Carmela. He's gone, and you're here. It's a different world for you now. Someday you'll forget him."

Rising on one elbow, Carmela shook her head. "You're wrong, my friend, but that's not your fault. You don't yet understand passion. Once you've tasted it with the right man, you'll see. Without it, life is pale."

Ariel twisted a blade of grass between her fingers,

uncomfortable with the feeling Carmela's words spawned. That was part of the attraction she felt for Christopher. Whenever they were together the world was sharper, its colors brighter. It wasn't only when he kissed her; the feeling could be sparked by their conversation. Just being near him made her see the world differently. She'd expected life to go on just as it had once Christopher returned to England, but listening to Carmela she realized it wouldn't. She'd miss all the things he'd introduced to her. The ideas, the respect, the easy camaraderie, they were all things she'd never encountered before in a man.

And the kisses, the warm curls of attraction that steamed her insides when she was in his embrace, she'd miss them, too. She was surprised that those feelings didn't scare her anymore. She thought of them now as cozy, comfortable things. Feelings that were more natural than beating her way through life on her own. With a sinking heart she realized when Christopher left he'd take all those things with him, and she'd miss them dreadfully.

"So when do you see him again?"

"Tonight," Ariel replied, knowing exactly who she was talking about, and all at once tired of denials. "He's taking me to the Casbah to see Yazid and Suleiman."

"What do you want with those two?"

Ariel laughed. "You only have one use for males in your life, Carmela. But there are other reasons to see a man besides "passion.""

"Humpf," Carmela huffed, shaking the grass off her pantaloons as she rose. "Maybe, but Moulay El Yazid is Daiwa's son. If I were you, I'd keep my distance."

"I only want to know that he and Suleiman are safe. Besides, he's been very kind to me."

226

Carmela gave her a hard look. "When has Mohammed El Yazid ever been kind to you?"

Ariel faltered, momentarily unable to think of a way to avoid explaining their alliance to her. "He's been understanding about my wish to stay here."

"Then, you still do not want to marry the Englishman?"

Ariel hesitated. "I care for Christopher. He's kind, and handsome, and . . . I'm sure he'd make a wonderful husband, Carmela. But our lives are too different. I just can't leave El Bedi. How I feel about Christopher isn't going to change that."

The Gypsy concubine's full lips curled into a knowing smile. "Now I see everything," she said, starting back the way they'd come. "You are falling in love with him."

"I'm *not* falling in love with him!" Ariel insisted, running to catch up with her. "You and your overwrought romanticism!"

Carmela continued down the grassy path, unperturbed. "He is handsome, and strong. Every woman who sees him swoons; it's natural that you're crazy for him, too."

"I know him better than any of those women. He's a liar and a conniver."

She shrugged. "So are all men, *mi amor.*"

"He only wants his treaty, not me."

Carmela stopped and looked at her with one black eyebrow cocked. "Oh, he wants you. If that's what you're worried about, you can stop."

"What are you talking about?" Ariel demanded.

"Do you remember the *fantasia?* He rode boldly up to the tent and stared right in, do you remember?"

"Of course," Ariel replied, wondering how she would ever be able to forget that night.

"I thought he looked at me. But as soon as our eyes touched I knew I was wrong. He was looking for someone, but it wasn't me. I know that look. A man doesn't look like that when he's searching for a friend, or for a possession. He was looking for his *amor*. His lover."

Ariel stopped in her tracks, staring at Carmela's back as her friend handed her basket to an odalisque and disappeared inside the palace. Carmela could take the most obvious thing and twist it around until it reeked of passion. Ariel, at least, could see things as they were. Christopher had agreed to marry her because he thought she was in danger, and—despite his denials—she was certain that expediting the treaty had played a part in his decision. Ariel didn't deny that Christopher found her company pleasant enough—most of the time, she amended, thinking of the way he had of looking right through her when he was displeased. But he certainly wasn't in love with her. They had struck upon a pleasant friendship, that was all. And there was still the matter of his duping her when she'd trusted him. No, he wasn't in love with her any more than she was in love with him.

With a self-fulfilling nod, Ariel started after her friend. But for the rest of the day, a melancholy mood pursued her that she couldn't shake off.

Yazid galloped across the barren steppe with an entourage of only one. Chen was the only man he trusted to keep his mouth shut about this meeting. Over and over again the Mongolian had proven he cared nothing about what he did in Morocco; thus there was no worry that he might use his information against them. He was as ruthless and cold a man as Yazid had met, and that suited his needs well. He executed orders to the letter and without compunction. The only time he had failed Yazid was with the infidel.

That imbecile eunuch of Ariel's had appeared out of nowhere to defend the man's back. He should have killed Siad Ben Bahkar when he'd had the chance years ago. But Raisuli's idea had sounded better. Who would have believed the giant Berber they'd caught spying on them would survive having his manhood taken from him? Yazid had been certain he would die a terrible death, which was better than killing him outright. But he had survived, and then that damned daughter of his father's lover had taken him in. The gelding needed his brain cut out as well. He still thought he was a full man, and because of him the Mongolian hadn't been able to strike the infidel from behind.

Attacking his flank, Chen had barely escaped, or so he claimed. Yazid hadn't stayed to watch for himself. He'd taken no chance of being seen close to the Mongolian. When he'd reached their meeting place, Chen had told Yazid that the infidel's scimitar had been like curved lightning, coming from all directions at once. He'd had to sacrifice his horse, sliding off the far side at the last moment so that the infidel's blade skewered the horse's belly rather than his. Then he'd disappeared on foot amid the horses and fighting.

The Mongolian had no respect for Allah's animal. But then, he was godless. A heathen. Occasionally Yazid worried about his association with the heathen, but he dismissed it. His great plan was for the betterment of Allah's world. He would banish the tainting influence of infidels that his own father welcomed on their soil. Now he would rid the Maghreb of the foul stench of Christians once and for all.

A tent had been set up in the grove of cypress that

229

stood oasislike on the plain. As they approached, the flap opened, and his mother appeared in the entrance. Even from a distance, her stance was rigid. Daily now she became more tyrannical, swollen with the certainty of his victory, and stuffed with lust for the power she would wield when he was sultan. Or so she thought. But he was a patient man. He had been patient for a very long time, and now everything was coming to him. Everything he'd waited for so patiently. His mother thought she was going to run the government. He knew that. She believed this would be her victory, that he would become one of her puppets like the viziers she plied with opium and wide legs. Well, he thought, let her. She would see her mistake soon enough. Victory was only days away. He could taste it. He could play the charade one more time. But this would be the last time he would be the obedient son for her, or for Mohammed Ben Abdullah.

Yazid galloped straight at the tent, pulling Sirocco to a stop so close to his mother that a cloud of dust billowed over her. The black eunuchs worked furiously with their ostrich feather fans to beat away the dust, but his mother never moved.

"What has kept you! I, your mother, have waited in the heat of midday at great discomfort more than one hour."

"Forgive me, Mother," Yazid said, his voice hard while he bowed deferentially.

Daiwa glared at him, letting her ruffled dignity settle. "Come inside, there is not much time. I must return."

Yazid followed her into the tent. For all that it was a temporary shelter, the tent was as richly appointed as any room in the palace. Thick Persian rugs had been

230

layered one atop the other, and hung along the tent walls. Pillows had been scattered, and a silver pot of mint tea with matching tea glasses was ready for them. At his mother's nod, a eunuch served them while four more stirred the air with fans. They were all dumb, their tongues cut out at youth for the very purpose they now served. One could not speak in confidence when there were tongues to pass tales.

"What news have you?" Daiwa demanded.

She did not bother with polite inquiries about his well-being, Yazid noted cynically. "All goes as planned."

"Then, tonight you take the Casbah?"

"No." Yazid took a long, loud sip of his tea and helped himself to a pastry. "I have decided to join the Bukhariyin in the desert for a few days before we take the fort."

"That is not what we planned!" Daiwa pounded one fist into the palm of her hand, the enormous rings on each finger clinking against each other with every movement. "We must take our victory now! The viziers and the others who are with us grow anxious. They do not see the Bukhariyin, nor do they see you leading them. At the palace all the talk is of Abdullah's victories, of Suleiman taking the Casbah and chasing the Bukhariyin from the city. They must see victory!"

Yazid stiffened, eyeing his mother coldly over the rim of his glass. He repeated his decision, emphasizing each word with frigid precision. "I have decided to join my forces in the desert."

"Why!"

"I do not need to explain this to you. I have been trained for combat all my life. You saw to that yourself, my mother. If the viziers are losing their spine, if they want to turn and run like mongrels, let them. When I

231

am sultan I will deal with them as I will all traitors. They will pay the price of their fear. Tell them *that*, if they are so anxious for news."

Daiwa glared at him, her eyes cold and angry; but she did not deny him, and that pleased Yazid greatly. She was beginning to fear him. That thought made him feel magnanimous, so he fed her some of what she wanted. "I have not met with the Bukhariyin since the revolt. They have performed based on nothing but our plans before the *fantasia*. If we are to succeed, they must see with their own eyes and hear with their own ears that I am with them. And that I am their leader. This is much more important than holding the hands of your viziers."

His mother smiled and nodded. "Very good, my son. I shall relate your message to the viziers. Now, tell me, how many days until you attack the Casbah and kill that meddlesome issue of a concubine?"

"Five days at the most. By that time, Suleiman will be complacent. He will suspect nothing. He won't even know what to do when we strike. He is the least of my worries."

"And then?"

"Then, I go on to El Bedi."

"You will send our signal first."

Yazid gave a barely perceptible nod. "As has been planned."

"Good. I am well pleased, my son. I await the day when you reign as sultan."

The muscle in Yazid's cheek ticked. She was dismissing him. His mother was as much a fool as all the rest of them. But his day was on the horizon. In a black haze he rose and strode out of the tent, not even bothering to bow.

232

As the sound of Yazid's departure faded in the still air, Daiwa settled back against a pillow and helped herself to a pastry.

"Shall I give orders to prepare for our return to the palace, O great Sultana?"

"No, Raisuli," she said, smiling to herself. "There is no rush."

Chapter Eighteen

Ariel hummed to herself as the little mare pranced beneath her, full of the adventuresome spirit that had taken hold of both horse and rider. The Casbah was quite close now; a good thing Ariel thought to herself, for the sun was hanging low in the cloudless sky. They'd have arrived hours earlier, but Christopher had surprised her by stopping at the souk as soon as they left El Bedi that morning. Even now the memory made a smile appear on her lips. Dressed in her white djellaba and turban, she'd been able to wander from stall to stall to her heart's content. Not a single man had leered at her or been scandalized by her exposed face. Occasionally her oohs and aahs, coupled with Christopher's attentiveness at her side, had caused a few sidelong glances. But her voluminous clothing hid her curved shape quite nicely, and she'd been enjoying herself too thoroughly to pay much attention.

As she was learning was always the case, Christopher had left nothing to chance. When she'd visited so many merchants that she couldn't remember which stalls she'd yet to see, her purchases were heaped on the back of a camel and returned to the palace. She and Christopher had continued to the outskirts of Meknes, where

Siad met them with a contingent of five guards. Ariel ticked off the items that would already be piled at the foot of her bed.

She'd chosen two beautifully woven baskets and a bolt of green brocade backed with silver for Chedyla. The fabric would set off her dark features beautifully. For Siad she'd ordered a pair of boots made of the best Moroccan leather. They would be ready in three days, and she planned to give them to him as a way of thanking Siad for protecting Christopher during the revolt. One merchant had shown her an exquisite pistol with inlaid ivory along the handle. She'd thought Yazid would admire such a weapon, but recalling their last meeting, she hadn't bought it. Instead she'd found gifts for Rhima and Carmela. Deep in the pocket of her djellaba was her gift for Christopher. It had been difficult to place the clandestine order, but while Christopher had been inspecting a particularly fine saddle, she'd whispered her hurried instructions to the merchant, arranging to pass by the stall for her purchase before leaving the souk. She smiled now, feeling the weight of the specially made amulets against her hip. They would be a fine goodbye gift. Despite the fact that she would be staying here when he returned to England, she wanted him to remember her. And the amulets would keep him safe. She would feel better about their parting knowing Allah would be watching over him.

"Are you having second thoughts?"

Ariel looked up to find that Christopher had finished talking to Siad and come up to ride beside her.

"No. Not at all." She smiled at him confidently, wondering why Christopher was always able to read her thoughts so easily. Tonight would be the first time she'd seen Yazid since the *fantasia*. Over and over she'd told herself that what had happened that night between them was nothing. Still, she couldn't rid herself of her apprehension. A quick shiver ran down her spine, and her mount tossed her head, sensing Ariel's nervousness.

"We can still turn back," Christopher told her, assessing the sunlight still left in the day. "We'd get to El Bedi just at nightfall."

Ariel shook her head adamantly, casting aside her worries. "If anything, I'm anxious to get there. It's been a long, slow ride up this mountainside."

"Has it? Then, I'll race you to the gates. Do you think your riding skills have come back to you enough for that?"

"Definitely," Ariel replied, delighted to have something to take her mind off Yazid. "And what's more," she added with a jaunty grin, "this little mare and I will leave that hulking stallion of yours in the dust."

"Then, would you be willing to make a wager?"

Ariel gave him an imperious look down her nose. "Allah does not condone wagers, Lord Staunton."

"Then, an agreement. Allah wouldn't object to something so innocent."

Ariel thought for a moment, then smiled and nodded.

"Supper." Knitting her brows, she looked up at him. "If you win, you can have supper with the princes—as I'm sure you'd like. But if I win, you dine with me."

Ariel was on the verge of explaining that the princes would never condone her eating with them in the first place. It wasn't a woman's place to eat with a man, but she stopped herself, deciding that either way she'd rather have supper with Christopher than eat alone. And she was too embarrassed to tell him the truth. "Agreed." Squeezing her legs around the mare's ribs, she left Christopher, the guards and Siad behind. She didn't look back, but leaned forward against the horse's neck. "He'll have to work hard to catch us," she said into one curved ear. "Run like the wind."

Ariel didn't have to urge the gray mare. The two flew over the dirt road. They rounded a curve, and the road turned sharply up the mountainside. The mare, named Babouche since she was as petite as the little slippers women wore, was breathing hard. Ariel gave her her head, stretching out over her neck until the scarlet tassels on the bridle tickled her nose. She pulled Babouche up before the gate amid shouts from the guards in the watchtowers. Christopher was right behind her.

"We come in the name of Sultan Mohammed Ben Abdullah to see the princes," Christopher called out in Arabic.

"Sohda Agadir?" one guard called down. "Open the gates!" he shouted to the men below. "The Sohda Agadir comes to meet with our princes!" As the gates were slowly rolled open, Christopher walked his stallion over to Ariel.

"You see, your stallion couldn't beat a daughter of the desert." She laughed gaily.

"You cheated," Christopher replied with a wry smile. "You didn't wait for Siad to say 'go.' Besides, I thought you would need this." He handed her the unraveled remains of her turban. Ariel's jaw dropped. He had stopped to pick her turban up off the road and had still arrived at the gate only a heartbeat behind her. "I suppose this means you'll want to have supper with me regardless of my winning."

Christopher gave her a surly smile. "Of course. But unless you want to create pandemonium among Suleiman and Yazid's well-trained corps, I suggest you get that turban in place before anyone inside sees you."

Ariel quickly wound the length of cotton into an expert turban, and by the time they were ready to enter the Casbah, she looked the perfect, if diminutive, apprentice guard.

It took much longer than Ariel had anticipated—nearly an hour—for them to be shown to the princes. Besides waiting for Siad to arrive, there were the throngs of soldiers and Berber loyalists who insisted on meeting Christopher. Apparently, Siad had been right about the following he'd won in the past three days. Coming up behind her, one Berber gave her a hearty slap on the back as he waited for his turn to speak with the Sohda Agadir.

"Allah smiles on you, boy, giving you to such a great warrior," the desert-toughened Moroccan said. "But you'd do well to disguise your adoration. You're looking like a lovesick girl. Allah forbids such relations between a man and a boy. And the Sohda Agadir needs a sturdy guard by his side. So toughen up, son."

Appalled by the man's implication that she'd been staring with adoration at Christopher, Ariel tried to hang farther back in the crowd; but Christopher said something she couldn't hear to one of the soldiers, and a moment later Ariel found herself grabbed by the scruff of her neck and lifted off her feet as she was handed from man to man.

"Here he is!" the same gruff nomad declared, setting her down beside Christopher. "Puny little desert mouse. If you're looking for a boy to sharpen your scimitar, I have seven sons who would be proud to do your bidding."

Christopher nodded at the Berber and laughed as he clamped his fingers on Ariel's shoulder. "I'll keep that in mind, but for now I'm well pleased with this one."

"I'm surprised he can lift your boots," a soldier called out, and the group roared with laughter.

"Don't let looks deceive you, my friend," Christopher

238

countered. "That's a warrior's first lesson." The men in the crowd murmured in agreement, praising the astuteness of this infidel warrior. At Christopher's bidding, a path opened in the crowd so that Christopher and Ariel could pass. And it was all Ariel could do to keep from kicking the shin of the Berber who'd called her a mouse.

When they finally reached the room that was the command post for the sultan's forces, it was only Suleiman who rose to greet them. "Lord Staunton, welcome. I'm honored to see you. I only hope Allah saw fit to send you with good news."

Delighted to see Suleiman, Ariel stepped forward, her male persona momentarily forgotten. "Suleiman, I'm so glad you're safe!"

The prince stared at her as his mouth dropped open, then turned to the two soldiers guarding the room. "Leave us." The minute the men were gone, Suleiman turned on her reproachfully. "What are you doing here? This is no place for a woman. Every one of the men in my army has looked upon your face. You are too old for such childish pranks!" Turning to Christopher, he continued. "Lord Staunton, I realize Ariel is your betrothed and as such is in your charge, but I am deeply distressed that you've allowed her to accompany you here. And dressed as a boy!"

"I thought that better than having her come dressed as a woman, Moulay Suleiman. And since it was either bring her with me, or have her sneak out on her own, I thought this was the better of the two options."

Ariel stepped in front of Christopher. "It was my idea to come. I was so worried about you and Yazid. I told Christopher I had to see for myself that you were well and safe. We've arrived safely, so don't reprimand me, please."

239

Suleiman shook his head, hiding a smile. "You are as stubborn as a camel, Ariel, and sometimes twice as obstinate. Very well, you are here, and I suppose there's nothing to do for it except see that you get back safely."

"You're not going to send me back right now!" Ariel exclaimed in distress. "We've just arrived, and I've brought things to stay the night. Christopher said we couldn't make the trip back in the dark. Suleiman," she begged. "Please, I want to hear all about the battles, and I haven't seen Yazid."

Suleiman looked out at the setting sun and shook his head. "It will be getting dark soon. I suppose there is no choice. I'll make arrangements for you both to stay. And I'll tell you what I can about the insurrection, little as that is. But I'm afraid you'll have to settle for seeing me. Yazid left this morning with a battalion of men."

"Left?" Christopher asked sharply.

Suleiman nodded. "At dawn. We have reports that the Bukhariyin have regrouped near the foothills of the Middle Atlas. It is my brother's intention to attack the traitors before they can reform their ranks and come back to Meknes. He believes he can destroy what is left of their forces in a surprise attack."

"It's a day's ride to the foothills, isn't it?"

The prince nodded.

Ariel listened carefully. For her part, she was having a hard time disguising her relief at knowing she didn't have to face Yazid quite yet. But she recognized the shuttered look on Christopher's face. Something was bothering him. Something he didn't wish to discuss with Suleiman. Although she was dying to know what it was, she knew that until she could get him to herself, there was no use trying to discuss it. Instead she turned her attention to the maps spread in the center of the rug. "Explain to me what is happening, Suleiman."

240

He smiled. "I always said you spent too much time with the tutors." Ariel smiled back. "After the initial battle at the *fantasia*," Suleiman explained, settling onto a pillow as he bent over the maps, "the Bukhariyin were beaten back beyond the city walls. But we erred in not pursuing them farther. They used the night to re-organize, and in the morning attacked with renewed strength."

Dropping down beside him, Ariel listened as Suleiman explained the various stages the battle had gone through, pointing out the locations of skirmishes and larger battles on the map. It was clear by the frustration in his voice that they'd repeatedly underestimated the insurrectionist's abilities.

"They always seem to know where to strike," she commented.

Suleiman looked up and nodded, a gleam of respect in his dark eyes. Christopher continued to look at the map, his gaze moving between the place where the Casbah was marked on the map and the estimated location of the Bukhariyin Yazid was on his way to defeat.

"Would the Bukhariyin attack Fez?" Christopher asked, never taking his eyes off the map.

"It's possible, but unlikely I think. The pasha of Fez is a weakling. It would be easy enough to oust him once they took El Bedi. He'd probably run off without a fight."

"Would he join them?"

Suleiman's head jerked up, meeting Christopher's level look. He nodded slowly.

"The only reason I can see that they would choose to camp between the two cities is if they could get supplies and possibly reinforcements from Fez."

"I will run the spineless leech through with my own sword," Suleiman vowed. "He is my father's uncle, and a more worthless man I have yet to meet."

"Let me take the guards who came with us today and a half score of your men tomorrow and I'll circle around behind the Bukhariyin. Then we'll know for certain," Christopher said.

"The mountains are treacherous. The Atlas are no place for men who aren't familiar with the land."

"I know my way through the mountains." Both Ariel and Suleiman looked at Christopher in surprise, but he offered them no explanation.

"Why don't you send a messenger to Yazid, Suleiman?" Ariel asked. "He could send men just as easily, and he needs to be warned. If the Bukhariyin are well supplied and have more men in their ranks, Yazid might be overtaken in the fighting." Christopher was watching her intently, and Ariel fidgeted, looking away as she waited for Suleiman to comment.

The prince pursed his lips. "Yazid must be warned. But if we don't know that my uncle has become a traitor for certain, Yazid could lose his opportunity to strike."

"He could be caught in a trap!" she exclaimed in agitation. How could Suleiman, who always put everyone else first, consider not warning the sultan's first son?

"Let me ride tomorrow, Suleiman," Christopher said.

The prince rubbed his palm across his forehead. "I must think on this. We'll discuss it later."

Ariel was about to protest, but clamped her mouth shut when Christopher shot her a warning look. She would simply speak to Suleiman later when Christopher was not there. Then she could argue for Yazid's safety without having Christopher staring at her as though she had two heads.

Suleiman clapped his hands twice, and the guards returned from their posts just outside the door. "Have two rooms prepared for Lord Staunton and his, ah, boy," he ordered. After the guards had left, he turned back to the maps, staring down at it indecisively. "It is so hard to know what to do sometimes. I will seek Allah's guidance now."

Ariel and Christopher took their leave, and as they headed down the cavernous hallway of the fortress, Ariel began to worry about just what sleeping arrangements the guards might deem suitable for a warrior and his "puny boy." She needn't have worried. After several twists and turns, they were shown to one of the towers where an enormous suite of rooms had been hastily prepared for them. Christopher was ushered into the large center room. A fire had just been set to warm the stone walls against the first drafts of the evening cold. Ariel began to step into the room when a broad arm prohibited her from further entrance.

"Your room is here," the guard pronounced, nodding to a considerably smaller door just to the right. Pushing the door open, she walked into a narrow room without even a slit for air in the wall and no fire.

"A fitting cell for a cheat," Christopher said, coming up behind her.

"I can't possibly stay here," she replied, trying to hide her chagrin. "Our rooms are connected. Suleiman would never allow that."

Christopher called to a slave, and a moment later he was scurrying off in search of another room for Ariel to spend the night in. "While you're waiting, I'm more than happy to share my fire for a while."

Ariel retreated agreeably back to his room which not only had a fireplace, but two windows and beautiful wall hangings for decoration. Ignoring the fire, she went to the wall, running her fingers across the fine weave of one of the rugs.

"Do you know much about rugs?" Christopher asked.

243

"I've never seen one like this. It's almost like a symbol of some sort." She traced the interwoven stems that led to a profusion of stylized orange and yellow flowers encircled by black swirls.

"It's probably the coat of arms of one of the old dynasties. I'm surprised it's still here. Someone must have overlooked it when the old powers were overthrown."

"It's beautiful. Powerful, yet peaceful." Ariel's hand followed the arc of the black circle, then stopped. Walking quickly to the edge of the rug, she pulled it away from the wall. A cloud of dust filled the room.

Christopher coughed as he came striding over to her. "What are you doing?"

"I felt something behind the rug."

Christopher helped her pull the ancient rug away from the wall, sending centuries more dust into the air. When they had shoved it more than halfway, they found a doorway in the stone wall.

"Where do you think it leads?" Ariel asked, curiosity sending prickles of excitement up and down her spine.

Christopher laughed and shoved the rug farther out of the way. "I don't think you've made any great discovery. It's obviously a door onto the ramparts. This is a tower room, probably reserved for the use of the sultan's family. I'm sure all the tower rooms have doors onto the walls; it's basic fortress construction."

Ariel's disappointment only lasted an instant. "Let's try it."

Obligingly, Christopher put his shoulder to the door. "Stand back," he said when it wouldn't budge after several tries. Giving it a good kick, the door burst open, and Ariel ran to have a look.

Just as Christopher had predicted, they were standing at the end of the west-facing wall of the Casbah. The wall was thick, and the walkway before them wide.

Ariel stepped out into the evening. The sun was gone, and overhead the stars patterned the blackness.

"There's something special about these ancient places," Christopher said. "Blantyre's like this."

"Blantyre?"

"My family's home. It's not a castle," he continued, "but it's a grand old manor house. My mother's ancestors have lived there for generations. There's something about knowing so many lives have passed through it. It's mellow, like the stone this is made of. You won't find any rough edges or sharp corners here, Ariel. Everything has been sanded by the wind until it fits together perfectly."

Ariel walked over to the wall, touching the Moroccan red stone. Listening to Christopher, she could picture the slaves fitting the newly shaven blocks into place, sweating under the same sun in a different century. He was right; time had mellowed them. The crevices between one block and another were barely discernable. She leaned lightly against the stone barrier and looked across the darkness.

"It's the same sky in England," Christopher said, coming to stand behind her. "The same stars. There are more clouds, and it's often chilly and damp, but there are balls and soirees and dinner parties where women are welcome—fawned over in fact. There are discussions on politics and theater, and rides in the parks. It's a different world, but it has all the things you're longing for, Ariel. Give yourself a chance to have those things. I can give them to you, and more. You only have to stop fighting me. You have to trust me."

His hands slid across her shoulders, caressing her neck. Ariel closed her eyes, shutting out the darkness, letting the images he conjured come alive in her mind. It *would* be wonderful to use her mind to debate important issues as she had today with Suleiman and Christopher, to hear the musical virtuosos of the world, to ride every day, to visit the village whenever she pleased without the cover of a disguise. Today had been a taste of what lay outside the walls of El Bedi, and she'd drank it in like someone who until that moment had only tasted musty well water and then sips from a mountain spring. All he was asking in exchange was that she trust his judgment. He wanted her to believe him when he told her he knew she would be happier there than here. Christopher knew both worlds while she knew only this one. Did she trust him?

Christopher's hands slid down around her waist, and he bent to nuzzle her earlobe. His kisses sent delicious shivers racing through her. But Ariel needed to think. She was too close to something important. She sensed herself on the verge of a discovery that had the power to change her life forever, and much as she would love to give in to the temptation of Christopher's kisses, she needed to hang on to this feeling right now, before she lost it. Turning in his arms, she tried to deflect his attentions as gently as possible.

"Christopher, please—"

"Anything you wish," he answered just before he covered her mouth with his. For a moment Ariel let the deliciousness of his kiss fill her, and the urge to push aside her thoughts and revel in the delights of his kisses was a powerful one. But she couldn't. She needed to think things out, and she needed to do it now.

Gently pressing her hands against his chest, she broke off their kiss. "Christopher," she tried again. He tipped her face up, and the tenderness she saw in his eyes sent a sensation of pure sweetness running through her. He only waited a heartbeat before dropping his gaze to her lips and dipping his head to catch them up in another kiss. If she gave in again, Ariel knew she was lost. Insistently, she pushed away from him. Not wishing him to think she was rejecting his advances outright, Ariel chose to separate them by stepping back against the rampart wall. Too late she sensed that something was wrong, that where there should have been a solid wall behind her there was nothing. She heard the scrape of stone moving upon stone as the wall gave way beneath the weight of her body pushing away from Christopher. She had the strangest feeling as she realized she was going to fall. Almost as though it wasn't her who was falling away from Christopher. She tried to regain her balance, to pull herself back toward him, but she knew that it was impossible. She'd depended on the wall being there, and now, with an awful certainty, she felt her balance slip away. She was falling from the collapsing edge of the rampart. A strangled cry came from somewhere. Ariel wondered vaguely who it was, and why the last sound she would ever hear was one she couldn't even identify.

"Ariel!" Christopher leapt toward her, his fingers fastening around one slender wrist. As she went over the edge, the downward pull of her weight yanked him forward, but he only locked his grip tighter, bracing his free hand against a sturdier part of the disintegrating wall.

More of the wall crumbled, and Ariel pulled away, trying to save Christopher from falling with her.

"No!" he commanded, yanking her against the hard red stones. Her feet dangled beneath her, her arm stretched to its limits. "I'm going to pull hard on your arm," he told her, squeezing his words between the effort of holding on to her. "It will hurt. Hang on, and whatever you do, don't look down."

Ariel squeezed her eyes shut, letting out a whimper

when he wrenched her arm. Then she was being lifted into his arms, scraped and bloodied, but safe on the solid rock of the rampart. She collapsed against him as he wrapped his arms around her. In the security of his embrace, Ariel could feel his arms shake from the effort of her rescue.

"Dear God," he whispered, pulling her tight against his chest. "Don't ever waste so much for want of escape from a kiss."

Ariel looked up, trying to tell him that she hadn't meant to evade his kiss so adamantly, but the effort was beyond her. Then, without a word, Christopher swept her up into his arms, bearing her to safety.

When she awoke she was in a strange room, and it was as dark as pitch. Her arm ached terribly, and Ariel shivered at the thought of how close to death she'd come. The embers in the grate barely glowed. She was about to nestle deeper into the down comforter when she heard a movement in the shadows. "Christopher?" she asked quietly. A black-gloved hand slid over her mouth, and she was suddenly inches away from the flat face of Yazid's servant.

"Shhhh." He held a finger in the air, staring at her with his hand still over her mouth until Ariel nodded that she understood. "Come," he said removing his hand just enough to allow her to talk.

"Where is Mohammed El Yazid?" she demanded.

"Come!"

"Does Yazid need to see me?"

The man nodded.

"Have you a message from him?" she asked.

"No message. You come with me."

"But how am I to know—"

248

"I take you to him before, *ya hagga.*"

Ariel nodded, but despite the truth of his statement, every fiber of her intuition warned her away from this man. "Where is Yazid?"

"We hurry. Time is precious."

"Wait outside," Ariel said, her decision made.

"Time is precious! No waiting."

"I can't ride dressed like this," she told him, her words clipped in irritation. "Wait outside, I'll be right there."

The man gave her a hard stare and slipped out the door. Ariel was out of bed in an instant. Searching through the dark, she located her djellaba, trousers, and boots. As she slipped out of the sheer nightgown, she wondered if Christopher had put it on her. The thought sent warm delight flooding through her, but she had no time to waste on such contemplations. In a matter of minutes she had donned her clothes. Snatching up the material for her turban, she gave it a quick look and then tossed it back on the chair. There wasn't time, and besides, they'd be riding in the dark, miles from anyone. She wouldn't need the head covering. Ariel stepped into the hall. Yazid's man was there, waiting motionless in the dark hall. There were no guards in sight, and it crossed Ariel's mind as strange that Christopher wouldn't have made sure the room was guarded in case of trouble.

He started down a darkened staircase she'd never seen before. "Wait," Ariel whispered. "I have to leave a message for someone."

His eyes narrowed. "No message."

"But I have —"

"No message, *ya hagga.* We go now."

For one miserable moment Ariel hesitated at the top of the stairs. She'd come here under Christopher's protection, giving him her word that she'd stay with him.

Her stomach twisted sickeningly inside her. If she woke him now, she knew he wouldn't let her go, and the flat-featured messenger had made it clear he wouldn't wait any longer. She wasn't certain why Yazid had sent for her. She suspected it had something to do with the marriage. Even though Ariel no longer harbored much of a desire to prevent her marriage to Christopher, she at least owed Yazid an explanation, and by going with the messenger, she could tell Yazid about Christopher's suspicions. She could warn him that he might be walking into a trap.

Despite her growing misery, Ariel followed the messenger down the winding stairs, out a hidden door in the Casbah wall and into the deserted Moroccan night.

Chapter Nineteen

By the time they came in sight of Yazid's encampment, Ariel was exhausted to the point of numbness. Having missed supper, she'd been starving most of the night, but now she was so tired she hadn't any appetite. Even the arm Christopher had stretched to the limit no longer seemed to throb. She pulled her horse to a halt, watching the first rays of sunlight filter upward behind the peaks of the Middle Atlas. What time was it? she wondered. Still in the shadow of the mountains, the camp was asleep. It occurred to her that Suleiman must have misunderstood Yazid. If he'd meant to attack today, he'd have the soldiers up and busy with their preparations. Ariel gave her head a hard shake, banishing her drowsiness; but the effect was only temporary, and the hypnotic lethargy crept back. Ariel nudged her mount forward and followed Yazid's yellow-skinned messenger down the winding path to the camp.

"You go in here." Pulling his horse to a halt, the messenger nodded to the tent before them. "I will tell the great moulay you have arrived."

Ariel nodded. She prayed Yazid would have the foresight to let her rest before asking to see her. She couldn't possibly explain Christopher's theories in the state she was in, and if an attack wasn't imminent, there was no need to rush her information to him. A few hours' rest would do her tremendous good. Dismounting, Ariel tied the mare the messenger had brought for her to a tent support and ducked into the tent. Immediately, a eunuch scrambled out from beneath his blanket and dropped to his knees before her.

"Beloved mistress," he began in a sing-song soprano voice. "I have been awaiting your arrival. Do not think I slept, no, I kept vigil as ordered by my master the great prince of our sultan. Tell me what I may do to ease the difficulties of the great journey you have completed? I am at your every service. Command and it shall be done."

Ariel smiled wanly at the profuseness of his welcome. "Right now I'd like a pillow upon which to lay my head. After I've rested a bit, we can see about a bath, if one is to be had here, and some refreshment. But for now, a bed."

"That is all you desire? A bed? How am I to serve you if you ask nothing of me? A bed, this is nothing."

"But that is what I want," Ariel repeated. "If you find that too simple a request, I can ask the prince to provide me with one."

"No, no!" the eunuch exclaimed, ushering Ariel to the raised bed covered with leopard skins and beautifully embroidered Berber wool blankets. "You needn't bother the mighty prince. I have such a bed as you desire right here. I have made it with the finest blankets in the land and added the softness of a wild cat's skin. You see, beloved mistress? I serve you well."

"I see," Ariel said, smiling. "Now I'll rest. When I wake in a few hours we can discuss the other things I mentioned." The eunuch scooted around her, pulling back the blankets before she could do it herself. She sat gratefully on the bed and bent to pull off her boots, but the effeminate slave swept her hands away with a flourish, seeing to the task himself. Ariel made no protests. She barely had the strength to pull her legs up onto the bed and curl her hand beneath her head before she fell into a sound sleep of exhaustion.

She woke with a start. Two men were arguing loudly in dialects that weren't familiar to her just beyond the wall of the tent. For a moment Ariel thought she was back at the *fantasia*, hiding from the Bukhariyin among the dead.

"Ah, you awaken, beloved mistress."

Ariel jumped as she pulled the blankets aside and looked at the eunuch. "What time is it?" she asked, getting her bearings at last.

"Such simple pleasures you ask of me when I have been trained to fulfill the most elaborate of desires." Ariel eyed him meaningfully. "It is past midday. The sun shall set in four hours."

"I've slept the entire day!" she gasped.

"This is so. But have no worries, beloved mistress. Mohammed El Yazid, the great emir, son of Mohammed our sultan, carrier of the blood of Mohammed the Prophet, has sent word that you are to join him for the evening meal."

Ariel relaxed, relieved that Yazid had not been waiting for her, nor, obviously, taken his forces to rout the Bukhariyin. "The bath?"

The eunuch smiled broadly, displaying a mouthful of ornate gold fillings that suited his taste in clothing and jewelry perfectly. "All is in readiness, beloved one." With a clap, he conducted a line of slaves into the center of the tent, where they set a copper tub, filling it with skin upon skin of steaming water. Another slave

253

bore a large mahogany chest which contained viles of oils and essences. The eunuch made his selections carefully, deliberating over each one as though the world revolved around the contents of her bath water. "Attar of rose to scent your golden skin," he chanted as the tent filled with the powerful fragrance. "Oils from the almond and hazelnut to soften it."

Laying back against her pillow, Ariel enjoyed the thought of being fawned over so extravagantly. When at last the bath was prepared to the eunuch's satisfaction, the slaves were dismissed. Ariel climbed out of her bed, dropping her dirty clothes on the rugs. She was too accustomed to the eunuchs in the harem baths and didn't think twice about being naked before this one. The water was hot, but she slid into it, letting out a long, grateful sigh as the heat enveloped her. The rose-scented steam would normally have been too heavy a scent for her tastes, but today it was intoxicating. "What's your name?" Ariel asked as the eunuch handed her a sweetly scented bar of soap.

"My name is Ahmed, O beloved. And I am here to make your every moment a delight."

"Where on earth did Yazid find you?"

"I come from the prince's own harem, mistress. I am the treasure of his wives and concubines. I prepare them for their hours with the prince, just as I prepare you now."

Ariel closed her eyes, letting the bath rejuvenate her.

"Shall I wash you?"

"No, thank you, Ahmed. Tell me," she said, opening her eyes as she began to lather one leg. "Have you overheard any of the prince's men? Do you know when they plan to attack the Bukhariyin?"

"I know nothing of such matters," Ahmed responded

lightly. "My concerns are for the prince's women. I know only of earthly pleasures. I know nothing of war."

"I see," Ariel said, disappointed. Not wishing to be completely uninformed when she saw Yazid, she had hoped to glean a little information from the eunuch. As it was, it looked as though Ahmed's only concern was to make her smell good for her supper with Yazid.

"May I feed you a fig, O beloved?" Ahmed asked, presenting a platter overflowing with chilled fruits and sweets.

Ariel sighed with delight, realizing it had been more than a day since she last ate. Surrendering to his determination to satiate her every need, she plucked the fig from Ahmed's fingers. Maybe, she thought, it wouldn't be so bad if she didn't know absolutely everything there was to know before she saw Yazid.

When the appointed time for her meeting with Yazid arrived, Ariel donned the requisite haik that covered her from head to foot and completely disguised the actual clothing Ahmed had selected for her. The moon-faced messenger arrived to escort her through the camp. As she walked behind him, Ariel tried to look unobtrusively around her. There were many more men than Ariel had imagined she'd find. She'd expected hundreds, but from what she saw there were thousands here. It was difficult to see, for she was expected to keep her eyes lowered at all times, and she could only catch glimpses as she crossed the open ground; but something struck her as wrong—something she couldn't quite place by the time they stopped before Yazid's tent.

"*Tisbahee, ya hagga,*" the messenger said, bidding her good night in his strangely accented Arabic. There were slaves captured from all over the world at El Bedi, but none like this moon-faced, yellow-skinned man. She didn't like him any better after having travelled with him than she had upon their first meeting. He was cold, his every move calculated. Yet she felt certain he was a man who would never stand on his own. A man who thrived only with a master.

Two guards stood at the entrance of Yazid's tent, bowing as she passed them. If her own tent had been opulent, it was a stable in comparison. She expected no less from Yazid; he was a prince. But with so many loyal subjects of the sultan dying in battles, and the seriousness of the mission Yazid had undertaken, she was a little taken back by the grandeur of the setting. The rugs were finer, and there were more of them; the tapestries on the walls, large and colorful. There was even a crystal chandelier, its candles spreading a soft glow in the center of the tent. Centered against the back wall was an enormous bed strewn with pillows. And the skin of a majestic lion was spread against the wall at its head. At the foot of the bed, a low table had been set, but nowhere could she see the prince.

"Yazid?" she whispered.

"The haik does you no justice, sweet Ariel. Take it off and let me see you." Ariel started forward, staring into the corner that his voice had come from. "No!" The command stopped her in her tracks. "There, where I can see you."

"Yazid," Ariel said uncertainly. "Let me greet you. I've come a long way."

"There will be many hours for greetings. Now, do as I ask and remove your covering." Self-consciously Ariel unlatched her veil and lowered the hood. "Your hair glows like honey and spice," he whispered from the shadows.

The sweet tangy smoke of a hookah drifted from the corner. Ariel hesitated. "Yazid—"

"I grow impatient." Anger tinged his voice as he interrupted her. Taking a deep breath, she did as he asked. The important thing was to tell him about the pasha, she reminded herself. What did it matter if he wanted to look at her? The hookah could do that to people. It could fill them with lethargy and strange desires. Gathering up the discarded haik, she held it in front of her, uncomfortable in the clothing Ahmed had dressed her in.

From the darkness Yazid snapped his fingers. The black robe was suddenly snatched out of her hands by a guard she hadn't noticed before. Ariel jumped. Then, locking her jaw, she let her arms fall to her sides and tilted her chin proudly upward. She concentrated on the lion's regal head and its bared teeth snarling from the wall.

For a moment Yazid said nothing. She could feel his gaze on her, and her skin began to crawl with revulsion at the humiliation he was subjecting her to. But she wouldn't cower. She had come at Yazid's bidding, breaking her promise to Christopher. She would bear this indignity for the sake of the lives that might be saved, for the sake of the sultan's success against the Bukhariyin.

"That is better," Yazid said at last, his voice low; almost breathless.

Keyf, she thought, silently attributing his behavior to the opium.

Yazid appeared from the shadows, moving slowly as he came toward her. He was dressed in a long coat heavily embroidered with metallic threads and slippers to match. He wore no turban, his dark hair neatly groomed and his mustache freshly clipped above a thin smile. He circled in front of her, his gaze everywhere on her body at once. "Leave us," he said, and the slave who'd taken the haik shuffled quickly out of the tent on the heels of another faceless servant who'd lurched from the shadows.

"You are incomparable," he said, reaching out to finger her midnight-colored shawl. Stepping closer, he inhaled the rose essence Ahmed had insisted on dotting at her wrists and bosom. With one hand, he drew the drape from her shoulders, revealing the short-cropped silver vest that barely covered her breasts.

Despite the tent's warmth, Ariel felt gooseflesh rise along her bare midriff. The silver and diamond girdle around her hips was cold and heavy, and she silently cursed Ahmed for convincing her to wear this outfit. She'd give anything to be swathed in her djellaba at this very moment. "Yazid," she said, trying once more to end his demeaning inspection. "Am I here for you to sniff at all night, or was there some other reason you sent for me?"

Yazid pulled back, his green eyes glittering angrily as he glared at her like a dangerous desert beast.

"I have news for you about the revolt. Suleiman was sending a messenger in the morning," she lied. "He's probably still hours from your camp while I'm here now. Don't you want to hear it?"

Yazid's eyes ran over her once more before he retreated, turning back to the darkness for a moment before answering. "So you have news. But of course, you do. You know so much, little Ariel. Always at my father's feet, always listening, always watching with those innocent eyes. Always quiet and obedient until you hear every morsel. And then you just slip away like a little hare." He lowered himself onto a pile of pillows and waved his hand. "Come and sit with me, sweet Ariel. Tell me what you know."

Relief flooded through her. The worst was over. Yazid had had his moment to humiliate her; now they could settle down with the important matters. The longer she was here, the more anxious she was to finish with Yazid and start back for the Casbah. She had so much to explain to Christopher when she returned, and there were apologies to make. She settled on a cushion opposite Yazid and tried to smile. "Christopher and I rode to the Casbah late yesterday."

"Do you think I do not know that? I know everything," he bragged. "Nothing happens within the palace that I do not know of; that I do not allow to occur."

"Suleiman told us about your plan to defeat the Bukhariyin here in the foothills," she continued, ignoring his comment. "Christopher felt that if the pasha of Fez had joined the rebels, you and your forces might be in danger."

"Is that what the English duke said? That I might be in danger?" Yazid threw back his head and laughed. "He is more of a fool than I thought."

"He didn't say that exactly," Ariel corrected. "He said it didn't make sense that the Bukhariyin had camped near here. I was the one who thought you might encounter danger."

Yazid's eyes narrowed. "He is suspicious, then, the infidel?"

"He thinks the pasha may be with the Bukhariyin."

Yazid relaxed against the pillows, smiling maliciously. He clapped his hands, and the two slaves reappeared, serving tea and the first course of their meal. One of the slaves stepped over to Yazid presenting a small gold bowl. Yazid dipped a tiny spoon into the white powder and sprinkled it over his tabbouleh. He looked up, and Ariel shook her head, declining. Yazid shrugged. "As you wish. It heightens one's senses. The meal will be finer than any you've ever tasted, as will everything you experience through the *keyf.*"

Ariel declined again, concentrating on her supper. Yazid became engrossed in each bite of food, rolling it in his mouth as though each taste was a new one, and the meal progressed in silence. At last pastries and fruit were served along with more tea, and Ariel decided that she had to broach the subject of her marriage.

"Yazid," she began slowly. "When your messenger came for me, I thought you might have done something about my marriage to Christopher."

Yazid smiled. "I have."

Ariel closed her eyes as misery filled her. Only a few days ago she would have delighted in those words. This was what she'd wanted, what she'd prayed for. But not anymore. Her few days with Christopher had changed everything. Her only mistake had been in not realizing how completely it had changed *her.* Being in this camp made her see, as if for the first time, all the things Christopher had been trying to tell her. She didn't want to walk with her head down, hidden beneath a haik everywhere she went. Nor did she wish to be an object of admiration as she'd been tonight. Something to stare at and fawn over. Something to brag about, yet dismiss at the merest whim. She wanted to be treated as a person, someone with a mind.

In a few short days she'd grown accustomed to being with Christopher, to the genial friendship they shared, the laughter, even the arguments. The world he described in England was a world she wanted to see, and although she was still afraid of going so far from her home and being among people who might judge her unfairly, she knew Christopher cared for her. With him at her side, she'd have a safe haven to run to. Now all she wanted was to tell Yazid she no longer needed his help, and get back to Christopher. "Yazid, thank you for what you've done in my behalf, but I've decided that marrying Christopher would be the best thing for everyone."

Yazid's hand jerked in midair, and he grit his teeth as hot tea splashed over the rim of the glass, burning his flesh. "So you've changed your mind, sweet Ariel? Rather than humiliate a stomach-crawling, asp infidel, you'd disgrace my father and our country with your lust?"

"What are you talking about?" Ariel gasped incredulously.

He rose so quickly that Ariel jumped up, every muscle poised for flight. A moment ago he'd been a dazed, harmless half-man satiated by his drugs, but in the breath of a second he'd become a creature of prey, stalking Ariel as he rounded the table between them. She stepped back, nearly tripping over the cushion she'd been sitting on a moment ago. "The sultan wants me to marry him. I'll be doing what everyone's wanted from the start."

"Is that how you show your gratitude for the life you have been permitted here, by throwing yourself at any man who passes by?"

"How dare you!" she gasped, seething with anger and humiliation.

"How dare I? I am the sultan. I am the savior of the Maghreb. How dare I? I dare *anything!* It is you who dares too much."

261

"You may be sultan someday, but that day has yet to come," Ariel retorted. "Until then, your father rules the land. He has given his approval of this marriage, and it shall be." She couldn't believe that she was arguing for the right to marry Christopher. A handful of days ago Yazid had been comforting her, her only ally. Now he was demanding that she go through with terminating the betrothal. Why? Why did he care whether or not she married Christopher?

"You think you'll be free of our laws. After all, you're not a Moroccan, Ariel. Not a true believer of the Faith. You've always refused to bend to the laws of our people. Now that you've had a taste of freedom, you think that gives you the right to become like them."

"I don't think anything of the sort," she protested angrily. "I'm not Arab or Berber, but I've tried to be a Moroccan."

"You're no different than your mother," he shouted, his shoulders hunched forward as he stalked her. A malicious gleam shining in his eyes, he turned full force on Ariel. "The wives and concubines, the true daughters of Allah do not want you around them. They are either scared by your iniquities, or repulsed by them. You should have been put in your place years ago, or else you should have been sent back to England. But it's too late for either of those things. You are full of evil. Just as your mother was."

Ariel stared at him. How could he say such a thing about her mother? Her mother had sparkled and shone. She'd brightened everything around her. Evil? There hadn't been a gram of wickedness in her. "Whatever you say about me, Yazid, this has nothing to do with my mother. It wasn't her fault the sultan abandoned your mother and the others to be with her."

"She was a witch. She could cast her spell on any man, and make him lose his mind with desire. She could make a man do anything in order to have her. My father stopped listening to his counsel; he refused to receive my mother. He listened to Caroline. Always, Caroline. He was her monkey on a leash, and still she wasn't satisfied. She wanted more. She wanted all men to desire her."

"You're wrong," Ariel cried. No one could speak so about her mother. It wasn't true. It simply wasn't true. And no matter what Yazid said, Ariel knew that truth in her heart. "My mother was none of those things. She was sweet and kind. She had no choice but to stay here. My father—"

"She was evil!" he screamed. "She cast her evil eye on me. She made me insane with lust for her. She toyed with me. She smiled at me, and spoke to me. I sat at her feet in the gardens and read poetry to her. And then, when I came to her, when I was ready to spill my seed alongside that of my father's, she turned me out!"

Ariel struggled to stay on her feet as she reeled under the impact of his words. She shook her head in mute denial. She had to escape before Yazid could flay her with more words, before he touched her with his eyes again—before she broke into a thousand pieces. She spun wildly, bolting for the doorway. Two enormous guards appeared from nowhere, dragging her back to Yazid as they held her between them.

Yazid stepped forward, a smile of feral rancor on his face that filled Ariel with fear. "I had to kill her."

"No-o-o-o!" Ariel's scream reverberated against the walls of the tent. Struggling against the guards' hold on her arms, she denied Yazid's words. "You're lying! She died of desert sickness. I was with her!"

He only laughed, throwing back his head in victory. "I poisoned her. Slowly. Oh, so slowly. No one knew. Even Caroline didn't know. I killed her because she was temptation. I could think of nothing but her. Her face, her skin, her hair." He reached out, gathering Angel's long tresses in his hand, and let it run between his fingers like sand. "But she tricked me," he whispered. "She came back. She became you."

The cry that issued from Angel's lips was born partly of fear and partly of agony. Murdered. Her beloved mother had been murdered by a maniacal fanatic. As his words sunk into her soul, Ariel was overwhelmed. She had turned to this same man for help. She had conspired with this man. He had touched her. Kissed her. And no matter how repulsed Ariel had been by his advances, she couldn't stop the feeling that somehow she desecrated her mother's memory even by being in the same place as Yazid. Suddenly she felt dirty. Had her mother also been disgusted by Yazid's affections? No, Ariel knew that Caroline would have been patient and understanding of a young man who was enamored of her. She would have gently rebuffed him, explained to him that she cared for him, but not in those ways.

She'd be alive right now if not for Yazid's insanity. And Ariel's whole world would be different. So much would be different. All the years of being alone. All the times she longed to reach out and touch her mother, hear her voice. All those years lost because of Yazid's lust. And now, somehow, Yazid thought that she was Caroline.

"You should have been sent away as soon as she died. Then she could not have come back to haunt me. You were crafty, though. You stayed away from me once you started to become a woman. You hid in your room

264

with those stupid, besotted servants to keep you company. But then the infidel came, and you needed help. You knew I'd help you, didn't you? You knew once I saw you, really saw you, I'd know. And I'd help you. But this time you're not going to refuse me, sweet Caroline. This time I'll have you. Such is the power of Allah's will."

"She didn't tease or bewitch you, Yazid. She was kind to you, that's all. She was lonely for company perhaps, and you were, too."

He towered over Ariel, and she swallowed hard, hiding her fear in the face of his rage. "I am heir to the throne. Within me flows the very blood of Mohammed, founder of the Faith." His voice rang as he advanced on her. "And you! You are *nothing!* The seed of a fool English lord ill-spent upon an unfaithful wife. I shall have my final revenge. You shall be everything your mother refused to be. You will bow to me. And you shall satisfy my desires; you shall crawl to me and beg for my favor."

She hated him. She hated him with a hatred that turned her cold. What kind of animal was he that he could reap such satisfaction from killing? He was as demented as his grandfather had been, and he wanted to avenge his battered, insane ego on her. "Never!" She spat the word at him. "I'll never submit to you."

"Shut up," Yazid snapped, a feral sneer curling his lips. "I've had enough of your prattle. I have a taste for a woman's true uses." His smile grew thin and sure. "Do you even know what they are, dear Ariel?"

Reaching behind her, he grabbed her hair by the ends. Her head snapped back, and Ariel willed her tears not to flow. Yazid ran the back of his hand along her cheek, his voice silkily menacing.

"It's far more than a stolen kiss from a simpering fop.

You need a man who will teach you what a woman was designed for. Why her place will always be beneath a man."

As he leaned over her, his face mere inches from hers, fear knotted her stomach, but with it a steel resolve was born. He might be able to force her beneath him, but she would never submit. She would never crawl to him in the way he predicted. He thought he knew her, yet he knew nothing about her if he didn't know that.

Yazid's finger slid roughly down her face, imprinting a hard groove on her cheek. Ariel flinched, pulling away from the heartless caress. "My wives, and my harem, dare not speak unless bidden. They know their place. If they don't—I beat them until I know they'll never forget." His pale green eyes were savage and cold as he pressed his lips into a flat smile.

"Don't touch me, Yazid. If you want to rut with one of your wives, then go do it. If you look at them with such violence in your eyes, if you touch them with such rancid desire, I pity them."

His hand cracked against her face with a force that sent her reeling backward despite the guards holding her arms. "What a little fool you are. Who do you think will stop me?"

"Your father will," Ariel retorted, lifting her chin defiantly. "He'll never allow you to do this. Never."

"My father," Yazid sneered. "That snivelling man of learning you admire so much? Caroline also thought he was so wonderful. Always telling me to listen to him, to be like him. Talking about his vision for the Maghreb. I listened, but I only hated him more for her admiration. He wants unity with the Christian world; he invites the infidels to rob us of our treasures and calls it commerce. *We don't need them!* We are Allah's people, the moon and the stars and the planets. We are power and might and greatness beyond their wildest dreams. And we shall be always. My father will not stand in the way of our might."

Ariel's head began to buzz as Yazid's words fell into place beside all the other things that had nagged in the back of her brain since she arrived. The sleeping soldiers, the thousands of men, the opulence of these quarters, as if this tent had not been erected last night, but weeks, perhaps months before. And, suddenly, she knew.

The two men on either side of her were Bukhariyin.

"You've betrayed him," she whispered incredulously. "You've betrayed your own father."

Yazid smiled at her triumphantly. "No one can stop me. Not from becoming sultan, and not from having you. Tomorrow, we ride back to the Casbah. Already my envoy is on his way to Suleiman with my message. He will be expecting us. He'll think the line of Bukhariyin are captives.

"The fool. We'll ride right into their open arms, and we'll cut them down. The blood will flow like a river, and then I'll ride into my father's palace and do it again. Once he's dead, the new regime will begin. The infidels will be annihilated, the soil of the Maghreb cleansed of their taint with their own blood. There will be no more commerce, no more treaties. Morocco will rule from strength as it did before my father bound us hand and foot to the infidels. We will become greater than we have ever been, and my name shall be written in the book of greatness beside Ismail."

"You killed them," she whispered in horror, recalling the macabre scene she'd witnessed as she'd searched

among the bodies for Lord and Lady Belmeth. "All those innocent people. I was in the tents; I saw the massacre you caused. What kind of beast are you?"

"I am a lion!" Jumping onto the bed, he wrenched the skin from the wall, holding its fierce head erect. "The mightiest of animals! I kill any who defy me, any who corrupt my kingdom."

"You are insane."

"Are you afraid, sweet Ariel?" he asked, glaring at her. "That is good."

"I'm not afraid of you, Yazid," she said, despite the knowledge that she was lying. "I'm revolted by you."

He leapt off the bed. "We have the long, long night before us." Coming to her, he pressed his lips against her neck, then looked at her, watching for some reaction. Ariel remained perfectly still, refusing to give him any indication of the emotions he had stirred in her. Turning away, he walked to one of the chests pushed against the wall. He returned with something in his hand, and smiled rancorously at Ariel. "Tell me, Ariel. I give you this one chance to agree to satisfy me willingly. Do I have your word?"

"I told you, Yazid. I will never submit willingly to you. The thought of your touch revolts me."

"Then, you'll learn submission." Opening his hand, Yazid revealed two sets of leather thongs. "There is no escaping the laws of Allah, sweet Ariel. I was born to be your master." With a sharp jerk of his head, he directed the Bukhariyin guardsmen to take her to the bed.

Ariel prepared to fight. If they were going to bind her to the bed, she intended to fight every step of the way.

"Moulay Mohammed El Yazid!" The messenger's voice was low and filled with urgency. "I beg your

268

mercy for disrupting you, but you are needed." Yazid's reaction was obscured by the shadows, but Ariel could feel his attention shift away from her. She shuddered in relief as the heat of his assault turned to his servant.

"What is it! What has happened of such importance that you interrupt me now!"

The messenger's gaze slid to Ariel, and then back to Yazid:

"Don't worry about her!" Yazid snapped. "She is of no concern, and she will be less so after I have finished with her tonight. Tell me why you've come or get out."

"There is fighting, Moulay."

"Again! Arab and Berber alike have sworn their allegiance to me. They have no right to disrupt my camp."

"It is not as it has been before. The rift is great, sire. The tribes from the south say they will leave tonight if you do not punish the others for their insolence. You must come now. If you do not, your cause is lost."

Yazid threw the thongs onto the bed in disgust. "Return her to her tent," he ordered. "Stand guard there until I call for her. And you, sweet Ariel," he snarled. "Be sure Ahmed keeps you as lovely as you are right now. My appetite has been whetted, and I am hungry for all of you." Grabbing her chin, Yazid kissed her, a hard, punishing act that bruised her.

Ariel jerked her face away, staring pointedly at the walls.

Grinding her jaw between his fingers, he wrenched her head around, forcing her to meet his cold, green glare. "I will see that every last shred of your defiance is gone before the dawn." Ariel glared back at him, refusing to let him see her fear. Yazid let go of her chin. Grinning, he slowly dropped the palm of his hand onto her chest. With a snap, the thin silver clasp that held

269

her vest together broke between his fingers. He pushed the brocade away, exposing her bare breasts, and slowly, coldly cupped his palms around each one. His smile widening, he squeezed her flesh, never taking his eyes off her face, watching for her reaction. Ariel remained motionless, refusing to let him see her revulsion.

His hands began to travel downward again with sickening intent. Past her ribs, over her navel, to the flat of her stomach. At the uppermost edge of her pants, where the diamond girdle rode low on her hips, he stopped. Suddenly, his fingers dug into the delicate girdle, and he yanked her forward, pulling her hips against him while he rotated his pelvis against hers, grinding his erection against her. He stared at her, laughing.

"I am glad you refuse to come willingly. I will enjoy seeing the pride seep out of you like water from a leaky skin.

"Now take her!" He thrust her back at the guards, like a discarded, used, plaything, and left.

Chapter Twenty

With a rough shove the Bukhariyin thrust Ariel into her tent. Ahmed jumped up, his dinner scattering in all directions as he ran to her. "O beloved!," he said, falling at her feet. "What evil happens here that you are returned to my service? Does not the great prince find you all things? Do not say that Ahmed has somehow failed in his duties, that my great master was dissatisfied."

Ariel stared at him, wondering how she could have been so blind to something everyone else seemed to take for granted. "You knew he'd brought me here to become one of his concubines."

"But of course," the eunuch replied, looking up at her like a confused pup. "Why else would my master bring me with him?"

"I don't know," she whispered.

"Why would he furnish a tent so lavishly and order all things necessary for many nights of couching pleasures?" Ahmed continued, trying to help her understand what was eminently clear to him. "Why would he bring a woman here, to the foot of the mountains?"

"To talk to me!" she nearly shouted. "To be glad of my company, to listen to what I have to say!"

"Why would he do such a thing, O beloved? Why would a great and powerful man seek the worthless counsel of a woman?"

Ariel stared at him, soaking in his words, understanding her world for the first time. A half-crazed giggle welled up inside her. Why indeed? Why would any man, Arab or Berber, bother with a woman except to bed her? Ariel's hysteria erupted into hollow laughter, and the eunuch eyed her as though she'd lost her mind. He was half right, she thought. She'd lost the part of her mind that understood and accepted such reasoning.

"Oh, Ahmed. I'm the one who's been wrong. All this time, so wrong. No Moroccan would bother with a woman to *talk* with her! How could I have been so blind." Tears of hilarity born of exhausted frustration rolled down her face. "Once we're used for their purpose, they want nothing more to do with us. We're shunted behind the locked doors of the harem. Discarded for someone new until she, too, joins the harem." Her mood changed as she spoke. The laughter faded and was replaced by bitter acknowledgement of realities she'd spent her life pushing firmly away. "And woe to any woman who wins the heart and ear of a man. She's feared and cursed. There's no rest for her, even among her own kind, until she's destroyed." Ariel paused, her shoulders sagging under the weight of her new perspective. "That's all the hope there is for a woman here, be discarded or be destroyed."

Her anger was spent. The world she'd so carefully constructed to keep her safe and happy lay shattered around her. Slowly Ariel sunk to her knees, her fingers grasping as though she meant to somehow gather up the shards of the world she'd believed in and to somehow reconstruct it. Her hands shook, and she steadied them against her legs, gulping in a ragged, defeated breath. And then her tears came in earnest—hot tears of grief that coursed down pale cheeks. She cried for the world she'd lost in one swift and terrible hour. And she cried for herself, mourning the innocence she knew was gone forever.

All the while Ahmed stood silent in the darkening tent. When at last Ariel's tears began to subside, he turned away, busying himself in his corner. Drawing a steadying breath, Ariel dried the last of her tears with the back of her hand and looked around the tent, studying it all with new perspective. The clink of glass vials and the distinct smell of flowers came from the eunuch's corner. He must be concocting some love potion to drive Yazid to new heights of passion, she thought wryly. Something to make him forget she'd just denied him. But Ariel had no intention of giving either Ahmed or his master the least opportunity to see their plans to fruition.

She had no illusions left. Certainly not about her current circumstances. She'd jeopardized the lives of everyone she loved by coming here—the sultan, Chedyla . . . everyone. But Yazid had made a mistake. He'd told her too much. He believed once she was in his camp, she would be a captive, someone powerless to stop him from taking what he wanted from her and her guardian. But he underestimated her. Ariel would do anything to correct her mistake. She had to put the information she had to good use. She might not live to see those she loved again, but somehow she would survive long enough to stop Yazid. For a moment Christopher's face flashed before her, and her heart, if it could bear to break any more, ached at the thought of how she'd wasted those precious hours with him. Why

273

hadn't she listened? Why had it been so important to deny everything he'd said?

Rising, Ariel crossed the tent, coming to a stop before the large trunks Ahmed had lined against one wall. "What do you have in these?"

Ahmed abandoned his mixing and measuring to scurry across the room. "Ah, beloved, these trunks contain the tools of seduction. The clothing, the powders, the jewels to make a man's desires come alive."

"May I see?" Eagerly, the eunuch threw open the first trunk, allowing Ariel to peer in. It was filled to overflowing with silks and satins. Many had been sewn into provocative outfits similar to the one she wore; others were simply long, fluid drapes. Ariel lifted one from the trunk as an idea formed in her mind. "How does one wear these?"

Ahmed smiled in delight. "Beloved mistress, I see you now understand the ways of Allah's world."

"I do, indeed," Ariel replied, smiling back at him. "I want to please the prince. But since we've gotten off to such an unfortunate start, I'm afraid I will need some very special way to make him desire me."

The eunuch pursed his lips thoughtfully. "Yes. Yes, I see. You will need more than just your beauty and charms, incomparable as you are. The prince must see how willing you are, how very eager."

Ariel nodded. "What pleasures him more than anything else, Ahmed? What does he want from his concubines that they rarely give him?" Ariel didn't know what it was she sought. She only sensed that there must be something she could do, some way to stop Yazid, to catch him unaware. If she could lure him with the promise of sensual pleasures, and if she remained alert, she might find the opportunity to disarm him. Perhaps, she could feed him more *keyf* and render him senseless long enough to escape. If she could just warn Suleiman. If she could just arrive at the Casbah an hour before Yazid, she could help.

"There is one thing that the master loves more than any other pleasure," Ahmed told her. He hesitated, hovering indecisively over the chest.

"Tell me," Ariel coaxed. There was so little time. Any moment now the Bukhariyin might return for her. If she went unprepared . . . Ariel pushed the unthinkable out of her mind. She would do whatever she had to if she could stop Yazid; otherwise she would fight him to the death. "If it is his special delight, then surely he'll forgive me when he sees how I intend to please him."

"It will not give you pleasure, O beloved, this delight of my master's. It is his great fascination, but it is a dark delight he seeks over all others."

A chill ran down her spine, but she swallowed back her fear, pressing her entreaty. "I'm not afraid, Ahmed. Show me."

The eunuch closed the silk-filled trunk and moved to the farthest one. He opened the lid and slowly lifted out a gold box encrusted with gems. "This will please Mohammed El Yazid, great prince of all Morocco," he said quietly. "This box contains his greatest pleasures."

"What is it?"

The eunuch eyed her, hesitating.

"If I don't know what it is I take to him, how will I be able to prepare myself?" she prodded. "How will I know what to do?"

Ahmed set the box on the ground between them. Crouching on his heels, he sprung the latch and lifted the heavy, gold lid. Inside, laying on the scarlet velvet lining, were five objects. They were as beautiful as any jewelry she'd ever seen, and infinitely more chilling. They were golden cuffs — two small cuffs to fit delicate wrists, two larger cuffs for the ankles, and a fifth cuff, more ornate than the others. For a moment Ariel couldn't take her eyes off them, and she realized the danger she faced. At last she looked up. The eunuch's gaze met hers, and a silent acknowledgement of what she was about to enter into passed between them.

"What does he do once he shackles me to the bed with them?" Ariel whispered.

The eunuch lifted the fifth cuff from the box. The front of it was thicker than the rest, covered with an intricate design forming a circle around an enormous sapphire that lay in a bed of flowers. Ariel gasped audibly.

Ahmed looked at her in surprise. "You know what the fifth cuff contains?"

"Contains?" Ariel shook her head. "It's the design. I've seen it before."

"It is the symbol of the Saadians."

Ariel shook her head. "Who are the Saadians?"

"Who *were* the Saadians," Ahmed corrected in his lilting, effeminate voice. "They ruled all this land, all of the Maghreb before Ismail the Great broke the dynasty and became sultan."

Ariel looked at him in surprise. "I saw a rug with this same design in the Casbah."

"Then, you have found something even the sultana knows nothing of. But then the fortress is much older than El Bedi; it was built in the days of the Saadian sultans."

"How did Yazid get this box?" Ariel said, as much to herself as to the eunuch. "Christopher said the rug was probably overlooked when the treasures of the old

276

rulers were recast into objects for Ismail's palace. Something as precious as this wouldn't have been omitted." She looked up at Ahmed, her mind leaping to the only possible conclusion. "This could only have escaped if someone hid it."

The eunuch nodded. Suddenly he did not look as simple as Ariel had assumed. He was old, the corners of his eyes creased with lines, his knuckles knotted with age. He hid his years behind soft, hairless skin and flirtatious manners. How did he know so much about the history of the Maghreb? Who had he served before Yazid? She realized that like so much in her life, she'd made him into what she wanted him to be, never seeing what he truly was.

"The sultana is of the Saadians," he said.

"Daiwa?" Ariel stared down at the cuff, then slowly lowered the lid of the box. It was there, too—hidden amid the pomp and flourish of an overzealous artist, but there nonetheless, a field of flowers nestled in a circle of Arabesques. She looked at the old eunuch and waited, hoping for the story. Compliantly, as though he'd waited years for someone to ask, he began to talk, his voice becoming lyric and sing-songy as he unveiled the tale only he, Daiwa, and Yazid knew.

"I served the sultana's mother. She was very beautiful, and the sultana was her image." He closed his eyes, remembering. "Their coloring was so dark and Arabic, with bodies that swelled and dipped in a manner that invited a man to touch them. But they lived poorly, just the two of them with me to see to their needs. There was no husband, and Daiwa, the child, never asked such questions. She never asked how they had come to have a eunuch. She never asked why she was kept away from the other children. These questions were forbidden. Such a beautiful girl; but one who had no lineage, no bearing to attract a sultan's attention. Not even a pasha would look at her twice. Then, one day, everything changed.

"Her mother had suffered a long and painful illness, but she wanted no doctors, not even an Imam. No attention was to be drawn to her. When at last she knew death was coming, she called for her daughter. She told her about the old sultan, the last of the Saadians. You see, she was the daughter of a royal concubine. She had been born after the Saadians were defeated by Ismail. Her mother, the last concubine to lay upon the old sultan's couch, should have been destroyed with the others when Ismail took the throne, but there was a young warrior who was entranced by the concubine's charms. He took mercy on her, or perhaps he hoped to bed her himself, and he helped her escape. Only afterward did the concubine, Daiwa's grandmother, reveal to him that she carried the sultan's seed in her belly. He should have killed her, but the young are foolish . . . I mean no offense, O beloved," the eunuch amended quickly. Ariel smiled and shook her head, urging him to continue.

"Instead he ran, and the concubine, wise for her years, ran also, but in the other direction, and months later she gave birth to a girl-child. Like the sultana, the girl was kept away from the other children of the town. She did not mind, though. She knew who she was, and that she was better than the others. When the concubine saw her growing into a beautiful woman, she began to plot. One day a young man appeared at their door. He had good blood lines; but he was head-strong, and his father was a very strict man of the Faith. The concubine had promised him the pleasure of a beautiful

278

virgin in exchange for a servant. The young man brought me as his gift. I was quite young, but the concubine was pleased. The girl was shy; but the young man was handsome and strong, and soon they became lovers.

"He came many, many times, and the concubine allowed their mating. There was no talk of marriage, nor of the girl becoming his concubine. I believe the young man thought himself the luckiest of Allah's warriors. Then one day the concubine called him to her room. Her daughter was with child; and the warrior was to come no more. He wanted to take the girl to his home, raise the child. I believe he was in love. But the concubine would have none of this. I was too young to understand all that happened then, but years later I came to understand that the concubine had wanted only one thing. She was determined that the line of royal blood continue. This was her revenge for the years of fear, destitution, and loneliness she had suffered. She would see the Saadian dynasty continue.

"The sultana was the result of the mating, and the dynasty did continue." Ahmed stopped to rest, and Ariel blinked, suddenly aware of the trancelike state she'd fallen into as the tale unfolded.

"But how did Daiwa then come to the attention of Mohammed?" she asked. "It's almost as though the hand of Allah moved them."

Ahmed smiled. "Fate? Kismet?" He shrugged mysteriously. "Perhaps so, O beloved. Her mother had been taught by her own mother to fear the new rule, and she tried now to instill this wisdom in her daughter. Now was not their moment, she warned. Their duty was only to continue the bloodline. She must find a man of pure, strong blood and seduce him. This was the obligation she passed to her daughter. But Daiwa did not hear this. Her mother died that same night. The young girl, my new mistress, looked at the squalor and poverty in which she lived and dreamed of her grandmother's life in the palace. Within her ran the blood of kings, and on that night I heard her vow to regain what was rightfully hers. One day her own would again sit upon the sultan's cushion.

"She could not read; but from that day forward she searched the marketplace for books about the concubines' art, and she studied the illustrations. She went to old hags and mystics, anyone who might teach her the tools of seduction. She learned to use the kohl and other powders to transform herself into the most desirable of creatures, and she learned every technique imaginable to pleasure a man. One day, sorting through her mother's belongings, she came upon the golden box. I do not believe the sultana ever used the instruments it contains. She did not need to.

"Through her own devices she had won the eye of the head eunuch at the palace. She found ways to pleasure even him, and he agreed to recommend her to the sultan, since she was indeed still a virgin. The sultan kept her as his favorite for six months, and then she bore him a son. Mohammed Ben Abdullah was very pleased. He made her his first wife. Many years passed, and the sultana was very happy. She had everything she wanted. She was Hatum Kadin, and her son would be sultan. Her bloodlines would be redeemed. Once more a Saadian would rule Morocco, and not even the sultan would know."

Ahmed rested for a moment. The strain of the long story had brought a sheen of perspiration to his hairless upper lip. Taking a long breath, he readied himself to continue, but before he spoke Ariel knew what his next words would be. "Then the English woman came."

He nodded. "It was different with the English one. This was not a concubine to comfort the sultan's needs. She came here with another man's seed lodged in her belly. She did nothing to make herself enticing. She hid her body in voluminous clothing and disgraced herself by going bare-faced. Yet the sultan was drawn to her as a fly to a sweet. The sultana would find Mohammed sitting beneath the fig trees telling the English one his dreams. She had only to speak and the sultan would make it so. Daiwa feared her. She feared the power of a woman who could entrance a man with her mind rather than her body. But she was patient. She had seen many infatuations pass while she remained Hatum Kadin.

"Then, one day the sultan called no one from the harem to his bed. This continued for many days, and at last the sultana learned that the English woman had couched with the sultan. She was insane with jealousy that night. I stayed with her when everyone else ran in fear. She wept, she rent her clothes, and vowed upon the holy one's name that this one woman would not defeat her. The sultana did all within her powers to poison the mind of the sultan against the English woman, but it did no good. In the end it was Allah who solved my mistress's problem and made her die."

Ariel sat numbly beside the gold box. It was too easy to recognize the parts she was familiar with to deny the old eunuch's tale. The only thing Ahmed didn't know was that it hadn't been Allah's hand that stayed her mother's link with Mohammed Ben Abdullah. It had been Yazid's. "When did Daiwa give Yazid the box?"

"She made a gift of it upon his seventeenth birthday.

281

He had become strangely despondent, and she hoped this token of his birthright would bring light back to his eyes. He bore the blood of not one, but two sultans, and she wanted him to know how great was his future."

"And . . . ?" Ariel dreaded what she knew she was about to be told, but she was no longer afraid. Kismet. Perhaps Allah's hand was directing all of them. Tonight the circle would be closed. Was the law of Islam right after all? Was an eye for an eye truly the justice Allah sought? If she killed Yazid tonight, her mother's death would be avenged, the dynasty that should have died over sixty years ago would at last be wiped out, and Mohammed's vision of prosperity and unity would continue unchallenged. Perhaps that was why she had stayed all this time in Morocco; because she was the instrument by which God's hand would move.

"He loved the box," Ahmed was saying. "He could not take his eyes off of it. But it was the contents that he wanted. Unlike his mother, it was not the emblem of his Saadian ancestors that he loved. It was the cuffs. The sultana tried over and over to tell him how important the box was — that it alone had been saved from Ismail's destruction. But my master had eyes only for the cuffs. At last, the sultana told him what she knew of the cuffs and their purpose. His thanks were heartfelt, but they were tainted. He lusted for the pleasures of using the cuffs; he cared nothing for the meaning of the box."

"You still haven't told me what the fifth cuff is for," Ariel said after a long silence had passed between the two of them.

Ahmed placed his thumb over the sapphire and pressed lightly. Faster than her eyes could follow the movement, a tiny dagger sprang from a hidden casement. "It is a tool of excitement," he said quietly. "He

282

will use it to titillate you, and to arouse himself. You may bear tiny cuts after tonight. He may even go so far as to injure you more substantially."

"Could he kill me if he wished?" she whispered, staring at the tiny blade as it glittered in the firelight.

"The blade can kill. But I do not think the prince would do this. His pleasure is not in killing. It is in inflicting pain upon the helpless."

The blade could kill.

Ariel closed her eyes. It was her only hope, yet the thought of being helpless against the deadly blade overwhelmed her. Could she wield it against Yazid? Could she plunge it into his heart intending to kill him or at least render him incapable of following her? To fail meant certain death. To succeed was murder.

But in the end, there was no choice. Ariel lifted the little dagger from the eunuch's hand. It fit her grasp perfectly. Replacing it in its compartment, she tested the release, over and over watching the blade shoot out of its sheath, learning how best to hold it.

"You will take the box?"

Ariel didn't answer, instead she simply slid the cuff up her arm.

Ahmed watched her thoughtfully. "The prince will be pleased."

"I'd like to be alone, Ahmed." Obediently the eunuch retreated to his corner, carrying the golden box and its remaining four cuffs with him. Ariel faced the back of the tent and dropped onto her knees as she pressed her forehead to the rug. "Allah, forgive me for what I am about to do," she prayed. The arm cuff was heavy and cold against her skin. She squeezed her eyes closed, praying harder. "I do not want to be your instrument of violence. If there is any other way, help me find it."

283

Christopher stood in the darkness, watching Ariel kneel over an elaborate box that was certainly worth a large portion of his family's substantial fortune. He'd slipped into the back of the tent, intending to get Ariel out of Yazid's camp unseen. Later, when they were safely beyond the prince's sights, he'd reprimand her for running off so foolishly. But instead of finding a frightened young woman who'd learned a lesson in trust, he was staring at a seductress about to fly into the arms of her lover.

With each passing second, Christopher's control was slipping. He watched her slide the gold arm band into place, and heard the eunuch praise her choice, telling her how pleased the prince would be. Fury slammed through his chest. His fingers flexed around the hilt of his scimitar. He wished nothing so much as that the narrow handle could have been his fiancée's lovely throat. His fiancée. His future wife. He'd come here to *rescue* her! Knowing the enormous void between the reality of Morocco and what she believed it was, Christopher wasn't surprised she'd felt compelled to warn Yazid about the pasha. Still, he had been furious that she'd sneak away in the night without a second thought to the danger. But he was the one who'd been an innocent, trusting fool. She'd run off to *join* Yazid. *Bitch!* Conniving, two-faced, lying witch.

No, he corrected himself. She hadn't lied. From the first, she'd told him she wanted nothing to do with him. She'd sworn her allegiance to Yazid. He'd been the one who wanted to believe she'd changed her mind. He'd invested more time and energy than he cared to recall convincing himself that she enjoyed his company and trusted him. And now he was getting exactly what he'd asked for. She was flaunting his stupidity and trust in his face. But even if he'd been a fool for trusting her, he knew a traitor when he saw one, and she'd pay the Islamic price for her treachery. He'd be the one to see to that. She could count on someone else to play the fool for her from now on. He had all the proof he needed that Yazid was leading the Bukhariyin revolt, and Ariel was here with him. If he couldn't take the leader right now, he'd at least take his accomplice.

Ariel rose and walked to the center of the room as Christopher watched, not willing to believe what he saw despite his vow to remain unaffected. She was scarcely dressed. Her sleek, golden midriff was bare, and the silver vest she wore was scant cover for her ripe, curving breasts. Despite his resolve, his body reacted, making him even more infuriated at his own lack of control. *Damn you. How dare you pray like a humble virgin when you have the heart of a harlot.* At that moment he wished he could turn and walk away from Ariel Lennox forever. Forget he'd ever met her, forget he'd ever kissed her or smelled the jasmine that filled the air wherever she walked. But as the king's emissary, and with England promising to be an ally to the Moroccan sultan, he couldn't do what he wanted to do. He would take Ariel back to her guardian and let him deal with her duplicity. He'd be a widower before he was even married.

Yazid's messenger would be back any moment. Ariel knew she'd already had more of a reprieve than Yazid had intended to give her. She must be ready. She couldn't think about anything else. She would need every sense at its sharpest in order to make the first move against Yazid. She had to use the dagger first, before he used it on her. Before she became his plaything, a vehicle for his distorted pleasure. Before it was too late to warn the sultan, and Suleiman, and Chedyla, and Christopher. She shivered, and crossed her arms in front of her to ward away the sudden chill.

Christopher. She tried to push him out of her thoughts. She needed to be here. She couldn't afford daydreams now. But it was hard. She wanted so badly to see him, to tell him she was sorry for running off with Yazid's strange Mongolian servant. Sorry that she hadn't listened to her heart. Ariel shook her head and paced toward the back of the tent, trying to clear away Christopher's image. He seemed so close. She could almost feel his presence—that air of leashed control that was always about him, the overpowering maleness of him.

Ariel stopped dead in her tracks, every muscle rigid. For a second she couldn't make out anything in the shadowy corner of the tent; then she glimpsed a movement. As silent and awesome as a sleek panther, Christopher stepped into the light. Without thinking, Ariel ran to him, her heart nearly bursting with joy.

"Don't you look enticing," he mocked through clenched teeth, holding her at arm's length. "A most delectable morsel for your lover."

"My lover?" Ariel shook her head adamantly. "Thank God you're here. Yazid wants to—"

"Wants to what?" Christopher leered maliciously. "I think I have a very clear idea of what Yazid wants. I have half a mind to leave you to him. You deserve what you'd get. But that would be too easy. After all, you'd be getting everything you want, wouldn't you? No," he said, his viselike hold nearly bringing tears to her eyes. "I think it will be much more equitable for you to face your guardian. Do you know what the punishments for your crimes are in Morocco?"

"My crimes?" Ariel stared up at him in disbelief. She opened her mouth to explain and then stopped herself. She watched Christopher's jaw knot as he stared at her with utter contempt. Ariel closed her mouth without a sound. When she'd seen Christopher standing in the shadow like an apparition she'd wished into reality, she'd thought he was the heaven-sent answer to her prayers. She'd thought she conjured him up by the sheer power of her need for him. But the man before her wasn't her savior. His beautiful blue eyes shone like cold crystals of fury. Ariel had grown up among the strongest of the strong. She'd seen fierce tempers and fury, jealousy that threatened lives, and retribution that occasionally ended them. She'd endured Daiwa's hatred and Raisuli's contempt. But never in her life had she encountered such tightly controlled rage. And never had scorn touched her so painfully.

Deep inside her an icy hole bore into the pit of her stomach. She wanted to cry. She wanted to break his angry hold and throw herself at him, melt the cold shield of hatred he wore and find the kind, warm man who had kissed her with passion and love. Love, she thought. Yes, he had loved her. And now, because she was here, because he thought she was Yazid's lover, he hated her. He didn't want to hear the truth. He had his own.

"Exactly what are these 'crimes' I'm being accused of, and who accuses me?" she asked, stepping away from him. "Or have you decided to judge me on your own, Lord Staunton?"

"I don't need to," he snapped. "Mohammed and all of Morocco will see to that. Now change into something you can ride in," he ordered. Then, running a scathing appraisal from head to foot, he added, "Or weren't you planning to be out of bed so soon?"

Ahmed shuffled out from his corner. In a slice of a second Christopher spun around, his scimitar nothing more than a silver flash in the lamplight.

"No!" Ariel screamed. The eunuch staggered forward. The sword impaled in him up to the hilt, protruding from between his ribs at his back. She ran to him, bracing her hands under his arms as he fell.

"Your djellaba, O belov—" His last word was lost in a gurgle. A stream of blood dribbled from the corner of his mouth, the snowy djellaba spilling on the floor.

"He was just a slave." She glared up at Christopher, her eyes glazed with angry tears. "He was *kind* to me. Do you understand the meaning of that word?" Ariel couldn't stop her tears, although at that moment the last thing she wanted was for Christopher to see her cry. She didn't want him to see her vulnerability. "He may have been Yazid's slave, but he was kind, and honest, and loyal . . ." She didn't go on; there was no point. Carefully, she laid the still head on a makeshift pillow, using the clothing Ahmed had intended for her.

"He could have been one of Yazid's guards," Christopher replied, dragging her up from the floor.

"But he wasn't," Ariel stated flatly.

"You'll have to leave him. There's nothing that can be done now."

"How dare you? How dare you come here accusing me, and then murder a man, an innocent man, without an ounce of remorse."

"Ariel." He yanked her away from the inert body, his

288

face cold and implacable. Snatching the djellaba from beneath the eunuch's head, Christopher stuffed the bloodstained clothing into her arms. "You're coming with me. Now." With a hard shove he pushed her through the slit he'd cut in the canvas, following on her very heels. And then Ariel heard the guards push aside the flap, and the scream of the Mongolian as he found Ahmed.

Chapter Twenty-one

It took less than a minute for the Bukhariyin to find their escape route, but it was all Christopher needed. Grabbing Ariel around her waist, he threw her onto Hannibal's broad back at the same time he vaulted up behind her. The black stallion sprung forward, eager to be away from the shouting band of pursuers. If Ariel hadn't grabbed a handful of the stallion's mane, she was certain she'd be lying at Yazid's feet at this moment, since she was in the air more than she was on the horse's back such was his speed and power.

Hannibal negotiated the narrow passage between tents in great, bounding strides. Just as they reached the outer limits of the camp, a group of enormous, black-skinned Bukhariyin appeared from behind the last tent, blocking their way to freedom. Ariel pressed her body closer against the animal's neck as he plowed fearlessly into them, scattering many with his slashing hooves. She heard Christopher's scimitar sing from its scabbard and felt the hard, downward thrusts of his arm as he cut down one warrior after another. Foot by foot they won their freedom, and just as she began to believe they would defeat the band of traitors, Ariel felt a hand close around her foot.

The hand dragged her from Hannibal's back, pulling her to his side as she frantically tried to free herself. She kicked, twisting her leg. A delicate, silver slipper Ahmed had given her fell to the ground, but her assailant's fingers held tight around her ankle, separating her from Christopher's forward progress. In another moment Hannibal would be through the crowd of guards, but she would remain behind. *Don't let them take me now,* she prayed.

Suddenly Christopher's arm was around her waist, hauling her back. He pulled her forward with him while the hand around her ankle pulled her down with equal force. Ariel screamed in pain, certain that she would be rent in two by the very forces that had clashed in her soul with such fury. Her head dropped to Hannibal's side, Christopher's arm cutting off her breath as the stallion strained forward against the hand that held her foot. Through a blur of tears she saw the human manacle, its thick, black fingers wrapped in a stranglehold around her ankle. The acrid scent of his sweat assaulted her senses; the dirt beneath his nails became the central focus of her vision. With a slowness that had the imagery of a dream about it, Ariel saw the Bukhariyin's free arm rise, his scimitar gleaming in the moonlight.

Ariel knew she must either fall into his hands or risk Christopher's life. Then, as she was about to release Hannibal's mane, Ariel caught sight of the glimmer of gold on her arm. She pulled her fingers free of the black mane, searching for the smooth surface of the sapphire. The instant she touched it, the tiny dagger sprang free. Using the last dregs of her strength, Ariel drove the blade into the black flesh of the Bukhariyin's hand. She heard the howl of pain, but her mind barely acknowledged it. They were free.

Hannibal lunged past the last of the Bukhariyin and sped across the dunes, bound for escape. Ariel felt Christopher's arm tighten around her. He pulled her into the secure hollow of his lap. How could he continue to protect her, she wondered, after all the trouble she'd caused them? But Ariel hadn't enough strength left to even contemplate that mystery. Closing her eyes, she let her head droop with exhaustion. "I'm sorry," she whispered against Christopher's chest. But her words were lost in the tangle of the stallion's black mane.

She must have dozed. When she opened her eyes again, they were climbing through the steep foothills of the Lower Atlas. The night was as black as pitch except for the stars, which seemed so close she might have touched them with a brush of her fingertips. Hannibal loped along at a comfortable gallop, but she could tell by the stallion's labored breathing that they had come a long way. "Christopher, where are we?" she asked softly.

"We're near the Ras El Ma."

"Hannibal is tired," she said. "And you must be, too. Is it safe to rest for a bit?"

"We can't stop now. There isn't time. Someone has to take a warning to the sultan and Suleiman. And, besides," Christopher muttered, "I need a bandage."

Ariel jerked around, prompting Christopher to grunt in pain as he yanked her away from his right side. "Hold still, damn it, or you may succeed in killing me yet."

"You're hurt! Stop and let me help you," Ariel urged.

"If we were in the middle of the Sahara, I wouldn't let you lay a finger on me. While you batted those golden eyes of yours and crooned over me, you'd probably be inching a dagger out of your boot."

"I would never do such a thing."

"Tell that to the African you skewered." Christopher made a sound that might have been a caustic laugh if he'd been in less pain. "I'm sure you'd do the same to me given half a chance. Then you could run back to Yazid and tell him all about it while the two of you gloated over your success."

"You're wrong," Ariel began, but Christopher dug his knees into Hannibal's side, cutting her off as the stallion reacted.

"Save your lies, Ariel. I've had enough of them to last a lifetime."

There was no time for Ariel to defend herself. Ahead of them a single torch had multiplied into dozens, and as they rode into the small Berber village, shouts of greeting and concern filled the night. Christopher pulled Hannibal to a stop before the largest tent, and a handsome young Berber ran up to them while another grabbed the stallion's head.

"My brother! What brings you here in the middle of Allah's night!"

"Take her, Fatim. And watch her," Christopher instructed, dropping Ariel into the Berber's arms. "I need your mother's help." He slid off the stallion, leaving a slick trail of blood down Hannibal's side, and collapsed in the white mountain sand.

A cry of female voices went up from behind the tent flaps, and a moment later Christopher was surrounded by a brood of women. One, older than the rest, wasted no time examining his wounds. Then she stood and gave sharp orders to the others. Ariel watched Christopher as the wave of anguished women carried him into the largest tent. Most of the remaining people filtered away, either gathering around the tent entrance to overhear news of Christopher's injury or returning to their own tents.

Ariel turned to the young Berber Christopher had called Fatim, uncertain as to how she should proceed in this situation. As it turned out, she was required to do nothing. Waiting only until Christopher was inside the tent, the young Berber set her away from him and bowed courteously.

"Forgive my brother's lack of respect. Even a wife should not be treated so. Especially a new wife. He has the stubborn head of a camel, and he knows little of our ways despite all I have tried to teach him."

His mouth curved into an infectious smile as he straightened, and Ariel smiled back despite his erroneous assumption that she and Christopher were wed. She had the distinct feeling that the women would want very little to do with her, but here, at least, she felt certain she had an ally. "On the contrary," she said, "I fear he knows much of our ways and that he had good reason to be angry."

The Berber's head jerked to the side in surprise. Eyeing her with keen interest, he leaned forward to whisper. "This may be true, my lady, but you must never tell him so to his face. You must speak with my sisters. They have refined the art of constant criticism to its highest form. I can see you need some instruction in this area. But that can wait. For now, come, I will see that a place is found for you to rest."

* * *

Ariel watched Christopher's fitful sleep. The angry red swelling in his left shoulder had all but disappeared beneath the fresh bandages that she had helped change earlier in the morning. Safira, Fatim's mother, had assured her that he would recover perfectly, making some comment to the effect that a mere lead ball certainly could not fell a man who carried as much of Allah's *baraka* as her English "son." But Ariel was not so certain. This was their second morning since arriving at the Berber camp, and Christopher still hadn't awakened. Gently dusting a strand of hair from his forehead, Ariel rested her hand on his brow, reassuring herself for the hundredth time that there was no fever.

Then, for as many times in as many days, she berated herself. What a complete fool she'd been, putting her faith in Yazid when instinct had warned her against him. Like so many other things, she had made Yazid into what she wanted him to be, refusing to see the real man. A sound at the doorway made her look up. Fatim, his arms waving in the now familiar salute of enthusiasm, strode in. Not bothering with any formalities, he settled onto his haunches beside her stool.

"And how is my brother today? Is he still sleeping like a lazy bazaar beggar?"

Ariel bit her lip, never taking her eyes off Christopher. "I'm worried, Fatim. I know your mother says he'll be fine. But he barely moves."

"That is the sign that all is well, sultana. If he tossed and had fits in his sleep, then indeed he would not be well. But this sleep of his, the sleep of the drugged, it replenishes him. Soon he will be awake, and you will yet have your chance to be a wife."

During the long hours of watching and waiting, Ariel had explained to Fatim's family that she and Christopher, although betrothed, were not yet married. As she'd expected, Fatim's sisters had absorbed this news with ill-concealed relish. Only Fatim, Safira and Khalif al Rashid had shown appropriate distress. Funny how much she was still hoping to becoming Christopher's wife. But Ariel realized that things had changed considerably, and she had changed along with them. It was as if her veil had been covering her eyes all these years rather than the lower portion of her face. Christopher had lifted that veil, despite how stubbornly she clung to it. The tenacity that was so much a part of him had won out at last. Except, she was very afraid it had come too late.

Christopher had come to her aid time and again, proving himself beyond measure. Yet she'd scorned him, and that knowledge filled Ariel with remorse. Their dinners, the surprise trip to the marketplace, their trip to the Casbah—all the times they'd spent together were highlights in an otherwise dull existence. Even the way he'd brought Sami back to the palace with her the night of the *fantasia* was special. These were things a Moroccan man would scorn, just as a Moroccan man would eventually scorn her because she desired such things. And two nights ago, Christopher had risked his life to rescue her from her own stupidity.

"He won't forgive me, Fatim," Ariel whispered as she caressed the stubble of beard on Christopher's face.

"He shall see the truth of what happened in the mountains. Only first he needs to assuage his pride."

"I've endangered the lives of everyone I love," she

296

continued, unencouraged by his words. "And I broke my promise to him, Fatim." She looked at the young Berber, hoping to find some balm to soothe her guilty conscience. "I promised I would stay with him, and instead I ran to Yazid. I don't think he'll ever forgive me."

Fatim stood, stretching his legs with exaggerated casualness. "You can overcome this."

Ariel listened, but her face reflected disbelief.

"Ayyiee!" Throwing his hands helplessly in the air, Fatim stalked across the tent and back again. "What my sisters could teach you if they weren't so covetous of your man!" He leaned close to her. "You are a woman, a beautiful woman. He is a virile man. And I think he has been without a woman for many months." He paused, letting his words hang in the air before continuing. "He may be very angry, but this I know beyond doubt. He desires you greatly." He strode out without another word, but Ariel was positive he winked at her before he left.

Running her hand across the furred expanse of Christopher's bare chest, she wondered if Fatim was right. Could she redeem herself to Christopher by giving herself to him? No, Christopher would see through such a guise and despise her for it, even if it was done for love. As she contemplated her dilemma, Ariel didn't notice the first movements of Christopher's eyelids. His hand snapped out from under the sheet with the speed of a coiled snake, making her gasp in surprise. Locking strong fingers around her wrist, he pulled Ariel hard against his chest and stared at her with eyes as icy as a mountain stream.

"Who the hell let *you* look after me?" he demanded.

"I've helped Safira care for you the past two days. I

don't know much about medicine and herbs," she said, recoiling at his look of disbelief. "But I've tried to follow her instructions—"

"So I could live to see you dupe the sultan the way you've duped me?" he snapped.

Ariel's jaw dropped, and for a moment she could only stare at him in disbelief. "Why would I ever wish to 'dupe' my guardian?"

"So you could become Yazid's sultana." He tightened his grip on her wrist until Ariel was afraid he meant to snap it in half.

"No," she said, shaking her head emphatically. "I would never, never, betray Mohammed. My mother loved him. He's been the only father I've ever known."

Christopher thrust her away from him with such disgust that Ariel could barely breathe in the face of his contempt. "Christopher," she said, forcing her voice to be even despite the growing panic she felt rising from the pit of her stomach. "Clearly, you know that I willingly left the Casbah with Yazid's servant. But I swear to you, I knew nothing of Yazid's treachery. I believed just as you did—just as Suleiman did— that Yazid was fighting with the sultan's troops. I never suspected until I arrived at his camp that he could be the leader of the Bukhariyin."

"And I suppose next you are going to tell me that you were dressed like a bazaar whore because you were getting ready to escape and take your new-found information to Mohammed."

"I was—"

"At least give me credit for being something on a higher order of intelligence than the baboon the two of you took me for," he declared icily as he cut her off.

"Please, Christopher," Ariel begged.

"Get out!"

Ariel backed away from him. He shot her one last condemning glare, and she fled from the tent. She collided with Fatim, nearly knocking him over in her haste to escape the hatred she'd seen in Christopher's face.

"Where are you going, running like you have just seen a djinn?"

She continued past him without a word, running on legs that would barely carry her — away from the man she had hoped loved her.

"Praise Allah's good will!" Fatim clapped his hands together enthusiastically as he ducked under the tent flap through which Ariel had just fled.

Christopher winced as he shifted his weight to ease the stiffness in his shoulder. "I'm not in the mood to discuss Allah's will with you, Fatim."

"No? Was it not Allah's will that you eluded a hundred Bukhariyin guards?" he asked, lowering himself onto the stool Ariel had just abandoned.

Christopher scowled. Fatim could be a damned nuisance when he wanted to be. "You're going to have to ride for Meknes, Fatim, and tell the sultan that his son and heir leads the rebels."

"And how shall I convince the almighty sultan Mohammed Ben Abdullah that I am not a madman who has wandered out of the Sahara?"

"Mohammed will listen to you. He listened before. Your warning about the revolt saved his life."

Fatim muttered, rolling his eyes. "And if I say that his beloved English ward is at my father's camp, he will think I am the one who kidnapped her from the Casbah."

"She wasn't kidnapped from the Casbah."

299

Fatim's brows shot up, but he only shrugged. "Perhaps not, but it was still Allah's will that she go there. How else would we know that Yazid leads the Bukhariyin?"

"The only 'will' that was involved was Ariel's. She's determined to do exactly as she pleases, no matter who gets hurt by her actions."

"You perhaps?" Fatim suggested.

"She didn't shoot me, although I wouldn't put it past her."

"I didn't mean your shoulder." Fatim jabbed his finger into Christopher's bandages as he rose. "It is not the wound of the flesh that hurt a warrior so much; it is the wound in the soul. You should know such a thing as this, my brother. Or have you perhaps only given such injuries and never before received one?"

Christopher rubbed his shoulder. "With friends like you here, it'll be a miracle if I ever recover."

"What is the wound of your soul, my brother?" Fatim probed. "It is a raw one, I know."

"You've been in the sun too long, Fatim," Christopher commented icily. He had no intention of baring his soul to anyone, including Fatim.

"I do not think that is so. I've seen it before in you, this pain. And it is a great injury. So great that it stands in the way of your marriage to this woman."

"Get out, Fatim. Go write poetry under some palm tree. This is very simple. Ariel is not to be trusted. Nothing more, nothing less. And all the poetry and stargazing in the world isn't going to change that."

Fatim bent his nose to the sand floor of the tent in exaggerated obedience. "As you command, my brother. But I think it is you, not I, who cannot see for the strength of the sun in your eyes."

300

He was out of the tent before Christopher could respond. But the rumbling growl that followed the young Berber out of the flap only caused him to smile to himself.

Lying on the pallet in his tent, Christopher was not nearly so pleased. It didn't matter what Fatim thought. He didn't know Ariel the way Christopher did. She was not to be trusted. He'd found her with Yazid twice, and that implied there had been other times when she'd managed to see him without being caught. He thought of how violently she'd argued her desire to stay in Morocco. Loyalty to one's homeland was something he understood. But he was revolted that Ariel was willing to make a whore of herself to get what she wanted. He'd been wrong about Ariel from the start. Like the ladies of the *ton*, she sold her body to the highest bidder. The only difference was that for her it wasn't money and mansions, it was Morocco.

And Fatim's claim that his past had anything to do with this was completely idiotic. Because it was Stephan who was being trained to take over the title and Blantyre, Christopher had enjoyed far greater freedoms than Stephan. The eldest son was always under the watchful eye of their father while Christopher had been free to do as he liked. And for the most part, he had. Nothing Christopher had done garnered more than a passing interest from their father.

He had learned not to lean on anyone. And not to wait for anyone's approval because there wasn't any coming. Christopher had been away from the country when his father died. By the time he returned, the excitement had long since died down, and Stephan

301

was the new Duke of Avon. Lying in his tent in the mountains of Morocco, Christopher remembered standing at his father's tomb as though it were yesterday. He had brought flowers. An asinine idea because, as Christopher looked at the cold gray marble, he'd felt nothing. Nothing at all.

After standing there for three-quarters of an hour, he took the flowers back to the house and gave them to his mother. The next day he sailed out of London, and for two years he kept himself busy in countries far warmer and more attractive than England. He occasionally returned to London, but they were infrequent forays. It was only when he received his mother's letter telling of Stephan's death that Christopher came back for any length of time. That was when he discovered that Stephan had gambled his way through every establishment, reputable and not, in England. And to add a bit of spice to the whole mess, he'd also slept with every politician's wife in the House of Lords.

Since then, Christopher had put all his energies into restoring the family's depleted resources and reputation. With this mission he would finally regain the favor of the king toward the house of Avon. It was something Christopher could not have cared less about, but which he wanted very much for his mother.

No, there was nothing in his background that needed fixing. It was his present that needed correction. And that could easily be accomplished by removing Ariel Lennox from both his present and future. Christopher intended to do just that.

Ariel stood knee-deep in the cold mountain stream,

her borrowed caftan drawn between her legs and tucked into her waistband to keep it above the rushing waters. She and two of Fatim's sisters had come down to do the wash, but the girls had worked their way downstream, claiming to be chasing wayward pieces of laundry. Ariel knew otherwise. During the three days she'd been at Khalif al Rashid's camp, none of the girls had made any attempt to befriend her. And with Fatim on his way to El Bedi, she was feeling the effects of her banishment keenly. At least Christopher was sitting up and eating well today, or so Safira had told her. Since he'd banished her from his tent, Ariel hadn't had the strength to go back. She didn't relish the thought of another argument with him. She was still bruised by their last one.

Bending over, she rinsed the burnous she'd been washing and then waded to the stream's edge to beat the heavy woolen garment against a rock. Exhausted from the back-breaking work, Ariel lay the burnous with the rest of the laundry. Massaging the ache in her lower back, she looked down the deserted stream. Fatim's sisters had undoubtedly finished long ago. They were probably back at the camp having a good laugh over her ineptitude, she thought grimly. She stared out over the water; it wasn't very deep here, and it seemed like a lifetime ago that she'd last had a bath. Yet even that bath, with Ahmed's oils and scents, only served to make her feel dirty in retrospect, and she felt a sudden need to wash away the memory of her night with Yazid.

Quickly Ariel stripped off the caftan, pulled the colorful cotton scarf off her head and dropped it on the bank. Although the current wasn't strong, she could feel it tug against her thighs as she waded into the

303

stream. Ariel lowered herself into a deep pocket behind a large boulder. The first shock of cold made her gasp. How different this was from the harem baths where the water was hot and the air filled with steam. She could feel the surge of the current caressing her breasts, and running against the sensitive place between her legs. Pulling her hair out of its thick braid, she ducked her head underwater, letting fingers of water drag her long tresses downstream. Emerging once again, Ariel gulped in warm mountain air. Her body tingled all over. She'd never felt so awake! Jumping to one side, she peered into the water to see what tickled her foot and caught a glimpse of a fish nibbling her toe. She wiggled all ten toes, and the salmon darted off. Laughing, she dipped her cupped hands into the stream and let water spill down her face and chest, enjoying the exhilaration of its cold journey over her flat belly and thighs as it returned to the stream. She dipped her hands in again and this time drank deeply.

The water was a balm for her soul, renewing her for the first time in days. With Fatim on his way to Meknes, Mohammed and Suleiman would know by nightfall of Yazid's betrayal. Ariel had fulfilled her vow to warn them. But she'd paid a high price. As she stood in the stream, the vision of Christopher's face filled her thoughts. His hatred was so deep, so tangible to her, that she held no hope it might change. Perhaps with time, she thought hopefully. But she had no time. As soon as they returned to El Bedi, Christopher would leave. The treaty had only to be signed, and now with the war there was every reason for Christopher and the Belmeths to return to England. It was no longer safe in the Maghreb. And here in the mountains, where they might be together and learn to trust agâin, he wouldn't let her near him. Fatim's sisters fawned over him, leaving her no chance to speak with him even if he would listen.

Despondent once more, Ariel found her footing in the stream and began to wade toward the shore. It was only when she'd reached the bank that she realized she wasn't alone.

"We're leaving." Christopher stood not ten feet away, coldly watching her from the embankment.

Ariel stared at him in disbelief before she regained her senses enough to yank her clothes off the rock. She pulled them on over her head, jerking the caftan into place over her dripping body, completely oblivious to the fact that the soft cotton clung to her damp curves in a way that created an effect on Christopher that was hardly any different from seeing her walking naked out of the stream.

"Your shoulder—" Ariel said, trying to fit the strange pieces of this puzzle together. Just one day ago Christopher had regained consciousness, and she could see by the way he favored his arm that his injury was still painful. And now he was standing here announcing that they would be leaving within the hour. Carefully stepping out of the stream, she repeated her comment. "You're still hurt."

"Never mind me. I don't trust Yazid. And with you as my captive—"

"Your captive!"

"—he'll change his plans," Christopher continued as if she hadn't said a thing. "Fatim doesn't know enough of the details to be convincing if Mohammed should have second thoughts. I need you as proof. The sultan may not want to believe his heir is capable of treachery."

305

Ariel stared at him, her mouth open. "So I am to be your proof?" she repeated in disbelief.

"Everyone, including Suleiman, knows you fled from the Casbah. Fatim can verify that I returned with you from the mountains outside Fez; that should explain very well where you were. And besides, you'll be there to tell Mohammed everything you know."

"Under my own will?"

"Or mine, whichever you prefer."

"Why, you jackal!" she hissed. "Do you think you can bend the will of every living thing if it suits your purpose? I will do what I do of my own volition. You can drag me across the Sahara if you like, but when I stand before Mohammed I shall speak my own mind. And you'll simply have to wait until then to find out exactly what that is."

"One way or another, Ariel, you'll tell Mohammed the truth," he stated frigidly. "We're leaving in an hour, be ready." And with that, Christopher left her to fume wordlessly after his departing backside.

Ariel raged at his callous treatment of her. His words smarted like a well-directed slap in the face. Any illusions that he might listen to her died as she gathered her pile of laundry and headed toward the camp. The load was unwieldy and heavy with water, and her caftan clung to her legs, making her progress unsteady at best. By the time she reached her tent, half of the hour Christopher had allotted her was gone. She was of a mind to take her own sweet time and let Christopher wait; but she could all too easily imagine him dragging her half-clad all the way to El Bedi, and she thought better of such a childish revenge.

As Ariel discarded the wet caftan and slid on the

cotton pants she'd worn on their ride to the Casbah, her mood turned from angry to recalcitrant. The truth was she knew exactly why Christopher was behaving so angrily. If their positions were reversed, she might have jumped to the same conclusion at Yazid's camp. Hadn't she done that very thing when Yazid told her the man she'd put her trust in was none other than the duke she hoped to elude? She stopped midway through the job of tucking the pant legs into her boot tops. She'd never given Christopher a chance to explain, although he'd tried several times. The awful truth, she acknowledged, was that she still didn't know why he had concealed that information from her or what had happened between the time he promised her the duke wouldn't marry her and when he reversed that decision. However, Ariel was certain now that Christopher hadn't intended to marry her until something had changed his mind. Not because of any proof she'd seen, but because that was Christopher's way. He wasn't the type to deceive. He'd rather bear whatever came of his often brutal honesty than twist the truth to suit his purpose.

She was as guilty as he of stubbornly refusing to listen. How foolish they both were, she thought sadly. Stubborn. So bent on having their own way. And how alike.

No, she corrected herself. In that one sense they were alike, but beyond that they were quite different. Christopher didn't trust, but she trusted too much. He attacked the world with determination while she had spent her life hiding from it. With him, Ariel had begun to reach out more. With Christopher she knew she'd see and do things she'd shun on her own. And she had something to offer Christopher also—the trust

307

she'd refused to give him while she bestowed it on everyone else. She could give him that now, and slowly, with time, she might win his trust. If it wasn't too late. Ariel pulled the djellaba over her head, and as it dropped into place, she felt the amulets still at the bottom of her pocket. She gathered them in the palm of her hand. They were a thousand times more valuable to her now than on the day she'd bargained for them. She wanted him to have them; she wanted him to wear them with pride. But if she didn't do something, reach Christopher somehow, they would never lie against his chest in that intimate spot where his heart would warm them.

Outside she heard the families of Khalif's clan gathering. Quickly replacing the amulets in her pocket, she tied the sash around her waist and reached for the turban cloth, ripping off a short length. She wrapped it around her head, tying it at the base of her neck, and let her hair cascade down her back in a straight sheath. She had no bags to take. She had borrowed all the clothes she'd worn here, and nothing could induce her to touch the harem dress Ahmed had preened over the night of her appointment with Yazid. Taking a deep, steadying breath, Ariel left her tent.

As she'd expected Christopher stood in the center of a circle created by Khalif's clan. Aziz, the youngest of his daughters, was making a spectacle of herself, leaning against Christopher's arm as she stared doe-eyed at him. Ariel wondered why he allowed the girl to cling to him like that. Certainly it must irritate him; he wasn't a man who would admire fawning females. As she watched the scene, it occurred to her suddenly that perhaps Aziz had reason to be so possessive of Christopher. Was that why she and her sisters had

308

been so hostile? Did they believe she had usurped something that belonged, by rights of past possession, to Aziz? The question lodged in her mind as she said her goodbyes, and it would not leave.

When she reached Khalif and Safira, Ariel clasped both their hands in hers. "Thank you both so much."

"You owe us no thanks," Safira replied, smiling gently.

"But I do. I'm a stranger and suspected of infidelity to the sultan. You had every reason to treat me as a pariah. Instead you embraced me. I swear to you both that I love Mohammed. I would cut out my own tongue before I would betray him."

"It is not necessary that you say this for our benefit, although we are pleased by your loyalty," Khalif told her.

"Allah's light shines from within you, my child," his wife added, patting Ariel's hand. "There is no evil in your heart. We will pray that Allah helps you convince those who do not see with our clarity."

Ariel smiled, tears of appreciation shining in her eyes. She wanted to say more; but her words caught deep in her heart, and she knew the tears would come first if she tried. Behind her, she heard Christopher's voice issuing her orders. "It's time to go, Ariel."

Chapter Twenty-two

Their ride took them through far different country than Ariel had crossed travelling between Meknes and Yazid's family's camp days before. During her escape with Christopher, they had ridden far into the hill country of the Rif to find safety in Rashid's community. When she had ridden with the Mongolian, although he had seen to it that they stayed off the main roads, they had passed along the common route between Fez and Meknes. Frequently they'd seen the makeshift camps of nomad Bedouin herders as well as a few small Berber villages. But Ariel had yet to see a single sign that anyone had traversed this route recently. It was nearly sunset, and she was tired and sore from the relentless pace Christopher set. What was more, her back ached where the muscles cramped from holding herself rigidly away from his chest.

When she'd leaned back against him at the start of their journey, he'd pulled away from her with a hiss of quickly indrawn breath, as if her body was a white-hot ember, the very touch of which burnt his flesh. Since that moment, Ariel's pride hadn't allowed her to seek the comfort her muscles so desperately needed. The image of Aziz languishing against Christopher

310

still rankled her. His easy acceptance of Aziz's touch when he couldn't bear even the friction of Ariel's clothing against him hurt. Ariel set her teeth on edge recalling how the girl had leaned against his thigh in the most wanton fashion. It was a miracle Christopher hadn't fallen to the ground under the press of her ardor. But Ariel must ride hour after hour inches away from him and never touch him, even by accident. All because she chose poorly when the Mongolian had appeared in the darkness.

Ariel felt Christopher tighten Hannibal's reins, drawing the stallion to a walk, and she looked more closely at their surroundings. This was the first time since they'd left Rashid's camp that Christopher had slowed their pace. They were at a tiny oasis, so small Ariel hesitated to label it so. But there were two date palms, which meant that there must be water of some sort. As they drew closer she saw that there was indeed a spring, larger than the date palms indicated.

Christopher dismounted. "Get something to drink." Without so much as a glance in her direction he strode away from the oasis toward a tufted mound of soil. Ariel glared after him, but she had no choice except to do as he'd ordered. She'd be fool-hardy beyond imagination not to refresh herself while she had the chance. Sliding off Hannibal, she led the stallion with her as she walked to the edge of the spring. The water was crystal clear and as cold as snow. She let the stallion drink and then cupped her hands, helping herself to a long sip. As she quenched her thirst she eyed the tussock Christopher had disappeared behind, wondering if he intended to go on from here or if they would spend the night. If they were to go on, they would have to change their riding positions, she decided with determination. Her back couldn't take even one more hour of the strained posturing.

Away from Ariel at last, Christopher continued the war of wills he'd fought with himself all day. Ever since he'd gone after her at the stream to announce their departure, he'd waged a losing battle against the effect she had over him. He'd expected to find Ariel engaged in a pile of dirty linens. Instead he'd found her frolicking naked in the mountain stream. The effect had been immediate and severe. As she'd waded to the shore, he'd watched the seductive sway of her hips, drank in the fullness of young, ripe breasts and the glittering reflection of sunlight on her wet thighs. She was beautiful beyond imagination. Watching her emerge from the water, one could almost believe she was an innocent water nymph. But Christopher knew better. And that was the issue that continued to infuriate him. He knew, only too well, how much to the contrary her personality was, yet he still desired her.

Having her so close that he could smell the fresh scent of the stream on her skin and watch the glimmer of the desert sun on her hair had made the day's ride a living hell. Unbound, the amber mass had played against his cheek, twining itself about his arms as if binding him to her in a tangle of desire. When she'd leaned against him, using his chest to ease the discomfort of the ride, he'd felt her warmth surge through him as though he'd been struck by a lightning bolt. Since then, he'd taken pains not to touch her; but it had been hours now, and his desire for her had yet to wane in the slightest. The white-hot power of her closeness singed him, but its heat only fed his desire.

Straightening his clothing, Christopher headed back to where Ariel stood beside Hannibal stroking his neck as her lips moved in conversation with the stallion. "Are you often taken to sharing intimate discussions with animals?" he asked, coming to stand beside her. The golden color of her skin was sweet torture, and he stepped closer still, punishing himself for wanting her by demanding he resist his most base urges.

"It's been a long day, and I've barely had ten words with anyone. It seems I'm not fit company for people, so I thought I'd try enticing this handsome stallion into conversation."

"I'm sure Yazid would be interested in what you have to tell him."

Ariel swung around to glare at him. "I have nothing to speak to Yazid about. Nor have I conspired against Mohammed. Rashid and Safira believe me. Why won't you?"

"Because I know you better. I saw you."

"Things, even things we see with our own eyes, are not always as they appear. Many a man has ridden for an oasis in the distance only to discover his eyes deceived him."

"My eyes did not deceive me, Ariel. You did."

"As you wish, Your Grace." Ariel turned as if to walk out toward the plain, leaving the sting of his title to remind him of his own deception.

Furious, Christopher laced his fingers around her arm, pulling her against his chest. "Mine was a well-intended, temporary use of your own misled judgment. I did not, ever, practice deceit in order to better myself as you have."

"Have I, Lord Staunton?" Ariel shot back, glaring

313

at him as fiery sparks of anger glistened in her eyes. "Have I practiced deceit? Or is it your own illusions that are the deception? What proof have you at all of my treachery? That you found me in Yazid's camp? Yes, that was wrong. I admit so freely. But I went there innocently, hoping to protect him."

Christopher watched her face change, growing soft with anguish as she searched for words. Her eyes settled to a warm glow as their fiery embers mellowed. When she spoke again, her voice was a whisper, her breath a gentle fan of warmth in his face. "I knew nothing."

Christopher felt himself drowning in the golden depths of her eyes. He knew he was losing the battle, perhaps even the war. With the will of a thousand less-disciplined men, he pulled himself back from the maelstrom of desire. "I can't believe you."

"Why? Were your lies less real than mine? What makes them different? Although I know you didn't intend it, they hurt me. When you first told me you were not the duke, you thought you were aiding me. You knew no more of Yazid's plans than I, and yet look how his revolt has changed everything—even the impact of your words. Innocent words turned painful. You never intended to marry me, so you thought what could be the harm? And I never intended to jeopardize the sultan's success. Now, in the light of all I know, I realize how foolish I was. But now is not then. And you can't forgive me for not knowing what was to come." She stepped back, looking at him with new understanding in her eyes.

"That's it, isn't it," she said, scrutinizing his face with her golden gaze. "Christopher, who in the world will give you satisfaction if that's the criteria of your

314

forgiveness?" Without another word, she walked past him.

"We'll camp here for the night," he announced to the general area, refusing to look at Ariel. Irritated at her and at himself, he began to unsaddle Hannibal. He rubbed the stallion down, setting his anger against the animal which braced all four legs against the attack of his master's care. Why did she never do as he expected? She might have screamed, or pouted, or demanded, and she would only have hardened his resolve against her. Instead she had seen deep within him to dark places he didn't care to look anymore, and left him uncertain of himself when *she* was the one they had been discussing.

Ready to wipe away the saddle marks from the gruelling ride, Christopher turned to the spring, intending to soak a rag with fresh water. Ariel sat on a rock at the water's edge, absorbed in her own thoughts as her feet dangled in the spring. She had pushed up her pantaloons, and above the water surface her long, slender legs swung in slow circles. As his gaze devoured her, she looked up. Her eyes met his, weaving a web of seduction around him that numbed his mind and set every sense aflame. All the guile and dishonesty that had passed between them since the day they'd spent at the trysting pool evaporated. All that remained between them was a passionate need that refused to be tamed.

He wanted her. She was becoming an obsession, and he couldn't afford that. He needed to be clear-headed again. He had to be able to see her for what she was, a need that was becoming impossible with this haze of lust blurring his reason. If he lost this single battle, what would it matter? he asked as he stood rooted to the sandy earth across the pool from her. He would win in the end. Why should he deny himself the pleasure of making love to her? Hadn't she already given her virginity away? And to a man possessed of the lowest morals. He needed to empty his mind and his heart of Ariel Lennox, and there was only one way to accomplish that. He would prove to himself that she was no different than any other woman. It was only because he denied it that his desire had become an uncontrollable hunger. Now he meant to have it satisfied.

Pulling the colorful Berber blanket Safira had sent with him from behind his saddle, Christopher shook it open with one fluid snap and let it flutter to the ground. Ariel dared not break the thread that connected their gaze. Although more than three meters separated them, she could see the way his eyes had darkened. She knew that look. In the garden, at the trysting pool, and a thousand times since — whenever they had been together — she'd looked up to find that gaze on her. Every time before it had filled her with an uncomfortable mixture of excitement and apprehension, and she'd run from it as fast as her heart could carry her. But seeing the look now, she rejoiced. As though Allah put his words on the wind and bore them to her, Ariel heard Fatim speak to her. Despite everything Christopher said, he wanted her. And if he still desired her, perhaps he didn't believe quite so completely in her dishonesty.

And she wanted him. He'd rebuked every attempt she'd made to breach the chasm that yawned between them since he'd found her in Yazid's camp. She had tried reasoning with him, asking for his forgiveness, admitting her own wrongdoing. None of those things

316

had won her his trust or forgiveness, but perhaps through passion she could reach the part of his heart he had closed to her. She knew such things happened. It was every concubine's fervent dream. Couching with the sultan was the doorway they hoped would lead to love, and all their skills were directed toward that end. Would it be so wrong to let him make love to her first and hope that trust came after? Ariel had no answer, but every instinct within her urged her forward. She stood, her movements slow and unwittingly seductive. She dared not take her eyes from his, fearing the spell that bound them would be broken.

Her legs moved beneath her, but she couldn't have sworn that they carried her there. Somehow she arrived beside him, damp feet on the soft, woolen blanket. She waited, but Christopher didn't move, neither bending to kiss her nor turning away from her. He only stared into her eyes as though fighting a private battle of wills while he held his arms rigidly at his sides. Ariel didn't know what to do. She'd come this far, but never having approached a man before, she had no idea how she should proceed. What must she do to spark a reaction from him? Her desire to touch him was overwhelming, and tentatively she laid her hand on his chest — just where she knew the rhythm of his heart would be strongest.

Her touch bolted like a shot of lead to his very core as the need Christopher had held tightly in check burst from its confinement and tore through him like a cyclone. A man possessed, he pulled her into his arms. With half-open lips he assaulted her mouth, his tongue already deep in its warm recesses before their lips were fully met. Ariel leaned into him, her body pliant and warm as it molded to the hard contours of

317

his own. A moan tore from deep within, his body reacting immediately to the willingness of her. Slender fingers slid across his shoulders, skimming the short hairs at the base of his neck in an action that sent a shudder of desire snaking to his loins. Her every action was exquisitely full, every movement meeting his, matching his own uncontrolled ardor with a fevered response of her own. Dragging his mouth away, he buried his lips against her throat, inhaling her sweet fragrance. "I want you," he whispered. "God help me, despite all I know, I do."

He pulled her closer, the granite expanse of his chest pressing against her breasts, steel against velvet, and looked down at her, his eyes lit by a desire that made Ariel's senses reel. Encasing her with his arms, he covered her mouth with his in hungered urgency, then lifted her as easily as if she were a child, cradling her against him for a moment before she was lowered against the blanket's fine weave. Stretching out beside her, Christopher threw one leg casually over her hips and drew her intimately against him, his mouth capturing hers once more. She felt his hand caress her buttocks, fitting her to him, making her feel his desire hard against her, and then his fingers were at her waist, easily freeing her knotted sash. The warmth of his hand against her flesh drew a moan from her lips as his thumb brushed the tip of her nipple, tantalizing it with tender enticement until she felt it harden, cresting obediently beneath his ministration. Laying open her djellaba, he leaned back on one elbow, blatantly admiring her.

"Temptress." The word was a ragged whisper against her mouth as he bent to kiss her again. His kisses wandered lower, trailing along her neck, and

318

the tip of his tongue painted a line along her shoulder as the white cotton slipped away. His hand cupped her breast as his mouth closed on the jutting peak of her nipple. Ariel gasped at the surge of indescribable pleasure that his mouth sent coursing through her. Through a thickening haze of desire, she urged his mouth upon her with fierce need. He nibbled gently, then lavished equal attention on the other, suckling until fevered chills bolted one upon another through her and her breathing came in quick, uneven gasps.

The demand in his kisses softened, his lips brushing against hers as they explored the breadth of her mouth. His tongue flickered across her teeth, running along the inner edge of her lip, then dipping into the well where lower lip met upper. His mouth pressed hers open, and she yielded as she had before; but while his first kisses had held more demand, these gentle caresses struck deep and true to her soul. Immediately, his tongue began an intimate exploration, caressing the moist inner walls of her mouth, drawing her tongue into titillating play.

Ariel's fingers splayed across his back while beneath them she felt his power. He was a mass of contradictions. Hard sinew and muscle. Soft, velvet blue eyes. Intense, bold, and demanding. Gentle, warm, and enticing. The kiss gave birth to a thousand offspring as he showered her face with their warmth. Her eyelids. Her brow. The sensitive skin where her jaw met the lobe of her ear. An indefinable urge rose from the molten heat within her. It was exciting. Tantalizing. Overpowering. And she wanted much more, something beyond what they shared at this moment. She felt an indefinable need blossom within her. And with an innate and ageless knowledge, she knew what it was. And where it would take her.

Christopher dragged his mouth from hers and gazed down at the flushed golden tone of her cheeks, the heightened pink hue his kisses had brought to her lips, the languid way her gaze followed him. He pulled his tunic over his head, discarding it in a ball somewhere behind him. When he stood to remove his pants, her eyes followed his every movement. There was none of a virgin's embarrassed turning away, and he realized suddenly that he'd still harbored some hope that she had told him the truth at least about sleeping with Yazid. It didn't matter, he reminded himself tautly. What was about to happen had been as inevitable as the sun's passage across the sky since the moment he'd first kissed her in the garden at El Bedi.

Naked, he returned to the blanket, kneeling at her feet as he gently hooked his thumbs over the waist of her pantaloons and slid them off. Casting the pants aside, he turned back to her, and his breath caught in his throat. She was golden from the tips of her toes to her head, so finely sculpted that if he didn't know the treacherous bent of her heart, he would have believed she was perfect. Her hair lay about her head like a pagan crown and matched to perfection the dark golden thatch of curls at the union of her slender, young legs. As he eased down beside her, he let his fingers trail a path upward along her leg from her knee to the place on her inner thigh where he knew the skin was sensitive. His palm brushed across the lightly furred triangle of her womanhood as he moved to caress the other thigh, letting his thumb slip against her mound, stroking lightly the intimate folds there.

Ariel tensed, startled by the power of her reaction

320

to his touch; but as his mouth captured hers in a heated kiss and the gentle probing of his fingers increased, waves of warmth began to wash over her, and she relaxed, giving herself completely to his care.

"That's better," he murmured against her ear. "Or hasn't Yazid ever bothered to satiate you? Too bad. But I doubt your past lover cared about that."

Through the haze of desire that threatened to engulf her, Ariel shook her head, mutely trying to tell him that he would be the first in every way. But Christopher paid her feeble protest no heed, and she couldn't fault him, for she paid little heed herself. The roar of molten heat within her had blocked out even the sound of her own moans of pleasure as her body responded of its own accord to the ancient rhythm that coursed through her. Christopher covered her body with his own, and she arched to meet him, driven by a longing powerful beyond the ages, and far beyond the scope of her meager understanding. She had only instinct now. And need. As she arched again, Christopher rose with her. She felt his manhood poised between her legs, and knew that she would be incomplete until their union was met. Then, when she thought she would die from want, he drove into her.

At her cry of pain, Christopher froze. He held himself immobile, still sheathed deep within her while his mind was caught in a vortex of conflicting emotions. But when he would have withdrawn, Ariel cried out in protest, her arms pulling him back. The desperation in her eyes spoke the one thing he could understand when all else had ceased to be comprehensible. He began to move inside her, slowing his drive, controlling his own need as he skillfully helped her find the release she so desperately sought. Ariel matched his rhythm, and he couldn't suppress his wonder as her passion drove his control to the brink of his ability.

Ariel's hands rode Christopher's hips, then traced across his back as she arched against his deepening thrusts, searching. And then, as they moved together, her wild searching found satiety. The world exploded into a thousand lights as pleasure complete, total, and all-consuming spread through her. She tightened around Christopher, unwittingly using her own pleasure to create his. He drove into her once more, burying himself deep, deep inside, his powerful body convulsing as he poured himself into her.

Still within her, he rolled until she was relieved of his weight and brushed his cheek against hers, pressing a kiss to her forehead as he held her. Ariel laid her head against his chest, and he drew a ragged breath. His breaching of Ariel's virginity and the searing heat of the union that followed struck deeply at Christopher's conscience. "Why didn't you tell me?" But he already knew the answer. She *had* told him. Again and again, though he wouldn't listen. He'd accused her of every conceivable crime—treachery, treason, and whoring. It didn't matter to him that he hadn't used the exact words; the intent had been the same. Yet knowing that he had accused her wrongly, Ariel had still been the one to cross the sand. She had come to him, aware that he was about to take her virginity. And she had given it. Wincing, Christopher thought of the things he'd said to her even as he made love to her, trying to hurt her even as he loved her. "I'm sorry, Ariel," he said softly, tilting her face to his.

She pressed a kiss against his chest before looking

322

up at him. "It was mine to give, and I gave it willingly to you. Better that than to have it taken by someone else."

Christopher started to correct her. To say that he was sorry for thinking she'd conspired with Yazid, but the words caught in his throat, unspoken. She moved, parting them intimately, and although Ariel snuggled close in his arms, he felt the chill of the night air drop like a wall over him. When her even breathing told him she was asleep, he slipped from beside her, covering her with the loose ends of the blanket, and walked to the water's edge. Long after the moon had risen high in the sky he sat there, telling himself that it didn't matter that Ariel had gone repeatedly to Yazid, choosing the prince over himself.

But it did matter.

She had told him the truth about being with Yazid, but that didn't explain her other actions. It didn't explain why she'd stolen out of the Casbah in the middle of the night. And despite the fact that he desired her, and that she'd come to him freely, he still didn't trust her.

Chapter Twenty-three

El Bedi's gate no longer lay open as it had for more years than Ariel could remember. She counted over a score of heavily armed guards eyeing their approach, and her heart broke at the terrible changes Yazid's ambitions had wrought. Belatedly, she ran her fingers over her djellaba, smoothing wrinkles and fussing over dirt stains, but there was nothing she could do to make her appearance justifiable to these men. She was sitting in Christopher's lap, dressed as a boy sans turban, or veil, or anything to cover her face. It was a futile effort, so she settled for folding her hands in her lap, and prepared for the worst.

Christopher felt Ariel square her shoulders and adjust her chin stubbornly as he pulled Hannibal to a stop. Despite his anger, his chest tightened in acknowledgement of her bravery. Whatever she had done, she possessed an inner strength that he understood only too well. She'd given his distant attitude a single questioning glance today, and then had settled in front of him for the long journey home. But unlike yesterday she'd leaned back against him the entire ride, a silent, yet constant, reminder of what had passed between them.

"I'm an emissary of King George III of England,"

Christopher announced to a guard who'd separated from the rest. "And acting as an agent for Moulay Mohammed and his son, Prince Suleiman."

Although he had never seen the Sohda Agadir before, the guard acknowledged the authority of the infidel with eyes like ice from the mountaintop immediately, for his description, and reputation, preceded him. Only a fool hadn't heard the tales of this warrior's great feats in defense of the sultan, and Asani prided himself in knowing every detail of such legends. Bowing low, he salaamed at the same time he indicated that the gates be rolled open to let the giant stallion and his riders pass. He asked nothing at all of the golden woman who rode before the Sohda Agadir. She was, of course, the sultan's ward and the great warrior's betrothed. He knew that tale as well. It was not for him to disapprove if the Sohda Agadir wished her to dress as a man and bare her face to the heavens. But it gladdened his heart to know his own wife would never see such a thing.

"So it wasn't just me you came after in Yazid's camp," Ariel stated quietly as they made their way along the palace drive.

"I came because Mohammed feared for your life."

The hope that he truly cared for her had sprung full-grown in her heart last night, but now it withered like a plucked rose deep inside her, pricking her heart. She'd dared to dream she had reached beyond his icy shield. Dared to step to a different melody than the one they had played over and over since meeting.

But it hadn't been enough. And now she knew the price she would pay. By surrendering to him, she had given him the power to hurt her as surely as she had withheld it from him until now.

Despite her dread of the pain he could inflict, her next words were past her lips before she had time to think or arm herself against his reply. "And you didn't care anything for my safety?"

"I came because Mohammed and Suleiman asked me. And because something of mine was missing."

Humiliated to the core, Ariel squeezed her eyes tightly shut. "I'm just a possession, then? That's what I'll be when you return to England with me as your wife?"

Christopher heard the anguish in her voice and steeled himself against it the same way he'd steeled himself against her warm body as they rode. He had willed himself to ignore the enticing view of her full breasts when he'd glanced down and found the neck of her djellaba blown open by the wind. And he willed himself to ignore the tug at his heart now. If she was a traitor, she wouldn't live to accompany him to England.

And if Mohammed found her innocent of that charge? Christopher would admit that he desired Ariel, but that was all he'd admit. He wouldn't even contemplate the possibility of Ariel going with him to England. Last night had not remedied his desire for her. He still wanted her. Even as he denied himself, his body responded to the mere thought of her.

"If you go to England with me, you will be my wife. It's not uncommon in England, as here, for a man and woman to make a marriage of convenience, or in this case, a marriage of political advantage." He was amazed at the matter-of-fact tone in his voice as he described the very kind of marriage he despised.

"But you said it was different in England. You said at the trysting pool . . ." Ariel stopped short, realizing how very long ago that had been—perhaps not in days, but in the passages they had traversed. Then she had not known who he was, only that he was handsome, and charming, and had the power to entrance her with his kiss.

And he'd had no reason to distrust her.

All her choices had lain ahead of her then. Why had she chosen so foolishly? she thought as her eyes filled with tears of frustration.

They continued to the palace in silence. Christopher never responded to her last, unfinished thought, and Ariel rode in silence, lost in the hopeless vista her future presented. By the time they arrived at El Bedi there was one thing she knew for certain. She would rather spend the rest of her life with Christopher's contempt than live even one day without him.

"Allah be praised!" Chedyla's cry was followed closely by the duenna's embrace as Ariel stepped into her room. "I thought never to see your sweet face again, my child. Thanks to Allah your beloved has brought you safely back to us."

Ariel backed away from Chedyla, eyebrows knit in frustration. Christopher had given her into Siad's care as soon as they'd reached the safety of the palace, and Ariel had no idea when she would see him again. "Why did you call Christopher my 'beloved'?" she asked deliberately.

"Is this not what he is, child? I am an old woman and have seen much. I know the desires of your heart better than you do yourself. Besides, fate directed you."

Ariel no longer had the energy to deny her feelings,

especially to Chedyla. The old concubine was far too wise to be fooled, and Ariel realized she wasn't really very surprised by Chedyla's declaration, only chagrined that she had taken so long to realize it herself. "I've lost his love," she told the duenna quietly. "Lost it at the very moment I found it.

"If this is fate," she continued in defeat, "then it has chosen to play a cruel trick on me." Heart weary and exhausted, Ariel fell into her duenna's arms, her tears at last breaking through the barrier she'd so carefully erected during the day. She poured out her anguish, recounting each episode between Christopher and herself. And she pinned the guilt upon her own stubborn pride, blaming it for the rift that lay between her desire and reality.

Chedyla clucked softly, stroking Ariel's long tresses as she rocked her like the child she'd comforted so many years before. After her mother's death, Chedyla had known that time would heal Ariel's wounds. But there was no time for these wounds. Their world was crumbling around them. Ariel could only find safety and happiness in her mother's country far across the seas. But even there Ariel would not find happiness if she lived without the love of the man to whom she had at last given her heart. Chedyla would do anything to spare her that heartache.

Her old, knowing eyes gazed out beyond the ornate bedroom, and past the balcony with its gardens below. She looked far beyond, to the great, unending sky of the Maghreb. "Sometimes," she whispered, "a man must be given a special gift by the woman he loves. Even a great warrior may have a hidden fear in his heart, and he cannot see the way until he knows that he need not fear his love."

"What could I ever give him to mend the rent in his trust, Chedyla?"

"That is only for Allah to reveal." Taking Ariel's smooth hands in her own gnarled ones, she continued. "You will know the answer only when Allah chooses to reveal it."

"It was that way with my mother, wasn't it, Chedyla?" Ariel said, interrupting the moment of quiet. "When she chose to stay at El Bedi, she gave Mohammed the greatest gift she could offer. She gave him her life."

Chedyla nodded. It was as though a torch had been lit and the world illuminated for Ariel. Her tears evaporated as her understanding grew. "That's what made their love strong enough to survive all the forces that worked against them. They trusted each other."

"Without it there could be no love for them," Chedyla replied. "Only fear, and anguish, and doubt."

"Yet with it, they were invincible."

"It is the true way of love, my child. Yet so few see it."

For several minutes Ariel was quiet, absorbing this new-found knowledge. Then she looked up, locking Chedyla's dark eyes with hers. "When did you see it, Chedyla?"

"It was long, long ago, child. Before I ever came to the sultan's palace or dreamed of living in the luxury of the royal harem. But it lives with me still. And that is how I know."

Bathed and fed, Ariel let Rhima slide an emerald tunic over the sheer blouse she wore over her harem pants. She was anxious to see Sami. After crying out

329

her frustrations to Chedyla, she felt able to turn her mind to things other than Christopher for the first time in days. "I'm going to check on Sami now."

"The boy thrives," Rhima assured her.

"Have his parents come forward yet?"

Chedyla came to weave Ariel's hair into a long braid, and shook her head. "I fear he shall not be reunited with his family."

Ariel thought of Christopher's comment about Sami's family. "Maybe he was meant to be lost in the melee, Chedyla."

"The hand of Allah moves, and it is not always for us to see the reasons why."

"So I am learning."

Running anxious fingers through his silvering hair, Robert paced the room another time. "I don't know how to get Mohammed's attention. They've created so many barriers to keep everyone away from him, and I can't seem to determine a way to break through them. By God, I must be getting old. I don't even know who 'they' are," he declared bitterly. "Except that they're very close to the sultan, and they wield enormous power. I swear to you, Christopher, I've used everything within my ability and knowledge to speak with Mohammed Ben Abdullah, but it's all come to naught."

"I, too, have been unable to see the sultan, though I have declared my message of greatest import," Fatim added from where he sprawled on an armchair across from Christopher in the Belmeths' sitting room. "But I know who it is who thwarts us."

Robert stopped in his tracks, pinning the Berber with a stare.

Fatim shrugged, subdued by the seriousness of their situation. "It can only be Daiwa. She is like a swarm of hornets. She is everywhere at once, and whatever she touches is poisoned."

"What makes you say it's Daiwa?" Christopher asked. He agreed with Fatim's assessment, but now wasn't the time for guesses. If the Hatum Kadin was responsible for isolating Mohammed from any outside information, then she was conspiring with Yazid. It made perfect sense. From inside the palace Daiwa could get Yazid all the news he needed to make his moves flawless. And they had been. She could prevent Suleiman's field information from reaching Mohammed, which explained why the sultan had no interest in meeting with either Robert or himself. He probably didn't even know Fatim was at El Bedi.

"I do not know, my brother. I only say what Allah's wisdom tells me. Has not your betrothed dealt often with the treachery of the first wife?"

Christopher nodded.

"Then, should we not seek her wisdom in this matter?"

"No." Christopher's response was as flat and unyielding as a wall of stone.

"Aiyyee!" Fatim leapt from his chair, arms flying wildly in an agitation that forced Robert to step out of his way or risk a blackened eye. "You are as hardheaded as a woman. How can I call you my brother with honor when you act like a stubborn camel? You would let my country rot beneath the stinking hand of the Bukhariyin before you would ask her for help! I am beginning to think it is true what they say about the English!"

"And that is?"

331

"Never mind. As I am bound, I have condemned such talk, but if you ignore any chance to save the Maghreb, it shall be upon my family's name! And that would be very hard to forgive."

Christopher stared him down icily. "You're free to seek Ariel's help, Fatim. But I choose not to. Robert," he continued, directing his attention to his uncle. "I'm going to speak to Mohammed. One way or another I'll get through. Can you get a message to Suleiman?"

"I believe so."

"Good. Warn him that Daiwa may be helping Yazid and that he and his men are needed at the palace." He raked another glare over Fatim. "At least one of us should succeed in reaching the sultan's ear. The question that remains is whether or not Mohammed will believe us."

The Hatum Kadin strolled leisurely toward a small copse of lemon trees in the walled garden. Within it was a small bower of climbing hibiscus. A very private place. Perfect. Stopping, she removed the tiny dagger she wore at her waist from its golden scabbard and cut a single bloodred rose. She didn't bother to appreciate its heady fragrance, but held it at arm's length. "Flawless," she crooned in her husky voice. "A faultless blossom brought to the culmination of its life on the first day of the new regime. The day my bloodline is returned to its rightful throne." She threw back her head, exultant as a surge of power poured through her. "At last. At last, today, it shall be mine. I shall have my revenge on Mohammed for spurning me. I shall have revenge on all Morocco for sending my family into exile and letting me grow up in a hovel, less than the lowest of men." Behind the trees' narrow

332

trunks she caught the movement of a black tunic and smiled, triumphant.

She stepped into the copse and offered her son the rose.

Yazid slapped the blossom away. "You are late, my mother."

Unruffled, Daiwa merely crooked a carefully penciled eyebrow. Normally she would not stand for such treatment by Yazid or anyone. But this was their day of triumph, and he was the agent of her success. This once she would let him have his way.

"I took extra care dressing. I shall be at my most glorious when I stand beside you in victory." Her caftan was deepest purple, shot with threads of gold and heavily laden with gems at the cuffs—for Daiwa never wore anything that a woman of lesser station could have possessed. Even her rings were more numerous than usual, the very finest in her collection.

"It is time," she said, lowering her voice.

"Yes. My men are gathered just outside the palace walls. When I signal them, the palace shall be breached. Without my father as their rally call, his forces shall be like butter in the sun."

"And tomorrow we shall reign." Bending to retrieve the rose, she continued. "With you upon the throne, and my influence among the Bilad al Makhzan, the country will be ours within the day."

"Not ours, Mother."

She froze with her hand suspended in midair above the blossom where it lay on the grass, then straightened carefully. "Of course. You shall be sultan. I am only a woman. But I am your mother, and as the mother of the sultan, I shall hold a place of even greater honor than is already my right."

"No."

It was a flat, simple statement spoken without the anger or temperament she knew flowed so readily in Yazid's hot blood. Daiwa spoke carefully, testing this unforseen change in her son.

"You are my issue, Yazid. Prince or no. Without me, you would not be sultan."

"Ah, but you are wrong, Mother. Once I would not have been sultan without you. Once I needed you. I needed your lies. And I needed your treachery. But now I shall be sultan with you, or without. It is mine to take today, and no one shall deny me my right.

"Except you, my dear mother. If, indeed, I was to place you in such an exalted position. If I gave you such power, how would I trust you? I have seen your devious nature firsthand. Why, it was you who taught me never to trust, and never to give power to anyone. So you see, what you envision is quite impossible."

"How do you think you will hold the viziers, Yazid? They will break and run like the cowards that they are if you do not have me. They know me. I am the one they have followed these past months, not you." She eyed him smugly, certain she had the upper hand. She had played such games of power many times, and always she had come out the victor. Still, she admired her son for his gall. Was that not how she had bred him? But he was still a pup while she was a master of the game at which he attempted to best her. He could not win.

"They will learn to follow me."

"I think not, Yazid."

"But they will, Mother. They will think of you, and any doubts will be banished."

"Then, I will be in a venerated place in your realm,

or it will not be as you say," she threatened, making it clear that she would not cooperate without the price she demanded.

"Oh, yes," he replied softly, moving as if to embrace her. "An exalted place, beloved mother. But not beside me, beside Allah."

The dagger slid between her ribs so smoothly. She was surprised at its warmth as it drove to her heart and sliced away her life. The blade was painless, though its effect was immediate, for her vision was already blurring. She slipped to the ground and was assailed by the scent of the rose. What had happened to her perfect plan? The dying was painless. It was her own stupidity that burned like hot poison in her soul. So close. She had come so close. Oh, how Allah must be laughing, she thought. Laughing at them all.

Ariel started down toward the rooms that had been converted into a nursery for Sami. Except for herself and Siad padding silently behind her, there wasn't a soul to be seen.

As they wound into a little-used portion of the palace, Ariel wondered if Daiwa had ordered her charge put in such isolation, or if Chedyla had been trying to protect Sami from Daiwa's long and deadly reach. Either way, they were far from the main traffic of the palace, and the hallways were eerily forsaken.

She was excited about seeing Sami. It would be wonderful to cuddle the little boy again. She'd grown used to the feel of his small frame upon her lap as she read stories to him or helped Rhima ready him for bed. But as she rounded the corner it wasn't Sami she found. Instead she came face-to-face with the Mongolian.

For a moment she stared mutely into the cold, soulless eyes of Yazid's mercenary; then as his scimitar slid like a silver snake from its scabbard, the scream that had frozen on her lips found voice.

Siad jumped in front of her, his own scimitar arcing before him. "Run, O beloved! There is treachery in the sultan's palace. He must be warned!"

Even when she heard the bite of steel upon steel, she didn't look back. There could be only one reason for the Mongolian to be inside the palace walls. Like a wraith borne on wings of fear, she flew down the hallway, knowing she must reach Mohammed before Yazid.

Chapter Twenty-four

Although Christopher stood perfectly still in the anteroom outside Mohammed's study, his mind was racing. He should never have let Fatim go after Ariel. What if she *could* condemn the Hatum Kadin? Fatim was just the type to let her confront Daiwa with their suspicions. And smart as Ariel was, she had a face as transparent as her harem pants tended to be. Even if they tried to be diplomatic in their questioning, Daiwa was adept at deception. She would read through Ariel in a moment, and she had that henchman eunuch.

If Siad was with them, they would have a chance. But Ariel was as likely as not to ditch her only source of real protection if she felt he might not approve of her activities. He was weighing the liabilities of abandoning the sultan to intercept them, when the door burst open and Fatim strode into the room, wearing a scowl that did nothing to settle Christopher's rampant imaginings.

"Where's Ariel?" he demanded.

Fatim threw up his hands helplessly. "I could not find her."

"What do you mean you couldn't find her. She's supposed to be in her rooms," Christopher stated, his voice dropping to a growl.

"But she is not there. She has gone to see some child."

Christopher's jaw tightened in fury. When he got his hands on her again, he intended to tie her to the chair of any room he left her in for more than two minutes. In his entire life, Christopher had never met anyone who put so little worth in her own word. How many times had he told her, no *asked* her, to stay where she would be safe. And she had said she would.

While he was worrying about her, she was traipsing through the palace playing marbles with a child. It was probably her idea of a good way to while away the time until Yazid's army overran the palace. But it wasn't going to be that easy for Ariel. Not if he had anything to say about it.

And he intended to have a great deal to say about the outcome of this day.

"Have you had success in gaining the sultan's ear?" Fatim asked.

"I think we'll be invited to see him at any time."

"And how have you accomplished this impossible feat, my brother?"

"It seems I've developed into something of a legend," Christopher replied dryly. "Everywhere I go in this place the guards and servants are bowing and mumbling strange things I can't quite make out. By the time I arrived here, they already knew I was coming. Mohammed sent out a messenger to say he'd see me shortly."

"This is always the way with you, Brother," Fatim declared in exasperation. "I am called to perform feat upon feat of bravery and devotion without acknowledgment or praise while you achieve a single act of bravery and all the Maghreb carries words of your praise upon its lips. Sometimes, my brother, I do not like you at all."

At the other end of the room, the double doors that

led to the sultan's study opened, and two guards bowed ceremoniously, indicating they could enter. "Fatim," Christopher warned as they crossed the room, "remember that we probably won't have much time with Mohammed, and we have news he's not likely to enjoy hearing. Try to restrain your natural penchant for talk and stick to the essentials."

Fatim gave Christopher a ludicrous grin. "I will do my best for you, but it is most wise not to ask the impossible of one's friends."

It was the first time Christopher had been in the study since he'd signed the marriage documents. Less than two weeks had passed since he'd allowed himself to be beguiled into a marriage contract by a pair of golden eyes and Ariel's seemingly innocent seductiveness. He had thought he was saving her. And he'd thought that in those eyes he could find the thing he'd given up hope of ever having. But as it had always been, he'd found that the love he wanted was always the love that spurned him. His father had taught him that lesson. It was the only one he'd bothered to teach the extra son. And Christopher had learned it well. He preferred relationships where he held all the cards. Relationships in which he didn't care if the woman came or went. Dalliances he controlled. And he intended to continue the policy that had served him so well for so long. He would marry Ariel. But he had no intention of touching her ever again. He would reserve his affections for women who couldn't come close to reaching his. That was all he wanted with her, he told himself as he waited for the sultan's acknowledgment. Beyond that, he had no interest in her at all.

The sultan stood with his back to them, looking out over the gardens as he clasped one large brown hand in the other. It was several minutes before he turned to them.

"I welcome you both," he said with subdued enthusiasm. "Lord Staunton, you have come from seeing my sons. Tell me how they are."

"Suleiman is in good health, Moulay Mohammed. His troops await the order to put an end to the revolt. But I have no news of El Yazid. He was not at the Casbah."

"So it is with all leaders," Mohammed declared. "They must be at the front of the army, showing the men for whom they fight."

"Some rulers lead through knowledge and forbearance," Christopher countered. "Isn't that the lesson you've brought to your people?"

"There will be time for temperance later on. Now the country must be won back. If we do not accomplish that, then there will be nothing to lead to peace. I have learned over the years that there is no right or wrong. The sun has many shades of gold."

"But some things *are* bad, Moulay. The Bukhariyin, for instance, seek an evil purpose."

"They are not evil, Lord Staunton, only misled."

Christopher had hoped that the philosophical bent of the conversation would somehow soften the message they had brought. But Mohammed was too willing to forgive, and what was more, Christopher had no idea how much time they had until Yazid attacked El Bedi. He knew it wasn't long enough to try to win the sultan over in this discussion.

"Moulay Mohammed, Fatim and I bear information which we would not wish to give if it wasn't absolutely necessary. There is no way to say what must be said except to be straightforward. You've brought peace and prosperity to a land that for a thousand years has been rent by war. Now someone is trying to destroy that.

Fatim and I know who it is. So does Suleiman."

Mohammed listened carefully, then looked Christopher straight in the eye and nodded. "Tell me."

"It's El Yazid."

The sultan whirled away from them, his arms clamped across his chest as he paced to the balcony doors. For a long while he stood immobile. At last he sighed heavily and, without turning, acknowledged Christopher's message. "I did not wish to believe this could be so, but I am not an old enough fool not to have considered this possibility. So now we must wait and see."

"What?" The word was nearly a shout torn from Christopher in disbelief.

The sultan turned back into the room and gave them a wry half-smile. "Yazid is young, and he has always been full of lust for the days when the power of the sultan was absolute. He does not believe in a government. The Bilad al Makhzan and Bilad al Siba would not exist in his world. He alone would determine the future of the Maghreb. Perhaps this is a good lesson for him. After this he will see that the old ways are not so good. Perhaps, he will listen to me with more respect when all is finished."

"Mohammed, he is leading the Bukhariyin. He needlessly murdered innocent people at the *fantasia*. As we speak, he marches on El Bedi," Christopher argued.

"He comes to talk," Mohammed declared cryptically. "And I caution you in your discourse, Lord Staunton, for he is my son and my heir."

"You have two sons."

"But only one heir."

"In your eyes, Moulay." Christopher waited for some response, but the sultan had moved back to the balcony window to stare out over the gardens. Christopher un-

341

derstood that they were being dismissed, but he couldn't leave yet.

"Do you intend to turn the throne over to him?" he continued after several minutes. "I can promise you that the treaty will be nullified if Yazid takes the throne. I have to make my report to the king."

"I will not give him my throne, Lord Staunton. There are other ways to fight insurrection besides with the sword. I will send him on Jihad."

Fatim shook his head imperceptibly at Christopher. "Great Moulay, I do not think Jihad will enlighten the heir."

"Have you made Jihad?" the sultan asked.

"Yes, Moulay. Two years ago. It was a journey of illumination for me as it is for most men. But it does not change what a man is."

"It need only change how he sees Allah's world," the sultan stated.

Christopher could see that there was no use in continuing their meeting. Mohammed had made his decision. If he succeeded in somehow coercing Yazid into a position in which he was forced to go on Jihad, then the danger would be put off for a while. But Christopher knew that as long as Yazid was alive and free, he would plot against his father. Fatim was right. You couldn't change a man's basic nature.

Christopher walked to Mohammed's side and extended his hand to the sultan. "I wish you luck, Moulay."

Mohammed turned to take his hand in a firm grasp, and their eyes met over the handshake. In that wordless communication much was said between them, and they parted with respect for one another.

"I shall nullify your contract Lord Staunton. But the treaty shall hold fast. The Makhzan will not deny me

342

once Yazid is on his way to Mecca.

"In the blink of Allah's eye the world changes, Lord Staunton. This I have come to understand well," Mohammed Ben Abdullah called after them.

Christopher nodded, then turned and headed for the door with Fatim in his wake. But as he reached for the door, it was opened from the other side at the exact same moment. And in that moment, Allah blinked.

Christopher stood face-to-face with El Yazid. For one second their eyes met, and purpose clashed against purpose with the friction of lightning bolts. Then Yazid's loathing was masked, and he looked past Christopher as though he didn't exist.

"My father!" he proclaimed, and strode to embrace Mohammed.

Christopher quietly closed the door, remaining in the throne room. He didn't care what the sultan believed. He knew better than to think Yazid had come here with good intentions.

"Send these infidels from us, Father. We have much to discuss about the Maghreb and the blood of Allah passed down to us from Mohammed."

Mohammed Ben Abdullah glanced quickly at Christopher and Fatim. But he only smiled at his son and clasped his shoulders in an embrace. "Lord Staunton is betrothed to my ward, and the other is the son of my great ally, Khalif al Rashid. They are surely as family and welcome in my presence."

Christopher could see Yazid seethe inwardly, yet the prince quickly covered his fury with a smooth smile. "Then, let us view the setting sun. I would have a word with you, my father, in at least some privacy."

The sultan led the way to the balcony, stopping where Christopher and Fatim could still see him clearly. Fatim leaned over to Christopher. "I do not think Mohammed's faith is as great in Yazid as he would have us believe."

"I trust him even less," Christopher replied. As he watched the men on the balcony, Christopher's thoughts returned to Mohammed's last statement. The engagement would be nullified. He no longer had to worry about his obligation to Ariel or the sultan. He had been freed from that. And that was something to celebrate. From the first, it had been nothing but an error. His instincts had been correct when he had told Robert he'd have nothing to do with the marriage.

The marriage had been forced on him. And forced on Ariel, who had made it clear from the onset that she wanted nothing to do with him. If she hadn't very nearly fallen into his arms the night of the ball, the negotiations would be completed, and he'd be on his way back to Blantyre. The fact that things had at last been put right should have pleased Christopher immensely. But he felt no sense of relief.

Instead, an emptiness seeped through him. All he could see before him were images of Ariel — the sparkle in her eyes and the soft music of her laughter. His mind filled with memories of her spontaneous, unself-conscious nature, and the knowledge that at any moment she would do something completely unexpected — something extraordinary that would cause him to catch his breath in wonder. He would miss those things.

But she would miss nothing about him, he realized, shaking himself from his juvenile fantasy. It was Yazid she wanted, standing not ten meters away from him, plotting against everything Ariel had benefitted from through the sultanate, plotting against everything that she wanted. She had made it clear at every opportunity that she wanted no part of him. She'd even gone to Yazid at the first possible chance. And Christopher, himself, had provided her with that opportunity because of his calf-eyed lusting. No, Ariel wouldn't lament the broken engagement. She would rejoice.

Christopher was jolted from his thoughts by Mohammed's shout. Fatim was at the balcony a step before him, and the two crashed through the open doorway together just as Yazid drew his scimitar.

"I am meant to be sultan of all the Maghreb! You old fool," the prince ranted as the crescent blade swung in a wide arc through the scorching air. "I shall not go on Jihad! I shall be sultan, and no one, no one shall keep me from it. It is mine. Allah brought it to me through the rite of my birth. You would destroy our strength. You make us soft as the pasty infidels who swarm into our ports and rob us of our God-given gifts. No. No one shall stop me this day. Look well on it, my father. For it is your last."

Mohammed made no attempt to protect himself; he never even raised his arms in defense against the glistening blade of death Yazid wielded. It was Christopher's scimitar that blocked the downward death swing of the heir's knife.

"No!" Mohammed shouted. "You shall not defend me against my own son!"

Christopher saw the light of anger spark at last in Mohammed's face. He parried Yazid's stroke and passed the scimitar to Mohammed. "Then, defend yourself, Moulay."

The older man moved with an agility that belied his age. And it surprised Yazid, for as the sultan laid a solid downward thrust against his sword, the heir fell back a step.

"You shall not take back all that I have built here," Mohammed declared, advancing a step on his son. "You have the blood of your mother's greed in you. You

345

shall never rule this land. Not so long as I am alive to stop you."

"I have the blood of the Saadians, the rightful line to the throne."

Mohammed missed the target of his scimitar as he reacted to Yazid's words. "What?"

Yazid stopped for a moment, and smiled victoriously. "You never knew all this time that my mother's only goal was to see you killed and to put her own issue on the throne. She was the last of the Saadians. A princess in her own right. You, and your father, and your grandfather stole it from her. Through me she would have had it . . . if only she had not been so selfish. Instead she lies dead in the gardens. As you shall be. As Caroline had to be."

Seeing the disbelief spread across his father's face, Yazid threw back his head and laughed. "Poor Caroline. If only she'd given me the slightest attention. But it was all for you, so she died the most horrible of deaths. Poison."

For one second silence filled the air like the heavy precursor of a storm; then Mohammed's rage and anguish burst from behind the dam he had erected eight years before. The battle cry that issued from his lips filled the palace, shaking crystal chandeliers and reverberating through the gardens of El Bedi like an ominous portent, and there was no one within the palace walls who did not hear it and shiver at the sound. He raised Christopher's scimitar high above his head and charged his son and heir, throwing his still-powerful body against Yazid with a force that sent the two men rolling across the mosaic tiles of the balcony floor.

Ariel heard the cry, too. With her heart in her throat she burst through the doors of the throne room and raced toward the open doors of the balcony, searching for the source of that malevolent cry. At the balcony's edge, she stopped short, staring at the body that lay so still on the glistening tiles.

Time seemed to suspend itself. In the gardens below, Ariel could hear the unnatural gaiety of birds in song. She felt the warmth of the afternoon sun as it poured down on her bare arms. Yet a numbness spread through her body until she felt nothing except where her heart was being torn from her very soul. Ariel pressed the back of her hand against her mouth, swallowing back the bile in her throat as she watched the scarlet stain spread across her guardian's chest.

It was Christopher's scimitar that stood impaled in Mohammed's chest, and on either side of his motionless form stood the two men who had shattered her dreams. Her head began to buzz as though a swarm of ten thousand hornets had gathered inside her brain, and Ariel felt the world tilt crazily.

This could not be. She would not believe that this could happen.

Later, when Fatim told her how she had screamed, how the sorrow and anguish of her voice had broken the heart of every living thing for a thousand miles in all directions, Ariel could not recall uttering even a sound—for the numbness had spread through her completely by that time.

She ran to Mohammed's still figure like a frightened child. Her fingers caressed his chest where the lifeblood seeped in an ever-widening stain through his jewel-studded tunic. She'd laid her head on this chest night upon night after her mother's death. Only with Mohammed had she felt safe enough to sleep. With her head resting against his broad chest, he had quietly reassured her that Allah had a plan for them all in this world. The resonance of his deep voice vibrating against her cheek had made her feel safe again. And she had believed him.

But now the pillow she'd depended upon was silent and growing cold. And his promise grew cold as well, for she could no longer see Allah's plan for her. The world she loved had turned upside down. The things she treasured and trusted had become ghoulish caricatures, tarnished and misshapen, and not at all what she'd believed them to be.

Certainly Allah did not condone this horror. This could not be the plan that He had for her. As surely as the peaks of the Atlas rose in the east, He mourned the murder of the man who had been her only father. And she saw quite clearly what she must do.

Ariel knew that what she did afterward came from a source within her borne of an absolute knowledge. She did not have to think about it. She knew. Slowly, Ariel pulled herself from Mohammed. Turning her face away from the sultan, her eyes met those of the man who had destroyed all her dreams. His eyes were sour with envy and hatred, emotions well suited to their color. She couldn't imagine how she had ever put her trust in him. Or why she hadn't seen it before. But whatever her failings in the past, she wouldn't let it go on. When she ran to him she had but one purpose; she wanted him to feel the pain of what he had done. She went at Yazid intending to rake her nails across his face and wipe away the smug triumph there, intending to destroy his triumph as he had destroyed everything she had loved and cherished.

From the other side of the balcony Christopher saw only one thing. He saw Ariel run straight from Mohammed's dead body into the arms of the man who had killed him. As he watched, his heart curled like a dried leaf. Throughout everything that had passed between

348

them since their first meeting, somewhere deep inside Christopher had harbored a belief, a seemingly indestructible belief, that Ariel was not really the heartless mercenary she sometimes appeared. But as she ran to him, and Yazid's arms went around her, that belief died, leaving Christopher devoid of any feelings for her at all.

Was it really only moments ago that he had been mourning her lack of affection for him? Had he really questioned for even a portion of a second her motives, thinking that perhaps he had misjudged her? The enormity of his foolishness appalled him, and the shell around his heart hardened. Christopher knew then that the inevitable had finally come to pass. He would never again trust. As he watched her run to Yazid, Christopher felt the shell close around him. It was too much of an effort even to hate her.

Yazid watched Christopher's face flatten into an unreadable mask as Ariel flew at him. Despite her bared claws, Yazid's arms slid around her in a caress that only Ariel could feel clamp around her like steel bands. "How sweet, my love, that we may share our triumph. Today all the Maghreb is ours!"

Ariel struggled against him furiously. "You—" But Yazid cut off the stinging retort she intended for him, smothering her words with a kiss that brought the bile rising in her mouth with ferocity. Ariel tried to push him away, to scream out. At last she was able to tear her mouth from Yazid's repulsive kiss. Gasping for air, she parted her lips to scream a denial of his accusation, but the point of a blade pricked her side, drawing silence from her instead. Then, for the first time, she turned to look at Christopher. She had known he was there, just as she had known instinctively that although it was his sword impaled in Mohammed's chest, Christopher had not killed her guardian. But her thoughts had been so completely on her loss, and on Yazid's guilt, that she hadn't done more than glance at him since entering the room. Now, as she looked at him, any hope that he would understand her situation died.

Yazid pinned Christopher with a triumphant glare which was only returned with bland indifference. "So, perhaps we have reached the impasse, Lord Staunton."

"How so?" Christopher responded with indifference.

"I have everything I desire, and you, who have gambled to thwart me, have nothing. You have no treaty, no woman, and, I think, no dignity in your God's eyes. You have nothing left here. Your time in Morocco is done. But because you have lost so completely and so dishonorably, I see no point in killing you. Instead, I have a mission for you."

"I see."

"Leave my country, Lord Staunton. But take a message back to your king when you go. Tell him that the Maghreb is the lone star in Allah's sky. We form no alliance with countries who seek to sap our strength for their own purposes. Infidels only weaken us. Tell your king to stay away from my shores and my waters. Unlike my father, I shall show no mercy to infidels, no matter what their claims of innocence."

"You should be tried for murder, Yazid. If it was within my power, I would see to that."

Yazid snorted. "You try my benevolence, infidel. Get out of my sight. Should our paths cross again, I will kill you myself."

"You tried so many times before, Yazid. Are you sure you're capable of doing it?"

Yazid's eyes narrowed into green slits of hatred. "It is only the knowledge that by living you will suffer more, that allows me to free you. You are weak in one way, infidel, and I have found that place in you." He eyed him for a moment and then smiled wickedly. "I have the one thing you desire. And you shall have no peace from this day forward knowing that her body is mine to command."

Christopher looked at Ariel, and the cold indifference she saw in his eyes hurt her as nothing else could.

"You're wrong, Yazid. You have nothing I desire."

The ache in her heart caused Ariel's knees to go weak, and she slumped against the point of Yazid's dagger until it pierced her flesh. Only the sting of its steel cutting into her drew her mind from the pain of Christopher's contempt. But even its bite did not stem the drain upon her. She no longer cared what her fate was to be. If she ended up in Yazid's harem, or worse, butchered by the ruthless tools of pleasure Yazid craved, it no longer mattered.

Christopher looked away, his face a study of indifference as Yazid pulled Ariel closer against him in order to keep her upright. It was Fatim who at last spoke in Ariel's defense.

"Let her go, Moulay. You have all of the Maghreb. What is one simple woman to you now?"

Yazid sneered at Fatim, curling his lip at the young Berber. He pinched Ariel's face between his fingers until her cheeks grew white with pain. "Let a rare jewel such as this go free? You let your simple mind show too easily, Fatim al Rashid. No, this one I have waited too long for. I shall use her well and often, and she shall cry for mercy before I have finished with her." He laughed.

Christopher's head snapped up, every sense suddenly alert.

Yazid's laughter escalated until it roared his contempt. Snapping the dagger from its hiding place, he laid it against the slender column of Ariel's neck. "You have lost again, Lord Staunton. Lost what you did not even believe you had. I shall have such pleasure. While a thousand women beg for my merest glance, she dared to deny me. And while I am satisfying myself on her, I will relish the knowledge that I have had what you desire. I will make her cry out your name, and then I shall make her curse it to damnation."

He glared at Ariel, the last vestiges of his mask of affection stripped away. "You shall learn to regret the day you ever met Lord Staunton, little Ariel. At last you shall learn your station in the world of men."

Ariel made no attempt to defy him. She had lost. She had gambled with fate, attempting to change its course. But all she had done was cause the destruction of everything she'd sought to keep. She only wanted it all to be over.

Fatim ventured a quick move toward Ariel, and Yazid's blade drew a thin line of blood across her throat before Christopher pulled him back. Ariel saw his sharp frown at Fatim, and her heart broke again. He didn't want Fatim to waste any efforts on her. She didn't blame him really; there was so much of greater importance to be done.

"I'm afraid we must go now," Yazid announced with a grin. Fatim started forward once more, but Christopher grabbed his arm and shook his head. "Let him go, Fatim."

Ariel's eyes never left Christopher's face as Yazid backed her out of the throne room with the point of his dagger still pressed against her throat. She wanted to memorize everything about him. She would need those memories for what was to come.

Chapter Twenty-five

Robert, who had entered unseen, was the first to speak when the door closed behind Yazid and Ariel. "Will he take her back to the mountains?" he asked.

"He'll take her to the closest place that can be secured," Fatim stated knowledgeably. "What do we do, Brother?" He directed his question to Christopher, who gave no response. He stood motionless, staring at the closed door.

Frustrated with Christopher's lack of response, Fatim burst out with his own assessment of the necessary action. "Moulay Suleiman must rally the royal guards. We can attack Yazid on horseback wherever he sets up his camp. I know the mountains like the flesh of my own hand. I can help Moulay Suleiman in this." As if he had conjured Suleiman up with his thoughts, Fatim pointed to the line of troops racing toward the palace. "See, he comes even now!"

Robert joined him at the balcony railing, grimly shaking his head. "He's too late for Ariel. I understand that the palace is rife with unused passageways. I'm afraid he's escaped with her."

In less than twenty minutes, Suleiman had joined them in the throne room. His anguish over the death of his father was profound, but he wasted little time with his mourning, determined to see the sultan's dreams continue rather than be crushed by his half-brother's blood lust. Suleiman explained that like Christopher, he too had suspected Yazid's infidelity, and had posted watches all around the city. When Yazid had been spotted riding for the palace with only one other rider, Suleiman had immediately rallied his troops.

"How will you catch him now?" Fatim demanded.

"For a while I shall not worry about Yazid. I left only a minimal guard at the Casbah, and I must return there as soon as I secure El Bedi from the possibility that Yazid will return again."

"But the sultana! Yazid has her with him. My ears will not believe the words that you will leave her to him!"

"I have split what troops I have between the Casbah and El Bedi. I cannot divide them yet again," Suleiman said quietly. "Not even to save Ariel. My obligation now is to the Maghreb. Ariel, of all people, would agree with this." The prince turned an understanding face to Fatim. "We will save Ariel. But first I must see to the needs of my people."

Fatim stared at Suleiman before waving his arms in exasperation. "You must find a way to achieve both these goals at one and the same time, Moulay. Even the simplest man can see that Yazid, may Allah condemn the poisonous juices of a snake that flow through him, will waste no time with Ariel. He shall take pleasure in causing her great pain."

Gaining no response from the prince, Fatim's face turned scarlet with distress. "This is not to be allowed! I shall go myself! No! I shall collect my clan and sneak up upon the snake in the desert! I cannot let this happen to the sultana!"

In his growing frenzy, Fatim had forgotten the stone

figure standing beside him. But Suleiman had not. With each word that passed from Fatim's mouth, Suleiman watched Lord Staunton's muscles tighten until the flat plane of his cheek twitched with the effort of his control. Suleiman saw Christopher's anger and understood its power. He, himself, never felt such depths of emotion. His mind was like his father's, ruled strongly by temperance. His was a reasonable mind that dealt with reasonable commodities, things such as knowing that he must put Morocco and the good of its people before Ariel—and understanding that Yazid would destroy himself. Suleiman's goal was, and had always been, to save the Maghreb from being destroyed along with him.

He had understood this from a very young age. Every time Yazid had beaten him in riding or weaponry, Suleiman had understood more clearly where his destiny lay. Yazid was far too reckless. Everything came too easily to his brother, and the price was Yazid's lack of discipline. His bid for the sultanate could never succeed because his impatience left many chinks in his armor. Suleiman had only to wait patiently, plan carefully, and he would find that vulnerable place. He was not proud of this fact. He had no lust for his father's throne. Nor for his half-brother's death. He only wanted the Maghreb to survive, and that could only happen if the country followed the course his father had set it on, a course of trade and education. This was his destiny. He saw clearly that such was Allah's plan. And Suleiman was willing to follow Allah's vision. He had only to allow fate to lead him.

In this way, he and Christopher Staunton were much alike. Lord Staunton possessed an intensity that Suleiman would never have; however, in other ways he was much more like Suleiman than Yazid. While his

355

emotions were strong, he possessed control of those emotions. He planned carefully, and he had great patience when looking toward his goals. For these reasons, Suleiman had been much in favor of the union between Ariel and Lord Staunton.

Ariel knew so little of temperance and patience. She was like a small desert whirlwind that whipped about furiously, tossing sand in all directions as she searched for something she did not understand. He loved Ariel, but she needed someone who would love her for those things that were so unique and admirable in her—her integrity, the strength of her commitment, and her fathomless capacity to love. And someone who could teach her patience and where to place her trust.

Christopher Staunton understood what it was to desire something. He knew what was required to fight for something worth having. He understood things of value. Suleiman did not worry overly much about Ariel's safety. He had no doubt that Christopher Staunton knew Ariel was a thing of value.

"Well, while you both stare off into the clouds," Fatim interrupted Suleiman's thoughts with an uncontrollable fit of annoyance, "I am going to do something. I cannot stand by and let the son of a viper succeed in his plans." He stormed off, his djellaba flapping behind him. He didn't make it halfway across the room before Christopher stopped him with an icy command.

"You'll do nothing, Fatim."

But the young Berber was in a fit at the lack of reaction or emotion from the other men. "You!" he shouted, turning on Christopher in a rage. "You are no brother of mine. I dismiss you from the bonds of honor that have united us. You have broken them!"

Crossing back to where Christopher stood motionless, he wagged a long brown finger in his face. "You are an idiot. You should be begging for alms with the others who have lost their wits in the desert sun! She loves you. She is more beautiful than the sun, warmer than a gentle sea breeze, softer than a newborn ewe. She has risked her life for you. I have seen her sit by your sickbed night and day, caring for you, worrying over you, praying for you. Yet I have seen her take nothing but abuse from you.

"Yes! Yazid will abuse her physically, but you have abused her long before this with your words. With the daggers in your eyes. With your lack of trust.

"For you she must prove herself time upon time. And always there is a flaw. Something she has done that is not perfect. But it is not she who has failed. It is you, my brother. You could not find the strength to trust her." His speech over, Fatim sealed his meaning with an unforgiving glare and spun to leave.

"I know, Fatim."

His voice was as flat and hard as the sea at dawn. The pain that had at last shed its mask lined the haggard pallor of his face. Bowing his head, Christopher ran his fingers through his hair. "I saved your life once, Fatim. Now I need you to help me save hers." His eyes were haunted as he searched his friend's face. "I let her walk right into his arms. Right into a death trap."

Clapping a hand against Christopher's bowed back, Fatim's unsuppressible nature resurfaced. "Let us not waste Allah's precious time with remorse, my brother. Ariel awaits us. And I, as you know, am always glad for a good fight."

In the black of a starless night, Fatim squatted beneath the small olive tree as he watched the solitary figure on the only escarpment that looked down upon the

Casbah. The wind was cold tonight, whipping down out of the Atlas to shake the scant cover of the tree's branches. An ill omen, Fatim decided. But not for them. The omen was for those in the Casbah below.

Yazid had been smarter than any of them had suspected. He'd gone immediately from El Bedi to the Casbah, taking the minimal guard Suleiman had left behind. Yazid now controlled the fortress, and with it the clear view of all who approached. It would be impossible, Fatim thought, to get Ariel out of there. It would take all of Suleiman's army, an army Fatim knew he would not commit to save one small woman, to overtake the Casbah. He could not even allow himself to think of the atrocities Ariel would suffer before Suleiman had formulated a plan and was prepared to attack the Casbah. Impossible, except for the man with him.

Fatim did not know how long they had been on the escarpment. Since long before the Imam had called for evening prayers. Hours had passed, and Christopher did nothing but stare down on the fortress, watching it like a desert hawk watches the mouse's hole. The freshening breeze pressed his black djellaba tight against his broad shoulders until the material whipped in front of him like folded wings awaiting the moment to soar. He was a barely discernible outline against the darkness, more an eerie djinn than flesh-and-blood man. More the spirit of a cause than mortal being.

But despite the specter he appeared, torturously human emotions racked Christopher's soul as he watched the bonfires burning in the courtyard of the Casbah. As he memorized the location of each sentry and guard, he relived in his mind each of his transgressions against Ariel. Time and again he had punished her for pursuing her own dreams instead of forsaking them for his.

358

Each scene burst to life before his eyes, illuminated by the flames below. He had allowed her to believe that the man she was to marry was someone else, yet when she discovered his lie, he had expected her to simply understand. He had humiliated her in front of Yazid, punishing her because he'd found her in his arms without ever asking if it might not have been a sisterly embrace she bestowed on a man who was like a brother to her. He had thought from that moment that he had reason not to trust her, but had he ever truly trusted her?

Fatim was right. He trusted no one, and although Ariel had given him her trust by putting her future in his hands — he had not trusted her. Instead he had judged every encounter as a test, trying to determine when she would prove him right. When she, too, would confirm that she was not to be trusted. He had driven her to Yazid with his rage and coldness. He had judged her without reason. And now she was Yazid's prisoner — the captive of a man whose hatred had robbed him of reason or remorse. He had been a fool, Christopher admitted as he raged against himself. Because he wanted her so completely, he had done everything possible to deny it. Because he needed her love, as he had needed his father's, he had made it impossible for her to prove anything except that she, too, would put someone else before him.

The encampment within the Casbah was settling down for the night. Fewer Bukhariyin moved about, and the bonfires were less bright now. Despite Christopher's anguish, doubt raised its ugly head within him again as he watched the Casbah. Perhaps Ariel was in Yazid's chambers right now, a willing lover. She could be, even now, kissing Yazid as she had kissed him, making love to him while they planned for their new regime.

359

Angrily Christopher shook the vision from his mind. He had been a prisoner of his father's legacy too long. It was time to strike a new pathway. Loving someone meant trusting them, and he knew one thing with certainty. He had fallen in love with the sultan's golden-eyed ward.

Fatim jumped up as Christopher whirled away from the cliff and strode toward him. "Now?"

"Now."

"Allah Akbar! my brother. God is Great!"

"One hour, Ariel."

Ariel glared at Yazid in defiance, refusing to let him see the hopeless fear that enveloped her as the prince paced the tower room.

"One hour and my generals will all have received their instructions. Then I'll expect to see you in my rooms." He smiled at her, an ugly smile meant to frighten rather than disarm. "And be certain, my sweet, that you have prepared yourself well. I want no concubine who stinks of my father's household in my bed."

"You'll never have what you wish from me, Yazid."

"Ah, but I shall. And I will enjoy it all the more because you will try to keep me from it. It has been a very long time, little Ariel, since a woman was fool enough to deny me."

She tossed her head angrily and continued with a bravery she didn't feel in the least. "You may be able to force yourself upon me, Yazid. But it makes no difference, because what you truly want I have already given to another man."

Yazid's eyes narrowed, and in an instant he was across the room. Grabbing her by the arm, he yanked her against him and stared into her eyes. Ariel forced her face into a mask of triumph that she hoped confirmed her words.

"You lie." He moved as though to release her, and then suddenly pulled her back, wrenching her shoulder and digging his fingers into her flesh. Ariel's head snapped back, and her heart jumped into her throat in fear. "You would not be such a fool, Ariel. I take no man's leavings. If I find tonight that you have let another man have you, I shall kill you with my bare hands. And if that man was the infidel, then what you shall suffer will be worse than death."

He cast her away with such force that she flew against the wall. Her head smacked against the stone, and the world exploded into bright colors. As she slid to the floor, her face broke into a smile. Perhaps she would die now. That would be a fine trick on Yazid.

But thirty minutes later, Ariel stood before the bronze grillwork that made her room her prison. Her head throbbed terribly, and her mouth still tasted of blood where she had bit her lip as she hit the wall. But she was alive. It would have been too easy, she decided, to have died so simply.

Beyond the grillwork, she could only see darkness. She knew that the night spread out onto the plains surrounding Meknes, and that should have soothed her. But it no longer felt as safe as it once had. Her home, the place she loved above all else, was not her home anymore. She had worked so diligently to stay here. She had been so determined, so single-minded in pursuing her goal, that she'd never considered the possibility that it wasn't hers to decide. Her home had been taken away from her — not because she'd been married and sent away, but because of something entirely different. She realized now that Mohammed must have had some knowledge of Yazid's plans. But instead of trusting the man who had raised her, she had stubbornly refused to cooperate. Since then, very little had gone right.

She left the window, turning instead to the fire that crackled brilliantly in the hearth. Only the things without emotion continued unaffected by the day's events. She, however, had been changed forever. There was no need to look out into the night. Christopher was not coming this time. When she had faced Yazid at his camp outside Fez, she had prayed to be rescued, and Christopher had appeared as though by her very wish. But this time he wouldn't come.

Even if his only reason for coming was revenge, as it had been when he'd dragged her out of Yazid's camp, she still wanted him to come. She wanted to tell him that she loved him. And it seemed to her as though he must have loved her a little. The day he had brought her here to see Suleiman, she had believed that he loved her. And at the oasis, when they had been united as one beneath Allah's sky. Then, too, she had believed he loved her. She knew she loved him. But she also knew she had betrayed Christopher.

Ariel's pride rose in her breast in protest at that thought. She'd always told him the truth — except when she'd left the Casbah with Yazid's messenger. And even then, she'd wanted to tell him, but there hadn't been any time. With a sigh, Ariel pushed her pride away. It no longer mattered who was to blame, or who had lied to whom. She had lost Christopher. She had her wish; she would stay in Morocco forever now. But now she hoped that forever wouldn't be very long. She wanted Yazid to tire of her quickly, and she knew that she would fight him to the very end. Forever seemed a very long time without the person she loved.

A person was so much more to love than a land, she thought. How silly she had been to believe otherwise. How could she have thought that a place, a view, a building could give her what one look from a pair of midnight eyes could give her. She had believed that she could be happy with the inanimate, but once she felt the heat of his life force beside her, she should have seen how desolate the landscape was without him.

If only she'd had a chance to tell Christopher, she thought. But he hadn't even looked at her in the throne room. Ariel thought of Chedyla, and the words she had spoken to her only days before. Sometimes a person must give something more precious than words to the one they love. Her aching head was forgotten as she sunk onto a tasseled pillow and smiled sadly into the fire. It was the first good feeling she'd had all day. She had done something good. Yazid had her, not Christopher. Christopher was probably already on his way to the harbor in Salè with Anne and Robert. They at least were safe. She had done that. She had given Christopher something of value. His freedom. It was freedom from Yazid and freedom from her as well. By keeping Yazid here, Christopher could escape. That was good. He could go back to England and his life. That, too, was good, for that was what he had wanted. She could prove her love for him this way. Christopher would never know it, but she would. And that was the best thing of all.

She looked around the tower room. At least Yazid had put her back in the room she and Christopher had shared for a few hours. Here they had discovered the secret doorway. She recalled the sunset they had witnessed from the battlement. If she had it to do again, she would run straight into his arms instead of backing away. Ariel looked over at the Saadian tapestry hanging on the wall. It seemed to billow in the breeze, as though the doorway they discovered was once again open.

Shaking her head, she looked away. She would not attempt to escape fate again. This time she would face it bravely. This time she would walk into it with her head up and her heart open. That was her gift to Christopher. That he should have his world back while she would stay in hers.

Ariel drew her knees under her chin and curled her arms around her legs, warming them against the chilly night. The Saadian tapestry billowed and flapped again, and Ariel felt the cold on her back in a sharp gust. She closed her eyes, banishing the thought that rose in her brain. *Don't be silly,* she told herself. *You are only wishing again for something that you may not have.* But another voice in her brain spoke, a new voice. It spoke of trust, of faith. *Trust yourself, Ariel. Trust fate. Trust Allah. And sometimes the thing that doesn't seem possible, can be.*

Slowly Ariel turned, waiting to open her eyes until she could look fully at the tapestry. She held her breath, wanting to believe in this new voice, yet so afraid to let go of the old. She opened her eyes, and stared at the tapestry. It hung straight and still against the wall. There was no breeze, no open door, no Christopher. She sighed, closing her eyes against the pain that hope had caused in her heart. Better not to hope, she thought. Better just to sit in the dark and wait.

"Are you praying again? You only pray when you're in very serious trouble."

Ariel's eyes flew open. Her heart began to pound in disbelief at the vision that stood against the grilled window. He was there. Real, and whole, and more wonderful than she could ever have dreamt him to be.

She flew into his arms with the inevitability of a mountain stream running to the sea. Their union possessed a power neither had ever known before, as if at last each had found that part that had heretofore been missing from their souls. Christopher's arms closed around her with healing warmth, and Ariel absorbed it like a balm that soothed her parched soul.

"Christopher . . . ," she began, but he pressed his finger against her lips, quieting her.

"We only have a few minutes. There will be a lifetime for explanations." He swept the great black cape over her and nodded toward the tapestry. "Thank the Saadians for at least one thing."

As Ariel stepped in front of Christopher, the crown of her hair brushed his chin. Unable to control the need that burned in him, he swept her into his arms. Ariel melted into his embrace. Her body molded to his without resistance, and they knew a sweetness even their dreams had not prepared them for. Ariel looked up at him with love and trust, and a faith that nothing could defeat. She encircled his neck with her arms and pressed onto her toes, drawing his head down to her lips. Christopher dipped his head to receive the kiss she offered, and the union of their lips was far sweeter than anything either had ever tasted before.

"I love you," she whispered. Her tongue darted between his lips, and he groaned, racked by the sweetness of her surrender. Christopher pulled her hard against him, one hand cupping her buttocks through the sheer silk of her harem pants while the other crushed her against him.

"You've entranced me like one of Fatim's djinns, except no spirit could drive me to such distraction. I will gladly take what you are offering, but . . ."

Ariel's nutmeg eyes pierced him with a look of sublime understanding. "I hope the trysting pools in England are as private as El Bedi's because we have much pleasure to share. And I have a great many amends to make."

Christopher groaned, surrendering to the bonfire of desire that raged in his soul. His lips captured hers in a kiss, and she returned it, taking them to a place beyond all imagination. She was his. Not as a possession, not as a bauble to be shown about. She was his as his life was his. Inevitable and right. Ariel filled his empty spaces and satisfied needs that had caused him pain his entire life. Somehow, with her in his arms the circle was complete. He could let go of the anger and pain of his childhood. He filled those spaces in his heart with her love. Golden-eyed, beautiful Ariel. A seductress without guile, a woman who knew only of loyalty and pride. And she was at last willingly in his arms, saying words he had scorned ever needing to hear. He crushed her to him, and silently repeated her words to himself: *I love you.*

The tower room doors crashed open at the very moment their lips parted. In an instant the space was crowded with Bukhariyin wielding scimitars and muskets. They were huge, any one among them an equal match to Christopher. But there were ten of them.

And in the center stood Yazid.

Ariel turned in panic, wanting to bolt through the secret doorway to freedom, yet riveted to her spot by her fear. She knew Yazid was beyond anger. Knew that there was no escape. Yet beside her she could feel Christopher's calm.

"No one dares to touch a possession of Mohammed El Yazid, sultan of all the Maghreb."

"Prince Yazid," Christopher acknowledged with icy control.

"Sultan Mohammed El Yazid, infidel."

"I don't think so, Yazid. Not yet."

366

"I am sultan of all from the western sands of the Sahara to the shore. Within me runs the blood of Mohammed and from him the blood of Allah himself. No man dares to defy me." He turned his attention to Ariel. "And no woman who defies me shall live."

"A king doesn't hide behind his soldiers," Christopher taunted. "If you truly deserve the title you've stolen by murdering your father, then prove it. Fight me."

Yazid's eyes glinted yellow-green in the candlelight. A slow smile spread from one corner of his mouth to the other. With the speed of a snake, his scimitar flashed from its scabbard, and he sliced a swath from the space in front of him. "Gladly, infidel. I shall gladly see your tainted blood flow like a river across the sands of my country. I shall make you the first. And when you are defeated — the great Sohda Agadir — " he jeered, "then I shall turn the streets of the towns and the waters of the ports crimson with the spilt blood of infidels. Man and woman, and the issue of their unholy flesh, shall I destroy until my land is cleansed again. Until you and your kind are forever banished from Morocco."

Christopher didn't acknowledge a word of Yazid's speech. He merely nodded toward the Bukhariyin.

"Go," Yazid commanded. "This infidel is mine alone."

Conditioned by years of utter compliance, the Bukhariyin filed dutifully from the room. Not even one looked back or held his scimitar unsheathed in case of trickery. But Christopher could think of nothing he wanted more than to make Yazid pay for the wrongs he had committed against Ariel. Knowing that he had even touched her was enough to make Christopher's blood boil. Yazid would pay for his crimes. Tonight Christopher intended to have his payment in blood.

Ariel slid up against the wall as Christopher's scimitar sung from its scabbard, trying to make herself as small as possible. She didn't want to distract him in any way. Although his demeanor was deadly calm, Ariel could feel the white-hot intensity of his mind and his absolute concentration as the two men began to circle the room.

Yazid smiled insolently. "Come taste my blade, infidel."

You are a fool, Yazid, Ariel thought.

The prince laughed and took the offensive. His scimitar arced through the air, but Christopher slid easily away. He answered with his own blade, catching Yazid off guard with the speed and deadly accuracy of his aim. The sound of steel upon steel rang through the air as the two men clashed. Yazid was forced to parry Christopher's thrust, stepping back to regain his balance. But his retreat was short-lived. Spinning around, he faced Christopher, this time with both hands wrapped around the hilt of his scimitar, all traces of hubris gone. He glared at Christopher with a hatred that emanated from him like waves of heat. Slowly, he lifted the scimitar over his head.

"Now you will die, infidel."

He brought the blade down with all the power of his body behind it. Christopher moved away, and the blade smashed into a mahogany table, splitting it in two. Yazid wasted not a second in recovering, slashing the sword sideways as he moved aggressively in on Christopher.

Do something, Ariel begged Christopher silently. Why did he let Yazid make all the moves? Why did he constantly back away, only using his scimitar to parry Yazid's stabs and slashes? Again Yazid moved toward Christopher, his scimitar ripping through the air with the skill that had made him a legend throughout the

Maghreb, and Ariel's heart caught in her throat. Christopher had been the one to throw out the challenge. He had dared Yazid to fight him. But now he wasn't fighting; he was letting Yazid dominate him. He was letting him win. Yazid's blade moved like lightning, seemingly everywhere at once — always moving, always forcing Christopher back. Christopher was nearly against the wall; one more thrust from Yazid and he would be blocked in with nowhere to go but into the scimitar's path. *Please,* she prayed. *Please fight.*

Yazid also saw his opportunity. A feral grin spread across his face as the blade in his hand arced toward Christopher. Slicing the air, he leapt forward, intending to carve the infidel's heart into a thousand pieces. Then suddenly the Englishman was moving. Not toward the wall as Yazid had expected, but directly at him. From nowhere the infidel's scimitar struck at his own, coming upward with a motion that pulled the hilt from his hand and sent his sword clattering across the stone floor. Yazid whirled away from the Christian blade, but he felt it separate the fine muslin of his tunic and then sting his flesh. He twisted away and turned to face the Christian, but as he did he realized the infidel's trick. It was the Christian who now cornered *him,* and the Christian whose scimitar danced before him like a deadly serpent.

Barely able to believe her eyes, Ariel watched the sudden reversal of swordplay. In the matter of a second, Christopher had changed places with Yazid. He had been toying with Yazid, letting him believe he was winning while Christopher lured him to a place where he could entrap him with a single, swift movement. Now it was Christopher who held sway over Yazid, but Christopher had none of Yazid's boastfulness. He was deadly calm. And deadly serious.

"So, Yazid, now do we talk?" Despite Christopher's conversational words, his tone brooked no refusal. The tip of his scimitar pointed directly at the prince's heart, and his eyes never left his captive.

Instead it was Yazid who smiled, his eyes narrowing in smug self-assurance. "I think I shall have to refuse you, infidel, as always." Before his words had even crossed the room, the doors from the hallway burst open. The Mongolian attacked Christopher from behind, jabbing a dagger into his shoulder before Christopher had a chance to react. In the same instant, Yazid dove for his lost scimitar, triumphantly twirling it over his head as though he was again at the fantasia. Christopher slammed himself against the stone wall, crushing the smaller Mongolian between his weight and the stone. Yazid's servant slid dazed from Christopher's back; but he had done more damage than even he knew, for his dagger had reopened Christopher's shoulder wound and added to it. Trying to stem the flow of blood, Christopher held his shoulder with his free hand, still wielding his scimitar in the other.

"Ariel," he called as he squared off against Yazid. "The doorway." He didn't need to say more. Ariel flew to the wall tapestry, yanking on it with all her strength. The age-old hemp holding it to its spot gave way, and the rug crashed to the floor, sending clouds of dust billowing through the room. Ariel wasted not a second scurrying over the massive rug. She set her hip against the secret door, and it opened easily. Christopher was right behind her, nearly sweeping him with her as they fled Yazid. Behind them Ariel could hear Yazid's fiendish laughter following them.

"Run!" he shouted. "There is no escape for you. Infidels, all! I shall see your heads upon the spears of my guards and bury your corpses in the walls of my palace. There is no defeat for the mighty!"

Ariel knew Yazid was right in one sense, for there was nowhere to go. The battlement ended in another door at the far tower, but like its twin, it had probably not been opened in a hundred years. There would be no escape there. Behind her, Christopher stopped, and Ariel turned, grabbing for his sleeve. He was as pale as death, and the blood seeping from his wound had turned his black djellaba heavy and slick.

"Give me the scimitar," she demanded. If they were to make their stand here, she would be with him. Ariel had lost everything, but she would not lose Christopher so long as there was a breath of life within her. Christopher ignored her demand, stepping in front of her to shield her from Yazid. Ariel could see the sheen of the thin layer of sweat that lay over Yazid's face. It added a look of lunacy to the maniacal gleam in the prince's eyes as he bore down on them. Christopher lifted his scimitar, and Ariel knew it was the last of his strength. For the third time in nearly as many days, she prayed for a miracle. Twice Allah had heard her, but this miracle she needed more than any of the others.

Seeing Christopher's feeble effort, Yazid could not resist laughing. "Be afraid, infidel. Now you see the wrath of Allah!" Brandishing his scimitar, Yazid leapt for the wall of the battlement. His feet landed a mere meter from the spot where Ariel had nearly plunged to her death only days before. And as it could not bear her weight then, so it could not now bear the weight of Yazid's strong, youthful body. The ancient red stone crumbled beneath him, and he had time for nothing except to fill the night with a scream of fury. And then there was nothing but the sound of the wind in the starless night.

Chapter Twenty-six

Christopher sat up, resting his weight on his good arm as he watched Ariel. She was curled up by the fireplace in his room, reading. "Is your book so engrossing you can't be lured away to tend the wounded?" he inquired innocently.

"Are you truly interested?" she asked without moving.

"Yes. Tell me what it is you're reading?"

Ariel cleared her voice and quoted,

" 'Awake! for Morning in the Bowl of Night
   Has flung the Stone that puts the Stars to Flight:
      And Lo! the Hunter of the East has caught
   The Sultan's Turret in a Noose of Light.' "

"The Rubaiyats," Christopher stated.

Ariel set her book on the table and crossed to his bed, settling on the covers beside him. "They're beautiful, but nevertheless I am at your every disposal, sir. What may I do to ease your discomfort?" she asked, cocking her brow mischievously, for she knew well enough that

Christopher was recovering quite nicely. All he required was rest.

Slowly, he ran his fingertip along the curve of her jaw. "Just you."

The roughness of his skin against hers was enough to send a shiver coursing through Ariel. As his fingers followed their course down her neck, she knew unerringly where he meant to guide them, and she sighed, wanting him to continue yet knowing he must recover his strength. "Christopher," she murmured.

"At the Casbah," he whispered huskily. "You gave a promise."

"Yes. But you are not well yet."

"How do you know how well I am?" he asked. "It was a promise."

"And one I want to fulfill more than anything, my love, but—"

"I am waiting."

Ariel looked down at him. His eyes had gone dark with desire, and her fingers longed to reach out and touch his bare chest where the sheets had fallen away revealing the broad expanse of sculpted muscle there. With a sigh she leaned over him. At least she could kiss him; then he would know she meant to keep her promise. Her lips grazed his parted ones, and as they did the tip of his tongue ran along her mouth. Ariel groaned against the effect that smallest movement had on her. Closing her eyes, she parted her lips and kissed him again, this time giving him entrance there. The moment his tongue met hers, she knew she was lost already. Never in her life had she needed something as she needed him. It was a need that never ceased, never ebbed. She had not in reality been reading the afternoon away. Instead Ariel had sat across the room watching the man she loved sleep, and it had taken every ounce of her will not to climb beneath the sheets with him, for she could not stop the sensation that even to be in the same room with him was not to be close enough. She needed his touch.

He drew her to him, pulling her down on top of him until only the thickness of her tunic separated them. Even through its fabric, Ariel could feel the taut muscle beneath his skin, and her nipples hardened with desire. His kisses intensified, and she met his ardor with equal of her own. Catching his lower lip between her teeth, she teased him, demanding that he react as she did to his caresses. A groan escaped him, and his kisses became an assault. He pulled her closer, turning so that her head lay upon his pillow and he was above her. His fingers crept beneath the silk, and Ariel thrilled at the warmth of his hand at her breast, teasing her nipples until she could not bear the fire that he built within her. She arched toward his hand, wanting more, needing him closer.

Christopher moved away from her. Their lips parted, and Ariel lifted her head off the bed, not wanting to lose the warmth of his mouth on hers. Her eyes fluttered open, and Christopher looked down at her, the intensity of his desire etched on every plane of his face and in the rigid lines of his shoulders. Slowly he lifted the tunic over her head, tossing it heedlessly onto the Persian carpet. With the same measured slowness, he drew her pants down to her feet. Kneeling at the foot of the bed, he ran his hand softly across her toes, then bent to kiss them, each in turn. His tongue burnt a trail of raw heat up the inside of her leg, stopping only to kiss the delicate skin at the innermost crease of her thigh. As Christopher plied his kisses there, his thumb stroked at her most sensitive place, eliciting shudder upon shudder from her. Ariel could feel the wetness between her legs

374

as his touch released a thousand butterflies within her stomach. Hypnotically, her hips began to move in rhythm with the commands of his fingers.

Then, warm and gentle, his lips replaced his hand — meeting his own wetness with hers, mingling the two until one flowed into the other without distinction. Christopher swept her away from all reality to a place where nothing existed except this moment, this union between the two of them. But Ariel wanted more. She needed more. Moaning, her fingers moved across his shoulders, and Christopher rose up, coming to her as certainly as the waters come to the shore. Poised above her, he was magnificent. Masculine and powerful. Every sense within her was drawn to him. This, as nothing else, was the bond forged between them from deep within their souls. For a moment time seemed suspended as their eyes locked and a knowledge passed between them that bespoke the ageless pull of two people who knew beyond question that they were destined for this union.

Ariel moved beneath him with an urgency she could not define, knowing only that she would not be whole until they were one. He moved between her legs, and she could feel the hardened maleness of him there. Her gaze raked over his body before returning to meet his own, certain as she had been at the oasis that this was meant to be. Then she lifted her hips to meet him. There was no pain as there had been before. This time there was only the pleasure of becoming whole. He entered her, filling the cavity within her. Warm flesh within warm flesh. And for a moment they remained there, motionless, basking in the completeness of their union.

Then Christopher began to move within her. With long, sure strokes he alternately filled her, then pulled nearly completely away from her. Each time he drew away, Ariel moaned and arched upward, desperate not to lose his warmth. Each time, as her hips arched upward, he came back to her, filling her completely, drawing her farther into the fiery passion that threatened to consume her. And then the ball of fire burst within her, sending fingers of melting heat outward to every crevice of her body. Ariel clung to him, gasping for breath as Christopher drove into her again. In response Ariel tightened herself around him, and felt the intensity of his strokes change. Christopher's breath came in short, rapid gasps, and a bead of sweat dropped onto her breast. Ariel locked her legs around his hips. With a cry Christopher shuddered within her, holding himself as deep inside of her as he could press. They remained locked together for long, silent seconds.

"I love you, Ariel." Christopher's voice was a whisper weighted by the depth of his emotion. "I will love you forever."

"And I you," she replied. Her eyes filled with tears of joy, and a gentle smile touched her lips. Christopher smiled in return. The smile of a man at peace at last. Still within her, he lowered himself to one arm and drew her close to him. Her cheek lay against his chest, and deep within it she could hear the still-rapid beating of his heart. Closing her eyes, she sent a prayer of thanks to Allah. This was the finest pillow she would ever know.

Chapter Twenty-seven

The morning sun dried the last drops of wash water from the ship's deck as the final barrels of water, food, and supplies were carried aboard. The slaves, bent beneath the weight of their burden, were dressed in the scarlet sash and white tunic and pants of the sultan. Ariel stood at the foot of the planking nervously watching her trunks being carried to the captain's cabin.

"You are having second thoughts?"

"No," she replied, shaking her head in response to Carmela's question. "But it will be the first time I've set foot off the soil of Morocco. I guess I'm a little scared."

"Pshaw! There is nothing to be scared of! Wait until you smell the salt air, the sea breeze in your hair! Ah, there is no feeling in the world like this," Carmela crooned. "I cannot wait to feel these things again."

Ariel skewered her with a doubtful look. "I thought that you came over here in a slave ship. How was it that you experienced the 'sea breeze in your hair'?"

Carmela lowered her eyelids until she looked her most sultry. "The captain was a beautiful man. How could he resist the chance to share his days with a hot-blooded Gypsy woman who was inconsolable?"

"Well, on this trip be certain that you stay far away from the captain. He has a wife."

"You gloat." Carmela pouted. Then, flashing a broad smile, she hugged her friend. "Never has the Imam married two people so much in love. The glow is still about you."

Ariel smiled in agreement. She had certainly never felt so wonderful. Shielding her eyes from the sun, she watched Christopher and Suleiman chat on the aft deck of the ship. Sultan Suleiman, Ariel reminded herself. Morocco couldn't have wished for a better successor to Mohammed. In Suleiman, his dreams would continue, and the Maghreb would flourish. A shadow of sadness crossed over her features thinking of Mohammed. If Yazid hadn't led a rebellion, Suleiman would not have become sultan, and Suleiman would be a far better leader for Morocco than Yazid. But the bloodshed and loss had been so great. So many people had been killed in the name of power and greed. Her guardian was dead. Yazid was dead. Even Daiwa had been discovered murdered in the rose garden. Such a high price for Morocco to pay.

She cleared the bad memories out of her head with a shake. She'd promised herself that she wouldn't look back. Everything lay ahead of her now. She was Christopher's wife, and although so much unknown lay ahead, she knew that as long as he was there with her she would be happy.

The last of the trunks went up the ramp as Christopher and Suleiman came off the ship. Suleiman clasped both her hands in his and smiled down at her with all the affection of a true brother.

"Allah's *baraka* has always been with you, Ariel. I know it will follow you to your new home. You must remember to send books from England for the libraries. With you to select for me, Morocco shall soon have the best of England's new authors and poets."

Ariel nodded, unable to speak for the tears that knotted her throat. "I'll miss you, Suleiman."

"Do not miss me. This is my world, and I must stay here as surely as you must now leave for the new world you begin." He smiled at her tears and shook his head gently. "You must remember this. At night, the stars that look down upon you are my stars as well. Through them you shall always know I am here." He kissed her lightly on the forehead and then stepped off the dock, walking serenely away before she could try to hold him back.

"He is so much like Mohammed," she said to Siad, whose presence she could feel beside her. "So certain of his destiny."

"He will be a great leader," Siad replied simply. "For greatness lies in deeds done and not words spoken, beloved mistress."

Ariel turned to him. "Then you, Siad, are a great man indeed." The eunuch bowed, graciously accepting the compliment. "And I'm not your mistress anymore. You're free now, I told you that. You have more than fulfilled your service."

"So you have said, mistress. But what shall a graying eunuch do if not serve his mistress?"

"I have spoken to Suleiman about this. He would be pleased to have you at his side. It is yours to decide, but either way, you are a free man."

The big man bowed again, but even with his face turned away, Ariel heard the catch in his throat. "So it shall be."

"Thank you, Siad," she said softly. "I will feel better knowing you're with him."

The eunuch rubbed his eyes abruptly. "There is too much sand in this land!" he complained. "I must now wash this grit from my eyes, belov—Lady Staunton."

Christopher curled a possessive arm about her waist as Siad stalked off. "Carmela's already aboard, and the breeze is strengthening, darling. I think it's time to leave"

Ariel nodded, looking at the shore and the land she was about to leave forever. "I still have to say goodbye to Chedyla. You've sent the trunks for Sami with Fatim?"

Christopher nodded. "Safira is bound to think he's a very spoilt little boy."

Ariel laughed. "Not nearly so spoilt as he'll be living with Fatim's family."

"If Fatim is any measure, I agree. Now go on, Chedyla is waiting for you."

"Won't you say goodbye to her?"

"I already have. And I've spoken to Suleiman about her as well. She'll want for nothing for the rest of her life."

Ariel looked up at Christopher with gratitude. He gave her a gentle nudge and nodded toward the shore where her duenna sat patiently under a tree.

"Go on," he said.

Ariel walked slowly down the dock and silently took a seat on the bench beside Chedyla. The old woman's eyes were closed and they did not open when Ariel sat down. Instead she reached out and wrapped one gnarled hand around Ariel's, pulling it into her lap. They sat for several minutes, silent, yet communicating. Ariel could feel the calm and safety of Chedyla's presence seep through her, and she was grateful for it, especially at this moment.

When Chedyla spoke at last, her voice was serene and free of tears or regrets. "It is as it should be."

"Is it?" Ariel asked quietly.

Her duenna opened her eyes and turned to her, a smile on her lips that reached to the depths of her soul.

"Yes, my child. The circle is complete."

"Then, this is not a sad goodbye."

"It is a joyous goodbye."

Ariel smiled, realizing that Chedyla was right. She kissed the wrinkled cheek beside her. "Goodbye," she whispered. "I love you." She had gone only a few steps when she heard Chedyla call softly to her.

"May Allah keep you in his hand always."

The hull boards groaned as ten corsairs pulled Christopher's ship from the shallows of Salé harbor. As the ship began to run in the deeper water, sailors unlashed the sails from their spars, and Ariel listened with excitement to the sound of the sheets snapping as they caught the freshening sea breeze. She took hold of Christopher's arm as the ship heeled to the wind. He looked down at her inquisitively.

"Are you excited?"

"I'm excited and nervous and scared and sad all at the same time," she replied. The ship heeled again, and Christopher pulled her close against him.

"It takes a while to get used to, but by the time we reach London you'll have a fine set of sea legs."

Ariel put her hand on his chest to balance herself, and beneath his crisp linen shirt she felt the amulets she'd had made for him at the souk. She smiled. "You're wearing them."

"I'll wear them to my grave, darling."

"Then, you'll wear them for a very long time because I have years and years of plans for the two of us."

"And do they include many hours of 'couching'?" he teased, running a finger across her mouth.

"Many, many, my lord."

Christopher's eyes clouded, and he looked at her seriously. "You don't regret leaving your home?"

Ariel looked out over the aft of the ship to where the shores of Morocco slipped away in the glare of the morning sun on the water. The whitewashed buildings and palm trees faded in the haze until it seemed to Ariel that the port town could almost be a thing of her dreams. A mirage created by flight of fancy. Far behind the town, the peaks of the Atlas rose through the clouds; somewhere between the two she knew was Meknes, and within it stood El Bedi — beautiful, glittering, and magical. There she'd created a world in-between, a place where she was neither Moroccan nor visitor, not a part and yet not totally separate. She'd woven her world of gossamer dreams and held it together with the determination of one too young and too idealistic to know that what she tried to do was impossible.

Sighing, she turned to look out at the sea before them. They were headed for a land of which she knew nothing. But she believed Christopher when he told her there were no windows with beautiful bars, and no laws that kept her apart. No gardens where concubines lived like beautiful, well-tended flowers waiting only to be plucked. And she had Christopher. Ariel felt his arm tighten around her, and she looked up, smiling. His eyes still held their question, and she knew the answer meant everything to him.

"Will you love me forever?" she asked softly.

"Forever and ever, my love."

"Then, I shall never miss my home, for wherever your love is shall be my home." And then Ariel saw no more of Morocco fading in the distance, for her husband crushed her against him, drawing her into a kiss of such promise that there was only tomorrow for her, and the promises that she gave him in return.

PASSION BLAZES IN A ZEBRA HEARTFIRE!

COLORADO MOONFIRE   (3730, $4.25/$5.50)
by Charlotte Hubbard
Lila O'Riley left Ireland, determined to make her own way in America. Finding work and saving pennies presented no problem for the independent lass; locating love was another story. Then one hot night, Lila meets Marshal Barry Thompson. Sparks fly between the fiery beauty and the lawman. Lila learns that America is the promised land, indeed!

MIDNIGHT LOVESTORM   (3705, $4.25/$5.50)
by Linda Windsor
Dr. Catalina McCulloch was eager to begin her practice in Los Reyes, California. On her trip from East Texas, the train is robbed by the notorious, masked bandit known as Archangel. Before making his escape, the thief grabs Cat, kisses her fervently, and steals her heart. Even at the risk of losing her standing in the community, Cat must find her mysterious lover once again. No matter what the future might bring . . .

MOUNTAIN ECSTASY   (3729, $4.25/$5.50)
by Linda Sandifer
As a divorced woman, Hattie Longmore knew that she faced prejudice. Hoping to escape wagging tongues, she traveled to her brother's Idaho ranch, only to learn of his murder from long, lean Jim Rider. Hattie seeks comfort in Rider's powerful arms, but she soon discovers that this strong cowboy has one weakness . . . marriage. Trying to lasso this wandering man's heart is a challenge that Hattie enthusiastically undertakes.

RENEGADE BRIDE   (3813, $4.25/$5.50)
by Barbara Ankrum
In her heart, Mariah Parsons always believed that she would marry the man who had given her her first kiss at age sixteen. Four years later, she is actually on her way West to begin her life with him . . . and she meets Creed Deveraux. Creed is a rough-and-tumble bounty hunter with a masculine swagger and a powerful magnetism. Mariah finds herself drawn to this bold wilderness man, and their passion is as unbridled as the Montana landscape.

ROYAL ECSTASY   (3861, $4.25/$5.50)
by Robin Gideon
The name Princess Jade Crosse has become hated throughout the kingdom. After her husband's death, her "advisors" have punished and taxed the commoners with relentless glee. Sir Lyon Beauchane has sworn to stop this evil tyrant and her cruel ways. Scaling the castle wall, he meets this "wicked" woman face to face . . . and is overpowered by love. Beauchane learns the truth behind Jade's imprisonment. Together they struggle to free Jade from her jailors and from her inhibitions.

Available wherever paperbacks are sold, or order direct from the Publisher. Send cover price plus 50¢ per copy for mailing and handling to Zebra Books, Dept. 4207, 475 Park Avenue South, New York, N.Y. 10016. Residents of New York and Tennessee must include sales tax. DO NOT SEND CASH. For a free Zebra/ Pinnacle catalog please write to the above address.

LET ARCHER AND CLEARY
AWAKEN AND CAPTURE YOUR HEART!

CAPTIVE DESIRE   (2612, $3.75)
by Jane Archer
Victoria Malone fancied herself a great adventuress and student
of life, but being kidnapped by handsome Cord Cordova was too
much excitement for even her! Convincing her kidnapper that she
had been an innocent bystander when the stagecoach was robbed
was futile when he was kissing her until she was senseless!

REBEL SEDUCTION   (3249, $4.25)
by Jane Archer
"Stop that train!" came Lacey Whitmore's terrified warning as
she rushed toward the locomotive that carried wounded Confed-
erates and her own beloved father. But no one paid heed, least of
all the Union spy Clint McCullough, who pinned her to the
ground as the train suddenly exploded into flames.

DREAM'S DESIRE   (3093, $4.50)
by Gwen Cleary
Desperate to escape an arranged marriage, Antonia Winston y
Ortega fled her father's hacienda to the arms of the arrogant
Captain Domino. She would spend the night with him and would
be free for no gentleman wants a ruined bride. And ruined she
would be, for Tonia would never forget his searing kisses!

VICTORIA'S ECSTASY   (2906, $4.25)
by Gwen Cleary
Proud Victoria Torrington was short of cash to run her shipping
empire, so she traveled to America to meet her partner for the
first time. Expecting a withered, ancient cowhand, Victoria didn't
know what to do when she met virile, muscular Judge Colston
and her body budded with desire.

*Available wherever paperbacks are sold, or order direct from the
Publisher. Send cover price plus 50¢ per copy for mailing and
handling to Zebra Books, Dept. 4207, 475 Park Avenue South,
New York, N.Y. 10016. Residents of New York and Tennessee
must include sales tax. DO NOT SEND CASH. For a free Zebra/
Pinnacle catalog please write to the above address.*